The Tayl

Death of An Ordinary Guy
Sainted Murder
Twelfth Night "On The Twelfth Night Of Christmas"
Pearls Before Swine
Horns Of A Dilemma

HORNS OF A DILEMMA

Jo A. Hiestand
& Paul Hornung

P.O. Box 275
Boonsboro, Maryland 21713-0275

This novel is a work of fiction. Names, characters, places and incidents either are the product of the author's imagination or are used fictitiously. Any resemblance to actual persons, living or dead, events, or locales is entirely coincidental.

Horns Of A Dilemma Copyright © 2007
By Jo A. Hiestand & Paul Hornung

All rights reserved. No part of this book may be reproduced or transmitted in any form or by any means, electronic or mechanical, including photocopying, recording, or by any information storage and retrieval system, without the written permission of the Publisher, except where permitted by law.

First Edition-June 2007
ISBN 1-59133-205-2
978-1-59133-205-3

Book Design: S. A. Reilly
Cover Illustration © S. A. Reilly
Manufactured/Printed in the United States of America
2007

To The Six Pack. We've shared music, camp, spaghetti, laughter and adventures. Though you're incognito in this story, you've a very obvious part of my life. I don't know what I would've done without our friendship and music. I'm glad I never had to find out.

Jo

To Jo, for her wisdom and patience as my writing deadlines occasionally came and went due to scheduling conflicts.

To the real Alexa, for her love and patience as my household duty deadlines often came and went due to writing conflicts.

To my parents. They have provided me a path to becoming a better person and to always help others. I promise here to follow that path.

Paul

Acknowledgements:

First of all, thanks to Ryan Cramer for suggesting the "horn" part of the "dilemma." A nice break from the "usual suspects." See, Ryan? Your degree in Criminal Justice has finally paid off! Ongoing thanks to Stephanie and Shawn Reilly, publishers, for their continued support, encouragement and broad shoulders. Thanks to friends who were always there, listening and caring — Jackie Boyd, Madaleaze Cramer, Beth Early, Chris Eisenmayer, and Cindy Greer. Thanks to police officer Dan Davis for answering questions while wrestling with a coot. And thanks to those whom I entitle and consider my Brilliant Bunch: Dr. Ruth Anker, for answering medical questions in the midst of acquiring a new associate; Detective-Sergeant Robert Church and Detective-Superintendent David Doxey (ret.), Derbyshire Constabulary, for tethering my cops and nomenclauture in England while house-hunting and struggling with new computers; and Paul Hornung, for all other "cop stuff" — emotions, insights, motives and the original idea of King.

    As always, any errors are mine.

    Jo A. Hiestand
    St. Louis, February 2007

Thanks to Steve for teaching me how to be a good cop. I am still watching and learning from you on a daily basis. Your field training duties will never be over, my friend.

    Paul Hornung
    St. Louis, February 2007

Characters

Villagers:
Richard Linnell: owner of villager launderette
King Roper: friend of Richard, visiting village
Lloyd Granger: vicar of St. Michael's church
Darlene Granger: wife of Lloyd, secretary
John Granger: son of Lloyd and Darlene, works part-time in launderette
Conrad Quinn: friend of John's
Colette Harmon: aunt of Conrad, realtor
Ian Harmon: husband of Collette, security guard in Macclesfield
Noel Dutton: hair stylist and owner of village hair salon
Rita Dutton: wife of Noel, hair stylist
Toni Dutton: daughter of Rita and Noel
Frances Cresswell: Rita's mother, living with Rita and Noel; part-time cashier at hair salon and at tearoom
Page Hanley: health club personal trainer
Harry Willett: brother of Page
David Willett: brother of Page and Harry, visiting village
Tad Mills: artist friend of David

The Police and Personnel of the Derbyshire Constabulary:
Detective-Sergeant Brenna Taylor
Detective-Chief Inspector Geoffrey Graham
Detective-Sergeant Mark Salt
Detective-WPC Margo Lynch
Constable Scott Coral
Sergeant Adam Fitzgerald
D-Constables Byrd and Fordyce
WPC MacMillan
Jens Nielsen: Home Office forensic pathologist
Faye Usher: Home Office forensic biologist
Dean Hargreaves: civilian Scientific Officer employed as police photographer
Detective-Superintendent Simcock

Chapter I

They hung witches some time back, during the superstition-swathed years of the early 1600s. Up around Bakewell and farther north into Scotland. Hung evildoers on gibbets, their bodies chained to the pole as if afraid they would escape even in death. Hung up at wastelands and village outskirts and crossroads. A tacit message: 'Traveler, shun the road to ruin.' Creaking corpses swaying in the wind, as though they had become a wagging, cautionary finger. Hung out in rain and snow and baking sun, crow-pecked and mid-day silhouetted like a black sun in an eclipse. Hung around the scenes of their crimes, viewable day in and day out, loitering throughout a slow-grinding year. Eerie shapes slowly materializing like specters through fog-choked dawns and black-as-hell nights.

Witches—practitioners of black magic, partnered with the devil. Possessing the ability to conjure and enchant, to ruin crops, sicken livestock, take human life— all manner of mischief to beleaguer the Living. And before we had finished this case, I would swear we were plagued with a newer form of the old devilry.

The devilry manifested itself as a monstrous boulder and murder—both at the foot of a holy place. This hallowed spot was the churchyard of St. Michael's Church, a late medieval edifice of gray stone squatting near the zenith of a heavily wooded hill. The building shone eerily against the blackness of the March evening, seeming to float above the dark clusters of shrubs and winter-dead flowers hugging its foundation. Moonlight broke sporadically through the ebony jumble of clouds, flooding selected earthly objects with a silvery iridescence. So intense was this contrast of darkness and light that police work lamps might have illuminated the scene. Then, as quickly as the light had identified the church, it shifted, abandoning the massive structure to the unease of encroaching shadows. Fading into the darkness and the dense wood beyond were the bell tower and its menagerie of gargoyles, centuries old, stanch affirming icons amid Doubt. Below and to the left of the tower the graveyard's tombstones poked through the inky curtain of night, emphasizing this bizarre yet suitable spot for a death, mutely advertising previous travelers on life's journey and tonight's rude betrayal of the Holy.

"Rather grim, isn't it, Taylor?"

"Sir?" I jerked my head up from my contemplation of the dead body to stare at the speaker.

Graham had come up beside me when I had returned, rather sheepishly, from physically expressing my horror of the crime scene and the condition of the body, and now stood beside me. His tall frame cast an even longer shadow under the flood of light from the police lamps. He was dressed casually in jeans, cream-colored Aran knit pullover, and once-white trainers. Both shoes and jeans were streaked with mud, and there were dark stains on the elbows of his pullover, as though he'd been wrestling in a marsh. His chestnut hair was mussed and speckled with mud. Mud also dotted his cheeks. Graham looked as far removed from my well tailored, quiet boss as I could ever imagine. Not that I ever had. I was about to ask the reason for his casual attire when he nodded toward the body. "Bloody awful, isn't it? No pun intended. I nearly lost my stomach, too."

I nodded, the back of my hand against my lips, as though that would stem the abdominal churning. Right now I was merely thankful that Mark and any of my other male colleagues hadn't witnessed my less-than-dignified lurch to the nearest tree, for I'd taken enough ribbing years ago as the only female in a male-dominated police class. I didn't want this latest escapade to become new material in their joke book.

But the murder scene was beyond a joke. And that it *was* murder wasn't even questioned. Even from my position several meters outside the crime scene tape I could tell it was murder. Blood seemed to be everywhere, flung about by the obvious attack. Blood splattered the face of the huge boulder, the muddy ground and nearby grass. It lay in irregularly shaped splashes, pointed like crowns on the rough stone, or in elliptically tailed blobs that indicated a great rate of travel, and therefore a great violence. It lay in spots and blobs so numerous in some areas that they seemed painted on. It lay in streaks that had run down the boulder's face to leave brilliant crimson, pencil-thin stripes against the light gray stone. Blood pooled beneath the body, which was sprawled on the ground, face down, next to the boulder. The blood was thick, scarlet, and threw back the reflection of the work lamps, as water in a deep pond at night appears black and substantial. The pattern of this blood splashing indicated the victim had been attacked viciously, repeatedly, with a heavy object. Most of the blows had been struck on the back and right side of his head—the common location for a cowardly, surprise attack. I had no need of a postmortem examination to realize his scalp would be lacerated and chunks of his flesh and hair would be missing. His skull was a bloody mess.

I said, "Do you know who he is?"

Normally, I would have supplied the information to Graham—I being a detective sergeant in the Derbyshire Constabulary and, therefore, arriving at a scene before Graham, my immediate superior. But this case was already proving itself unique. And adding to that was the fact that Graham had been here while the murder happened.

Which doesn't mean he witnessed it. If he had, I and the rest of the CID team wouldn't be poking about for clues. But Graham had participated

HORNS OF A DILEMMA

in the village event prior to the murder, discovered the body and called headquarters. Can't ask for much more from a detective-chief inspector."

Graham nodded, his gaze on the police constable cordoning off the crime scene. The blue and white police tape fluttered in the breeze that swept down the hill and stirred the boughs of the conifers and oaks. It held the scent of an imminent storm.

Responding to my question, Graham said, "Yes, I know him. Enrico Thomas."

"Former mate of yours?"

"Not at all. I'd never seen him before. He's a newcomer to the village."

"Sir?" I know I shouldn't have asked, since it was bordering on personal information, but he had opened the door, as it were, and anyway, I wanted to know everything about him. Love is like that.

He looked at me, his green eyes dark in the light from the work lamps. "Hollingthorpe. This village, Taylor. I used to live here as a child."

"Did your family move, then?"

"No. My parents continued living here even after I entered university. It was only after they retired that they eventually left."

"So this is your first visit back in some years."

"Not really. I'd return while they were here, during holidays, summers and such. And I've come back several times since then, when there was something special going on."

"Like tonight."

"Yes. But it's not the same, is it? Coming home, I mean." He paused, waiting for a response, perhaps a confirmation that he hadn't somehow missed out on something. How could I give that when I wasn't part of his family?

I smiled tentatively, not knowing what to say. Instead, I sought the anchor of police work and said, "And what was special about this evening? You merely mentioned on the phone that you were here, doing something in the village. You didn't state exactly what it was."

He gestured at the boulder, which sat like a beached whale in the churchyard. I estimated it weighed about a ton. "Turning the Devil's Stone. That's what brought me back."

"Pardon?" I blinked several times, trying to recall anything in my eclectic store of knowledge about a stone or the devil, but I couldn't.

Graham smiled. "That great hunk of rock, Taylor. The boulder in our crime scene. The Devil's Stone. Every year on Ash Wednesday the villagers of Hollingthorpe gather their crowbars and ropes and collective strength and turn over the stone. We...oh, good. Glad you're here, Salt."

Mark Salt, a detective-sergeant in the constabulary's B Division, as was I, came up to Graham. Mark was tall, muscular, and not only conscious of his boyish good looks but also of their effect on women. I'd struggled during our early acquaintance to steel myself against both aspects. Graham, while handsome in a mature, lead actor way, did not use it as a lure as Mark did.

Graham seemed unaware of his affect on the opposite sex—particularly me. As much as I battled openly with Mark to stay out of his clutches, I battled with myself to hide the affect Graham's attraction had on me.

"Right. Evening, Salt. I was waiting until you arrived to brief you and Taylor on the situation," Graham said, turning slightly as Mark joined us. He glanced at his watch, said something about 9:30 being the usual time lately to begin investigating cases, and doled out the facts.

"I was actually here for the stone turning event."

"Which began..."

"At six o'clock tonight. There were about a dozen of us in attendance—all villagers or expatriates, such as I."

"Would you happen to know who they are, sir?"

"Yes, but I'll give you names later. We assembled in the churchyard, near the boulder, here, prior to that. The event lasted nearly an hour. After that..." He paused, aware of my note taking, which signaled my hand had healed from last month's accident and that I was 'back to normal.' He stared at the dead body, as though wanting to include it in the conversation, since it was the reason we were here. After taking a deep breath, he continued. "After that, being Ash Wednesday, there was a short worship service inside the church at seven o'clock."

"And that lasted..."

"Approximately thirty minutes."

"So everyone left at half past seven."

"No. We stayed for refreshments in the church hall—tea, rock cakes, assorted biscuits, milk. This was available to all the worshippers, not just those of us who had participated in the stone turning."

I nodded, writing silently and swiftly, my mind already forming questions to ask about the event.

Graham continued. "The group started to break up after eight o'clock. Maybe closer to quarter past. Obviously I didn't consult my watch—I didn't know I'd have to be my own witness! Anyway, I stayed on for a bit to talk to some old friends."

"When did you leave?"

"Some time between 8:15 and 8:30. Well, it was before the half hour tolled on the tower bells, at any rate."

"And you rang up the station around quarter to nine," Mark said, stepping out of the way as two Scientific Officers ducked under the police tape and went over to measure the boulder. Several more SOs carried over a large tent, muttering about the daft scene. "I'm assuming," Mark continued, "that our victim was part of your group and didn't disappear before the service began at seven. That would narrow in not only on the time of the murder but also on a suspect."

"I don't recall specifically if he was in attendance at the service," Graham said, "but I saw him in the hall afterwards. He had a cuppa, I know. Other than that..." He grimaced, as though mentally reliving some of the admonishments he'd given witnesses whose memories weren't particularly good. He cleared his throat and said, "Well, I don't know when he left. Like I said, I wasn't exactly scripting everyone's movements."

Mark nodded, glancing from the boulder to the church. "Pinpoints the time of murder, I'd say. Refreshments around 7:45 or 8:00. He may have left when you say people began leaving a bit after eight o'clock. And you discovered him at 8:45—forty-five minutes or so. Can't ask for much more, unless we have a witness!"

Graham snorted. "How many people seeing such a violent attack would step forward? Hell, I'd be cowering beneath the bed clothes or packing for a fast getaway."

"If you don't mind a question, sir, how did you come to discover the body? If you left the church hall between 8:15 and 8:30, but didn't ring up the station until 8:45...that's twenty or twenty-five minutes unaccounted for. Sorry, sir," he added, his face suddenly flooding with color.

I stared from Mark to Graham, wondering how Graham would take this tacit implication that Mark was questioning his boss's whereabouts, and thus his involvement in the crime.

"Don't mean to be impertinent, sir." Mark's face had gone white.

Graham nodded, giving Mark a quick smile that said he understood. "I *did* leave, yes. I had walked from the church down to the pub. I took the path."

Mark and I turned to follow Graham's gesture. A well-defined footpath proceeded from the church's door, headed north towards the wood, skirted the perimeter, then dropped over the brow of the hill toward the east. It looped lazily through the village, sauntering past the pond, square, and old market cross before climbing the boulder-dotted tor and disappearing into the hazy distance north toward Youlgreave.

Graham said, "The path leads to The Floating Hog, the local pub. It's actually part of a walking path that winds through the district. This is just the village section of it."

"Do you know any more of it? Have you walked it?"

"Just a short distance, Taylor. It branches outside the pub, halfway up the hill. The fork that enters the wood goes northwest before it disappears behind the trees."

"But you didn't walk it last evening."

"No. I'd gone down to the pub, where I have a room, intending to spend an hour there before heading to bed."

"Intending...but something brought you out again."

"Yes. I thought of something I wanted to ask the vicar. I didn't know if Lloyd was at the church or at the vicarage. I assumed the latter, since we'd called it a night by then."

"So you didn't hike up the trail."

"No. I walked up the High Street until I came to Green Acre Road. I turned down that, went a bit of a way before cutting up the hill toward the vicarage."

"Which is why you passed by the boulder," Mark finished. "It isn't near the path from the pub."

"And why I spotted the body. I then rang up Silverlands."

I looked up from my writing and found Graham staring at me. I said that it was fortunate that he had wanted to talk to the vicar, or the body might not have been discovered until the morning, and by then any clues may have been obliterated.

"Let us applaud my woman's intuition, then," Graham said, smiling. "Or whatever prodded me into action."

"Did you go up to the body? Is there anything you saw that can help us?"

Graham turned his gaze to the body, as though envisioning his discovery. He said, "The attack must have just happened. He was lying face down, as you see him, Taylor, his arms slightly out from his body. I went up to him, not knowing if he would be alive or dead, and touched his neck. The body had not cooled. I didn't turn him over or touch him other than to confirm he was dead. From what I could see while bending over him, he had injuries to the side of the neck and to the back and side of the head."

I nodded. I had seen that much and I hadn't approached the body.

"The skin had multiple lacerations."

"Explains the profusion of blood," Mark said.

"The blood had run down the side of his face and had pooled beneath him."

"Could you tell anything from its state, anything to pinpoint time of death?"

"Just that it was still dark red and liquid." Graham raised his head and stared at me, his eyes devoid of the subtle humor that usually lay behind them. "Odd, isn't it, how some things stick in the mind? That bright red color seemed more real to me than anything else in that scene. The body seemed other worldly, but the blood..." He rubbed his forehead, closing his eyes for a moment before continuing. "That's all I can recall from my cursory look. Jens will obviously give us greater detail."

I said, somewhat hesitantly, that if Enrico had been lucky, he would have died instantly. That it might have been slow torment if he had lain there, knowing he was dying, feeling the pain from his injuries.

Graham seemed not to have heard me, for he said, "God, what a night."

Although the three of us had not entered the inner sanctum of the crime scene, Graham instinctively stepped back several feet as Dean Hargreaves, a Scientific Officer, moved a photo lamp and plunged us into darkness. He angled the camera and fired off several close-up exposures of the deceased's head wounds.

I turned away, not wanting to lose my stomach now that Mark Salt was here. Even though Mark and I were working out our personal problems and seemed to be headed toward friendship, I didn't want him to perceive me as weak. I'd taken enough harassment from him while in school.

HORNS OF A DILEMMA

Graham asked Dean to get a photo of the deceased's hands. "There could very well be defense wounds on them," he said. "But I doubt it."

He wouldn't have had time to defend himself since he was attacked from behind, I wanted to add.

"I couldn't make sure when I first saw him," Graham added, "and I didn't want to disturb him and possibly compromise the scene. I can get into enough trouble without deliberately setting out to do so."

He could've been talking about me—either my illustrious police career or my home life. I'd experienced trouble both places. My penchant for bird watching while on duty had yielded me a reprimand; my family had never really embraced me after I'd chosen the Force for my job. It seemed I was always the odd man out—succumbing to the lure of nature when I should be attending to police work, following a studious rather than an artistic path. The scientific, ugly duckling in a family of creative swans. My brother, the concert pianist; my sister, the opera singer; me, the disappointment to my father and regret to my mother. My career did not reflect gloriously on my parents as newspaper reviews, concert venues and compact discs did. I produced no headlines in the entertainment section, no photo for the scrapbook, no ticket stubs framed and under glass—nothing to hold on to and cherish. Nothing grand that got me noticed so that my father could brag to the neighbors. I was the youngest, the runt of the litter and, as such, should have been drowned. And, some nights sitting alone at home, I still wish I had been.

Dean moved the lamps again, throwing Graham and Mark into silhouette, and squatted in front of the body. The click of the camera shutter boomed in the quiet.

I pulled myself out of the morass of self-pity and said, "So you didn't hear the victim call out, then?" I gazed at Dean, hoping Graham wouldn't see my reddening face.

"No," Graham replied. "Don't even know if he had time to. From the cursory look I gave his head, I'd say he didn't know what hit him."

"Especially in the dark," I added, nodding and squinting at the cloud-covered sky. It felt suddenly colder. I shivered and said in a small voice, "Wonder if his attacker hid behind the boulder."

"I'm more worried about where he's hiding *now*."

Chapter 2

The murderer had a big lead on us—at least an hour. Even if he were a villager, which implied that, being local, he should have been close at hand and therefore readily accessible for apprehension, he well might have left the vicinity and gone God-knows-where. And, just because Graham hadn't seen a visitor at the stone turning event didn't preclude there being none in the village. A visitor could have been staying at the pub or a bed-and-breakfast or someone's home, attacking our victim while the participants were in the church hall. And Graham would not know.

Dean finished photographing the body and area around the boulder, then nodded to the Scientific Officers who were waiting to set up the tent. It was a necessity if Graham wanted to protect his job and the scene, for not only would it house the crime scene and preserve whatever clues were left, but it also would shield the body from prying eyes. By which I meant the press—television, radio and local newspapers. At times, they seemed to emerge from thin air, as though possessing a sixth sense about such events, but in actuality sat monitoring the police channels, descending upon the village in the first few hours like vultures to a carcass. And the next thing we'd see would be the body and the gory details on the BBC newscast, followed days later by Graham in uniform and walking a beat. I watched the SOs unfold the tent before I asked Graham how he wanted us to proceed.

"I'd like to find out about our victim, Enrico Thomas."

"Knowing a bit about him or his history may give us a lead on his attacker," I agreed.

"Mark, why don't you and Margo begin asking people living closest to him—you'll have to sort out where that is. Taylor and I will talk to the vicar."

"Does he know Enrico?"

"I haven't the faintest. But since Enrico was part of our jolly festivity tonight, he may have well been a churchgoer, so the vicar may know him. I'll see to the incident room after we tackle the vicar. It'll probably be in the community center, but I'll set it up somewhere. Any questions?" He looked expectantly from me to Mark, was answered with a shake of our heads, then said, "Right. Let's see if we can come up with something, then." He gestured toward the church, indicating I should precede him. Mark walked over to Margo, and they took the path toward the pub and into the village.

HORNS OF A DILEMMA

"I asked the vicar to wait here at the church," Graham said, coming alongside me as we skirted the cordoned area. Here, away from the powerful police lamps illuminating the crime scene, the night seemed unnaturally dark, as though black could be blacker. Somber clouds obliterated the moon, and although a few stars poked through the celestial mask, they did nothing to break the gloom. Graham had switched on his torch and we wove our way through the gray tombstones bursting through the darkness like pranksters yelling "Surprise!" The white diamonds of the police tape appeared to be dancing in the ebony night, the blue sections of tape mingling with the surrounding blackness. "I thought it would save us a bit of time if we didn't have to hike to the parsonage," Graham said, his voice startlingly loud beside me.

"Is he a friend of yours, sir? Do you come back often to see him?" I asked, brushing against a yew bough. "I was wondering if you make it a point to keep up with friends who still live here."

"I don't make yearly pilgrimages. Haven't the time or the inclination, to be truthful. Without my parents or my best mate here, the place has lost most of its pull. But I have known Lloyd Granger, the vicar, for some years."

"So he's not a childhood friend."

"We've become friendly through my trips back here. Nice enough chap. About your age, I reckon."

Thirty-five-ish. I asked about Lloyd's family.

"He's married and has a son. And, other than expounding on his hobbies and theological beliefs, that's about it. Good, he's left the door open." Graham pushed open the wooden south door of the church and, since he had the light, I followed him inside.

Once we quit the porch and emerged into the nave, Graham switched off his torch. The lights in the south aisle were on and, although not as brilliant as the police work lamps, they were far better than the torch. Graham nodded to a dark haired man, who rose from the nearest pew, and introduced me.

"This is Detective-Sergeant Brenna Taylor, my colleague and right arm," Graham said, his voice echoing against the stone walls and carved columns.

Perhaps under a difference circumstance I would have smiled. Even felt my heart rate elevate, for I'd never heard him refer to me as his right arm. But it never manifested; tonight's matter was too serious. And meeting the first of those involved, however remotely, brought this sickeningly and vividly into perspective.

Lloyd beckoned us to some chairs in the back of the aisle, and after we were seated explained that he really knew very little about Enrico Thomas. "I should like to help you solve your case," Lloyd said, his dark hair prominent against the background of whitewashed wall. A fresco above his head showed its age, the paint flaked and faded in areas. The faint drip of water whispered from an undisclosed spot in the north aisle. *Probably the roof*, I thought, remembering the dozens of church roof appeal signs I'd seen. Water was insidious, appearing dozens of yards, perhaps, from its entry. I wondered how long this had been happening and if they were close to repairing the damage. Most of the building's interior was carved stone, marble or brass, an implied belief that the structure was as dependable and ever lasting as God. But nature always battled human endeavors; rain and wind lashed out at buildings and landscapes, sun faded and dried and cracked. I glanced at the wooden beams spanning the ceiling, feeling insignificant in this vast space, feeling the eons the human race had pondered about the heavens and theology. Perhaps we'd be seeking Divine Intervention before long. I gave one last, quick look at the gold brocade nave altar cloth, then refocused on Lloyd as he leaned back in his chair. The wooden chair legs scraped across the stone floor, sending sharp reverberations sailing up to the rafters. I wondered if angels lounged up there, awakened from sleep.

"…help with your case not only because I knew Enrico and liked him," Lloyd continued, "but also because no one should get away with murder. I know there is a God and, therefore, retribution in the afterlife for sins—and I should be content with that! But I think humankind needs to punish the evildoer. If we didn't, we'd be a mass of criminals in a chaotic existence." He stared at me, his dark eyes trying to read my impression of him, perhaps. I nodded, agreeing with his philosophy. Had Graham felt like that? Was that why he had forsaken his clerical robe to don a police officer's uniform?

"When did Enrico move here?" Graham said.

Lloyd looked at the south door, as though expecting Enrico to walk through it, then said, "One month ago, though he'd been seen in the village one month prior to his move."

"So," said Graham, calculating the time, "right around Valentine's Day."

"I can't be certain of the exact date, though I do remember because we obviously don't get many newcomers to Hollingthorpe."

"And, like any village, those who do come are instantly recognized."

"Yes. We pounce upon them with welcoming phrases and homemade bread and invitations to join everything in town, from the church choir to the rambling club. Darlene chats up the wife, if there is one, which there wasn't in this instance."

"Widower, divorced?"

"Enrico was single. Oh, Darlene's my wife," Lloyd said, leaning toward me. "She always has a list of clubs and activities that she suggests that might appeal to women. Children, too."

"But," I added, guessing, "Enrico had no children."

"Childless. I know my son, John, was disappointed, for he was hoping for a new mate since Enrico seemed to be about my age—40 or thereabouts. So," Lloyd shrugged, as though not knowing what else to relate. "Other than that…"

"Did Enrico mention where he moved from?"

HORNS OF A DILEMMA

"No, though I got the impression it was from a large city. Not necessarily London, but some city. Manchester, Liverpool."

"Why? Was it something he said?"

"Just a cultured air about him, like he'd know any answer to an operatic or fine art question posed to him. Intelligent, product of a large university. Is this making any sense?"

Graham nodded without speaking, his eyes never leaving Lloyd's face.

"Which isn't to say you can't be a cultured, intelligent person living in a village! Lord, I don't want to imply that! I'd have half our residents throwing stones at me if I meant that! But he had sense of having been reared among the classics."

"So," Graham finally said after considering the news, "as you said—London, Manchester or other large metropolitan area."

"Of course he wasn't a native of any of those. But, then, you heard him speak, didn't you, Geoff?"

I looked up from my note taking. I so seldom heard Graham called by his first name that it was startling. Especially during a police investigation. But this was Graham's home, and I would probably hear him referred to as Geoff or Geoffrey many times before the case ended.

Graham nodded and said that he couldn't quite place the accent. "Which would've narrowed down our search. Enrico never spoke to you, Lloyd, about where he came from? Not even casually, something dropped as in reference?"

"Like 'I sure miss the mangoes of Jamaica'?"

"Or 'I wonder how long it will be before I get used to June being summer instead of winter.' At least we'd know in which hemisphere to make an inquiry."

"No, Geoff. Not that I can recall. Something like upside down seasons would surely have stuck in my mind. I'll have to pray on it."

Graham nodded and exhaled loudly. I'd worked with him enough to know that he was frustrated that a potentially good lead such as this had evaporated.

I said, "Do you know where he worked? Perhaps we can speak to his coworkers."

Lloyd leaned forward. "Now that I *do* know about." He smiled, perhaps pleased that he was some use after all to his friend.

"I assume it was fairly local, since you said he's been in the area for two months," I said. "Although I have heard of people living in the area and working in London, staying there for the week and taking the train back home for the weekend."

"Nothing like that, Brenna. May I call you Brenna?" Lloyd smiled sheepishly. "Geoff's mentioned you several times, and if he has such high regards for you...well, I'd like to get to know you." He glanced at Graham. "Or if you think I shouldn't...being on duty and this being a murder investigation..."

I said I'd like to be called Brenna, and he relaxed. "He had a part-time job," Lloyd said. "In the village bookshop."

"Was that all he could get, the part-time work?"

"He seemed content with that. He said it gave him time to do what he wanted to do, plus gave him a chance to get to know us."

"He could live off a part-time wage?"

Lloyd shrugged, as if to say he had no idea about Enrico's finances. "Of course, I barely knew him, but he seemed very happy to have the job. He was semi-retired."

Graham hadn't seen that one coming. He blinked and said, "Rather young to be semi-retired, isn't he? You said he was about forty. How did he make his money, assuming mummy and daddy didn't hand it to him through some inheritance? Internet company? Rock star?"

"No. Nothing so privileged as a family fortune, I'm afraid. Rather glad, too, if I may editorialize for a moment. Enrico was very grounded, as if he'd struggled for everything he had."

Graham nodded. "Wealthy folks may work, but I don't think they know the hard times that people do who depend on a paycheck. And I'm *not* saying wealthy people are all insensitive swine."

"Of course not! But no matter how hard they slave away at an office, people with money don't know the panic or desperation that comes from needing money for a new fridge, let's say, and not having it."

"So Enrico had enough money to live on."

"I didn't know his financial status, but he had a nice car and clothes, moved right into his house…and —"

"Pardon me. How do you know about the house? Did Enrico tell you?"

"Not in so many words. He said one day that he was glad he didn't have a mortgage and could use that money for charities."

"He didn't say which ones, I suppose."

"No. Afraid not, though he did ask me if I knew anyone in the village or surrounding countryside who had been struggling to make ends meet. But why would someone mention the charitable work if he didn't mean to follow through on it? What would be gained by such a lie?"

"We ask that all the time in police work," Graham said. "We usually find out when we arrest the bloke for murder."

"Only in this instance, he's the victim. Pity."

"So," I said, bringing the questioning back to Enrico's employment, "he made his money in…"

"Don't know. I just know he was happy with his half days at the shop and had loved this village. Perhaps he made money in computers. They've opened up a lot of career opportunities, haven't they?"

"Why did you suggest computers? Because the dot-com companies were so successful for a while?"

Lloyd stared at my notepad, as though weighing the pros and cons of his statement becoming Official. He said rather slowly, "Merely because he seemed to be computer savvy. More than your average person who uses it

HORNS OF A DILEMMA

for typing letters or keeping household accounts. He would help me if I'd got myself into a bind on some software program. He set up an e-mail account for me, too, and was planning to set up the church website. Not many people could design a site and become the webmaster, I think."

"Did he mention how he had become so literate?"

"No. At least, not to me. Perhaps he talked more freely about that to his neighbors. I just know I was impressed not only with his knowledge and skill but also with his willingness to help. Just because a man's got free time doesn't mean he will give freely of that time."

"So he wasn't a big one for playing golf, for instance," Graham said.

Lloyd frowned, maybe thinking about Enrico's activities since moving to Hollingthorpe. In the brief silence I could hear muted voices of some of the Scientific Officers working outdoors, see the swift splash of light as a work lamp swung across the stained glass windows to focus on something. Perhaps in the graveyard. A voice called out for someone to hold the end of the tape measure steady, then faded as the speaker walked away.

"He didn't seem the sport type," Lloyd said, glancing at the windows. The intense colors of the glass had sparkled briefly under the luminescence of the lamps; now they sat muted and dull in the dim air of the church. "You know what I mean, Geoff. Not the rah-rah go-team type. While he wasn't the classic trim bloke you associate with a cyclist, say, he wasn't dripping with muscles either. Well, you saw him." He grimaced and shook his head. "Sorry. I don't mean his—" He gulped. "You saw him tonight."

"Very healthy physique, yes."

Lloyd smiled tentatively now that he was past the verbal slipup. "I never saw him with golf clubs or cricket bat or bike or even hiking gear. I'd classify him as the quiet type who used his spare time reading or gardening."

"Standoffish, then?"

"No. That's too strong. He was quiet, to be sure, but he was friendly enough when you engaged him in conversation. He worked in the bookshop for only two months, but he was already very popular among the patrons."

"Any social visits for tea?"

"Not to my knowledge. But he may have done so with his neighbors, as I said. You'll have to ask them."

"So besides working in the shop, helping you with your computer and launching the church website, is there anything else you know about Enrico? A man has to do *something* to fill twenty-four hours."

"He traveled some."

"Like abroad, to see family?"

"Can't have done. He was always gone no longer than a day. Never longer."

"Was this frequent?"

Lloyd scratched his chin. "Of course, mind you, I've only known him for two months. But maybe three times since he came."

"Not like the second and fourth Wednesdays, for instance."

"That would suggest an appointment with a physician or something, I take it. He seemed healthy, but even people with cancer look normal."

"Did he always head the same direction when he left? I mean, did he always head west on the B5053, for instance?"

Lloyd shrugged. "I don't know, Geoff. I wasn't keeping track of the man. I wasn't suspicious of him nor was I overly interested in his routine. I just know he would leave for a day, then be back the following one. And while I didn't see him depart many times, I'd either see him drive back or hear from someone in the village that Enrico was gone."

"Did he take off work for that, or work around his part-time schedule?"

"I don't know. You'll have to ask his employer."

When Graham had thanked Lloyd and we were again outside, Graham turned to look once more at the boulder. Now that I had formed a mental image of Enrico's life, the boulder seemed more ominous, as though it were prowling there, waiting for another victim. I walked up to Graham, feeling suddenly frightened. He said, "So if the man isn't a football fan, isn't undergoing chemotherapy, has free time from his part-time job, is a computer expert, is living alone and independent, is not burdened by money worries, is reticent about his past, what have we got?"

I stared at his eyes, afraid of the idea taking shape in my mind. A car door slammed in the distance and the rattle of a wheelie bin lid slid up the hill. I opened my mouth, hesitated, then said, "A drug dealer?"

Chapter 3

"I hate jumping to conclusions," Graham said, "but that's my impression, too."

"There could be other 'occupations' that would fit, but I can't think of any right now."

"He certainly seems to have hidden himself away in this village. Well, we'll gather our data and then see what fits." He punched a phone number into his mobile phone and moments later was talking to Margo, a detective-constable in our section. "Would you mind delving into Enrico Thomas' background? Nationality, previous employment, that sort of thing. You know what to do." He grinned, as though Margo had said something amusing. When he rang off, he said, "Taylor, why don't you question Darlene, Lloyd's wife? She should be at the vicarage."

"Since she was part of the welcoming committee when Enrico moved in, she may know little bits about him that will help us. Certainly."

"I'll talk to Richard Linnell in the meantime. Then we can join forces again and tackle Enrico's house."

"Who's Richard Linnell?" I asked as we stopped beside the police tape encircling the crime scene. The body still lay inside the tent, waiting for the Home Office pathologist and forensic biologist to examine it. Several Scientific Officers still worked the area, for the area shone white in the surrounding night.

"Richard Linnell?" He looked at me as though I had just woken him up. "Oh, Richard owns the local launderette. It's been a tradition as long as I can remember for him to wash the muddy clothes of those who participate in the stone turning. We've tried many times to pay him for his service."

"Unusual to refuse money."

"He says it's his way of participating in the village custom. Of course, a number of the residents use his laundry to thank him."

"Seems a nice gesture."

"Especially since there aren't that many of us at the stone turning."

"But it's washing powder and hot water that his paying customers could have used." I glanced again at Graham's muddy attire and wondered if he'd trot those clothes down to Richard's. Graham had already mentioned he had a room in the pub, so he had brought other things to wear for his visit.

As if following my eyes, Graham said, "I know. Not particularly

15

professional, am I?" He flicked a patch of dried mud from his sleeve, then wiped his finger across his jeans. "I haven't had time to change. When I'd gone to the pub I had intended to change and have a beer, but then I needed to see Lloyd, so I hiked back up here. I expect I look rather disheveled."

"More unusual," I said, smiling. I pulled a facial tissue from my shoulder bag and handed it to him. "At least you can present a clean face to Richard Linnell when you talk to him."

Graham rubbed his face with the tissue, then looked at me. "Better?"

There was one spot he had missed. I held up my finger and said, "May I?" When Graham nodded, I licked the tip of my finger and gently applied it to Graham's cheek, took the tissue from him, and wiped off the mud. "Good as new," I said, pocketing the tissue.

"Now at least I'll frighten witnesses with just my questions." He smiled, then thanked me.

I nodded, murmuring that it was all in a day's work. Actually, my heart was pounding, for it was the first time I'd ever been so personal with Graham. I usually held my distance, not only for professional reasons but also because I didn't want to fan my ardor with a physical contact. But I really didn't want him talking to people with mud on his face. Lloyd's case had been a bit different; Lloyd knew Graham, knew that he hadn't had time to change clothes, knew that he had participated in the stone turning. Other villagers might not have that knowledge, and it wouldn't look particularly well for the senior investigating officer to go around looking like a leftover from the Ashbourne football tussle.

"I'll change when you've called it a night," Graham said, as though reading my thoughts. "Right now, we need to press on with the investigation. Are you fine with talking to Darlene?"

"Before I do, would you mind explaining the stone turning, sir? I feel disadvantaged not knowing what led up to the murder."

Graham leaned against a corner of the lych gate, crossed his long legs, and said, "Back before anyone remembers, the devil threw a boulder at our village church, St. Michael's. He chose St. Michael's church because St. Michael had thrown Satan out of heaven. I guess it's part of an on-going grudge match. Anyway, the villagers turn the boulder every Ash Wednesday to usher in their Lenten penance, believing that by doing something so seemingly impossible and back-breaking they demonstrate to the devil that humankind can emerge victorious for God—and also put the devil's nose out of joint. The stone weighs about a ton, I'd guess."

"How do you move such a thing as that?"

"With ropes and crowbars and a bit of human muscle. The villagers have been doing it longer than parish written records, which go back to medieval times."

"And it's turned every year?"

"Even during the war. There's a superstition connected with failure to turn it—something about tragedy striking the village—but I'm rather hazy on that. I suppose Lloyd could tell you if you're interested."

"I believe there's a village in Devon that does something similar. In November, I think. Or am I muddling my customs?"

"You're referring to Shebbear, I think, Taylor. They go in for a bit more demonstration than we do."

"Yes, I remember. In addition to turning their stone, they also ring a cacophony on their tower bells. Something about frightening off the devil before they turn the boulder."

"In their instance, they did *not* turn the stone one year during the First World War, and the following year the village and neighboring farms were visited with hardship after hardship. Fact!" he added when I looked skeptical. "Maybe there's something to the tradition after all." He shrugged, as though relinquishing mankind's futile attempt to understand God's ways.

"Maybe there's also some link between turning the devil's stone and the church's name," I said. "St. Michael is the mightiest of all the devil's adversaries."

"He's also the patron saint of churches built on pagan sites."

I gazed at the church, barely visible behind the spots of light from the Scientific Officers' lamps. The dim lights that had been on inside the church had been turned off, and the building was a black void, empty and abandoning us to our struggle with the all-too-real devil that had come to life tonight at the boulder. My fingers ran over the age-smoothed wood of the lych gate and I said, "This sounds like a chicken-or-the-egg situation. If you go with the pagan worship idea, the stone was here and part of their ceremony, then the early Christians came along and tried to dilute the situation by building a church on the site. If you go with the opposite view, the church was here first and the devil threw the boulder in hopes of destroying it. Which do you go with?" I asked it not because he had been a minister and I wanted to hear official Methodist canon but because Graham was a bit of a renegade, both with church doctrine and police procedure. I wanted to hear the opinion of a freethinking, unfettered man.

"I'd be destroying the lure of the custom if I said I favored your first choice," Graham said, drawing my gaze back to his face. He smiled, his right eyebrow lifted in jest. "But I'd be turning my back on my former occupation and sanctioned Wesleyan dogma, thereby believing in a fairy tale, if I favored your second choice."

"What's a fellow to do?" I said, half jokingly. I smiled, but I was disappointed. Sure, it was a frivolous subject and I was treating it in a light-hearted manner, but I had wanted to hear Graham's view and he was shutting the gate on the topic. My fingers slid off the rounded tops of the pickets and I turned, leaning against the gate. "So, how many villagers employ their manly strength in this episode?" It came out sounding like mockery, and I hadn't meant it to. I was merely upset that Graham had once again shut me out of his life, no matter if it was a tale about his family or an insight into his religious belief.

Either he ignored my sarcasm or hadn't noticed it, for he said quite civilly, "Approximately a dozen. It varies by year, of course—who's available, who's feeling up to it. And it's not only men, Taylor. Two women participated this year."

Thinking it prudent to stay away from sexist remarks, I murmured something about it sounding like a fun thing to do.

"We're limited by the size of the boulder, of course. There's room for a specific number of people around the thing."

"And when you're jabbing at it with crowbars and yanking at it with ropes, you need a bit of elbow room."

"You sound as though you've experienced it. So we've come to limit participation to twelve. I can't recall but one year when we actually had twelve people. Most times it's way less—eight to ten."

My gaze wandered briefly to the tent again, glowing inwardly from the police lamps. Before the boulder had been encased and had been backlit by the SOs working closer to the darkened church, it had seemed possessed of magical properties—whether godly or satanic, the onlooker could decide. But here in the blackness of night, with the tent glowing from the work lamps, it held either the white fire from hell or the shining halo of saints.

"I know them all," Graham said, drawing my attention back to him. "If that's what you were wanting to know with your original question. Perhaps not personally, like Enrico, but I knew all the stone turning participants. Which doesn't eliminate someone in the happy throng of onlookers from smashing Enrico's face in, granted. But at least we're spared the drudgery of tracking down visitors if they leave the village."

"There is that to be thankful for, yes, sir."

I glanced again at the lightless church. Lloyd had evidently gone into a different section of the building or had gone home. A SO working close to the south door said something to his mate about taking a measurement, and there was an answering remark that produced a sharp laugh.

"Well." Graham stood up and consulted his watch. "God, what an hour. We'd better press on or you'll never see your bed tonight."

"It would be nice to get acquainted."

"After you've finished with Darlene, meet me at Enrico's house."

"And that is...where?"

"Darlene can tell you where it is. I'm off to see what Richard of the Launderette can tell me." He pointed me toward the vicarage, which nestled at the farther end of the graveyard, to the west of the church, then he followed the paved walkway down the hill.

I remained at the lych gate for a minute or two, overcome with the darkness of the night and the lure of the setting. Heavy clouds creeping in from the west now obliterated the stars that had flickered overhead a half hour ago. A breeze had sprung up, carrying the scent of rain. A threat of frost lay behind the wind, for the temperature was falling. I pulled my torch from my shoulder bag and tucked it under my arm as I zipped up my jacket. The jacket's collar fit snugly against my neck but I pushed it even closer. I was trembling from either the chilled air or the gloomy surroundings.

Thinking it best all around if I got on with my job of work, I turned on

HORNS OF A DILEMMA

the torch and walked toward the vicarage. As I approached the edge of the graveyard one of the SOs called out to me, wishing me good luck with the Vic. He wasn't referring to the vicar, Lloyd. Graham was the recipient of 'The Vic', or 'The Vicar', the nickname born of ignorance and apprehension when he had joined the Force. Many officers hadn't known how to respond to a former minister in their midst. Some thought Graham would cramp their style, forcing them to watch their language or start each workday with a prayer. Others thought he would be a 'bleeding heart,' expressing sympathy for the rapist or murderer and pushing for acquittal in the spirit of Godly Forgiveness. But Graham had proven himself All Cop and had slipped into the ranks with such amazing speed and style that many whispered behind his back that he was actually god incarnate. The nickname was now just that—a pet name, a badge he wore nearly as visibly as his metal detective shield, signifying he had conquered ridicule and gained respect.

As I rounded the end of the graveyard, the beam of my torch caught the front of the parsonage, dragging it out of the shadows that embraced the stand of conifers and oaks by its western side. Although a separate building, it nuzzled the nearest group of tombstones, as though protecting them or emphasizing that even in life we are in the midst of death. It also echoed the church structurally, being built of light gray stone the same hue and type as that larger edifice. Diamond leaded windows gazed blankly from deep within their hewn sockets. The door shrank back from the outer wall, lurking in the black recess of the entryway, shut to the problems of the world. It huddled even more insecurely in the night shadows as I approached and swept my torchlight over the face of the house and the clumps of vegetation waiting to burst into bloom in the spring. I hesitated, staring at the dark mask before me, afraid Graham had been wrong about Darlene waiting up for me, when I caught a glimpse of a light in a back room. The light multiplied as I knocked on the door, and a moment later the front windows glowed in wakefulness. A light fixture over the door sparked into life and the door yawned open to reveal Darlene Granger.

She had not changed for bed, as the hour would have suggested, but wore a knee-length, exhausted cardigan over her sweat suit. On a plumper woman—me, for instance—the ensemble would have looked like a rescue mission from the rag bin, but on Darlene's figure it looked chic. She smiled, seemed momentarily startled to see a female instead of a male police detective, but welcomed me with a freshly brewed pot of tea, and settled me into an upholstered chair that threatened to lull me to sleep.

We were in the front room, a snug parlor of plaid curtains, blue carpet and picture-covered white walls. A coal fire flickered warmly in the grate, casting purple shadows on the far wall behind us. On the mantle, framed photos and miniature ceramic teapots mingled with several styles of religious crosses. Beside the front door, a wooden bookcase sagged under an overload of books. They seemed to be predominantly of theological, geographical and environmental subjects. They also gave forth the aroma of lavender, for a large basket of potpourri shared top space with a lit candle.

"I knew him only slightly," Darlene said, picking up her mug and balancing it on the arm of her chair. Brown-eyed and brunette, she was of medium height and still young enough in her mid thirties to hold on to her good figure. She rested her head against the back of her rocker, briefly closing her eyes, as if conjuring up an image of Enrico would help her define his personality. During the fleeting silence I could hear a mantle clock in the next room strike half past ten, and a radiator gurgled before settling down for the night. When Darlene again looked at me she said, "He moved here about a month ago, I think, although he'd been around the village before that."

"Before he found a house?"

"Yes. He'd been anxious to find a place here. He told me he'd tried in other villages, but he really wanted to settle here."

"Why was that? Did he have a friend here?"

"No. At least, I never heard him mention it. He'd fallen in love with the village, he said. He had looked around the district. Oldfield was another village—what's wrong?"

I had no idea I'd gasped, but I must have, to evoke that response from Darlene. Oldfield was the village in which we'd investigated a murder last month, the village in which a stranger had been asking to buy a house. Had Enrico been that stranger? I made an excuse that I'd choked on the hot tea, and asked her to go on.

"He was a pleasant man, and eager to become part of the community."

"Out-going, was he?"

"No. I don't mean standoffish or cold. Private, as though he didn't like talking about himself."

"He may just have been shy."

"Could have been. He was only in our midst for two months—one, if you count his actually living here."

"Maybe there hadn't been enough time for him to get over his shyness and open up to you."

She shrugged, as though unable to fathom others' personalities.

"So," I said, set my mug on the coffee table, "you never talked with him in line at the green grocer's, for instance." I recalled Graham's words about women sometimes knowing little bits about people, the little personal, chatty things most people let drop without realizing it. I knew first hand, too, about guarding your tongue, for I had been warned on a trip to East Berlin not to chat with bus drivers or museum guards. Something as innocuous as 'I know what you mean about being on your feet all day; my grandfather couldn't wait to get his gold watch from the Force so he could sit down for eight hours.' Any little bit of friendly conversation could contain hints about you and your family and job that could be traced. So I mentally applauded Graham's foresight about setting up Darlene.

Darlene shook her head. "He'd smile, talk about the weather and innocuous topics such as the children's playground fund or the price of

HORNS OF A DILEMMA

petrol or global warning."

"Nothing at all personal?"

"Nothing to give away his past or a hint of home life. He was friendly enough, like I said, but it was frustrating. I couldn't get close to the man as I felt a neighbor—and a vicar's wife—should. It's hard to help people if you don't know much about them."

"So in the two months, more or less, that he was here he never mentioned home or wife or kids or job?"

I must have looked hopeful, for Darlene smiled. "Not so much as a former pet."

"Well, thank you for—"

"But I did see the inside of his house once."

Her revelation stopped me from rising, and I unfolded my notebook, waiting for more. "When was this?"

"Second week he was here."

"What was the occasion that prompted your visit? Pardon me if I seem confused, but you said he wasn't particularly open with the neighbors. An invitation to his home hardly seems in line with your portrayal of him."

"Nor is it, if you're thinking about a proper invitation."

"What, then? Business related?"

"I suppose you could categorize it that way. Nothing at all like a chat over the back garden fence or afternoon tea. I'd gone over there to solicit his help with our well dressing tableaux for this summer. We'd already settled on a design last autumn, of course. Tad Mills has finished executing the actual working drawing for the panel, but Enrico had volunteered to put in dozens of hours doing the actual labor on the wet clay. If you've ever helped with a well dressing panel, Miss Taylor, you know how much time is required."

"So you were thrilled Enrico wanted to help."

"Volunteers are always needed! He loved that sort of thing, he said—anything to do with the environment and nature."

"Were there no other visits to his home?"

"I had planned to pop in to invite him to the stone turning, but I saw him at the green grocer's a few days ago and asked him there."

"Of course. He joined in, I take it from what Chief Inspector Graham said."

"Yes. He seemed the type to join village activities, in fact. Very interested in the residents—who everyone was, names and what they did for a living and their hobbies...he would have gotten on so well here. I already miss him." She pressed her lips together, as though forcing herself to not cry. She fumbled for a facial tissue. During the moment of silence, I glanced at the books on her side table. A biography of Churchill, a history of Tudor England, a large photographic book of animals, a world atlas, a mystery novel. The novel's front cover was curled back and the spine was cracked in several places, suggesting it had been passed around or was a favorite read of

Darlene's. *Or bought in a church jumble sale*, I thought, remembering where I was. After taking a deep breath, she said, "I suppose there's no one to contact, is there? Relatives, family?"

"Why do you assume that?"

She shrugged and stared at the crumpled tissue in her lap. "Just an impression. Nothing more. He never said a word about a wife joining him. I know he wasn't particularly chatty and he'd been in his house only a month, but he just gave me the impression he was here by himself."

"Maybe there's a wife or family somewhere else, about to join him."

"I hope not. His death would break their hearts."

"It's already affecting you, if you don't mind me saying so."

"I liked him! I've said that! From the moment he unpacked his last suitcase he became part of the village."

"That must have pleased your husband no end."

"So often people have no time for church or the customs associated with village life. And that makes it sad, doesn't it, that newcomers choose not to become involved in the community in which they live. I was particularly pleased that he did so. Perhaps more than Lloyd."

"Why is that?"

"Well, Enrico wasn't local. I don't know where he was from."

"Couldn't place his accent?"

"Not at all. And if the newcomer is at all standoffish, it sometimes creates tensions. So I was relieved when Enrico was accepted."

Perhaps he hadn't been, if he had been murdered. "Were you worried about physical repercussions?"

"You usually are, aren't you? I mean, there are Pakistanis and Indians—Asians, too—living in Britain, which sometimes causes class or culture problems, but I didn't get the impression at first that Enrico was either of those nationalities. He was light skinned, maybe even Caucasian, but there was a definite foreign look to him. His eyes and hair—you know."

Unfortunately, I did. Like the runt of the litter or the ugly duckling—the different individuals suffered harassment or were pecked until they died. "If he's different, he's discriminated against. I hope it didn't come to firebombs thrown through his window or name calling."

Darlene said most of the villagers had been accepting of him, if not outwardly friendly. "But there's always that fear that someone who's had a bit too much to drink will do something, either because he thinks it's funny or in retaliation for some international incident."

Punishing the innocent because they are available.

"Nothing ever happened. At least I never heard of anything like that, thank God. Enrico was a nice chap and I wanted people to accept him as he accepted the village. He jumped in full heartedly and never said no to any request for help, either monetarily or manually. He seemed very interested in everyone and everything going on here."

"So your only complaint was that he wasn't more open with his life and didn't come over for tea and such."

"You have to respect a person's wishes."

"And lifestyle," I added, then asked if anything inside Enrico's house had struck her as unusual.

"Why? You suspect him of something illegal?"

"I just want a full picture of the man. It helps flesh him out. And the more insignificant detail may prove an identity to his killer."

Darlene took a sip of tea, then put the mug on the table. She looked toward the room's far wall, as though envisioning Enrico's parlor, then turned back to me and said, "I don't think his house is going to help you any, then, Miss Taylor."

"Why is that?"

"Simply because he hadn't finished unpacking yet. So I don't know what he was like."

Chapter 4

I hadn't been expecting that. "Hadn't unpacked yet! In one month?"

Darlene nodded. "I don't know why it surprised me, either." She frowned and cupped her hands around her tea mug. I wanted to hold my hands out to the fire, but resisted. Not exactly good manners. "I suppose there's no law stating you have to unpack completely within a month of your having moved in. But he wasn't that busy. At least I don't think so. His part-time job at the book shop couldn't have occupied him that much to where he couldn't unpack."

"Maybe he was busy with something else. Clubs or a volunteer project."

She shrugged again, not knowing what encompassed Enrico's time. "Like I said, miss, I didn't know that much about him. He could've done something with his evenings, but even so, wouldn't you have found time to turn your house into your home?"

I wondered if anything in Enrico's house would give us a clue to his life or death. I thanked Darlene, asked for directions to Enrico's house, and left her standing in the darkened doorway.

Graham and Mark were already at Enrico's when I had finished suiting up and had joined them in the front room. So was a Scientific Officer, who was busy photographing the interior. Not that there seemed much to photograph. I'd never seen a room like this outside a hotel room. Or a furniture store. Darlene might be even more surprised to learn that in the ensuing weeks since she'd been here, Enrico still hadn't done anything to personalize his space. Nothing spoke of his individuality. We might just as well be processing a scene in that hotel room. Except this was more bizarre. I turned to Graham. "Where's all his furniture?"

"Good question. Perhaps it's coming later."

I stood just inside the doorway and stared, amazed that a month's residence had produced nothing beyond a wooden folding chair, a small two-shelf bookcase, a small table lamp, and a large upholstered chair. There was nothing else in the room; no area rug, no pictures on the wall, no occasional table, no television set. No miscellaneous items that bring the owner to the room, such as framed photos, magazines, or plants. The lamp perched on top of the bookcase, which was empty but for a local BT phone book. The entire room wouldn't have taken two minutes to clean and pick up. I walked over to the upholstered chair and picked up the only personal article in the room—a postcard. The card's front showed a brilliantly colored photo of a swimming pool at a large hotel. Luxuriant flowers and trees seemed to cascade down a hill. *The Colonial, Kenya* was inscribed in black ink on a yellow banner in the upper left corner of the card. Some hotel. Must cost my entire pay packet for one week's lodging. I turned it over and read the handwritten message. *Most incredible sunshine—I'm on nearly every xcursion they extol! Night, day, evening. Dina wanted an intimate trip, full of rapids. Canceled our night tour aboard canoes, though.* A dashed-off holiday greeting from a friend, most likely. I tossed the card onto the chair.

"How much is 'later?' He's been here a month," I said, watching Graham leaf through the phone book. His gloved fingers riffled the pages. "Looking for something, sir?"

"Anything," he said, giving the phone book one last look. He held it by its spine, fanned through the pages as he shook it, then put it back on the shelf. "I was hoping something would fall out."

"The only fall out we'll have is if we can't find anything about him. Have you ever seen anything like this, sir?"

Graham got up and we looked around the barren room. It looked like Enrico was moving out instead of in. "Maybe there's something in the kitchen or bedroom. Maybe his things haven't arrived. We don't know where they're coming from."

"Has anyone found a personal diary or anything? Bills, letters...?"

"A Scientific Officer is tackling the kitchen. I've got Mark—"

As though hearing his name, Mark called from the back of the house that we had better come in there quickly.

Graham was the first to enter the room and from his expletive I was prepared for something shocking. It was just as well that he had inadvertently warned me for I may have had heart trouble if he hadn't.

Mark was standing to one side of the wardrobe, the door open, the half dozen shirts and few trousers pushed to one side. He gestured inside with the practiced smoothness of a traffic copper directing traffic.

Graham preceded me to the wardrobe and asked what Mark had.

"You'll never guess, sir." Mark's voice and face may have remained calm, but his eyes gave away the plot, for they were alive with excitement.

"Then I'll spare us all a few hours and just look, shall I?"

Mark snapped on his torch and Graham peered into the wardrobe. An energetic 'Bloody hell!' boomed into the room and I came forward, leaned around Graham, and echoed his opinion.

A Sig Sauer, an expensive, top-of-the-line handgun, lay on the floor. Two magazines—possibly fully loaded—sat beside it, compounding the horror of potential scenarios.

I stepped back, looked at Mark, and said, "I hope this is all there is."

Graham turned toward us, his face unusually grim. "I pray to God that you're right, Taylor. We'll get the SOs to do a thorough search of the house, but right now I'll die of curiosity if we abandon it to the Scientific lads. What say we dig a little deeper into Mr. Enrico Thomas' life and give these rooms a quick glance?"

"Why the gun?" I said, finally shifting my gaze from it to stare into Graham's eyes. "I mean, why even have it? And such a high quality weapon. If he did target practice, why use something so expensive? It seems out of character for him, from what little I've heard tonight."

"He *was* a quiet chap," Graham agreed. "Maybe we'll get some answers during our search."

"Sir," Mark said, halting Graham at the bedroom door.

"Yes?"

"Sir, what do you think this is? I mean, your ordinary citizen doesn't keep a weapon. I know we've just found it, but you've talked to Reverend Granger, you've seen Enrico during the stone turning event. What do you make of it?"

Graham leaned his shoulder against the doorframe and gazed at the open wardrobe before responding. "I don't like making first impression opinions, Mark. You know that."

"I know, sir. But this is all so odd. The absence of furniture, the weapon and ammunition. I keep thinking of the other cases we've worked, not nearly as bizarre, trying to make sense of all this."

Graham exhaled loudly, rubbed the side of his jaw, and said, "I know the temptation to want to understand it before we've all the facts. I know how it can get inside your brain, drive you crazy, rob you of your sleep. So, if you swear not to hold me to this opinion when we've finished our case, I'll tell you my impression. I agree that it's odd—the essentially bare house..." He paused as we glanced about the room. It was no better than the front room; it held an inflatable mattress and sleeping bag and a wind-up alarm clock. The windows had no curtain or shade, and the sill was thick with dust. A single suitcase sat on the floor in the corner, its lid open to reveal a few folded jeans. Aside from that, it appeared that the remainder of his clothes, what there were, was in the closet. 'Odd' was an understatement. Graham continued, "...the weapon and ammunition is the proverbial frosting on the cake."

"If we hadn't found that, we could dismiss the other with the conclusion that all Enrico's furniture hasn't arrived," I said.

Mark agreed. "Perhaps it's in storage or he's waiting to see if he likes it here."

"We have the Sig Sauer," Graham said, "and the ammunition intruding like a cancer into a body, overshadowing the skimpy décor. So, what do I think about it?" He folded his arms across his chest and stared at me. His gaze didn't startle me—it was the intensity of fear beneath his next words that produced the shivers. "I wonder if Enrico was part of a terrorist group."

"Like a sleeper who comes into this village," Mark said slowly, "who

HORNS OF A DILEMMA

immerses himself into its life to become Very British?"

"Exactly. Just waiting for his orders." I opened my mouth, but Graham went on. "His being an apparent loner suggests he was hiding here, 'sleeping' if you prefer that jargon. That's what I think right now. Opinion, as I said, subject to change."

My voice finally slipped into the strained quiet and I said, "But, sir, he could be hiding for another reason."

"I agree. That's why I hedged my opinion with the option to change it." He smiled, but his eyes still held the underlying fear of his belief.

"The weapon could imply he's a criminal, and he's chosen this spot to escape detection and the long arm of the law. Perhaps he was planning something—a bank robbery, a security van hijack—only he was killed before he could execute his idea," I said.

Graham agreed that was another interpretation, but thought it unlikely. "Why not hide in a large city?"

"He could disappear into the crowd of humanity," Mark agreed, "and never be noticed."

"Whereas in a village, he's instantly spotted as a newcomer."

"His life is immediately under the microscope because people want to know about him—where he came from, what type of job he does, if he's married—and want to become friends with him."

"He'd have more trouble lying doggo in a village than in a city," Graham said.

"The same would hold true for your terrorist sleeper idea, then, wouldn't it, sir?" I held my breath. It was the first time I'd challenged one of Graham's theories and I didn't know how he would react.

He smiled again, this time with some life to his eyes. "Of course it could do! But if he were a criminal, as you suggest, and his target was a bank, then we'd have surveillance photos that we could broadcast and effect his capture."

Mark took up the crusade. "Sure. Even if he chose the less risky route of a security van robbery, he would still gamble on leaving some DNA evidence, such as a hair, that would tag him as our criminal."

"Which is why I opted for the terrorist sleeper. Even though he'd be known in the village, he could pack up and leave just before his escapade. Easy and quick because he's practically no furniture or clothing to abandon."

"And if he's good enough or if he chooses a target that's not heavily populated with workers or security cameras, he'd run a good chance of escaping detection."

"There'd be no link between him—a villager of how many years he had intended to stay here—to the explosion at the oil refinery, for example. Make sense?" Graham rang up the station and requested a firearm officer, then rang off and yelled for the photographer. "Get this room, will you? Photos and sketch. And the gun *in situ*. Thanks." He gestured toward the wardrobe, stepping out of the SO's way, and watched as the officer ran off several shots of the overall scene and close-ups of the gun and ammo. When he had finished, he began to draw a detailed plan of the room and the location of the gun. The Sig Sauer would remain where we had found it until the arrival of the firearm officer, who would move the gun and ammo and eject the magazine for safe transportation.

"I think," Mark said, "it's more likely Enrico was a sleeper waiting for orders from someone. You know how those berks work—they move in, become part of the fabric. You don't move to a village and wait merely to rob a bank, Brenna." He tilted his head slightly and looked at me.

I said that, given that explanation, the bank robber was a bit unlikely. "But every loner isn't a terrorist, Mark. There are hundreds—thousands—more felons than terrorists. What's a terrorist doing here, anyway? What's his target? I can't accept that. Enrico was a criminal, planning some robbery or kidnapping. Maybe he's got a partner, maybe he's acting solo. But even if he has a partner, that person doesn't have to be such mates with him that he lives next door. There are such inventions as the telephone, letters, and e-mail, Mark."

"Glad to hear it. But e-mails can be intercepted and phone calls can get crossed so other people can hear the conversation. Not a very secure method of planning a crime."

"So they don't use plain English, then."

"Oh, great. Talk in French in a village. That'll be subtle."

"They use a code, Mark," I said, getting exasperated. "Nothing obvious like 'D 17 X Zed 43.' But words or phrases that stand for something."

"Like 'My, how windy it will be tomorrow' meaning 'we start the operation tomorrow'?" Mark looked skeptical. "Could do, I suppose. Yes…"

"That way, it sounds innocent, doesn't arouse suspicion or call attention, and they can still communicate."

"And uses the village as a retreat?"

"What better place? He commits his crime, then runs back here to hide. If he robbed a bank in Liverpool, say, then runs back here to hide, I doubt the cops in Merseyside would think to look in Derbyshire for their robber. This village is a perfect retreat. It fits the felon's MO and is a much more likely scenario than a terrorist, Mark. They're more common."

"Common doesn't rule out possibility. It's not common for meteors to strike houses or twins to be born joined at the head, but it happens! I grant you your criminal, Bren, but I'm still betting on the terrorist angle."

"Fine. He could be one, but I just think that's a bit over the top. I should make you bet me that he'll turn out to be a robber or something similar."

"I know what you make, Bren. You can't afford to bet me." He gave me the smile that melted many feminine hearts, only I wasn't in the mood to respond. I asked, "So, what do we do about him? Discover a sketch of a

HORNS OF A DILEMMA

bank and a timetable when Security comes to work? Find a list of contacts that will more or less hint he's a terrorist?"

"That and hopefully instructions," Graham said, "though he's probably memorized both. Still, it's worth an effort. We need more hands than we've got. I'll get some lads over to search the house. They may come up with a list of his mates or a date circled in his diary or something like a smoking gun. British Telephone can at least provide us with the phone numbers that he contacted. That may lead us somewhere."

When we'd made a cursory examination of the rest of the house and found nothing more incriminating than a half-eaten orange, Graham locked the door behind us, shed his work overalls, and rang up Byrd. The clouds had settled in, blanketing not only the sky but also the land in utter blackness. Perhaps they and the late hour contributed to the paucity of people out and about, for I'd never heard a quieter village. The only thing up and moving seemed to be the murder squad. Points of light from police work lamps or torches pricked the darkness like winking stars. On top of the hill, the church and its sheltering grandfather trees were nearly invisible, compelling the village to pause and stare in wonderment at the apparent void—St. Michael's had been there earlier this evening. Had the devil spirited it away? If so, what was left in its stead?

I shook off the Halloween feeling that was quickly gripping me and concentrated on Mark. He had opened his mobile phone, perhaps to check incoming messages, and was staring at the keypad. After another few moments of contemplation, he flipped it closed but held it in his hand. He glanced at me, smiled, and asked in a low voice if I'd eat if he ordered something.

"We can grab something at the pub," I whispered, not wanting to interrupt Graham's conversation.

"There's still that dinner you promised me."

"Not in the middle of a murder inquiry, you idiot!"

Mark smiled, clearly having fun with me. He nodded slowly. "You're right. I would like to see you in something a bit more enchanting than a white moon suit."

"I was just waiting to see if Graham wanted us to return to the house," I said rather warmly, then removed the paper work clothing.

"If you want to squeeze in our date, I'd not be averse to you cooking. You told me once about your chicken with tomatoes and almonds. You'd never find a more gracious dinner guest, Bren."

"So, besides me paying for the groceries and doing the cooking, I can't think of another reason why that's a bad idea." I wasn't going to add that Mark might find Erik at my house. I didn't want Mark knowing I had a chap living with me. I'd endured enough of Mark's jokes during our police training days; I wasn't going to display my living arrangements to him.

Mark was about to remark on my comment when Graham ended his conversation.

Returning his mobile to his pocket, Graham stood on the front walk to the house, jangling the latchkey in his hand. The Scientific Officers who had charge of the body had taken the key from Enrico's pocket and given it to Graham so we could examine the house. Now Graham tossed and caught the key as he waited impatiently for Byrd to arrive and stand guard. While we waited, I asked Graham about his conversation with Richard Linnell.

"Our village launderette owner?" Graham said, closing his fingers over the latchkey. "I've known him forever. He was reared here, as was I. He must be a bit younger than I, so we were a few years apart in school, but we played on the same rugby team—strictly amateur, kid stuff in the village—and associated through other village activities. He's a nice enough bloke, active in village life. As I said, he washes the clothes of the stone turning participants each year. His parents, as did mine, moved from here on retirement. I think his are in Manchester in a retirement home, but I'm not certain. He's taken over the family business and is doing well."

"Let's hear it for our local, independent businessman," I said, meaning it. I was tired of conglomerations owning everything in sight, controlling prices and forcing folks out of their small businesses.

Graham ignored my editorial and said, "On a more personal level, Richard's never married but is dating a woman in Chesterfield. On an investigation level, I'll tell you that he was at the stone turning, at the church service, at the tea afterwards in the church hall, knew Enrico only superficially, and has no alibi."

"He has no motive that you know of, then, for the murder."

"No. But, then, I haven't lived here for years. Things may boil beneath the surface that don't erupt on my biennial visits. I'm no good as a witness. We'll have to investigate as we would any other case."

"Pity," Mark said, stamping his feet against the cold. He gathered up our three discarded paper suits and wedged them beneath his arm. "You could have wrapped this up quickly enough to impress Simcock."

Graham smiled. The name of our Detective-Superintendent usually brought some reactions from all of us on the CID team. While perfectly competent, Simcock could be a bit demanding at times, which irritated Graham, especially when he was working as best he could with uncooperative suspects and slow-yielding evidence. "Let's just hope we can wrap it up. Unsolved cases eat at my soul."

His statement left us quiet, as though each of us ruminated on our own thoughts of the bits of cases we'd left unsolved. Like the author of the letters plaguing Mark's sister-in-law. That had been in January, and the weather had been marginally colder than it was now. I blew a cloud of white breath at the black sky and searched again for stars. But the darkness held its own, tenaciously hanging on to sky and landscape. The breeze, sharper and colder within the last hour, still carried the threat of rain. Other than being uncomfortable for us, it would not bother the SOs working the crime scene. Another reason for the all-enveloping tent.

Mark must have been thinking the same thing, for he said, "Brilliant.

HORNS OF A DILEMMA

Just what we need—rain and more mud to tramp about in."

Graham nodded. "Of course, some years are worse than others with regard to the mud at the devil's stone turning. Usually the later Ash Wednesday is, the muddier the ground. Spring thaw and all that. It wasn't particularly bad tonight—more like falling on top of a granite slab. Never did like frozen ground, even as a kid. What's the time, by the way?"

"It's just gone half past eleven."

"Is that all?" Graham massaged his eyes, then blinked at me. "When did we start all this?"

"Half past nine, sir."

"Only two hours. Not nearly enough time. And the heavens are about to open up, which always makes working conditions fun. At least the lads working Enrico's house will stay high and dry."

"The SOs at the crime scene have the tent, sir," I reminded him.

"It still doesn't protect the entire area, Taylor. I dislike rain during the early investigation period. Who knows what it will wash away elsewhere?"

"The killer leaving behind a bit of torn cloth in the wood—yes, sir."

Graham glanced at his watch and sighed. "It would be smashing if Jens is already here."

"One good thing about having a copper at a crime scene," I said. "You don't waste time in bringing in the needed personnel."

"Not when it's obvious it's a murder, at any rate. I never knew a corpse yet who could bash himself on the head like that and hide the weapon."

Constable Byrd walked up to us, nodded to Graham, and said he was ready to stand guard.

"Walk around, Byrd."

"No hovering by the front door. Right, sir."

"Don't follow a timed route. Mix it up both with the time and the direction you take around the house."

"So if someone's desperate to get in, for whatever reason, he won't sneak in the bedroom window while I'm hugging the front gate. Got you, sir."

"Not that you would do, Byrd. You're an intelligent copper, which is why I requested you."

Byrd's 'thank you, sir' rumbled up from his chest in an eruption of gratitude. He pulled himself up to his full height—which was about five foot six—and nodded. His eyes, intensely blue and usually smiling, were alive with pleasure. If I had to say one thing about Graham, it would be that he was grateful for his team and showed it.

"Good. Even though a SO is still inside, I've locked the door."

"More security for her," Byrd said. "For the same reason—no one sneaking in and tackling her when I'm in the back garden."

"A firearm officer will be coming, too. Daniel Tudor."

"To deal with the gun in the bedroom. Right."

"I think that's everything. Now that you're here, Byrd, we'll get on with our job of work. I'll ring up Simcock and request an incident room here. While we're waiting for the equipment—" He broke off as I stifled a yawn, then said, "Taylor, why don't you and Salt get some coffee or something. Come back to the community center—that's where we'll set up shop if we're not interrupting something. Right."

He flipped open his phone, and Mark and I headed back to town in search of caffeine.

The pub was just closing as we arrived. Late night customers called out good nights in the cold, crisp air, got into their cars or walked to homes beyond the green. As the sounds of departing cars and footsteps faded, the grating of a stubborn door squeaked into the quiet and a startling strain of "Ave Maria" blasted the air before being quickly turned off. The Floating Hog was ancient—ivy and Virginia creeper scaling its stone walls, tiles the colors of mud and tree bark and sun covering its sloping roof. A sign depicting a well-rounded hog splashing happily in a wooden half keg of sudsy beer creaked in its rhythmic swinging above the door. The building crammed itself between a grocer on its southern side and a teashop to its north, with just enough space for the walking path to feed between the two. The path, Graham had said, wound up the hill to the church to the west and connected to the larger rambler's trail east of the village. Now, however, the trail lay dark and un-traveled, like a black snake waiting for the first rays of daylight to illuminate it and rouse it from sleep.

It was a good spot for the pub, I thought, envisioning the summer tourist trade of walkers who were not only thirsty after tramping through the glories of the Derbyshire Dales but also seeking overnight lodging. They would need to look hard and long to find a more atmospheric spot to quench both needs, for the building seemed accommodating on both fronts. Through the leaded glass windows I could see the publican and a barmaid carrying empty glasses to the bar; another person banked the wood fire and called over his shoulder to someone nearly hidden by an armload of blankets. Light from the lantern-like overhead fixtures spilled out the windows and onto the ground outside. Remnants of snow dotted the dark earth and pavement, giving the land the appearance of a bizarre chessboard. I tugged my jacket collar closer to my neck and was about to open the front door when Mark grabbed my arm, pulling me to a stop. I looked at him, about to ask what he was doing, when I followed his nod.

David Willett, whom we had met in December while investigating a murder during a St. Nicholas festival, was inside the pub and heading toward the door.

Mark stepped back, pulling me with him, and we stood in the darkness on the far side of the windows, waiting for David to come outside.

"Bloody hell," Mark whispered in my ear, his eyes on David. "How weird is this?"

"What?" I whispered back, feeling Mark's thudding heart against my arm as he held me closely to him.

"David Willett. Alive and kicking in Hollingthorpe. What's he doing here?"

"How should I know?" I said more loudly, only to be shushed into silence by Mark's angry whisper. "What's the matter now?" I murmured, feeling like a conspirator or child sneaking into the kitchen to raid the biscuit tin.

"I don't want him to hear us."

It could have been Margo and I doing this, I thought. It was more the thing she did. I shook my arm free of Mark's grip and turned toward him. "Well, he's going to see us as soon as he steps outside. And what's he going to think with us plastered against the wall? We really look nonchalant."

Mark bent over me, his voice barely audible as a car roared down the street. "I don't care how the hell it looks. I think it looks damned odd to see him here. I never had a good feeling about him since we worked on that case in Bramwell. He bothered me then and he's bothering me now. What's he doing lurking about?"

I tilted my head back so I could see Mark's eyes. They were dark and angry, full of fire. I said, "He's not exactly lurking. He's making for the door and doing nothing illegal as far as I can tell. Probably had a drink or two."

"There's a pub in Bramwell, if I remember correctly. Two, to be precise. Why can't he drink there? He'd be closer to home and not endanger anyone on the roads if he's drunk."

"Doesn't appear to be," I said, watching David say something to the publican and grab his coat from the coat rack near the front door. "Come on, Mark. You're acting like a flaming berk. If David sees us like this—"

"Trouble is, Brenna, you like the guy."

"So?"

"You've let him blind you."

"And you can see through his façade, I suppose."

Mark nodded.

"What *is* his façade, if you don't mind me asking? What's he supposed to be guilty of, besides playing St. Nicholas in the village festival?"

"I still have doubts about that book of his. Something nefarious went on with that, Bren."

I sighed. Sometimes Mark Salt could be as thick as two short planks. "Well, at least you don't suspect him of joining up with Enrico in a terrorist plot."

"Not yet, anyway. But how many leopards can change their spots?"

Chapter 5

David Willett chose that moment to leave the pub. I turned in what I hoped looked like a casual manner, as though I'd just been talking to Mark, and greeted David as he came up to us.

If he was surprised to see us, he didn't show it. Perhaps he'd heard from the publican that the police were already swarming over the village in the course of their murder investigation. He had no way of knowing Mark and I would be here, obviously, but at least he'd made the mental jump to recall our names from three months ago.

"I guess you're here about Enrico," David said, nodding to Mark.

"And why are *you* here?" Mark said, an edge to his voice.

"Simple enough," David returned, leaning against the window ledge and buttoning his coat. It was pea coat style, thick and woolen, and matched the color of his jeans. A lighter blue woolen scarf hung around his neck. When he'd finished with the coat, he drew some dark colored leather gloves from his coat pocket and pulled them on while saying, "I'm visiting my sister and brother."

Another surprise. I recovered quicker than Mark did and said, "I didn't know you had any."

"I'm full of surprises." He grinned, looking like a smartass who's beaten the rap, his teeth blazingly white in the light from the window.

"Give me another one," Mark said, stiffening. "What are their names?"

"I don't know why you have to know, but I suppose you need to take them off your suspect list." He glared at Mark, as though resenting another police investigation that involved him. When his eyes had traveled the length of Mark's figure, he finally said, "Sure. Why not? My sister's Page Hanley, my brother's Harry Willett."

"*Hanley?*"

"Yeh. Page was married, but got divorced—that's why the name discrepancy. Will that do?"

"How long you here for?"

"Couple of days. You want to know the exact minute I'm leaving?" His eyes widened, giving him an innocent appearance.

I knew this wasn't sitting well with Mark. If it had been Graham who was upset, his jaw muscle would tighten. Mark displayed his annoyance through the tone of his voice.

"Just the exact day, Willett. And narrow it down to a.m. or p.m."

David's lips curled into a smirk. "Why should I talk to you when I've got a real copper to talk to?"

Mark's eyes narrowed. "What do you think my warrant card says?"

"Boy Scout, for all I know."

"Who do you consider a real copper, if it's not me? Detective-Sergeant Taylor?" He gestured toward me. I know sometimes the female gender has an advantage in various situations—domestic situations and female problems quickly come to mind. But I didn't think this was one of them.

David said, "As nice a thought as that is, I wasn't referring to Miss Taylor."

"Who, then? The Chief Constable?"

"Scott Coral."

I know I drew in and held my breath. Mark was already annoyed; mentioning Scott's name, let alone asking for him, never produced leaps of joy in the best circumstances. This was tantamount to handing an arsonist a lighted match.

Mark said slowly, "Why do you want Coral? What can you tell him that you can't tell me?"

"Nothing."

"Then why—"

"I respect him."

The words seemed to slam into Mark as if they had indeed lit the fuse. He took a step toward David, but I shoved my hand between them and said that I'd ring up Scott to see if he was free. David nodded and exhaled slowly while Mark remained where he was, his fist shoved into his pocket.

"And how do you know Coral?" Mark asked. "How did you become so good mates with him? Drinking buddies?"

"No. Poker."

"I should've known it would be something like an alcohol problem or gambling."

"Poker *isn't* gambling." He said it so forcefully that he reminded me of Scott. The difference was that Scott and I had joked about it; David wasn't.

"Calling a drunk a social drinker doesn't alter the fact that he's still a drunk."

"And calling you a cop, a police officer for whom I usually have such high regard, doesn't alter my low opinion of you."

"Fine. In the meantime," Mark said, trying to steady his voice as I flipped open my mobile and punched in Scott's number, "would you mind if I ask you a few minor questions? Nothing at all suggesting a lawyer will be needed."

"It sounds like I'm a suspect. You keeping an eye on me, then?"

"You want the distinction of being prime suspect, Willett?"

David sighed and stood up, tucked the end of his scarf into the neck of his coat, and said rather thoughtfully, "It'll give me something to talk about, won't it—the false arrest, police brutality, civil action victory? Plus giving me an idea for another book."

"You writing some fiction thing?"

"No. A true crime book."

Mark muttered something about the book heading for the wrong section in the store, then asked if David had been at the stone turning tonight.

"No. First of all, as an outsider, I'm not invited. Second, I don't go in for that stuff. Third—"

"What stuff? Murder?"

David curled the right side of his mouth before saying, "I didn't know it was a yearly ritual, murdering one of the Devil's Stone turners."

"Escaped your book, didn't it?"

David snorted. "You trying out your comedic routine for the next copper benefit? You know damned well what I mean, Salt. I wasn't at the stone turning, I don't do that sort of physical he-man stuff, and I didn't even know Enrico Thomas. That satisfy you, or do you want to drag me by my hair to the nick and beat a 'confession' out of me?"

"Yet, your sister lives here. You could have participated in the turning through her relationship, if you'd wished to do."

"You're really trying to pin this on me, aren't you? How often do I have to say it, mate? I don't go in for that physical stuff. I've nothing to prove with playing the muscle-laden lad. Understand?" He stepped toward Mark, his index finger extended.

I closed up my phone, having got no answer from Scott, thinking David was going to poke Mark in the chest. I tensed, waiting for a fight. But David merely waved his finger, as though he were warning one of his school pupils.

I said, "When did you get to the village, David?"

The man turned to me, perhaps glad of the chance to de-escalate the situation, and said, "This morning."

"You take off from school?"

"Ash Wednesday. We're off for the day. I'm taking Thursday and Friday as personal leave."

"Gives you a nice bit of holiday with your sister. Five days."

"More, if I'm going to be sitting in jail," he added, turning his smile on Mark.

Mark took a step toward David and I quickly asked the location of his sister's home. David told me, watching as I jotted the address into my notebook, then said he'd welcome us anytime. "My brother's there too," he added as a postscript to the pertinent information of dates and places.

"He's not got a family of his own, then?"

"No. He's never married. You'll understand when you meet him. So, I'm free to go?"

"If you'll remain in the village—"

"Only because I'm visiting my sister—not because you throw an order at me, Salt. Now, get out of my way. I don't have time for your stupidity." He saluted Mark, nodded at me, and walked to the corner of the street.

"Smart ass," Mark said, his voice threateningly low. "Can't stand the berk."

"That's obvious," I said, shoving my notebook and mobile into my shoulder bag. "You could've exercised a bit more restraint in your obvious dislike of the man. You weren't exactly following suggested police conduct, you know."

"So I got angry. You've never been angry with someone?"

"Of course I have. But I didn't start off the interview with flames roaring from my mouth. God, Mark, you'll be lucky if he doesn't complain to Graham."

"Let him. I don't think Graham holds him in high esteem either."

"Even if you're right, that's no excuse. That could've turned ugly. We've enough to worry about without someone running to the media or the chief constable with tales of police brutality."

"I wasn't being brutal, Bren."

"Coming awfully close, then. And why'd you tell him to stay in the area? You know we can't enforce that."

"I just wanted to get under his skin."

I shook my head. "Why do you dislike David so much?"

"Because he's a liar and a cheat and a fraud."

"Anything else?"

When Mark opened his mouth, I said, "I'm joking! I know your opinion of him as an author, but you can't let that spill into this investigation. David might be innocent of Enrico's murder. We don't know anything yet."

"I know enough about David Willett to keep him under the microscope. If he gives me the slightest reason…" Mark made an impolite gesture at David's retreating figure.

I turned and tugged at Mark's arm. "Come on. The pub's closing up. I need some coffee."

The publican was headed toward the door, probably to lock up, when we entered the pub. We explained who we were, asked if there was anything hot to drink, and were rewarded minutes later with two mugs of hot coffee and two rock cakes.

"Darlene makes them," the publican said as Mark paid for us. "You know Darlene Granger?"

"Vicar's wife," I said.

"Right. Specially made for the Devil's Stone turning event. Rock cakes. She laughs about the name association—rock cakes and Devil's Stone."

"I hope that's where the similarity stops!"

"Damned right. You can't find a better rock cake in all of Derbyshire. But they need to be eaten. They won't hold over to tomorrow."

"Darlene must've been working on these for days," I said, taking a bite of the bun.

"Nicest person in the world, she is. Always busy helping folks. Doesn't matter what time of the day or night. She's always there. Nearly as busy as Lloyd, her husband."

"It sounds like she donned the collar when he did."

"She may not have bargained for it when they were first married, but she seems to be wearing it now."

Mark picked up a mug and handed it to me. "Well, I hope she doesn't mind it. Just because he's in the business, doesn't mean she wants to be."

"She doesn't seem to mind. Always cheerful, she is. Never heard her say a mean word about anyone. Now, can I get you folks anything else?"

I thanked him and apologized for keeping him open.

"It's a cold night," the publican said, giving the counter top one last wipe before throwing the towel over his shoulder. "We had a group of people after the event—villagers who just watched, mostly."

Remembering Graham's description of the tea afterwards, I said, "And the turners end up in the church hall, munching on their rock cakes and tea."

"Darlene always sees that I have another batch of the buns here. Not everyone feels comfortable going into the church."

"Not if they're not churchgoers."

"So to make certain all of us get included in the event, like, well..."

"She ensures that the people who come here also get some rock cakes. Awfully nice of her."

"Like I said, miss, salt of the earth she is."

"Well," I said as the barmaid turned off lights in the private bar, "I hate to hold you up from closing..."

The publican shook his head. "Not to worry. What's a few more minutes? Just so long as I don't run afoul of the law." His laugh bounced off the paneled walls.

"Why don't we go outside?" I said, turning to Mark. "That way, we won't hold up these kind folks. Can we just leave the dishes outside on a table? Is that all right?"

The publican said that would be fine, thanked me for my thoughtfulness, confessed it had been a long day, and turned the deadbolt in the front door as we left the pub.

"I just don't feel right about it," Mark said when we were sitting at one of the small outdoor tables. It was white wrought iron, heavy with scrollwork legs. The tabletop was of the same curly design as the legs. Bits of the paint had chipped off, leaving the black iron beneath exposed. We had righted two chairs that had been tipped onto the table edge and I had instantly regretted it. The iron seemed to brand the cold into my backside. Mark evidently didn't notice; he was still jabbering on about David. I swallowed a mouthful of coffee, set down the mug, and jammed my hands between my thighs.

We would've been warmer inside, of course, but in addition to not wanting to detain the publican any longer, I didn't want him hovering and

HORNS OF A DILEMMA

overhearing Mark's and my conversation. Sometimes one had to suffer a bit for one's principles.

"What don't you feel right about? Keeping him open longer than he should have been?" I took another bite of the rock cake and savored the tenderness of the pastry before swallowing it. The publican was right—tomorrow this would be like its namesake.

"This David Willett thing," Mark said after he'd taken a sip of coffee.

"Why? He seemed straightforward to me. He told us when he got here, when he's planning on leaving. He knows we can easily check that out, so he was truthful. You can't hate a man just because—"

"I don't feel right about the fact that David is in two different villages where two murders have occurred."

"So he's guilty by reason of association. Is that your thinking?"

"I don't believe in coincidence."

He was sounding like Graham. I shook my head, disbelieving the conversation. "You're over-reacting, Mark."

"Yeh? I thought I was being a good copper."

"Not that I blame you. It's the hour and the devil's stone bit."

"Ah. Nearly midnight, wintry night, no moon, a nefarious deed on a dark moor..."

"You're being overly dramatic, Mark. Cut it out. This isn't funny."

"I wasn't laughing, Bren."

"Though the setting would make anyone uneasy, I'll grant you. A moonless night..."

"A graveyard breathing down your neck..."

"A mysterious boulder..."

"The devil's stone..."

A puff of icy wind slid through the pub's patio and I shivered, though whether from the weather or my imagination of the crime scene, I don't know.

Mark scooted his chair closer to mine. The iron legs scraped against the flagstone, echoing against the side of the building. He put his arm around my shoulder. "Does this make it any better?"

"I think," I said, ignoring Mark's touch, which—I do admit—wasn't easy to do. "It *is* odd that David would be in two villages that each had a murder. I don't like pointing a finger at him, especially only hours into the investigation, but..." I looked at Mark to see what he was thinking. It wasn't about the case.

His face was only inches from mine. I felt my heart rate quickening and tried not to show it.

"This is nice," Mark said, his voice little more than a whisper against my ear.

"I didn't know you liked murder investigations so much."

"Now who's being deliberately obtuse?"

I opened my mouth to reply but Mark said, "You owe me something, you know."

This time I found my voice. "What? I don't remember borrowing money or—"

"You owe me a dinner date. Remember last month?"

Yes. In the car. I nodded. "I wasn't putting it off, Mark. It's just that I've been a bit busy. And besides, we've already been through this."

"I'd like to firm up a date. I know about our job. It can continuously get in the way of everything if we let it. Anyway, time's too precious. As exemplified this evening."

He didn't have to remind me that death could claim anyone at any moment. You didn't have to be a cop to understand that. And here, in the night, just below the hill that housed church and graveyard and dead body, it was all too evident. I stared at him. His eyes were barely visible in darkness, but I knew he was concentrating on my face. My voice faltered. "Uh, sure, Mark. Certainly. Any particular time?"

"Dinner time." His face was angled enough under the streetlamp so that his grin flashed at me.

I laughed. "How about one evening this week? Assuming we'll get time for dinner. It'll save you petrol and time. You know—we're both here, you won't have to give up a free evening..."

He withdrew his arm from my shoulder and turned so he could see me better. When he did, a shadow from his head fell across my face. He scooted a bit in his chair and I was once more under the light. "I'm not concerned with petrol and time, Bren. I want to spend an evening with you or I wouldn't have asked."

I murmured my thanks. "Just giving you the option, Mark. There's nothing wrong with saving either commodity."

"Let me worry about my petrol. So one evening this week, then? Super."

"It'll give you something to look forward to when you're knee-deep in mud."

"I'm hoping the Scientific lads will be doing that." He drained his coffee and asked if I were finished.

"Yes. Why the rush? You think Graham's timing us? He did give his blessing on our coffee break, you know."

"Of course he did, or I wouldn't be sitting here now, risking a reprimand. But I'd like to check out David's statement. You remember where his sister lives?"

I patted my shoulder bag and got up. "I've nearly a photographic memory, but the notes help."

"He's had time to prep her, but I'd like to go over there now. If he's really staying there, we won't be waking her up. He'll have just wandered home."

"Presuming he hasn't the key or goes stomping through the house, he'll be waking her up. Fine. Let's see how inventive Page Hanley is with her lies."

HORNS OF A DILEMMA

The house Page Hanley lived in was not much different from the others on the street—or in the majority of Derbyshire villages I'd seen. Light colored stone created an unbreaking line of house fronts that set back a dozen or so yards from the pavement. Patches of gardens crowded in between the pavement and house façade, declaring owner individuality in the way of arrangement and plant choices. A black iron birdbath, topped with a layer of crusty snow, stood in a corner of one garden, while a white trellis covered in brown rose cane loomed out of the darkness across the street. As Mark stopped his car in front of Page's house, I could see a small concrete bench and sundial near the front walk. Snow iced the rim of the bench, nearly blending with the whiteness of the concrete, its presence marked by the mounds that lay thicker near the dense backdrop of rhododendrons.

Empty of summery finery, white-painted window boxes snuggled against the street-facing windowsills, a brighter hue than the light gray stone of the house and hoary snow blanketing the ground. The front door, however, stood out like a fresh slash on an arm, blood red against the paleness of stone, perhaps lending another element of personality to this house in a row of sameness.

The front curtain fell closed as Mark pressed the doorbell. "Seems as though we're expected."

"I'd be shocked if we weren't."

"So would I. Willett has the personality of the eager tale bearer."

Mark might have said more, but the door opened and Mark focused on the woman standing before us.

Page Hanley mimicked her brother David's red hair and freckles, but she hadn't the same physique. Page was smaller but muscular from daily physical workouts. The benefit, she said, of being a personal trainer at a health club gym in Chesterfield.

She didn't seem surprised to see two police detectives on her doorstep at midnight. Perhaps she'd heard of the murder; perhaps David had told her we'd no doubt be dropping by. Whatever the reason, Page graciously sat us in sleep-inducing chairs in the parlor and answered our questions.

"I watched the stone turning," she said, bringing one of her legs beneath her and sitting cross-legged in the wide-cushioned chair. She looked as though she were practicing a yoga position. "But I didn't stay for the revelry afterward. I returned home as soon as they flipped the thing."

"Is that usual?" I asked.

"What—the watching or the leaving early?"

"Both. Either."

"Usual, yes. I don't do the tea bit afterwards because I don't attend church. And I don't do the stone turning because, although it seems to be 'all are welcome,' it's really an old boys' club. Plus, I find all that muscle straining a bore. I get my fill workdays at the gym."

I eyed the obvious muscular build of her upper torso.

Page laughed. "Yes, it's a contradiction. But one has to do with my health and the other has to do with the he-men in the gym parading their abs in front of me, trying to impress me into their beds. I don't want anything to do with them outside my work schedule."

"You're just there to help them through the weight lifting machines and the stair steppers and all."

"They can save their strength and woo someone else. I'm fine the way I am and have no intention at the moment to move into someone's bed. Or home."

I could understand why she wouldn't want to leave her house. It was snug and small and welcoming, furnished with pieces that could have been handed down for generations. Rather than being shabby, the furniture shone from polish, the upholstery showed no sign of wear. The room solidified under the hues of green and burgundy—rug, sofa, cushions and paintings. I could have easily snuggled into the cushions for the evening if I'd been allowed.

But I rallied myself and asked, "I'm surprised you go to the stone turning."

"It's part of the village, isn't it?" Page remarked. "Like Christmas Eve services and well dressing. I go to those, too."

I glanced at a silver framed photo of her helping with the well panel decorating and nodded.

"I like the custom behind it," she continued. "I just don't get involved in the physical aspect. Besides being the same as long as I can remember, rolling the stone one direction, then back the other way the following year, I don't like getting muddy. And I can't avoid it if I'm in the midst of that tussle." She examined one of her painted fingernails, then looked at Mark as he leaned forward.

"And your brother—"

"He arrived this morning. He always does."

"Always implying same thing each year."

"He'll leave Sunday. It's a nice break for him. We see each other a few times a year."

"Does he come here all the time?"

"Or I go to Bramwell to stay with him. Our brother, Harry, comes with me if I go to David's. But I know what you're getting at, Detective. David arrives, there's a murder."

"The entire village was probably in town tonight, so most everyone is under suspicion. It's not personal."

"David would hardly come to Hollingthorpe to kill Enrico, though. Especially within hours of his arrival! God, how daft is that!"

"Yes. To deliberately call attention to himself by coming here and then killing some bloke..."

She tilted her head and the light from the nearby lamp highlighted the reddish tints in her hair. "You'd have to be an idiot to do that. Anyway, why would David kill someone he doesn't know? My brother and I are the only people David knows in Hollingthorpe. Doesn't make sense."

"Did anyone see you or David at the turning?"

"You want alibis. I should think all who were at the turning would have seen us. Pity we didn't stop in the church hall for tea—sounds as if the vicar's oath would instantly clear us of murder suspicions."

"Did you know Enrico?" I asked, pulling her eyes from Mark's face to mine.

"Just to say hello to. Nothing chummy. Although we weren't next-door neighbors, I did invite him over for tea. When I'd heard he had moved in I presented myself at his door, with a basket of fresh-baked buns, a tin of tea, and an invitation to come over for coffee. I thought I'd have a few people over, introduce everyone—that sort of thing."

"But he shrugged you off, gave you indefinite maybes about when he'd come over," I guessed.

"He never did come. The first day turned into the first week, then into the second week...well, after a while you get tired of asking, don't you?"

"Either the person wants to come and takes you up on your offer, or he puts you off."

"Umm. Enrico was like that, putting me off. I wish he'd just come straight out and told me no thank you, instead of keeping that 'perhaps' spark alive in me." She grimaced and looked down at the carpet. "I'm sorry, because I think a lot of people would have liked to have known him. Really know him—not just to nod to in the bank, but to talk to. He never gave us that chance."

Mark stood up and thanked Page. I followed as he hurried out the front door.

"What's the rush, Mark?" I asked as I half ran to catch him up.

"What's going on in this village, Bren? Something's going on with this bloke Enrico."

"Just because he refuses tea at someone's house —"

"It's more than that, if you remember his house and that nice little Sig Sauer. Sounds like he's hiding something more than himself."

Later that night I rang up Erik to unload my day and stress—a nightly ritual when we weren't together on the weekends. Though his words were comforting, his voice wasn't. Which was odd, considering we were living together to offer each other comfort. When I rang off and lay back in bed, the first whispering of doubt seeped into my mind. Recalling it days later, I wondered if the whispering had already crept into my heart.

Chapter 6

Thursday morning dawned with a gray sky and my head aching. I'd got to bed somewhere in the wee hours after helping set up the incident room in the village community center. Jens Nielsen, the Home Office pathologist, and Faye Usher, the Home Office biologist, had arrived, done their preliminary examination, bagged and loaded Enrico's body into the mortuary van, and left with Graham to do the postmortem. It was the beginning of his usual 48-hour non-stop work routine. I had watched them leave with a feeling of relief and dread. Relief because one less felon was alive, and dread because this case could develop into something more than a murder investigation if Mark's terrorist theory turned out to be correct.

So at six o'clock that morning I was briefing the various police teams on the situation and giving them the postmortem results. These meetings were held early so we could get a jump on the day and know which way the investigation was headed.

I looked at the officers seated before me. Mid-career and late-career, cynical and optimistic, laid-back and inflexible. Married and unmarried, childless and parental. Droll and dull, rash and cautious, vane and humble. Yet no matter these officers' personalities or attitude toward the case, they were professional and extremely focused on the job of work. The faces might vary but the team titles didn't—leader of the house-to-house team, leader of the search team, leader of the Scientific Officers, leader of the outside inquiry team, incident team inspector, press officer. A lot of men and women concentrating their talent and experience on finding Enrico's killer. All anxious to get going, if the paper shuffling and clock glancing and sighs I now heard were correct indications.

I opened my mouth, ready to begin, but paused as a team leader hurried to take his seat, apologizing for being late. The faces before me stared blankly, neither expecting anything unusual nor hoping for an early break. The officers sat in several short rows, the metal chairs more or less evenly spaced, the floor beneath them already showing signs of the general jumble that would accumulate during our stay—paper cups, coffee mugs, notebooks, stacks of paper, mobile phones, caps and gloves.

I glanced at my watch, smiled, wished everyone good morning, and started with the facts to date. Then I read aloud the postmortem report. Once again I was thankful Graham had attended it. This time more than any other, for the injuries had been stomach-churning enough during my

HORNS OF A DILEMMA

scant view; I could not have survived the medical exam that was always up-close, personal and graphic.

"The victim was struck on the back and side of the head," I said, stealing myself to read through the vivid details. "These blows forced him to fall forward. Chief Inspector Graham found him face down, which suggests the victim did indeed fall like this. Livor mortis in the chest and fronts of his thighs—which we might expect to see in any other scenario but this—was absent due to the time of the body's discovery, being under an hour after his death. This also eliminates algor mortis as a means of establishing time of death. Even though Enrico Thomas was found outside at night, and therefore would have ordinarily cooled quickly—due to the quick discovery of the body it had not cooled sufficiently to give us a change in body temperature. The same can be said about rigor mortis—the body still reasonably being at normal body temperature, the extremities would still be flexible. Normally all these indicators would pose problems in establishing time of death, but, as I stated, Chief Inspector Graham can pinpoint death to within a forty-five minute slot."

One of the officers cheered and another yelled, "Thank God!" Most of the others looked more hopeful.

I smiled, then continued. "The skull was fractured at the point of contact with the crowbar, which is the murder weapon, by the way. The skin shows signs of a compression laceration that matches the size and shape of the crow bar."

"I suppose Jens did comparison tests with crowbars from the stone turning event," an officer suggested.

"Yes. It fits precisely. Since scalp lacerations bleed profusely, there was considerable blood pooling over the face and onto the ground. The underlying bone splintering is a depressed fracture, with the bone fragments driven into the soft pink brain tissue." I stopped and grabbed my glass of water in what I hoped would look normal. My stomach was beginning to tighten. After taking a long sip that gave me time to steel my mind, I set down the glass and continued with the report. "There are corresponding lacerations and bleeding on the side of the head—the right cheek and ear—and accompanying fractures of the cheekbones and nose."

"Any sign of defense wounds?"

"None. Our victim apparently did not see his attacker. Death was instantaneous, or practically so, due from a massive skull fracture."

When I laid down the report, the room was deathly quiet. Several officers still stared at their notes, others looked at the walls or out of the windows. The few who looked at me seemed suddenly to have aged or to have grown more serious than when they had arrived. An air of determination settled over us as we dealt with the details of the gruesome death. Someone muttered that at least that was one less scumbag in the world.

I gave each team its assignment and asked for questions.

The press officer said the only question he had was if there were additional personnel available to call up now that the report of the murder had hit the newspapers and television newscasts. "I don't mind dealing with the press," he said, "but now that our superstitious and thrill-seeking public are learning that there's been a killing at a pagan custom, we're being inundated with gawkers."

"They'll be hanging from the trees, mate," another officer chirped. "And climbing onto the rooftops to have a peek at the stone."

"We won't be able to control the area."

"There is that," the other officer agreed. "We'll have our hands full dealing with the devil worshippers and occult dabblers."

"It's already started, actually. One group's protesting that the devil's claimed his own for disturbing his stone, and another group's wanting to touch the damned boulder because it's obviously got some spiritual power, being that it just conked a bloke."

"And that's just for starters."

"I'll bet you anything you like that there'll be another crowd that's gonna come just to ogle at the murder site, and yet another group's gonna protest that the village ought to get rid of the stone, that a bit of demonism has no right being so close to a Christian church—never mind it being the church that probably interloped into the stone's turf. Hell, it'll be a circus!"

I told the press officer that he certainly could request help should he sense erupting fervor at the press conference, and added that if the crowds began swelling to an uncontrollable size, to ring up headquarters without delay. "We don't want a public incident on top of everything else," I added. He nodded, looked relieved, and referred to the fact sheet I'd handed out before the briefing.

One officer, a woman new to the team, asked if we had any suspects. I told her no, that we were just beginning our inquiries. She sighed, perhaps envisioning the questioning of dozens of villagers, and sat back in her chair. Another officer said that we were ahead of the game on this case. "I can't recall," he said, his voice deceptively lazy, "when we began a case knowing every one of the big questions." Several officers murmured their agreement, and I nodded. It was not often that we knew the answers to the four major categories in a case: cause, mechanism, manner and time of death.

There being no more questions, the leaders left the incident room to meet with their teams and begin their jobs.

I glanced around the room. Graham had not returned from the postmortem examination, and Mark and Margo hadn't shown up yet. I decided to steal thirty minutes in order to wake up fully.

Having showered, dressed and breakfasted in the pre-dawn hours, I now allowed myself some exercise to brush the cobwebs from my mind and restore blood circulation to my body. I'd felt nearly asleep during the preliminary investigation last evening, and the early rouse from my bed hadn't helped my situation. I wanted to be as alert as possible today. Now we were getting into the heart of the case. I returned to my room to retrieve

HORNS OF A DILEMMA

my forgotten ski cap, jammed it on my head, and left the building determined to make significant progress today on the case.

My walk took me from the pub, where the entire murder team had rooms, up the church hill and along the edge of the woods. Graham had said last night that the path was merely part of the larger one that rambled through the dales district. Besides giving me a chance to bird watch, the walk would also take me to the area where Enrico had been murdered, and I wanted to look at the scene in daylight.

The path angled sharply upward several dozen yards from the back of the pub, then evened off as it crested the hill. I huffed up the hill, pausing halfway in my trek to look back to the village below me. It lay like the capital letter H on its side, nestled between the church hill to its west and the river and mountains to its east. The main street comprised the shorter, vertical stroke of the H and carried the commercial establishments along its length before it metamorphosed into the busier A5012—a convenient thoroughfare linking it to the bigger burgs of Buxton to the west and Matlock to the east. The bottom stroke of the letter H ran for miles in both directions: the segment in the village cradling residences, with the village's community center and playground at the intersection of the vertical street. The northern-most street in the village actually dead-ended into the vertical street, running to the east with another group of homes and leading to the region's hospital and health club. The village green cozied up to the backs of the businesses on the High Street, an oasis of green open space in this sea of gray stone buildings.

The village had chiseled its existence from the limestone hills and forest that seemed to threaten it with its unyielding embrace. But the wood was slower to encroach upon the villagers than were the tumbling boulders that had spilled from the mountains flanking either end of the village. Time and nature both moved slowly in Hollingthorpe, customs and seasons following the calendar. A landslide or creeping vegetation might threaten, but the residents would prevail.

The path branched as I approached the wood, the right pathway entering the dense copse, the left section heading toward the church. I chose this path and stepped around lingering clumps of snow that had solidified. The light rain of last night had frozen and now coated the ground in a thin sheet of ice. It cracked and broke beneath my weight, announcing my journey to the birds. Black pellets of sheep dung confettied the ground near the church, oddly dark on the creamy landscape. Patches of close-cropped khaki-colored grass sprawled matted and muddied in the open spaces, a reminder of this past summer and a hint of approaching spring.

Now that I could see the entire church, I could appreciate its beauty and its setting. It seemed to have sprung from the rock face jutting out from the tor behind it and thumbed its nose at the constant danger of rockslides. Great masses of green from the surrounding wood added the only color, though this seemed in peril of camouflaging the structure. The copse was restrained in its enthusiastic embrace by the lawn, but again, the gray limestone threatened domination, for the headstones that popped through the mantle of snow or muddy grass echoed the mountain's front wall. A centuries-old yew tree shading the church's south porch brought the sylvan backdrop within touching range. In the feeble morning light, the stones of the square bell tower burst from the apparent flatness of gray, the sun illuminating the bumps and gouges of each hand-cut rock.

The boulder for the stone turning custom lay alone in the expanse of the churchyard, a solitary object devoid of neighboring trees or tombstones. The devil could easily have tossed this stone at the church, for there was nothing similar in the vicinity. The ground around the stone was a sea of barren earth pock-marked with footprints and holes—probably where crowbars had been jammed into the soil to lever the stone. It was as good as a photograph, frozen by last night's cold temperature into an exhibit for Graham's case.

But as petrified in time as the scene was, it also breathed. The walls of the crime scene tent undulated in the wind as if it inhaled and exhaled; the police tape that encircled the area flapped, the blue segments of the tape bouncing above the snowy ground to announce the spot before I could see the lone constable standing guard near the church door.

It was as I left the edge of the wood that I saw it. A single red rose. Lying on the frozen ground, the edges of its petals fringed with frost. A red ribbon tied around its stem was iced to the soil.

I walked over to Constable Fordyce and asked who left the rose.

PC Fordyce blinked several times and asked, "What rose?"

I pointed to the spot, several dozen yards away, and said, "*That* rose. When did that appear? A bit ago, judging from the frost."

Fordyce blinked again, turned slightly pale, and said, "To tell you the truth, Brenna, I never saw it. I can't imagine when it was left, for I never left my post all night. Well..." He swallowed hard and said rather slowly, averting his eyes from me, "Except for...you know. But I still had the churchyard in sight. I just stood near the edge of the wood, there." He pointed to the nearest tree, a sky-scraping oak, a youngster by the wood's standard, a prize for any tree-loving gardener. "I wasn't long. Maybe a minute. But I positioned myself so I could see the church door and the boulder, in case someone wanted to slip back to tamper with the scene. No one came by, Brenna. No one. I'll stake my job on it."

I thought that he might have to if Graham discovered Fordyce was lying, but said, gazing at the copse, "I suppose someone could have sneaked through the wood. There's no law stating you have to keep on the path."

"Probably came up from the village, by the pub. Then took the right branch, followed the path into the wood for a bit, then left the path and doubled back to the church through the trees." He raised his eyebrows, expecting my confirmation. I gave it.

"Could have done. Yes. That's very likely, since you were watching the boulder area all night."

Fordyce's sigh was audible even against the tower bells' tolling of the

HORNS OF A DILEMMA

hour. He allowed himself a slight smile. "What's it mean, that rose? If someone wanted to honor Enrico, why not just come up to me and ask if I'd put it outside the scene tape? Why leave it there?"

"I would have said it fell from a bouquet, but the ribbon on the stem implies it's an offering by itself. Well…" I told Fordyce that I would let Graham know and walked back to the rose.

The soil around the flower was not trampled or marked as the muddy area holding the boulder. Even when I squatted to peer at the flattened grass I could see no indication of a shoeprint. There was nothing readily discernable that would give a clue as to the flower giver.

I said as much to Graham when I found him in the incident room.

He looked like the man I knew—freshly showered, hair washed, clean tailored clothes. It had been a fascinating peek into his off-duty life, but I felt more comfortable with the working Graham. At least at this stage of our friendship.

"You're looking bright and cheerful," Graham said as I set my shoulder bag on the table that held his laptop computer. "Two hours of sleep becomes you."

I faked a smile and looked around the room.

It was no different from other many community centers—hardwood floor and painted wooden walls with windows mantled in wire mesh to ward off misbehaving volleyballs. A small kitchen, rest rooms and storage room for equipment led off the main room where we had set up shop.

"Constable Byrd has just made some tea," Graham said, as though interpreting my scrutiny of the room. "You want some?"

I said I'd get it, but wanted to tell him something first.

He raised an eyebrow, probably wondering what I could have that seemed so serious. When I'd told him about finding the rose, he said, "Someone must have loved Enrico very much. Or at least feels saddened by his death."

"Yes, sir," I said. "That's what I told Fordyce."

"I'll have to get someone up there." He looked around the room, walked over to WPC MacMillan and asked her to take photos and see if there was anything at all suggesting a clue. When she had left, Graham returned to our table and said that with any bit of good luck MacMillan would find something. "Despite the light rain we had in the early hours. But isn't that typical of police work?"

I agreed. "Why couldn't the person have handed the flower to Fordyce to lay closer to the murder scene, sir? If he or she was that upset about Enrico's death…"

"Afraid of becoming involved."

"Yes, sir. Once you identify yourself as being sympathetic to the victim, you're opening yourself to police questioning."

"How long have you known Enrico? Were you lovers or friends? When did you last see him? Did you see anything peculiar during or after the stone turning?" He grinned and shrugged, looking like a boy who's been caught sneaking a drink from his dad's bottle of whiskey. "It's logical, TC. We've got to ask if there's a link. An indifferent person won't purchase a rose as a memorial to a murder victim."

TC was the nickname that had grown from the derision Mark Salt had heaped on me during our police training days. Originally standing for The Cop in mockery of my passion to become the best copper in the Division, it had mutated both into initials and affection, its birth and connotation relegated to the haze of Things Forgotten.

I smiled, not so much from Graham's response but from his use of my nickname. All was right with the world when he was relaxed enough to call me TC.

But our world—and a few others, too—tilted drastically in the next minute when Lloyd Granger, wearing mismatched shoes and a coat thrown over his pajamas, rushed into the room, shouting that his son was missing.

Chapter 7

The room threatened to tip and dump me screaming through its windows into the snow outside. I held onto the edge of the metal table as my knees gave way. What was Lloyd saying? How could John be missing? It was only half past eight. We had just begun our day.

I glanced at Graham. His face had blanched and he was guiding Lloyd to a chair, calling for a cup of tea, asking Lloyd to speak more slowly. Lloyd collapsed into the chair, thudding against its unyielding back and gazing up at Graham's tall figure rather like a child seeking approval from his father. Graham laid his hand on Lloyd's shoulder, told him again to start at the beginning of his narrative, and sat on the edge of the table, bending forward to be closer to Lloyd, who was half crying, half babbling. I pressed my fist against my forehead, trying to stop the pounding. All the faces of all the missing children I had ever been involved with flooded my mind, their voices screaming to be found or avenged, their arms reaching for me.

I shook the images from my head and went over to the men. Lloyd was accepting a cup of tea from Mark, thanking him with all the sincerity of a drowning victim grasping a lifeline. Graham was grabbing his notebook and pen, waiting for Lloyd to begin. I sat down opposite Lloyd. A bit of color was returning to his face and his breathing had slowed. When he had taken a gulp of tea, he looked up at Graham and spoke in a strained voice.

"He's not at home," Lloyd said, turning his red-rimmed eyes onto each of our faces. He looked like he'd done more than cry; he looked as though he'd not slept. "John's not been home all night. I can't think of where he'd be!" He lowered his head as though seeking strength through prayer.

Graham said, "Were you aware of his absence last night?"

Looking up, Lloyd said, "No. If we had, we would have begun looking for him immediately, not wait until this morning."

"And when did you discover that he wasn't home? What time?"

"Around seven o'clock this morning."

"Is that usually when he gets up? Is that why you knew he wasn't home?"

"On school days he's up then, yes. Today he should've been up. When it got to be quarter past, Darlene went into his bedroom to wake him. She thought perhaps he'd forgotten to set his alarm. But he wasn't there!" Lloyd's voice rose again as he relived the panic.

I said, "Had he been to bed? Could you tell from the bedclothes?

Perhaps he just got up early—"

Lloyd shook his head. "His bed was made and there was the same depression on it that has been there since last night at tea time."

"Depression?"

"I was in his room last night to talk to him while he was changing clothes for the stone turning."

"Like old trainers or something?"

"Yes. He wears those when he's going to be doing dirty work, like turning the Devil's Stone in the mud, as was the case last night. He found them in the back of his wardrobe."

"And sat on the bed to put them on," I guessed.

"He'd pushed aside his pillow as he rummaged under it for his iPod. He sometimes stashes it there when he's listening to music."

"As he's falling asleep." I did the same thing, except it was with my transistor radio.

"I was talking to him, so I know exactly where he sat. Pillow, bed—it's all the same..." His voice trailed off, lower and fainter, as though he were defeated.

"Is there anywhere he might be?" I asked, fighting the anxiety creeping into my own voice. The face of Mark's nephew loomed large and clear in my mind, taunting me in a whine that I would botch the job of finding John. I swallowed, fearful Graham knew what was happening to me. He was concentrating on Lloyd's face, perhaps reading the anguish there and formulating comforting, hopeful words. I pulled my strength up from somewhere within my soul and said, "Could he be at a friend's home, perhaps? Did he have a project for school he was working on? Perhaps he went over to a friend's early to work on it."

"I *told* you!" Lloyd said, anger replacing his anxiety. "His bed's not been slept in. How could he be at a friend's house if he's not slept at home all night?"

His rage snapped into the air, startling those constables working nearby. The room grew quiet with the unease that mantles an embarrassing situation. A heartbeat, an hour, a day seemed to pass in a numbing stagnation of time. I could hear nothing but my thumping pulse, see nothing but a haze of missing children's faces, feel nothing but apprehension. A ringing phone and an officer's answering voice finally shattered the stillness.

Graham's lower, calmer voice broke into Lloyd's agitation. "Sergeant Taylor merely asked if John could be at a friend's. She didn't say he'd gone there this morning. If John hasn't been home, it's logical to assume he was at the friend's all night. Perhaps worked on a project later than they had planned, so he slept over, not wanting to come home in the dark."

He left unsaid that John may have stayed at his friend's because Enrico's murderer might still be about.

"Now." Graham paused as Lloyd mumbled his apology for letting his temper take over. "We need to know when you last saw him, Lloyd. That may give us a lead on where he went, or the time he left."

"Of course. I understand. Sorry." He clasped his fingers together, stared at his lap, then up at Graham as he said, "Last night at the stone turning. He participated, as you know, Geoff."

"Was he at the Ash Wednesday service or in the church hall afterwards for tea? I don't recall seeing him, but I wasn't particularly looking for him, either. I was talking to you and Darlene, as well as to one or two others."

I could imagine the church hall, done up in beige paint or simulated wood paneling. Long metal tables, stressed and nicked from years of use and abuse, and metal folding chairs would sprawl across the tired lino flooring. The huge tea and coffee urns would perch on one table, along with the plates, cutlery and cups. The food would sit on the serving hatch or on a decorated table, perhaps. A low stage might stretch across one end of the room, hidden behind floor-length faded curtains. Posters and photos would interrupt the otherwise bare walls, announcing church club meetings, the forthcoming talent show, and Easter Sunday egg hunt. But even if the room were drab, the people brought it to bloom with their friendship and concern for each other. The environment was invisible when love was present.

Lloyd said, "John attended worship, yes, but I can't recall if he came down for tea."

"Can Darlene recall?"

"Might do, but I can't ask her right now." He glanced over his shoulder, in the direction of the church, as though he could see her. "She's extremely upset, Geoff. Barely able to talk."

"Is anyone with her? A neighbor...?"

"Someone's sitting with her. I saw to that before I came here to inform you. I thought..." He took a deep breath, as though to gather courage for the ordeal. "I thought it best to tell you in person. I don't know why. The phone is so cold. I—I needed to be with friends."

I glanced at Graham, wondering how he took the compliment. Warmth seemed to flood his eyes. Was this clergy to clergy condolence, a bond like that which cemented fellow police officers? I abruptly knew it wasn't; it was the compassion of one friend for another.

"So he was around last night until the end of the service," Graham said, jotting down the time in his notebook. "That makes it...what? Half past seven, quarter to eight or so?"

Lloyd nodded, the color fading from his face. "We began around seven o'clock, I believe. Well, we usually do, don't we? It was short because it was a weeknight."

"So from 7:45, let's say, John is unaccounted for. I suppose he couldn't have said something to you or Darlene earlier in the day about him spending the night at a mate's house, and you've simply forgotten?"

"Not possible. *No.* We don't allow John to sleep over on school nights. It's a rule. John knows it."

"Perhaps he thought last night special. Has he ever challenged you before?"

"He's not that sort of lad."

"He isn't seeing someone, is he? I know he's sixteen, Lloyd, and that may seem young, but these days kids are sleeping together in their teens. I don't like it—and I know you and Darlene don't like it—but you've got to accept that it happens and wonder if John had a girl friend he'd be spending the night with."

Lloyd's body tensed and he glared at Graham as though he'd just accused John of stealing the church funds. "*John wouldn't do that!* You know him, Geoff. Frankly, I'm astonished you'd even suggest it."

"It's not so far-fetched when you know the statistics, Lloyd."

"You can wallow in numbers all you want, but John's not like that. He's had a solid church upbringing. He doesn't smoke or do drugs or run in a gang or have sex. He's been taught right from wrong and he's a good lad. He has no particular girlfriend, and even if he did—"

"He wouldn't sleep with her. Right."

Lloyd slammed his fist onto the top of his thigh. "John's better than that, Geoff! He doesn't go sneaking off in the middle of the night like some common hooligan wanting to do a bit of vandalism. He wants to go to university and make a career. He works more now, in school, than some men I know who are supposedly adults."

"What work does he do?"

"He works weekends and during summer holiday at Richard's launderette. He puts in a lot of hours, too. Even misses out on going around with his mates, he's that serious about his future."

"Who are his mates? Anyone specifically he's close to? You said he has no particular girlfriend, but does he have someone he likes to talk to?"

Lloyd seemed to think about his answer, perhaps wondering if he were about to land one of John's chums in the middle of a police investigation. He took another sip of tea before replying, "He's close to Conrad Quinn."

Graham frowned. "The name's unfamiliar to me. New family here?"

"No. Conrad's aunt is Colette Harmon. You know her."

"Right." He nodded, as though recalling the woman or some incident from his years in the village. "I didn't know she had a nephew."

"Conrad's a big lad. He's 19, a sports fanatic, and desperate to be Someone. Well, a sports star Someone."

"He doesn't live here in the village, I take it."

"In Edinburgh. He comes down here to Hollingthorpe a few times a year to stay with Colette and her husband."

"Does he get on with their children?"

"They have none, so it's nice for them to have Conrad visit. They're quite close."

"So Conrad's visiting now."

"Yes. He's not in university, so he can come down several times a year."

"Well," Graham said, closing his notebook and standing up. "I think the best thing to do right now is for you to go home, stay with Darlene, and wait until I ring you up with any news. I'll go to John's school and ask about. Perhaps one of his friends there knows where he is. He may even be there, Lloyd. Don't give up hope. Taylor—" He turned to me, his face paler than I'd ever seen it. "You and Mark rout out Conrad from his warm bed. He's at..." He scribbled down an address on a piece of computer printer paper and gave it to me. "His aunt's, Colette Harmon."

"Right, sir. We'll find out if Conrad knows anything about John's whereabouts, and then return here."

"Don't bother ringing me up on my mobile; I'll be back as soon as I finish at his school. I want this thing solved quickly. Thanks."

As Graham grabbed his car key, Lloyd said, "Geoff, you asked about girlfriends."

Graham stopped, looked interested, and waited for Lloyd to continue.

"He hasn't a steady girlfriend, in the real sense of the word, but he likes one girl very much."

"And who is she?"

"Toni Dutton."

"Her parents own the hair salon in the village, don't they?"

"Yes. That's them. John's dated Toni a few times. I just thought she—"

"Thanks, Lloyd. I'll talk to her." He grabbed his jacket, yanked it on, and squeezed his friend's hand before heading for the door.

The sun had not cleared the ridge of the eastern hills but it still managed to proclaim its presence by washing the treetops in lemon-colored light. The backs of the eastern-most buildings and the faces of the western shops along the High Street shook themselves from sleep, opened shaded eyes and peered into the street, discarding an icicle from their brows and yawning through gaping doorways. Tiny icicles fringed the edges of the canvas awnings folded flat against the store walls. The ice would soon shatter and fall to the pavement, I thought, when the awnings were opened. Steam rose from the slated roofs, the sunlight warming the cold, glistening tiles. A flock of sparrows chirped around an evergreen, glad of the sun's heat and looking for breakfast.

The High Street still wallowed in shadow, too entrenched by the line of shops and the backdrop of mountain to catch the early morning sunlight, and the night's chill lingered on the hard stone surfaces of store facades and concrete pavement. Frost and clumps of snow clung to the deeper, darker, colder places, reluctant to release its wintry grip. I stepped over a puddle of frozen water, resisting the urge to shatter its smooth frosty surface with the heel of my boot. A store keeper dragged out his sign, fresh with the day's specials chalked on its black surface, nodded to me, and pushed a handful of sludgy snow from the edge of the canvas awning covering the door. The snow plopped onto the pavement, fragmenting and splattering like the blood spotting at a murder scene.

Mark stopped abruptly to peer into the shop window. He pointed to a carton of beer. "Maybe we should get that for Lloyd. He might need that before this thing is over."

"That's not funny, Mark. Either the connotation that Lloyd should drink himself into insensibility or that he'll need it to get over John's disappearance. We don't know much yet—John could be at school."

"I wasn't joking, Brenna. I was thinking of a search party. He might want to provide something for the workers. It's long, thirsty work."

I apologized, acknowledging that he'd already been on enough search teams to know about that. "But let's hold off. As I said, Graham might find him at school."

"What the hell would he be doing at school if he didn't go home all night? Sounds like an idiot's chase, but if it makes the Vic happy..." He sniffed and started walking.

We'd just crossed the High Street when we saw the man standing outside the hair salon. He was a graying brunet, pencil thin with a prominent nose and chin. The knitted ski cap he wore was stretched out of shape and he was making faces at someone presumably within the shop. As Mark and I approached, the man leaned his forehead against the window and shouted insults.

"He needs to be taken in tow, I'm thinking," Mark said as the man grinned at us before resuming his name-calling.

"Either that," I said, "or snared in a net. Is he daft or angry?"

"Hardly matters at this point. You want to talk to him first, or should I just nab him?"

A man emerging from the bakery next door quashed my response, for he heard the shouting and rushed over to the agitated man, calling calmly yet firmly for him to stop. The shouter glanced at the newcomer—a tall, muscular man in his early forties—but continued voicing his opinions about someone inside the shop. When he pulled away from the newcomer's grasp, Mark hurried over.

"He's all right," the newcomer said as Mark introduced us. "He just gets a bit agitated at times. I'm Ian Harmon, by the way. I suppose you're investigating Enrico's death. Terrible thing, that. Shocking. We're so glad you're here."

"You need any help with him?" Mark said, nodding to the agitated chap. "Who is he?"

"Harry Willett. No, I'm fine, ta. I can handle him. Harry and I go back a long way, don't we, Harry?"

Harry grinned at Ian and stood with his arms at his sides, watching the sparrows hop along the curb. He pursed his lips, snapped his fingers and called, "Kitty, kitty, nice kitty."

"I'm surprised Harry's out this early," Ian said. "Usually he's about mid-morning. Maybe he slipped out."

"Slipped out from where?"

I nearly crossed my fingers, hoping Ian wasn't about to say a mental

HORNS OF A DILEMMA

ward.

"His home. He lives with his sister, Page. His brother's visiting for a few days. Perhaps David let him out."

Mark glanced at me, his lips pressed together. I knew he wanted to make a comment about David Willett.

"Harry is only let out at certain times, then?" I said. "It sounds as though he should be institutionalized if he's that dangerous."

"Lord, no," Ian replied. "Page, his sister, keeps an eye on him well enough, only lets him out after breakfast when there are enough people about the village to report to her if Harry gets into trouble. He's usually quite docile. I can't fathom why he's so agitated. Something must have upset him."

"You seem to know a lot about the family."

"I've known Page, Harry and David for years. Page lives just a few houses down from me."

Harry ran at the sparrows, scattering them in a rush of laughter and arm waving. The birds twittered in fright and landed on the gutter of the bakery. Harry stood below them, his head angled to stare at them, his mouth open.

"That wasn't a nice thing to do, was it, Harry?" Ian said, frowning at Harry. "You know better than to tease the birds."

Harry lifted his hands to his head and held them briefly beside his ears. Then he hugged his chest. "You can't hear me," he said, tilting back his head and laughing at the sky. "I can talk all I want and you can't hear me!"

"He turns off his hearing aids," Ian said, eyeing Harry. "He thinks that affects other people's hearing because *he* can't hear."

"Low IQ, has he?"

"Somewhat, but the main problem with Harry is his personality disorder."

"Psychopathy," I said, watching Harry lean his hands against the hair salon window and pull a face.

"Yes. Some days, as I said, he's worse than others. I usually don't see him out this early or this excited so early in the day."

"You keep an eye on him, do you?" Mark said.

"Just as a concerned neighbor would do. Nothing more."

"But you mentioned about being surprised to see him at this hour."

"Implies I'm his keeper, doesn't it? No. I get home from work at this time. I'm a security guard for a company in Macclesfield. I work nights so I sometimes meet up with Harry when I'm coming home. Nothing mysterious about it. I happened to be coming out of the bakery just now when Harry pulled his shenanigans."

"Does he get violent? Is he under a doctor's care?"

"Not as far as I know."

"Which one—the violence or the care?"

Ian smiled. "Take your choice. Page moved here about ten or twelve years ago. If Harry has any history of violence prior to their arrival in

Hollingthorpe, I don't know about it. He's been fine as long as I've known him."

"It would be a shame," I said, "if they had to leave a place they love because Harry hurt someone."

Harry plunged his hand into his pocket and withdrew a palm-sized rock. He turned it over in his hand several times, walked up to me, and said, "Devil's Stone."

Ian touched Harry's shoulder, drawing Harry's attention, and pointed to his ears. Harry grinned, nodded vigorously, and shoved the stone into my hand. He reached up to his hearing aids and turned them on. Ian patted Harry on the shoulder again and smiled. "Now we can hear you, Harry. Thank you. We like talking to you."

Harry grinned, exposing a mouth of beautifully white teeth. He touched the stone with his index finger and said slowly, "You can turn it. It's the Devil's Stone. You turn it and the devil can't come out."

I ran my finger the length of the stone, then flipped it over. "Like this, Harry?"

He nodded, his eyes staring at the stone. Then he tapped my arm and pointed at the church. "He's up there."

I glanced at Ian for translation, but Ian shrugged. "Why is he up there?" I asked.

"'Cause he can't go nowhere else."

"Does he live there?"

Harry shook his head and waved his hands. "He's up there. On the hill. Up there! He's waiting for me. He wants me to go there!"

"Who's up there, Harry? Who is he?"

Harry rubbed his hand across his lips, as though afraid to say the name. He shook his head again and snatched the rock out of my hand. He held it over his head and waved it in the air. "He wants me. He wants the stone. I have to go!"

Ian grabbed Harry's arm and turned him slightly so he was facing him. "Who is he, Harry?"

Harry waved the rock again as though it were a battle flag. "He wants me. I have to go now."

"Is it Enrico?" I asked, thinking perhaps Harry had seen the police activity last night, perhaps had hidden in the shadows to watch as Enrico had been deposited into the body bag and taken off to the mortuary. Perhaps even seen the murder. An experience like that might certainly be the cause of Harry's anxiety this morning.

Harry's eyes were large and shiny when he looked at me. He brought the rock to his chest, cradling it in his left arm. He shook his head. "No. Not Enrico. He's not there. It's the other man who wants me. The devil."

Chapter 8

"And what does the devil look like?" I asked finally, finding my voice. Mark was frowning, gazing at the church above us. Ian was blinking as though trying to wake himself from a dream. Harry was turning toward the salon window, ready for another round of face-making. I said, "Did you meet him? Last night, perhaps? Were you outside later than you should be and saw him?"

"He wants me," Harry repeated. "He asked me to come."

"When did he ask you? Last night? Did you see him last night by the big Devil's Stone?"

The village was stirring; nosey-parkers alerted by the media were snapping photos of the church yard and congregating as near to the Devil's Stone as the police tape would allow; residents were patronizing the shops along the High Street or driving to jobs or appointments or the larger neighboring towns. The pavement outside the hair salon was beginning to see a steady flow of people, several of whom nodded to Ian or spoke to Harry in passing. Not one person, I noted, seemed alarmed or surprised by Harry's demonstration. Evidently he was as much a part of the fabric of this village's life as if he were the personification of the stone turning event. Harry waved to a woman across the street and wished her Happy Christmas.

I asked Harry again about meeting the devil.

He frowned, pulled off his hat and rubbed the top of his head. Tossing the hat into the air several times, he said, "I want to go home now. I'm tired. I want my breakfast."

I sighed and looked at Ian. Maybe he could get some logical explanation from Harry. He was used to dealing with him.

Ian opened one of the paper sacks he held, reached in and brought out a jumbal. He held it out and asked Harry if he'd like one.

Harry nodded and grabbed it, saying he liked biscuits more than any other food.

"Yesterday it was sausage rolls," Ian said, sighing heavily. "I don't know how Page keeps her sanity. I really don't."

"I'd be bonkers in a week," Mark said.

"David, her brother, pays the occasional visit. He helps out somewhat, but it's not much."

"Aren't women usually the caretakers?" I said.

He looked at us, expecting some agreement. I nodded and Ian added,

"I sometimes feel with David the visit's more a duty call than wanting to see his sister or to give her a hand. He's clearly got no patience for Harry."

Mark said, "Perhaps that's why David rarely comes here."

"Or a guilty mind from not helping Page more," I said.

Ian shrugged, saying he wasn't privy to Page's or David's conscience.

"I want another jumbal," Harry mumbled, cramming the last of the biscuit into his mouth and holding out his hand. He pointed to the bag, grunted, and repeated his request.

"You can have another biscuit," Ian said, "only if you're a good lad and will let me take you home." As Harry nodded and reached for the bag, Ian said, "Will you let me take you home?"

Harry nodded, his eyes fixed on Ian's hand holding the biscuit.

I wasn't sure Harry meant it. He would probably agree to being tarred and feathered if he could have another biscuit. But he crammed his cap back on his head, grabbed Ian's free hand and cooed that they should go home. He grasped the jumbal as though he were Jason and it was the Golden Fleece. Falling alongside Ian, Harry babbled that he was ready to sit on Father Christmas' lap. Ian nodded and they turned toward the community center. A car passed, its window partially open, its radio flinging music at us as it sped up the High Street. Harry pulled Ian to an abrupt stop, pointed after the assaulting car, and cried, "I wanna hear the music!"

The car braked briefly opposite the village green, its brake lights a brilliant red in the shadow of The Floating Hog. Harry pointed his biscuit at the car and whined his request again.

"It's gone, Harry," Ian said, pulling Harry's arm. "See? It's turned onto Well Hill Road. We can listen to music at home. I'll get Page to turn on the CD. Come on." He strengthened his grip, his fingers turning white, and pulled.

For all of Harry's thin build, he was stubborn. He wasn't going before he was ready. He braced his body, leaned away from Ian, and shook his head, squealing that he wanted to listen to the music.

Ian sighed, glanced at me as though soliciting advice or handcuffs or a nightstick, and said he'd give Harry another jumbal if they went home. Evidently the music held more sway than food. Or he wasn't hungry. Harry tugged at Ian's arm and said he wanted the music.

Graham would have said God intervened at that moment. Maybe He was tired of hearing Harry's whine. Whoever took pity on us got my vote for Mediator of the Day. The tower bells of St. Michael's Church boomed into the air at that moment, turning Harry's attention from the departed car to the tolling bells. He relaxed his grip on Ian's arm, let his hand that held the biscuit sink to his side, and stared open-mouthed in the direction of the church.

"God's music," Harry whispered, his eyes wide and shining.

"Yes." Ian mouthed 'Thank God' at me, puffed out his cheeks in an audible sigh, and told Harry that if he was good, he could listen to the bells again Sunday morning.

HORNS OF A DILEMMA

Harry nodded enthusiastically, took a huge bite of his biscuit, and meekly followed Ian down the street, talking about wanting to be an angel when he grew up.

"Nutty as a fruitcake," Mark said, leaving the security of the bakery doorway to join me. "Daft. How old's he, anyhow?"

"Mentally or physically?"

"I can tell what he's like mentally. Sounds like one of my nephews before he began primary school. Daft."

"Looking at him, I'd say mid-thirties. Why?"

"Oh, I just like to know as much as I can about suspects in a case."

"You think Harry—"

"I think anything and everything about everybody right now, Bren. It's a murder investigation. Enrico didn't bash himself alongside the head."

"And Harry's as good a suspect as anyone in this village, you think?"

"Hell, yes. Until proven otherwise. Sure, I admit I'm looking at him more closely because he's mentally under-developed. Fine. Label me politically incorrect or a berk or whatever you want."

"But until we know Harry's history and medical condition, you've got him down as a suspect."

"Why not? He's just shown us he's capable of anger and hostility, and if he was at the church last night and actually saw someone—labeled him the Devil or St. Nick or his mother—he could have lashed out at Enrico in anger or hostility or fright. Maybe not on purpose. But he could have. So Harry's on my list of people to watch. All right?"

"Lovely. Just curious." I watched Ian and Harry turn the corner at Green Acre Road, by the community center. "You suppose we should get on with our job of work—"

"Say no more. We gotta keep Graham happy."

"It's not so much Graham as it is the residents. There are more of them."

"But Graham has the power to discipline."

I grimaced. I didn't need reminding about December's little reprimand. "Come on, Mark. We've got to question Conrad. He might know where John is."

Conrad Quinn, nineteen, tall and blond as a Swede, was sitting on the front step of his aunt's home, smoking, when Mark and I walked up. He crushed out his cigarette, leaving the butt on the doorstep, and stood up when I introduced Mark and myself, then frowned upon hearing of John's disappearance.

"God, bummer! I haven't the foggiest," Conrad said, scratching his chin. His fingers were tobacco-stained and the same color as the small yellowish bruise just discernable on his lower left wrist. "I like John. We're mates, ya know."

"Do you two get together other than when you visit your aunt, or only here in the village?"

"You mean like hols and such? No, just here. We've talked about bummin' together later on, but he's not left school yet."

"So, he doesn't go to your place, then? I thought he might do—summers and term break."

Conrad shook his head. "Hasn't the money, has he? He's workin' after school and such at the launderette, savin' his money for university. As much as we like palin' around, he's got his priorities. He's not one for squanderin' his cash." He tucked his shirttail into his jeans. "We've not been able to make it work. I got a job myself. I'm usually outta town when he's on holiday."

"So that's why he never comes to see you?"

"Yep. It's that simple."

"And what do you do that takes you away so much?" Mark asked.

Conrad grinned, as though he was proud of his job or mentally reliving a joke about it. He said, "Photographer's assistant. I help carry all the gear ter the sites, set up the lights, hold the reflector...supply all the muscles for the shoot." He flexed his bicep. Even beneath the pullover, a good-sized muscle was evident.

"Indispensable."

"Yeh. I am. He may frame the shot, get the desired mood, but if he didn't have me ter ferry the lights around—"

"There'd be no shoot."

"You got it."

"So you're here between assignments, I gather."

"Too right. Just got back from the Hebrides last week, so I'm stayin' with me aunt for a week."

"Bit of relaxation before trotting off again?"

"I used ter come durin' holidays when I was in school. We get on great together, so now that I've a responsible job, I still drop by." He waved to an older woman who was walking past the house. "Sure, Aunt Collette is family, and I wanna keep in touch, but it's more than that. I love 'er—and me uncle—so I come by whenever I can. And whenever it's fine with them."

"It's nice that you've got such a tight family," I said. "Some folks don't have that love or support." An image of my family shimmered hazily in my mind—my dad snapping my sister's photo and talking to her manager about box office take and house capacity and star billing; my mother cooking for days and then pushing the celebratory meal at my brother when he returned triumphant from a concert tour. At first I had told myself that it was because they were hardly ever home, on the road more than in the parlor, so of course mum and dad were glad to see them and wanted to hear everything about their concerts. But somewhere in the third or fourth year of this royal kowtowing I realized it was not their absence that churned out the dramatic parental response—it was my siblings. Their glamour, their spotlighted careers. My parents never asked about my job or me. I just existed, an unfortunate relative hanging on to the edges of the family.

"I know," Conrad was saying when I finally shook myself free of familial images. "Me mum and dad were over the moon with anythin' I wanted ter do after school. We've never butted heads 'bout a thing. Some lads I know aren't lucky by half."

"And your folks are okay with your absences?"

"Don't like it, but they accept it. It's part of becomin' an independent adult, isn't it?"

"You said you are just back from the Hebrides. Where you off to now?"

"Luxembourg and Germany."

"Been there before?"

"Naw. It'll be a first for me. Been ter Egypt, Spain and Sweden. It's first-class, this job. Where else can I learn and see so much? Better than a caravan trip any day."

"So," Mark said, getting us back to police business, "you don't know where John Granger is, then?"

Conrad's eyes followed the flight of a sparrow from a tree branch to the pavement where it drank from the pool of melted snow. A second sparrow chirped from the recently vacated branch, perhaps asking if the water was good. Conrad said rather slowly, as if thinking through John's comments, "No. I saw him last night, of course, at the stone turnin', but not after. Which kinda surprised me, ya know? I mean, I expected we'd hang out together, do somethin' afterwards. But he wasn't around."

"Did you talk to him in the church hall, or hear him talking to anyone?"

"I didn't stay for that. It was after the church service, and I didn't go ter the social. But I hung about for a bit after the turnin', wantin' ter talk ter John. Didn't see him."

"You didn't participate in the turning?"

"I watched it but left soon after it was over."

"Because you're not, strictly speaking, a villager even though your aunt and uncle live here?"

"That plus it looks too much like me own work. Liftin' and tuggin'. Too much muscle power."

"You save yours for your job."

"Too right. How'll it look if I go back ter work with a stiff back? Nope. I watched from the sidelines, keepin' outta the way and keepin' safe."

"But John joined in," Mark reiterated as I made entries in my notebook. "Did he seem anxious last evening or upset by anything?"

"Didn't seem to be. I stood with him for a bit before he joined with the group ter turn the stone, but he didn't say a thing 'bout anything botherin' him or 'bout leavin'. I don't know what could be botherin' him in school—if anythin' is."

"Did you take any photographs of the turning last night?"

"Sorry. I don't have a camera. 'Sides, Enrico was still alive during the turning', so what good would photos do ya?"

63

Ignoring the question, Mark asked if there was anyone at the turning that Conrad didn't know or whom he hadn't seen in a while.

"Well, Geoff was there."

Mark blinked, trying to connect the name with a villager. I put him out of his misery and said, "Geoff Graham?"

Conrad nodded and snapped his fingers. "Yeh. That's him. Used ter live here as a lad, then left when he went ter university. Haven't seen him for some time. I hear he comes back kinda regular, like, but this is my first stone turnin' in a few years. It was good ter see him again."

Having recovered his poise, Mark said, "Anyone else? Someone you didn't know?"

"Well, there was one bloke, I guess, though me aunt kinda knows him."

"And who is that?"

"King. That his name? Yeh. King. Don't know his last name. He's a mate of Richard's. You know Richard? Owns the launderette."

"We know of him, yes."

"Well, King's been here a few times, visitin' Richard. But he's known ter others in town. Me aunt and uncle, for one."

"Yes. Fine." Mark sighed and glanced at his watch. "So there was no one at the Devil's Stone turning, then, that was an obvious stranger in town. No one that either you or your family or friends didn't know."

"You want a bloke in a dark trench coat?"

I eyed Conrad, trying to discern if he were joking. "If he had 'Murderer' stenciled on its back, it would help, yes."

"Sorry, miss. There wasn't that many of us there. And I knew or knew of everyone. Doesn't get us any nearer to John's disappearance, does it?"

"So he could have talked to someone after the church service or in the church hall, and gone off with him, and you'd not know, then."

"Could have done, sure. But John wasn't that sort."

"What kind of sort?"

"Ter go off like that. Especially without tellin' his mum or dad."

"Would they let him go off if he did tell them? Especially on a school night?"

"I wouldn't think they would, but perhaps if it was an emergency…"

"What kind of emergency would John have? Not a pregnant girlfriend, I hope."

Conrad grimaced. "He wouldn't do that. Sleep with someone, I mean. He was brought up in the church, and while that doesn't guarantee stayin' outta trouble…" He shrugged. "I'm as much in the dark over this as you are, miss. I can't think of where he could be."

Ian opened the front gate to his home, stopped short when he saw us talking to his nephew, then hurried up, asking if anything had happened.

When I explained that we were investigating John's disappearance, Ian relaxed a bit. He glanced at the house, then at me, and said, "I hadn't realized John was missing. I haven't seen him since last Saturday morning, when I saw him going into the launderette. He works there on weekends, you know."

I said that I had heard that, then asked if Ian had been at the stone turning. "As I said, I'm a security guard in Macclesfield and I work nights, so I wasn't there. Collette was—my wife. I assume you want to know if I saw John there or heard anything. Unfortunately, no. As I said, I last saw him Saturday morning. What's that—five days ago?"

"Did you talk to him? Did he say anything about an appointment or if he wanted to go somewhere?"

"We just waved to each other. He was going into the launderette, as I said, and I was about to go into the green grocer's. Hadn't time for an exchange of confidences. Sorry I can't be more help." He turned to Conrad, squeezing the lad's hand. "I had to see Harry home. He's agitated this morning. Has your aunt left?"

"Quarter of an hour ago, I guess. She said she'll be home early if she can swing it."

Ian patted Conrad's hand, turned, bid us good morning, and went inside his house. The door closed with a solid thud, knocking loose a chunk of snow from the portico. The snow plopped onto the front stoop, positioned nicely for someone to step in.

"Your aunt's not home?" I said, mentally cursing our bad luck. Now we'd have to track her down somewhere.

Conrad said she was an estate agent. After giving us her office address in Buxton, he said that if he heard anything about John, he would let us know.

Collette Harmon's face slid from expectancy of showing a house to a client to disappointment at losing a sale. With perhaps a touch of anxiety thrown in. Not many people retained complete composure when confronted by two police detectives. She forced a smile, ignored the ringing phone, and motioned us to two chairs facing her desk. Her office was above a pub in the High Street, facing the market square. A large foyer on the ground floor just inside the outer door accommodated the entrance to the pub and flight of stairs that took clients up to Collette's office. The lower landing smelled of beer and fried chips and grilled lamb chops as well as lemon-scented furniture polish—odors ingrained into the wood paneling and curtain covering the glass in the door. A sign announced 'Harmony Surrounds You in a Harmon Home' in black and gold lettering, and indicated the means for procuring this Utopia was somewhere at the top of the stairs. Mark had taken the steps two at a time while I had followed more leisurely, glancing at the photos of homes and flats available for sale and to let. At the top landing more black-and-gold lettering adorned the Harmon office's frosted glass door. The hall accommodated one other door farther down its length and made room for two leather chairs outside the business' door, but the hall had the near-feel of vacancy, too-few clients and hushed conversations. Dust had collected in the corners and the floor had warped with age. It creaked beneath our footsteps like complaining arthritic joints. "Good as a burglar alarm," Mark said. He'd glanced at me from over his shoulder and nearly tripped over the small oriental scatter rug that gave the otherwise bare floor a touch of home and elegance, and implied classy properties waited behind the estate agent's door. A large portrait of an older man—the original Harmon?—hung on the wall to the right of the door. Mark had entered the office before I could read the brass nameplate on the painting's frame.

Collette leaned back in her upholstered chair, pushed aside a stack of brochures on her large wooden desk, and echoed her husband's and nephew's comments.

"I didn't go to the turning," she said. She grabbed a pen, as though needing the assurance of something common in the unfamiliar area of missing children. Her pink painted fingernails glistened beneath the light of her desk lamp, matching the gleam of her pearl earrings. "Earlier in the day I had intended to go, but around tea time I wasn't feeling well—a migraine—so I gave up on the idea and stayed home."

"Alone?"

"After Ian left for work. I had a cuppa, took a pill, then went to bed."

"Did you hear anything?"

"I suppose you mean from the church yard."

"Anything. Anywhere."

"I didn't hear Conrad come back from the turning. My medicine knocks me right out. I doubt if I would have heard Ian even if he yelled that the house was on fire."

I said I was sorry to hear that she had been ill, then asked if she had seen or heard of any foreigners in the village that day.

The tip of her left thumbnail slipped under the clasp of the pen and she wagged the pen back and forth several times before stating that she had seen Geoffrey Graham there that morning. "But Geoff's been here before, of course. He came Tuesday, I believe—before the turning. And that friend of Richard's...King, I believe he's called. Other than that, no. No one. Sorry." She pulled the pen from her fingernail, set it carefully on the top of the desk and glanced from me to Mark.

"So," Mark said, taking Collette's cue, "you don't know if anyone was there either to lure John away or make an appointment with him."

"No. But kids have all those electronic gadgets these days, don't they? Mobile phones, e-mail, chat rooms on the Internet...John could have set something up with anyone, I suppose. Kids are so secretive."

"Is Conrad like that?"

"What—secretive?" She blinked, her eyelashes catching the lamplight and creating fleeting shadows across her eyes. Like sunlight through the pines, or like a lie whispered and slipped in among the truth—fleeting and subtle, yet imprinted on the mind. Then she moved out of the light and the

HORNS OF A DILEMMA

effect vanished, leaving her eyes dull and ordinary.

"Or savvy with electronic communication."

"Mightn't be that at all. John could've used the phone. Or the post. Or talked to some mate at school."

"Does Conrad know what's going on with John? I know they go around together when Conrad visits you."

"Ian and I are always happy to have Conrad stay with us."

"Whose son is he? Your husband's siblings?"

"He's my sister's son. Sometimes she and her husband come, either with Conrad or by themselves."

"Sounds like a house-full."

"We manage. Well, you do, don't you? Being family and all, it may be a bit of an inconvenience and you're all in each other's way for some days, but you manage. Anyway, I'd rather have it like that then us split between our house and a hotel."

"And Conrad's visit?"

"Usually twice a year by himself—when he's between assignments, but sometimes it's more often. Ian and I always look forward to it—we'll be crushed when marriage or a different job ends his visits."

"You've no children of your own?"

"No. That's one reason why we love having him. He's the child we've never had."

Mark dropped me at the incident room and left immediately for Macclesfield to find out from Ian's boss if Ian had worked last night. Which left me to relate the meager information we had gleaned to Graham. He nodded, drawing capital Js and Es on a sheet of paper, asking questions that I could only answer with 'I haven't found that out yet, sir.'

He finally sat up, gave me an equally dismal account of his unproductive interviews at John's school, and tilted his head back. He ran the heel of his palm across his eyes, held his left arm out and glanced at his watch. "I thought it'd be at least teatime and it's not even lunch time. Time crawls when you've been up all night. So." His arm dropped to his lap and he sat up. "Right. Either this is a kidnapping—a crime of opportunity—or John slinked away without telling anyone. Which seems unlikely, as most kids confide in someone, even if it's to ask advice on how to get somewhere or get a loan of money."

"Has anyone looked at John's computer?"

"We've got someone working on that, Taylor. Though John's classmates all swear John didn't go in for chat rooms or correspond via e-mail with anyone but his known friends. He has a sort of girlfriend, Toni, but it's nothing serious. She's as upset as anyone about his disappearance."

"Do you believe her? That she knows nothing, I mean?"

Graham stared out of the front window, perhaps at the church on the hill across the road, perhaps at the brambling hopping along a tree branch. The bird wiped its beak against the limb, knocking the snow to the ground. Its dull orange breast showed up well against the sparse, white clumps. I wondered if that's what held Graham's attention for so long—the hope for a bright bit of news in an otherwise dull investigation. When he finally broke his gaze, he answered in a quieter tone. "Yes, I do believe her. She looked absolutely frightened. I don't know how she'll get through her school day."

I could imagine her haunted look, the eyes red-rimmed and dull, the cheeks drained of color. Anxiety usually claimed people like that—I'd worked on enough missing person cases to know the blank, hollow expression that spoke of sleepless nights and abandoned hope.

"She mustn't give up faith," I said before I realized it.

Graham turned toward me, his eyes alive with interest. "What?"

I felt my embarrassment flood my cheeks. I, who didn't attend church, who had felt uncomfortable on being partnered with a former minister, who didn't really Believe, was now speaking of faith? I raised my gaze from the tabletop and found my eyes locked into Graham's stare. I swallowed several times, trying to get my breathing back to normal, and said rather softly, "It's too soon to give up hope of finding John. Toni has to have faith that he's all right. She has to cling to that as tightly as she can. Without faith that God will see him safely home, she has nothing. She may as well not be alive."

Graham's smile slowly consumed his face and he grabbed my hand. I was going to add something else but at that moment a man burst through the door, glanced around the room, then trotted up to us and said, "You the coppers? I heard there were coppers in the village. I want to do something about John Granger's disappearance."

Chapter 9

I quickly pulled my hand from beneath Graham's and looked at the man. He was tall and reed-thin. But the thinness of his frame belied the strength that he obviously had. I had always thought Mark Salt in good shape, especially for a detective, and Scott Coral—a constable in our division—absolutely dripped muscles. Which he had to have, being a response driver and maneuvering less-than-cooperative offenders into handcuffs or into the back of his police car. But the man before us was Muscles with a capital M. His shoulders seemed a mass of small boulders; his biceps bulged beneath his thin jacket. Either he turned Devil's Stones daily like poker players flipped over cards or he was an Olympian weight lifter. But his thighs didn't seem developed enough for that. I forced my eyes away from his muscular neck to look at his face. His black eyes examined me frankly, as though sizing up my ability to be a copper. He didn't smile, and there was a faint streak of paler skin above his upper lip, as though he had recently shaved off a mustache. He was pleasant enough to look at, but I found myself trembling and every hair on my body rising in unexplainable fear. My fingers felt for the sides of my metal chair and I held on, listening as Graham asked the man what he wanted to do.

"Help the lad, of course," he answered, his voice rough with years of smoking.

"You know him, do you?" Graham asked, standing up and facing the man.

"Ought to. Seen him often enough. He works for my mate. He's a bright lad, just beginning life, as it were. I'd like to help find him."

Graham leaned against the table and crossed his long legs. There was a quick movement of his eyes—like a hawk watching a mouse—as he appraised the man before him. The motion was no more than the faintest glint of light skating across his green irises, the hint of interest or curiosity as his eyes moved, but it shouted to me that Graham was scrutinizing the man for some reason. In fact, every officer in the room was aware of the man's presence. Conversations ceased; the clack of fingers typing on computer keyboards stopped; coppers remained seated or standing where they were.

Scott Coral, I noticed, slowly angled his body toward the man, his left foot and leg slightly ahead of his right, his hips and chest in straight line to the bloke. He looked like he was ready to leap forward—an unusual, extreme stance merely because John Q Public had walked into the incident room. Scott's eyes narrowed, following every move, no matter how minute, as though sizing up an adversary or anticipating a fight. Or ready to explode. The man glanced constantly from Graham to Scott. A trifle odd because Scott stood at the next table, not involved in the conversation. Yet the man included Scott in the discussion, acknowledging his company. Or was it something else? Did Scott and this man know each other? The man turned, ever so slightly and ever so slowly, mimicking Scott's stance, smiling, yet staring at Scott. The two men seemed destined to remain like that, the tension flowing between them, when Graham spoke, bringing the man's attention back to him, however brief it was before he returned to stare again at Scott.

"I appreciate your offer of help. That's admirable...sir." The word came haltingly, late in the sentence, as though Graham were deciding on the title since the man hadn't introduced himself. I had a fleeting suspicion that Graham might know him, that the man had reinvented himself—for whatever reason—and Graham had forgotten the new name or title. Perhaps the man was minor royalty or an esoteric celebrity on holiday and was avoiding recognition. Or could have been a member of Graham's congregation, but Time had dulled Graham's recollection of the name.

The man grinned and brushed his fingers through his graying black hair in a slow, practiced motion. I sensed he did it to call attention to its thickness, as a come-on for women. He returned Graham's stare equally as boldly and said, "I don't know whether it's admirable or not. You would know, of course, being exposed to the public's reaction. *That* must certainly astound you at times. But thank you for the compliment...Sergeant? No! Nothing so ordinary. Of course not. I apologize. What are you—something rather lofty, I assume. Divisional Commander? Superintendent? Or should I play it safe and address you as Mister...*Graham*, is it?"

"Chief Inspector," Graham said, his jaw muscle tensing. "And hardly anything the public does astounds me."

"No, it wouldn't, would it? You've seen too much. But then, in your line—as well as a fire fighter or medical person—you'd have seen it all. I suppose you could still be bothered by nightmares from what you've encountered, though. Or are you immune to that? Do you have a good spiritual foundation to help you through all the pain and brutality you've dealt with, Mr. Graham? Or are you an atheist, reasoning that if a God exists He wouldn't allow such scum as criminals to exist?" He smiled, his eyes narrowing and steady on Graham's face. "Which brings up something I've always wanted to know: do you think criminals view their world in reverse? That is to say, do you think they look on coppers as scum and, therefore, don't believe in God because God allows cops to exist? Interesting idea, isn't it, Mr. Graham? Perhaps you know some vicar or minister who'd enjoy the discussion. Do you know any—anyone *qualified*, that is? Of course, you'd still be free to throw in your personal spiritual belief...if you have one." He grinned, tilting his head slightly so he viewed Graham at an angle.

My eyes darted from the man to Graham, wondering how he would respond. There seemed to have been an underlying sharpness to the man's words, as though he were insinuating something, trying to goad Graham into a fight. Neither man spoke, their eyes fixed on one another, like combatants sizing up each other before a brawl. The stillness lay heavy between us, collecting thoughts and tension.

I glanced at Scott. He had not moved, either his stance or his gaze. He still assessed the man as though he expected the man to yank a lit bomb from his pocket and hurl it into our midst. I tried to swallow but felt my throat tightening. The church bells struck the hour before Graham spoke. His voice was hard, nearly curt, as his tone shifted to a crisp, precise reply.

"I think we can leave my personal experiences and spiritual foundation for another time. The topic most important at the moment is the whereabouts of John Granger. You were wanting to help, I believe, Mr....?"

"Roper. King Roper. I neglected to say, didn't I? I am sorry! I had no intention of being rude. It's just that in the midst of concern..." He paused, as though gathering his wits from somewhere else. "Being a friend of Richard Linnell's, as I said, I've come to know John, seeing and talking to him when I visit Richard. I'd like to help—in any way I can." There was a flash of his tobacco-stained teeth before his lips snapped shut.

"That's kind of you...Mr. Roper," Graham said slowly. His jaw muscles jerked slightly, perhaps imperceptible to someone who didn't know Graham, then relaxed. "What were you thinking of? Forming a sort of search party?" Graham eyed King's figure as though assessing the physical stamina it contained. If I could have done so at that moment, I would have bet Scott that Roper was capable of any amount of physical stamina. I'd never seen such developed pectorals and biceps.

"Could do. I'm not averse to climbing about these tors. I've had experience leading merry chases. But actually I had in mind something more in the way of monetary help."

Graham's right eyebrow went up. He clearly was not expecting that. Neither was I. Most people assume the police will take care of everything, never mind if we have limited funds. It somehow appears as if by magic. King Roper was the first person I could recall who not only volunteered to help but who also wanted to donate money. He must really feel strongly about John's disappearance. "That's generous of you," Graham said. "What type of help—reward for information?"

"I could contribute to that, certainly. But I think the urgency of the event dictates I get some posters printed. You know—recent photo, age, height and weight description, phone number to ring up if you know anything...that sort of thing. I could get them run off and post them about the area. Richard would help with that, I know. Would that be of any help?"

"Certainly. If John simply ran away, someone would have spotted him.

The more eyes we have looking for him, the better."

"So that's what you believe right now—that he's run off?"

"You know something to the contrary?"

King shrugged, his neck muscles straining as he inclined his head. He looked at Scott and answered Graham's question. "Not likely to, am I? I don't really know the lad—not as a close family friend would, I mean. I hate to see children go missing. Either because of family troubles or because there's some child molester lurking about. I'd like to help however I can. Society's plagued by too many problems...and criminals." He tore his gaze from Scott, stared again at Graham, and said, "I just heard the news from Richard—this morning—who got it from Lloyd."

"Nice man, Lloyd."

"You think so? A bit of a lightweight when it comes to dealing with real life, perhaps, but nice enough. But, then, a lot of clergy are, I should think. I mean, they're thinking about Sunday's sermon or worried about decorating the church for Harvest festival or overseeing the children's pageant. Not exactly stuff beyond the church door, is it?" He held Graham's gaze, the smile still plastered on his face, and waited.

Graham said, "I've found that the church is a microcosm of the world, Mr. Roper."

"Really?"

"The church is nothing more than people, people who bring their problems and joys and concerns into the church congregation."

"And, as such, need to be dealt with."

"Sunday sermons try to address those problems, joys and concerns. Church holidays and children's activities try to set examples of what we should practice in our Monday through Saturday lives. It may seem light weight, but if you study it, look beyond the façade, it is all life lessons and helping hands."

Roper shook his head slowly. "God, what enlightenment! And from a detective, no less!" He laughed, throwing back his head. Yet, when he had finished, the mirth was gone from his face and he was looking again at Scott. After several seconds of silence, he said to Graham, "You've missed your calling, Detective. You should be applying your insight where it will do some good, not chasing after blokes who drink a tad too much or tracking down stolen paintings."

"But the excessive drinker gets behind the wheel, Mr. Roper. He takes to the road and drives his car into other cars or buildings, severely injuring or killing innocent people. Theft, no matter if it's something you value or not, is not merely forceful seizure of an object that you don't own—it's a break from the norms that society has laid down and declares 'This is how we will behave.'"

"Ahh. I see. We'd be no more than barracudas fighting over the same chunk of fish. We'd be constantly at war with everyone around us, on edge and watching."

"There'd be no peace."

"Each person on his own, sleeping with his umbrella, fearful some stronger bloke will steal it when a storm is brewing, eh?"

"Every rain storm isn't a hurricane, but we prepare."

Roper's laugh exploded. I glanced at Scott, who was still poised as if for a fight. Graham's face was impassive, his eyes drilling into Roper's face, perhaps trying to read the reason behind the conversation. Again, I felt a tension between the men, a hint to their history that I knew nothing of.

Roper said, "If you ever want to change careers, Mr. Graham, maybe I can put in a good word for you. I know a lot of chaplains."

"In the towns where you've lived?"

"That, certainly, but a few in prisons. My life's not been in vain, Mr. Graham. I've developed friendships that I hope will speak well and testify to how I've lived my life."

"And how have you spent your life? By helping others, giving to charities?"

"Robin Hood had always been one of my heroes, Mr. Graham. Rob the rich and give to the more deserving. Spread the wealth around."

"And your portion of wealth that you want to spread, helping search for John..."

"Like I said, I'm open to anything I can do. I've spent a good portion of my life helping myself. I'd like now to help someone else." He flashed a quick smile at Scott, then winked at me.

Graham was silent for several moments, as though considering various ways of employing King's offer. He exhaled sharply and said, "You talked to John at the stone turning last evening. Did he mention anything about troubles at home, or someone he was going to visit?"

King laughed, throwing back his head to reveal a small scar at the base of his jaw. It was about an inch in length and curved, as though a ring had slammed into his flesh and this was the resulting brand and reminder. "God, how observant you are! But, then, you're a copper, so why wouldn't you be?" He ran his finger across his upper lip. "Yeh, I was there, and you know I didn't participate. Well, I couldn't, could I, not being a villager."

"Did you talk to John?"

"Just in passing. Nothing more. We're not exactly best mates."

"Did you overhear him speaking to anyone about leaving home?"

"No. I don't eavesdrop and I didn't follow him around."

"But you watched the turning."

"And sat through the Hail Marys in the church, had a cup of cheer in the church hall afterwards, and then returned with Richard to his digs." He shrugged again, signifying that was all he knew. "Sorry I'm no Sherlock. But I leave that to you...and your lovely partner." He smiled, eyeing me as though I were a stripper and he wanted me. Or a copper and he held the upper hand. "But we all help where we can, don't we? Sorry not to hold the key to the hunt."

Graham's voice freed me from King's imprisoning stare, forcing the man's attention back to Graham. "Was this the first time you witnessed the turning of the Devil's Stone, Mr. Roper?"

"Yeh. Though not the first time I've visited Richard."

"You've just never coordinated your stay with the turning before?"

"Right. It's interesting enough—the story and all. But I've never made a conscious effort to come strictly for the event."

"Too bad you can't join in. It'd suit you."

I knew what Graham was thinking. King, who obviously reveled in working out, would have been in his element—straining his muscles, testing his body's endurance, competing against his own limits and setting the mark higher for the other, less physically fit participants.

King nodded, his eyes on Graham. Like a wolf hunting down a rabbit. "So, you live here, do you?" he finally said, his raspy voice breaking the brief silence.

"Used to." Graham crossed his arms on his chest.

"Ah. So you are one of the happy throng by right of birth or previous residence. You return each year for the melee, do you?"

"And where do you live, Mr. Roper?"

"Too many places, Sergeant. Sorry! Slipped up again. I beg your pardon. *Inspector.* Too many addresses for me to keep tabs of."

"I'll let me know about the posters, then, shall I?" Graham said, closing the conversation.

"Like I said, I've spent a good portion of my life helping myself and now it's time I took a different turn." He flashed his smile again, this time at me, and strode from the room.

Graham uncrossed his arms and stood up. "I can well believe that, Taylor. Too many places, indeed."

"Why do you say that, sir?" I said. "You know him? You didn't act like you did. He didn't seem to know you."

"Part of the game, Taylor. Rule Number One: Never give away anything. Especially to a copper."

I blinked, unsure if he were joking or not.

When I didn't respond, Graham said, "We're old acquaintances, Mr. Roper and I."

I frowned, trying to understand. "Did he forget who you are? You two have a tiff or something? Is that why you weren't slapping each other on the back?"

"I suppose you could classify it as a tiff. And the only thing I ever slapped on him were handcuffs."

"Sir?"

"King Roper has lived in a damn too many places—one of them being HM Prison Dartmoor."

Chapter 10

"I don't forget faces," Graham said as I was recovering from my astonishment. The tension in the room broke suddenly, completely, as Roper left. Officers resumed their work, conversations continued, Scott reclaimed his chair. I hadn't realized I'd been tense, but when I released the grip on the sides of my chair, I noticed that my knuckles were blanched and my fingers stiff. Graham exhaled heavily, his eyes on the door. "He talked about helping himself and now wanting to help others. I'll believe it when I see it. The only thing he helped himself to was other people's possessions."

"Sir?"

"King Roper, as he calls himself now, has a long criminal record of violent assaults and robberies. I knew him as Rupert Kingsley. He was just as obnoxious under that appellation as he is under this one."

"Rupert, Roper. Kingsley, King. Close. He'll have no trouble remembering his name when a cop asks him." I knew it was inane humor, but I was still thinking through the conversation. No wonder Graham hadn't answered King's implied question as to Graham's current residence. If you were a copper and wanted to live, you didn't hand your opponent a business card. "He have any convictions for murder?"

"Logical assumption, TC, seeing as how Enrico was bashed over the head and King Roper excels at head-bashing."

"He's got the muscles for head-bashing, sir. Is that why he's so physically fit?"

"God, I hope not. But he's never been even remotely connected with murder, so I don't think we should focus on him for Enrico's killer. Just because King is handy and likes to flex his muscles at a human target, we shouldn't automatically assume he's our man."

"Pity. What are his previous convictions?"

"Assaults connected with robbery and burglary—hardcore assaults with the victim barely alive if they resist."

"Lovely."

"Yes, isn't it?" Graham slipped into his jacket and grabbed his car key from the tabletop. "It's close enough to lunch time to call it that. I'm going to do a bit of work on my own, grab a bite, then come back here. Why don't you and Margo track down the personal information on Enrico after you've eaten? Where he's from, if he knew King. We can clue each other in when I return." He waved to me over his shoulder when I called to his retreating back.

As Graham left the community hall, the sound of traffic swept into the room. Just another reminder that life went on in the midst of death.

Margo came over to me and handed me my shoulder bag. "You heard him, Bren. Let's eat. I'm starved."

"You're always starved." I accepted my bag and walked with her. "How do you manage to keep your figure?"

"It's my metabolism, Bren. I've nothing to do with it. Well," she added, following me outside, "I *do* watch what I eat. It's a matter of choices, too. You know."

I nodded but said nothing. I was mad with myself for having only sporadic willpower to pass up a slice of cake or fish and chips. That always offered immediate comfort when I was in crisis. The nebulous husband of my dreams was too far in the future to persuade me to remain faithful to a diet.

We walked to the pub, more quiet than talkative. Normally we would have chatted about the case, but John's disappearance reduced our conversation to lighter issues, topics that released our minds and emotions, at least momentarily, from the current melodrama. After a five-minute wait, we got a table by the window. Margo sat down with a sigh that declared her mental exhaustion; I was just glad of the emotional break. Across the road, the village green was at odds with the calendar, undecided if it were early spring or late winter, for the area was a mass of ice-fringed puddles, soggy earth and small patches of snow. The snow hugged the bases of the bushes and clumps of rhododendrons, creeping into the foliage's shadow as the sun stretched across the ground and grabbed for the scraps of white. A few hardy bulbs poked volunteer leaves through the cold soil, testing the temperature and predicting the vernal likelihood and temperament. A dozen daffodils waved their yellow buds, shivering under a breath of wind, declaring it was time to move ahead with the season.

I reluctantly passed on the Lancashire hotpot and hot chocolate, ordered a tomato and cucumber salad with vinaigrette dressing, and chewed on a breadstick as Margo asked if I had set up a date with Mark.

"You owe him, Bren," she said, gripping the slender glass that held her mineral water. "How long's it been? A month, five weeks?"

"It was barely three weeks ago, Margo," I said, exasperation creeping into my voice. "Give me time to breathe! What do you want?"

"I want you to firm up the date and time. He's asked you out; you should reply quickly."

"What makes you think I haven't?" I said before taking another bite of breadstick.

It was the wrong thing to say. I knew that as soon as I saw Margo's eyes brighten and heard her intake of breath. She leaned over the table and said, "When? Where?"

She would have grabbed my hand, but luckily it held my teacup.

HORNS OF A DILEMMA

I tried telling her as nonchalantly as I could that Mark and I had talked about it and that it would be while we worked on this case. "We're to see how the days play out," I added. "Nothing fancy, so don't run back home for your mink cape. Besides, I think I'm allergic. And I don't think it's fair to the mink, in the long run."

"But it's a date, Bren. You can't go to a take-away."

"It'll be a step above that," I said, annoyed with the conversation and wondering where the waitress was with our meals. "Don't get so excited. It's my date."

"Well, *someone* has to get excited. You're certainly not acting like you are." She took a sip of water, eyeing me from over the top of the glass. "You're dreading it, aren't you? Why? Because it's not Graham?"

I flushed and was instantly sorry. "I like Mark well enough. It's not that. I'm just not the date type."

"And what's that mean?"

"You know what it means, Margo. We've been friends long enough for you to know."

"You're not exactly a well of knowledge. I always have to pry things from you."

"Maybe that's because the things you pry from me are things I don't want made public."

"And when have I ever broadcast anything that you've told me? You know, Bren, I think you're scared."

The waitress appeared with our salads, giving me time to take a bite, swallow and catch my breath. When she had left, I said, "Scared? What a daft thing to say! Why would you think that? I've agreed to go out with the man. I'd hardly call that being scared. Besides, it's a whole lot scarier asking someone to live with you—and I did that. Having Erik around on the weekends is certainly taking a huge step. It takes a lot of courage to make a commitment like that. Sure, we're not sporting wedding rings that concrete our devotion, but it still states a certain depth to our relationship. So I'd hardly label myself 'scared' if I took such a plunge." I pulled another breadstick from the ceramic container and broke it in half. A few breadcrumbs fell onto my salad.

"You *are* scared. Deny it all you want, Bren. Calling the sky pink doesn't change it from being blue."

I sighed. "Fine. Whatever you want. I'm scared. Only I prefer to call it nervous. Why shouldn't I be? It's hardly been any time since Mark was harassing me and calling me names. That didn't create such a superb beginning for a friendship."

"So he was a berk. But he's changed. He's not anywhere near as black as he's painted, Bren. You know that."

I quietly agreed, recalling Mark's concern about me in December, his all-too human emotions in January.

Margo took a bite of salad before saying, "But if you're not that keen on him, why not cultivate another relationship?"

"I'd hardly call what Mark and I have a 'relationship,' Margo. It's more like a truce. You think it's easy working like that, with someone who slung all sorts of names at you, who wanted you in his bed as he would an extra pillow or comfortable duvet?"

"I'd hardly think Mark would classify you as a pillow if you snuggled down with him."

I threw my breadstick onto the table. "You know what I mean, Margo. It's hard to shake the words and their pain from my mind."

"So, as I said, go out with someone else."

"Oh, great. Like who? I'm just overrun with offers for dates."

"I can think of three lads for starters."

"Like who? Blokes in prison?"

Margo snorted. "If you're going to approach this in your usual self-deprecating way, with your usual defeatist attitude—"

"Fine. Who are these men who are waiting on the sideline of my life, clamoring for my attention? Are they sane?"

"I know one who might not be."

I eyed her skeptically, wondering what was coming.

"He was kind of dotty about you, as I recall, Bren."

"Great. A lad from the mental ward. All right, I give. Who is this patient?"

"Adam. Remember? You were going to ring him up, if I remember."

I nodded, recalling my brief conversation last month with Scott Coral. Adam and I had definitely clicked, I'd guess you would say. Had Scott mentioned where Adam was now stationed? I closed my eyes, trying to remember.

"He's at Ripley," Margo said.

I stared at her grinning face. At times she had the most uncanny talent for mind reading. Nearly as good as Scott's ability to 'read' people.

"You can use my mobile if you don't have yours." She laid down her fork and started digging about in her shoulder bag.

"I've got mine, thanks all the same."

"So?" She leaned back in her chair and crossed her arms, looking like the cat that got the last bit of cream. Or a suspect who's just procured the services of a too-smart lawyer.

I may not be the brightest bulb in the carton, but I have sense enough to know when to admit defeat and retreat gracefully. I pulled out my mobile, punched in the phone number of the constabulary headquarters, and a minute later was talking to Adam. I was startled at the emotions that threatened to drown me on hearing his voice again. It washed over me, wrapped me in warmth and tingly sensations, so rich and deep that I would gladly listen to him read aloud the phonebook. When I found my voice, I asked how he was.

"Better, now that I'm speaking with you," he said, a hint of laughter beneath his words. "You still in the job, or have you finally found immense wealth and fulfillment doing something else—ditch digging or singing?"

HORNS OF A DILEMMA

I smiled, wishing suddenly that I could see his face. "Neither."

"To what? The ditch digging, singing, immense wealth or fulfillment?"

I laughed, not caring if Margo or the neighboring table was overhearing my conversation. Talking once more with Adam was like stepping outside on the first day of spring. I felt alive and incredibly excited, expectant of innumerable possibilities. I recounted family episodes (because Adam knew of my struggles), wildlife stories (because Adam had endured retellings of my bird sightings), and ended with a brief précis of my career highlights. Not that there were many, but I'd heard it was always good to end with a joke.

"Cheering as all this is," he said, "I doubt that you rang me up to amuse me with the kidnapping episode. And even as good as you are with reading body language, I can't believe you saw mine last week and deduced that I'd love to hear from you. So, what's the reason, aside from my incredible sense of humor and enormous good looks?"

Which wasn't far off the mark. Though Adam was average height and build, and his face would never be used for after-shave telly commercials, he exuded part charm, part sexual magnetism, part good spirits. Adam Fitzgerald drew people to him like greedy lawbreakers to a sting operation. It was enough to be in his company, to be counted a friend.

I told him I'd been thinking of our days working together, that I had remembered the fun we had had, and wondered what he was doing, if he wanted to go out after work for a drink some evening.

Margo punched me in the arm and hastily scribbled a note on the paper serviette, which she held up in front of my eyes. 'Dinner—NOT a drink!' I pushed her hand down and told Adam that Friday would be fine, made the arrangements of when and where, and rang off. I turned to Margo, my fingers gripping my phone. "Honestly! You didn't have to do that. I was doing fine without your backseat driving."

"You weren't. You should have asked him for dinner. A drink... God, Bren, that's not intimate at all. What can you talk about in a noisy pub?"

"For one thing, Margo, I don't even know if he's married or single. So I'm not going to ask him out for dinner! For another, there are other places to have a drink than in a noisy pub."

"Good. I couldn't hear that part of your conversation. You turned your back and lowered your voice."

"Glad to know the technique works. I can use it with suspects any time, now, and not worry."

"So, where are you going? Tomorrow evening, you said, but where?"

"I'm not going to tell you. You'll either follow me or get there first, disguise yourself and watch everything Adam and I do. I won't be able to relax knowing you're taking notes or making discrete hand signals at me."

"You forgot the photographs."

I speared a forkful of salad. "Stay out of it, Margo. Adam and I are going out for a drink. That's it for now. If he's single and we have a nice evening, perhaps we'll go out again. But don't crowd me. It's just a get-together. Not really a proper date."

"Speaking of dates…"

I frowned, dreading what was coming.

"Where did Graham go in such a hurry? I didn't know his little Insight could accelerate like that. He get a lead on something?"

Hoping to convey disinterest, I shrugged and tore my piece of French bread in two. "Haven't the slightest. He doesn't exactly confide in me, you know."

"Maybe you're not his pocket diary, but you're a team. He ought to tell you—in case you need to get hold of him."

"He's got his mobile." I would never admit it to Margo, but I was agreeing with every word she said. I had wanted to be included in his manhunt, or whatever he was doing. And I was aching for him to confide in me. Like team members should. Or, if I were brutally honest, like lovers would. But we weren't lovers, and I was wondering about the closeness of our team if Graham could go off to Parts Unknown without telling me. I buried my feelings once more and tore off another hunk of bread—as good a stress reliever as many others.

"Great comfort to you, Bren. He's practically by your side."

I popped a piece of bread into my mouth, chewed and swallowed it before saying that it was second best. "Maybe he thought of something and decided to check it out. Anyway, he gave us a job of work to do. We ought to think about that and not what he's doing." It sounded good, but I didn't believe it. And I didn't want to believe that he was headed for another date with Miss Beautiful, as he had done last month. So, I concentrated on my up-coming date with Adam, then took another half hour feeding bread to the sparrows on the village green. Mindless activities such as throwing out bits of bread are good for sorting through problems or mulling over mental lists, but are the devil's playground for concocting painful dramas. When I'd progressed to Graham slipping the ring on Miss Charming's finger, I hurried back to the incident room.

Between gabbing about Adam, our pets, upcoming holiday plans, and complaining about our dismal amount of free time, Margo and I busied ourselves with gathering the information Graham wanted. Even with computer-based records, the report wasn't as easy to assemble as I would have thought. I was about to throw my pen at the computer monitor in exasperation when Graham walked into the room. Wherever he had zoomed off to in such a hurry, either it had been close by or else the person he wanted to see hadn't been there. I'd barely had an hour with the computer to produce these meager results.

"I'm waiting for a phone call from prison records," he said as he came up to me. "If I'm not here and the call comes through, you'll know that it's for me."

I said I'd make copious notes and wondered what he was tracking down. Why hadn't he given the job to a constable, as he usually would have done?

HORNS OF A DILEMMA

He made no move to remove his jacket, but angled his head to read the sheet of paper beside my keyboard. The aroma of cold clung to him, and I fought the impulse to run outside and hike through the woods behind the church. Spring called to me, too, not just the emerging flora. His voice drew me mentally back inside. "Anything useful on Enrico? Or haven't you had time to look?"

"That's it, sir," I said, handing the results to him. There were two lines of type on the page. "Perhaps Margo's found something more." I paused as Graham scanned the sheet.

"So Enrico took up residence in the village one month ago," he said, reading aloud slowly. "Was seen in the area one month prior to that. Worked in the local book shop part time..." He looked up from the paper. "You have any former British address on him?"

"I don't. Margo's working on that."

"We could ask in the village, of course, but memories are sometimes shaky. Hmm. Moved into his house sometime last month. I want to know the exact date. 'Around January or February' doesn't work in a murder investigation."

"Margo's searching for a wife so we can notify her."

"It's obvious she's not living here with him. Besides the absence of any female attire at his house, no one here in Hollingthorpe talked about her. All I've heard about is Enrico. Any indication of a divorce? I just thought that might be the answer, since no one's living with him."

"If she does exist, we need to get her address quickly. She needs to know."

"Of course she does. Margo will find something. She's becoming quite the computer whiz."

Which wasn't exactly a compliment, as far as Margo was concerned. She wanted to be in the field, doing hands-on work, not inside in front of a computer. But we all served as our talents dictated.

He tapped the paper with his finger. "I don't like this."

"Sir?"

"The fact that we haven't found anything on him."

"Yes, sir. And uh, sir, that mobile phone of his..."

Graham's right eyebrow raised, echoing the expectation in his voice. "An SO found it in his house. What about it?"

"Well, sir, that mobile was his only phone. He had no house phone."

"Many people these days have just the one type of phone, Taylor. Young adults, especially. They take it with them wherever they go. That's not unusual."

"I wasn't implying it was, sir. What I *do* find disturbing is that we can't find a record of it. Neither of Enrico buying it nor of any phone calls. It's like he never had one."

Graham leaned forward to stare at the computer screen, as though the closer distance would produce different results to my records search.

"I thought it might be a foreign make at first—you know, like tourists always bring their mobiles with them when they enter the Kingdom—but it's a British model. Even if he bought it from someone, a mate of his or got it through his job—which doesn't make sense if he's a part-time bookstore clerk—he'd have to have records of his calls through the phone company."

"Unless it was loaned to him and the phone's real owner gets the monthly statement." He leaned back and shook his head. "Damnedest thing I've ever heard of."

"Yes, isn't it? I haven't had time, yet, but I can run a check for a driving license now. Was there one found on his body, or in his house?"

Graham nodded. "Fordyce mentioned it to me this morning. It's British, recently issued. And 'recent' means January of this year."

I nodded slowly, a hideous explanation brewing in my mind.

Graham went on. "Fordyce also found his British passport. It was recently stamped—and again 'recent' means just that: this past January. He reentered the Kingdom then, after spending several months in Zimbabwe."

"Africa?"

"I'll put someone to work on that angle of it. Perhaps we can find out something about Enrico through that channel, see if he has relatives there. Though, with our type of luck, it will have been a business trip."

"What kind of business?" I asked, my voice barely audible. Could Enrico be from Zimbabwe? He was certainly light skinned enough to be from northern Europe, but the villagers had said he'd had an accent no one could identify. And if he were a legitimate Briton, why could we discover nothing of his past life?

Graham seemed to be zeroing in on my thoughts, for he said, "Yes, it's like he didn't exist until two months ago. Who was it who sprang fully adult from her father's forehead?"

"Minerva." I again gripped the chair back, fear beginning to grab me.

"Ahh, yes. I'd forgotten. Favorite daughter of Jupiter, born from the mind, thereby symbolizing wisdom and skill. Fully grown and fully clad in armor."

"I hope Enrico doesn't come to symbolize skill in deception."

Graham cocked his right eyebrow, waiting for me to continue.

I said, "Yes, sir. I'm wondering if Mark was right when he said Enrico could be a terrorist, sleeping until he was needed."

Chapter 11

"So," Graham said, his voice holding the concern that had gripped him. "We have a man who wasn't born, apparently, until the beginning of this year. His driving license and passport say he's British, he's had a recent extended trip to Zimbabwe, and he's just moved into his house. He's been employed in the local bookshop for two months. That's all we know of him! Incredible. Do we have anything back on his fingerprints yet?"

"Yes, sir. New Scotland Yard ran them through their computer data base and—"

"Don't tell me. There's nothing on record. How about his car? We *know* he has a car—an Audi. To be precise, an A4 Cabriolet, phantom black. Nice convertible. The SOs found it in his garage. He has to have bought or hired it. I won't believe it if he stole it."

"We don't have a thing on it." I let the information and its implications sink in before I added, "Why would we be able to find an issued driving license but no record of his car? Neither a registration for the car's number plate nor a logbook. Nor a hire agreement, either." The insinuations were multiplying. I asked in a not too steady voice, "So, how'd he get his car, then?"

Graham slowly rubbed his forehead, as though he could stimulate his brain through the layers of skin, muscle and bone, and therefore arrive at a solution.

I could not meet his eyes; I was too afraid what I would see there, too frightened that his apprehension would fuel my mounting anxiety. Instead, I stared at the two simple phrases printed on the paper Graham had laid on top of the table and whispered, "He doesn't exist. He's a non person."

"Bloody hell." He said it so faintly that I might not have heard it if I hadn't been watching his face. But his eyes conveyed his uneasiness; they stared holes in the paper. Graham grabbed the phone and punched in Simcock's number. Moments later he was relaying our scant findings to our superintendent.

It wasn't so much what he said as it was his tone. Graham's voice was strained, even periodically threatening to quake, conveying his misgiving as succinctly as if he had yelled '*No one* in the 21st century doesn't exist. This situation scares the hell out of me!' And I echoed his words and alarm. If Enrico was a British subject, as his driving license and passport purported, then he would have been documented from the day of his birth. There would be a computer-full of his history—birth date, health history, education records, employment accounts, utility bills, housing addresses, banking or checking accounts, and credit card records. But there were none. It looked as if he were a Minerva, springing to life at the beginning of the year. And *that* scared us to death, for it signaled that Enrico or his employers had obliterated his true identity. A terrorist sleeper, I thought, recalling Mark's theory. And if that was true, how many other 'Enricos' were scattered throughout the Kingdom?

I stared at Graham, the fear palpable now that the situation was conveyed to a third person. It was as if giving voice about our suspicions and meager findings to another person threw the electrical switch on Frankenstein's monster. By talking to Simcock, we were watching our beast take its first menacing steps. Graham's knuckles had gone white as his hand gripped his mobile phone; his eyes had darkened, which always signaled either anger or deep concern. And though his voice was little more than a whisper, his words were razor-sharp, again conveying the escalating urgency of this case.

When Graham had rung off, he looked at me without smiling. I was unwilling to speak first, to intrude on his thoughts or vocalize our worry. A constable passed our table and nodded to us. Graham waited until the officer had grabbed his jacket and had left the building until he spoke.

"As you heard, Taylor, I related our findings to Simcock. He agrees we may have something major here. He also agrees we needn't throw the community, and our people, into a panic by announcing we've uncovered a terrorist cell. It's way too early for that. We don't know for certain, although it certainly looks like it."

I nodded, unable to trust my voice. Terrorist activities were certainly in the news, what with the London subway bombings and shoe bombers and militant-expounding clerics.

"As you also know, a photograph of Enrico was aired on the television newscasts the first night and printed in the newspapers. The press officer asked the media for help, appealing to the public for any information about Enrico's previous residences, employment, and so on. So far—"

"Aside from the usual nutters who phone in, we have nothing solid."

"We're to continue inquiries into his past, which means one-on-one interviews with the residents here as well as our computer investigation—although I will tell you now that I think that rather hopeless. If nothing as obvious as a birth certificate exists, we're dealing with a high-level organization that's planned this well in advance of two months ago."

Again I could merely nod. As Graham expressed the situation, my misgivings grew. Had we stumbled upon the makings of a terrorist plot? Even if it weren't that horrifying, if Enrico was a lone player and tracking someone for a personal vendetta, he would have a background, he would 'exist' via credit card reports, car sales or hires, birth certificate. He would not have taken the time—nor could he have accomplished it alone—to erase

HORNS OF A DILEMMA

his past. I shuddered, more afraid than I'd ever been.

"I want you to keep this to yourself," Graham added, bringing my mind back to the present. "You're not to talk of it to anyone else, got it? For now, this is just between Simcock, you and me."

Had I heard him correctly? "What about Mark? And Margo, and the other officers on the team?"

He shook his head. "No one—and I mean no other person, TC—is to hear of this. That includes Mark and Margo. Yes, you can well look shocked, but until we ascertain what's going on, I don't want anyone else to have this knowledge. Things leak out—unintentionally, to be sure, but it's too late to wish you'd not said anything when it becomes village gossip."

"Yes, sir," I said rather humbly.

"That also goes for family and friends. This information stays among us three. Understand?"

"Will you still put Margo on the computer inquiry, then? What's going to happen when she can't come up with anything on Enrico? How will we explain to her that he isn't a real person?"

"I'll come up with something. Don't look so worried, TC. I've had years of experience elaborating on the truth or creating white lies. My ministerial career taught me the finer points of polite falsehoods. 'My, that hat is becoming.'"

"You just don't say *what* it's becoming." In spite of the situation, I smiled, imagining Graham in his clerical robe, shaking hands with his parishioners, chatting after Sunday service, and trying to wriggle out of a difficult conversation. White lies seemed to be an accepted part of our society.

"But I won't lie to you, TC, and say that I'm not concerned. I'm scared as hell. But until we know more..." His eyes held my gaze, mutely finishing his sentence, emphasizing not only the seriousness of the case but also of his unspoken trust in me.

"Yes, sir," I said, my voice sounding strangely foreign in the quiet room. It was easy to rush our fences, to paint lurid, plausible scenarios. But until we knew more of Enrico, we had to wait.

Graham nudged my bag toward me. "Right. On to something we *do* know and can work on, then. Unless you're in the middle of something, Taylor, I'd like you to come with me. I want to question Richard about John's disappearance."

I pushed Enrico and his terrorist mates to the back of my mind, pulled on my jacket, grabbed my purse, and said, "You think Richard knows something, since John works at his launderette?"

"I have no idea, but we'll find out." He held the door open for me and I waited for him to catch me up.

The launderette was near the community center, where we had established the incident room. Its exterior was plain, unadorned stone; a sign gave the only indication what type of business it was, for there was no display window offering a peek at merchandise. Graham said something about minimal upkeep, then followed me inside.

It was a utilitarian room, devoid of decoration. White painted walls, white lino floor, and rows of white washers and dryers gave me the feeling of being in a hospital ward. Or the North Pole. Graham must have felt the same, for he whispered, "I hope we're in time to see the polar bear." Low, light-colored wooden benches squatted in the center of the wall-flanking machines, magazines and cheap paperbacks confettied their surfaces and the top of a small table near the door. A change-making machine and several large-print posters advertising prices of services and laundry products clung to the walls. The aroma of soap and fabric softener saturated the warm, humid air.

Graham introduced me to Richard, whose face was barely more vivid than his establishment. He didn't seem the type to revel in the stone turning custom, being of thin frame and slight stature. Still, he may have just participated from the sidelines, contributing his laundry instead of his muscles. He glanced from Graham to me, his eyes large and strained as though he'd been searching the woods for John. Despite the No Smoking signs plastered around the room, he lit a cigarette and took a drag before he asked if we'd heard anything.

"That's why we're here," Graham said, side-stepping slightly to avoid the exhaled smoke. "I'd like to know if you heard John say anything."

"*Say* anything? Like what?"

Graham repeated the same request every officer had probably asked. Richard shook his head, vehemently denying that he knew anything of John's private life or had heard any plans being made or any conversation. "And I didn't see him after the turning, either. I took the muddy clothing and left to get things washed. I was working here late, so I wouldn't have heard or seen anything, would I?"

That's what he'd say, I thought, *even if he were guilty of something*. The great desire not to become involved. I said it was a pity he hadn't noticed anything out of the ordinary for we might be able to find John more quickly if he had done.

Richard flicked the cigarette ash on top of a washer and said, "Well, now that you mention it, miss, I thought Lloyd or someone had lost his mind."

"Why is that?"

He halfway closed his eyes, fanning the smoke away from his face. In doing so, his hand hit a box of laundry powder. It fell to the floor where he ignored it. "Merely because there were more crowbars than I'd ever seen at the turning."

"Why was that?" I asked, wondering if crowbars were involved in John's disappearance.

HORNS OF A DILEMMA

Richard took another puff on his cigarette and said, "Don't know exactly. I expect he ordered too many. Or someone gave him a few, even though he had some. You'll have to ask Lloyd."

"How many crowbars are normally at the stone turning?"

"Half dozen or so. Not everyone uses one of the church's. Some bring their own."

"What do the people use who don't have a crowbar?"

"Rope, mainly. They drape it around the boulder and pull on that while the others shift it with the crowbars."

I nodded. It fit with what Graham had told me last night. "Is the vicar always responsible for collecting the tools for the Devil's Stone turning?"

Richard stared at the end of his cigarette. "Long as I can remember, yes. It's logical, isn't it?"

"In what way?"

"Well, the turning is in the church yard. It's a religious custom. Why wouldn't he be in charge of it all?"

"Does he make it a point to ask the participants to bring tools, or do people just do it?"

"There's no need to ask, miss. We've been doing this for so long, now, that everyone knows to bring whatever he's got."

Graham thanked him, and we walked up to St. Michael's, skirting the swelling crowd of onlookers, to talk to Lloyd.

Afternoon sun had broken through a haze of clouds and spotlighted the church roof in a flood of golden light. Beyond the building the forest hovered dark and menacing like an atmospheric backdrop to a stage play, nearly black against the downpour of sunlight. The gray stones angled sharp and prominent in the light, casting dense shadows that obliterated the depressions in the stonework. In a few hours shadows would smother the entire village and creep uphill, but the church tower would remain golden and rosy under the setting sun's radiance, perhaps giving the villagers one last reminder before slumber that God was watching over them through the night.

As we turned onto the path angling toward the church, a jazzed-up version of Beethoven's "Für Elise" floated downwind to us. It was an old Marian McPartland piece. I recognized it immediately, for my brother had played that record nearly non-stop as a teenager. This association with home was oddly comforting in the midst of the search for the missing boy, and my brother's face flashed before me, grinning and making up comical lyrics to the classic piece.

> *All I really wanted was some peace.*
> *But, for Elise,*
> *I'd get some sleep.*
> *Her snoring nightly burrowed in my ear*
> *until it's clear*
> *there's murder here.*

> *I'll spike her wine*
> *with ars'nic fine,*
> *entice her will*
> *to drink her fill.*
> > *Oh no! Oh yes! I did, I did, I did!*
> > *But crime don't pay, for look at what I've got—*
> *a chamber pot,*
> *a metal cot.*
> > *So now of course I'm sleeping with police,*
> *there's no release*
> *'till I'm deceased.*

The image of my brother's grinning face and his parody faded, leaving me feeling oddly alone and chilled. I pulled up the zipper on my jacket, which helped somewhat against the cool breeze. But I could find no immediate cure for my sense of loss and overwhelming emptiness. I glanced at Graham, three strides ahead of me, and wondered if the music had any associations with him. But his face was like finely carved stone, portraying nothing other than police work. I hurried up to his side.

The vicar was outside the church, sitting on a stone bench near the south door, mug of coffee in his hand, portable CD player beside him. He was dressed in faded jeans, a blue woolen Aran pullover, woolen jacket, and a corduroy cap. He called to Graham as we approached and punched off the music. Standing up, he asked us if we'd like something to drink. "You may not admit to it," he said, shaking Graham's hand, "but your red faces proclaim your frozen exterior. I've a pot of coffee made. Won't take any time to pour out a cup. Geoff, Brenna...?"

Graham looked at me, inquired, then said, "Nothing, thanks, Lloyd. Sorry to disturb your break."

Lloyd waved aside Graham's concern. "My time's nearly up, anyway. Doesn't matter." He tried to smile, to appear gracious, but his eyes held the haunted look of someone waiting to hear the worst possible news. His black jacket highlighted his ashen complexion.

"All the more reason for us not to have bothered you. I know it's precious."

Time off in any profession was precious, but perhaps more so to police officers, fire fighters, medics—anyone in the high-risk and high-stress profession. While I still had trouble seeing Graham as a minister, I could imagine him pulling a face or swearing in frustration if someone rang him up in the evening with an emergency. He did it in his office back at the station—just because he had changed careers didn't lessen his disappointment at losing his day off.

"I don't want you to get the wrong idea, Geoff," Lloyd said rather haltingly, as though searching for words that wouldn't damn him in a fellow cleric's eyes. He grimaced as he nodded to the CD player. "It eases the pain somewhat."

"Makes time pass a bit more quickly, yes."

"It takes my mind off—" He lowered his head and mumbled, "Well, it helps me focus on something other than his kidnapping. And death."

"We don't know that yet," Graham said. Again his voice was hard, exasperated by Lloyd's defeatist attitude. But it also revealed stubbornness, an iron will that refused to surrender to an outcome that befell a number of missing children cases. He believed in the methodical toil of police work, the pursuit of clues and information that led to the conclusion. And occasionally an old-fashioned miracle.

Lloyd mumbled something about being tired, and perhaps that was affecting his optimism, before asking again if we'd like coffee. Then, still assured we wouldn't, asked if we'd heard anything about his son. When Graham told him we hadn't, Lloyd slowly sank onto the bench. He removed his cap, ran his fingers through his hair, and looked up at us, his face flooded with sunlight.

"I'm sorry, Lloyd," Graham said, sitting beside his friend. "Wish I could produce him from my back pocket. But it's way too early to abandon hope."

"For you or me?" Lloyd asked.

"Both. We've just begun the investigation, and you shouldn't assume the worse. John could be at a mate's house, out for the day. We don't know. And because we don't, and because it's way too early in the inquiry, you shouldn't lose heart." He stared at Lloyd, as if daring a contradictory remark.

Lloyd nodded, said of course it was early, and thanked us for coming.

"Actually," Graham said, "I need to ask you about the stone turning."

"Oh, yes?" Lloyd eyed Graham, as though grateful for something to set his mind upon. He finished his coffee in one long gulp, then said, "About what? Who was there last night?"

Graham explained that a question had arisen as to the inordinate amount of crowbars used in the turning, and that Lloyd had actually bought more than was needed.

Lloyd smiled, perhaps relieved to be talking of the triviality of crowbars. "I bought some, yes. It was unusual, but there was nothing nefarious in it."

"I should think, crowbars being rather durable and this custom being rather old, that the village will have all the crowbars it will ever need."

"You would think so, yes. But some always get misplaced or 'borrowed' and never returned. I don't know where things disappear to around here. Hymnals, teapots, potholders, boxes of matches…amazing. They seem to develop wings when no one's watching and fly off to some great depository in the sky. But I'm sure you have the same problem at your office, Geoff."

"Certainly! Pens and pencils vanish from off my desk, the stapler goes missing. It's common in an office. But crowbars?"

"I know. It's absurd. Great, indestructible things like crowbars—vanish. I sometimes think we're overrun with poltergeist, the way things evaporate. Or, I could look at it as the hand from the grave."

"Pardon?" I frowned, not making the connection.

"Legal assistance or spritely mischief. The result's the same, Brenna." He smiled again, amused at my confusion. "St. Michael's stone turning is bound by a parishioner's will. We're given a yearly allotment for the custom. It must be spent that year or we lose it."

"So this year you bought crowbars."

"We always use some of the money for the tea and rock cakes and such afterwards, but we certainly can't use it all on food! Crowbars seemed a logical purchase, especially when I couldn't find many when I looked last month."

"Do you keep them all? I thought some of the villagers brought their own tools."

"If they have something, they'll bring it, certainly. But how many people have a crowbar? This isn't the good ole days of yore when this was a farming community and that was a common tool. The era of wagons and carriages have passed. And how many people pry up stumps and boulders in the course of their farming? They use tractors for that."

"So how do they go missing, if you keep them? Do they disappear immediately after the stone turning?"

"Not that I've ever remembered. They usually wander off throughout the year. You know—someone needs to pry open a stuck window, another person needs to open a rusted latch. Usual occurrences in a country community. You lend the tool and then forget about it. It happens. No one sets out with the intention of stealing."

"So many things aren't," Graham said. "But it happens."

"The road to hell…"

A robin warbled energetically from a tree and we stopped to listen, perhaps all of us reflecting on life and the scarcity, sometimes, of happiness.

"Were all your crowbars used last night, Lloyd? Or were some left in your tool shed, for example?"

"Are you thinking that the crowbar used to kill Enrico was stolen intentionally last evening for that purpose?" His face drained of what little color it had, and his hand went to his throat as though his breath had left his body.

"I'm just trying to fix all the players and whereabouts of the tools in my mind, Lloyd."

"Yes. Of course." He smiled tentatively, perhaps reassured. "All the regulars had tools."

"Either crowbars or rope."

"I tried to get some of the onlookers to participate, indicated we had crowbars if they wanted to join the turning. You know we had room for a few more at the stone."

"But you were unsuccessful."

"No one from the crowd took part. So I gave a crowbar to you..." He paused, looking at Graham as if he needed confirmation of his action in this nightmare.

"At least I had remembered to bring my leather gloves," Graham said, smiling.

"And I gave a crowbar to Enrico, of course."

"Why 'of course'," I asked.

"Well, he's no farmer and he's been here only two months. He hadn't any use for a crowbar at his house. So I concluded he wouldn't know to bring one even if he owned one."

"That's two accounted for," Graham said. "Any others?"

Lloyd rattled off a few more villagers' names, ending with "I thought David would join us."

"Was he was interested in the turning?"

"Thought so. He asked a lot of questions, seemed intrigued by the crowbars and rope. You know David Willett?"

"He's a history teacher," I said.

"And recently turned author. His first book was published not long ago."

"David Willet from Bramford?" Graham asked, clearly surprised to learn that David was in Hollingthorpe.

"That's him. He occasionally visits his sister and brother. Anyway, I thought at first David would take a turn, seeing as Page and Harry live here—and you know he has a right to participate based on that. But David declined, although I did see him looking later at the crowbars when we were having our tea."

"And the tools were...where?"

"In the church hall."

"Of course. In the corner nearest the steps."

"In a pile with the rope. I like to collect them immediately after the turning so I can keep track of them and they aren't left outdoors to get rained on. They were all there in one pile this morning when I went to shift them to the storage shed. I thought it odd because—" Graham held up his hand, halting Lloyd's words. "Pardon, Lloyd, but why do you say that was odd? We just agreed they were in the corner nearest the steps in the church hall."

"Because, Geoff, I remember when we went into the hall after the stone turning that one crowbar was by itself. Near the rest of them, but separated, if that makes sense."

"As though it'd been gathered up and the person put it down?"

"Yes. I thought it odd because what would it have taken, another three steps to put it in with the others? He could have even tossed it into the pile. But it was by itself."

"So you didn't gather it up, then. Do you know who did?"

Lloyd shook his head. "Haven't the faintest. I usually do it. That's why this is so strange—not only because I'm the one who normally hunts them down but also because the crowbar wasn't in the pile with the others. Is it significant?"

"But it was in the pile this morning? Who else has a key to the church? Would your wife have moved them?"

"I can't fathom who would have done it. I mean, it's so ridiculous!"

"Anyone else have a key?"

"Not that I know of. I suppose someone could have forced open a door or window to get inside, but why? To tidy up a pile of crowbars?" He frowned, not believing, either.

Graham said, "It's a bit far fetched, yes. I'll look for signs of forced entry in a moment. We can at least clear that up. Are you certain the crowbar was added to the pile?"

"Pardon?" The question clearly was unexpected, for his eyes widened.

"If the wayward crowbar is not as you last saw it, off by itself, how do you know it was thrown into the pile and not stolen? Did you count them?"

"Well…no. I mean, I just assumed, not seeing it, that someone had tossed—"

"You know how many you should have if they're all there?"

"Yes. Twelve. You want to see?" He stood up and turned toward the church.

Graham nodded, and I quickly followed the two men.

The small pile of crowbars and ropes was at the foot of the steps in the church hall. Graham put on the pair of latex gloves that I got from my shoulder bag, then picked up crowbars, setting them into a different pile as I counted aloud. When he had finished, I had counted ten.

Lloyd stared in disbelief, swearing that he had started the stone turning with twelve and he couldn't understand why two crowbars were now missing. Graham made a slow, precise tour of the hall, finally pointing to a broken window near the stage area and said it appeared to be the entry point. "Unless it was broken last night and you haven't cleaned up the glass yet. I don't recall it happening while I was still here."

Lloyd hurried over, stopped short when he saw the glass on the floor, and said it was the first he'd seen of it. "And I check to be certain we've locked all the windows and doors. No, Geoff, this wasn't done while we were here. Someone must have broken in." He turned slightly pale and stared back at the crowbars.

"I'll get someone out here to look for fingerprints, though we probably won't find any."

"Why break into a church to steal crowbars, Geoff? Why not just hide them after the turning and come back for it later?"

"That's what I'm wondering, Lloyd."

"Unless," I said, drawing the men's attention, "it was an afterthought."

Lloyd looked confused and Graham looked surprised.

I nodded. "Maybe whoever broke in and stole the crowbars didn't know earlier in the evening that he would need it. Maybe something came up after the crowbars had been collected, necessitating it."

"Heavens!" Lloyd said, the blood draining from his face. "But I saw the crowbar in the hall while Enrico was still here."

"Could someone have stolen it before he was killed?"

"There wasn't enough time for that! We were all here in the hall; we would've seen someone take it. And you discovered his body, Geoff, so you know about the time constraint."

"So," Graham said slowly, "the crowbars had to have been taken *after* Enrico's murder. And the question remains, as Taylor just said, why?"

I said, "Because he needed them again." I left unsaid the obvious, but the men had reasoned through to the conclusion.

Lloyd said, "Lord, I hope not! That would mean…"

"Yes, sir."

Graham asked Lloyd if he knew of any disturbances in the village.

"Surely you don't believe he's going to kill someone else, Geoff!"

"I hope not either, but what other implication do we place on the crowbars that've gone missing. If we hadn't found the broken window, I'd say the tools had been misplaced, as seems to be common here. But the window signifies that someone broke in and stole crowbars. I've no other conclusion at the moment."

Lloyd nodded, murmuring that it seemed logical and that he didn't know of anyone who hated anyone else. "Certainly there are little tiffs, but to be angry enough to plan a murder! And with such a tool!" He grimaced and glanced again at the crowbars.

"How about the visitors to the village? Obviously you can't speak about tourists, but how about the two regular visitors you have? Richard's friend, and Page's brother? I wouldn't think they'd be visiting that often, either to warrant becoming the target or instigator of murder."

Lloyd exhaled strongly. "Both are perfectly law-abiding people, as far as I know. I wouldn't think either man was here often enough or long enough to produce such anger in one of us. David, especially, seems so nice. I'm *very* disappointed David didn't join in. I thought he might."

"He seems exceedingly keen on local customs," I said, recalling his book.

"Asks all sorts of questions. Besides, his sister and brother are residents, as is his friend. Odd he wouldn't pick one up and join in, if he's that interested, don't you think?"

"And who is his friend?"

"Tad Mills. He's a fine artist. Very good, too. He did the illustrations for that book of David's. He's known David for years. A mutual friend introduced them when David first began writing his book. It's on Derbyshire customs. Do you know it?"

I glanced at Graham, wondering if he were going to mention something about our case this past December.

Without batting an eye, Graham said, "I'm acquainted with it, yes. And where does this other traditions-lover live?"

Chapter 12

Twenty minutes later, after Graham had rung up Divisional Headquarters and requested the crowbars be taken to the forensics lab and the window examined for prints, we were in Tad Mills' front room, hearing the same account that we'd heard from Lloyd. Tad's house hugged the northern edge of the village green, the first residence on Well Hill Street. His house also neighbored Enrico's, which made Tad's participation in all this—if there was any—a bit more important than knowing what time Enrico drove off to work in the mornings.

The house mimicked the others on the street, a building of gray stone and tile roof, a neatly kept exterior with a small front garden. A black painted wrought iron chair angled out from a corner of the front porch, a contrasting picture of dark and light created from the humps of snow still clinging to the arms and seat. I knocked the snow from my boots and followed Graham inside.

"I haven't seen David this trip," Tad replied to Graham's question. He leaned against the front door, staring down the hall, as though focusing his thoughts.

Tad was short, squat and blond, with a tattoo of a butterfly on his left wrist. His hair was in disarray, like he'd just woken up. Even his flannel plaid shirt was rumpled; half tucked into his jeans, half hanging out, the sleeves rolled up. I thought he and his pal David must have looked comical together, for David was tall and thin with brilliant red hair. He ran his fingers through his short hair, perhaps tidying up his appearance, and waited for Graham or me to say something.

The vestibule where we stood was wallpapered in pale gray and white stripes. A white radiator echoed the shape of the window above it and gurgled contentedly, throwing warmth into the cold that lingered around the door. A square pot of African violets sat on the windowsill, the flower's purple hue repeated in the purple, gray and blue rug. A white ceramic umbrella stand embraced the stairs that curved up to the upper floor. The fragrance of wet wool and hot coffee hovered in the air, making me simultaneously cold and hungry.

"David's staying with his sister," Graham said, glancing at the matted and framed pencil drawing of Toad's Mouth Rock. The gritstone boulder near Burbage Brook on the Derbyshire-Yorkshire border did indeed look like a toad, its mouth slightly gapping, its head turned skyward. "He's been here several days, I think. He's not called on you, then?"

"He's a busy, lad. We must've missed each other."

A sound like falling boxes clattered from some back room. Perhaps the kitchen. Tad seemed glued to the front door, staring at Graham, and showed no interest in investigating. I exchanged a glance with Graham and asked Tad if he were going to look into the disturbance, or would he like us to do it.

Tad blinked rapidly, gazed down the hall, then back at Graham. He opened his mouth, coughed and turned red.

"Daylight burglaries are not that uncommon," I said. "But there's no need to be frightened. We'll have a look, shall we?"

Graham followed me to the kitchen, with Tad hurrying behind us, calling that it was probably just his cat. I said that if that were the case, perhaps the cat was injured and that we ought to see.

As I approached the door, I asked Tad if he always closed up his cat in the kitchen.

"Only when I've company," he said, his voice blocked by Graham's tall figure.

"You shoved him in here, then, prior to our arrival?"

"Well, when I heard the door bell, I assumed—"

"Some of your friends allergic to cats, are they?"

"Not so much that as they don't like my cat jumping on their laps."

"I don't hear anything," Graham said. "Hopefully your cat's not hurt. All right, Taylor." He flipped on the light switch as I swung the door open, and we stepped inside the room.

David Willett had his hand on the doorknob, the back door angled open, the Venetian blinds covering the door's window swaying and banging against the door. A box of laundry powder was on its side on the floor where he had evidently knocked it over. He turned, red-faced and grimacing, and stared at us with eyes that mirrored his embarrassment.

"Going somewhere, Mr. Willett?" Graham said, walking over to the man, who bent over, picked up the box and slowly placed it on top of the working top. He patted the box as though it had been an expensive, valued object and had escaped destruction by breakage. Graham stood in front of him, his hands folded, waiting.

"Uh, yes," David said, forcing a smile and blinking rapidly. "I, uh, misplaced my current manuscript. I thought Tad might have found it. I came over to see if it was here, Tad," he said, leaning slightly to his left in order to see his friend standing behind Graham. His eyes darted sideways as his words rushed out in one long breath. "I came in through the back door, here, thinking you'd be in the kitchen, having a coffee or something. I was going to call out to you but when I heard voices I decided instead to leave and ask you about it later. I didn't want to disturb you, Tad. I thought about making myself a cuppa and waiting until you were free, but then I wondered if you'd be a while, so I decided to leave. I hope you don't mind my making myself at home."

The kitchen—a yellow rectangle harboring a small curtain-less window over the sink, a door and a wall of wooden cupboards—showed no tea or coffee preparation. The working top was empty of cups, saucers, spoons and coffee tin. The electric kettle was unplugged, the milk still presumably in the fridge. One chair, however, was angled out from the table, as though its sitter had risen in a hurry and had not shoved it back in place alongside its companion. There was also no scribbled note stating he had been there or would return.

"Uh, no," Tad said, clearing his voice. "Uh, fine, Dave. I don't think you left it here, though. I would've rung you up if I'd found it. I know you would've panicked if you'd misplaced it."

"What are you working on?" Graham asked, eyeing David. "Another book on Derbyshire?"

David coughed. "What am I working on? Now, you mean?"

"You both just spoke of your current manuscript. I assume it's a second book."

"Well, uh, I'm not sure I want to say—"

"If you're worried about plagiarism, you needn't be. I'm not a writer, and I don't think Sergeant Taylor, even with all her talents, has any designs on your idea. Have you, sergeant?" He looked at me, his right eyebrow raised, and smiled.

"I'd certainly like to read your book," I said, "if it's as interesting as your one on Derbyshire customs. But I'm neither a writer nor do I have the time."

Graham turned back to David, grinning. "There! What more assurance do you need from two officers of the law! Your subject matter is safe from theft. I know Sergeant Taylor would like to hear about your new book. And I'm also intrigued. Would you tell us?" He waited, his arms folded on his chest, looking as though he hadn't a thing to do other than talk with David Willett.

David sighed, stood up, and glanced at Tad before returning Graham's gaze. "I...it's, uh, well, it's kind of hard to explain—"

"If you'd rather not, of course we understand. We're interested, that's all. Fans of the author…"

"Yes, of course." David took a deep breath, looked again at Tad, and said, "It's about, uhh, curiosities of the Peak District." He slowly, nearly imperceptibly, let out his breath now that his brain had kicked in. "Right. That's it. Okay to say, isn't it, Tad?"

I turned to see Tad straightening a wall calendar, the month showing a photo of Stony Middleton's oddity, an octagonal church in which all pews face the middle—like theater in the round. A definite curiosity, this fifteenth-century building, and unique to Derbyshire. And Tad's tacit pantomime was a bit obvious. Still, David seemed to be breathing a bit easier now that he had his book idea.

I said, "Like Chesterfield's crooked church spire?"

HORNS OF A DILEMMA

He nodded and almost smiled. "That, of course, but also things like Mock Beggars' Hall near Birchover, and the yew tree tunnel at Melbourne Hall. I'm still doing research on most of it." He trailed off, perhaps glad that he had provided something sounding authentic enough to get us off his back.

I nodded. Too bad he wasn't going to write that book. I'd always been fascinated with the strange group of rocks that looked incredibly like an ancient manorial hall, especially at dusk. Perhaps due to their realism, the rocks had once been thought to have had associations with Druids. And the tunnel of yew trees, planted in Charles I's reign, was certainly odd. One hundred yards long and originally supported by a wooden framework, the gigantic hedge leads the visitor to an animal cemetery. I'd been cursed with too much imagination as a child, imagining Roundheads and Cavaliers fighting in the long tunnel, envisioning romantic meetings and elopements with the couples dashing on horseback through the dark arboreal avenue, their way lit by lantern light, the horses' hooves thudding on the damp earth. It was a strange object, the yew tunnel, and I had always wondered why it had been planted. Maybe David would write the book, now that he had mentioned it, and then I might have the police officer's eternal question 'Why?' answered.

Obviously feeling more secure, David leaned against the door, smiling and making small talk with Graham. Tad was anything but at ease, for he lingered in the doorway, his fingers wrapped around the jamb, his lips compressed. I gave up my adventurous speculations of smugglers' gold and escaping priests to refocus on police work.

"We were just talking about you," Graham said, concentrating on David.

"Oh, yes?" David shifted his weight to his other leg, suddenly wary.

"Your friend, Tad, had just been telling us before we came in here, that he hadn't seen you yet this visit."

"Yes," David said, fixing his eyes on Tad as though hypnotizing him into replying correctly. "I— I've been busy. I couldn't even get a chance to ring you up, Tad. This is the first few minutes I've been able to grab. Hope you don't think I was avoiding you."

"No," Tad said, glancing from Graham, to me, then to David. "Of course not. You've got your sister and brother to visit. I knew we'd get some time together. How about tonight? The pub good?"

"You didn't see each other at the stone turning?" Graham said, his eyes darting between the two men. "I understood you were both there."

"I, uh..." Tad swallowed. "I was there, yes, but I didn't get a chance to talk to David. He was, uh, with his brother and sister. He got away before I could say hi. And I got there a bit late, just as it was starting."

"Yes," David said, nodding vigorously. "My brother, Harry, was quite agitated last evening. Well, he always does get that way whenever there's something like the stone turning. He gets excited. He's a handful then. My sis needed help with him, so..."

Graham nodded, as though visualizing the scene. "I heard you were interested in the crowbars used for the turning." He waited for David to explain.

David stuffed his hands into his jeans pockets. The room was quiet except for the sound of his rapid breathing. A group of sparrows on the windowsill outside twittered enthusiastically before David said, "You're blowing it all out of proportion, Graham."

"And what is that?"

"The crowbars."

"You placing some significance on them, then?"

"*You* evidently are, or you wouldn't' be asking me about them."

"And what is their significance?"

"Murder weapon, isn't it? Didn't someone use a crowbar or something like it to whack Enrico over the head?"

"You seem to know a lot about the murder, Mr. Willett."

"Not any more than the next bloke."

"Does the next bloke believe that is the murder weapon?"

"Should think so. You lot have been asking questions all day long. I heard about it. The whole crowd down by the boulder is talking about it."

"And your interest in the crowbar—"

"Not to cosh Enrico with! It's a curiosity, that's all."

"You putting the Devil's Stone Turning in your book, then?"

David nodded, his face suddenly ashen. "I—It's a great custom. That boulder is another natural oddity, like the yew tunnel. I thought I'd include it in the new book so I looked at the crowbars and the rope. Enrico wasn't strangled with rope, was he?"

Graham merely looked at David, unsmiling, divulging nothing about the cause of death or the details surrounding the murder.

After several awkward moments of silence, David coughed, crossed his arms over his chest, and said, "Well, if he was strangled or beaten, why should you accuse me of Enrico's murder? I don't go around killing people I don't know. Or even those I *do* know," he added hurriedly.

"I haven't accused you of anything, Mr. Willett."

"As good as." David sniffed, his eyebrows lowering. "You asking about me and crowbars is kind of suggestive, don't you think? I didn't turn the stone—as you know, being as you were included in that modest group. I didn't whack Enrico with it. I just looked at them and the ropes. The stone turning will be in my book, you'll find out if you'll take the time to do a bit of research before jumping on people's backs. I'm about to write about it so I just went over to the pile last night to look at them. There's nothing more to it than that." To underscore his statement, he plopped down on the chair and glared up at Graham.

Tad yanked out another chair and sat next to him. He glanced at David, then thanked Graham for coming. As subtle a hint as any I've seen for us to be on our way. Graham murmured his thanks and we left the house

HORNS OF A DILEMMA

and the sound of their arguing voices.

"So why would Tad lie about not seeing David?" I asked as we walked to the pub.

The afternoon had advanced, throwing blue shadows across the land. Snow lay secure beneath the bushes and among the stalks of dry ornamental grasses, the sunlight too feeble to melt it. The shadows would deepen to indigo and black, stretching and consuming countryside and village until it so blended with the evening that you could not tell where twilight and shadow met. But for now, the whiteness of the snowy patches still sparkled in the late sunlight, and the ridge along the western horizon glowed golden and pink.

Graham opened the door of the pub, followed me to a table, then said, "That's just the first lie he told us, Taylor. I wonder how many more we'll discover."

Chapter 13

"Lies are not only a copper's bane," Graham said minutes later, taking the mug of coffee from the waiter, "but also the minister's. No matter what career I choose, no matter what happens in my life, it seems that I'm confronted by lies."

I watched him as he took a sip of the hot liquid, mentally choosing a saint to plead to that I wasn't about to do something stupid. Whether I'd chosen the correct saint or not, I had no idea. Hopefully St. Joseph of Arimathaea would be gracious enough to channel my request to St. Sebastian or whoever had jurisdiction over the subject. Had his ex-fiancée lied to him? I took a deep breath and said, "Police work I can understand. We get lied to all the time. But why would a minister encounter lies?"

Graham set down his mug and looked out of the window. He seemed to be recalling an incident or debating how much he should tell me, for he didn't reply for some time. In the interval, the everyday sounds of life washed over me: conversations and laughter, a door squeaking, dialogue from a television program, plates being placed on a table. Sounds so mundane and removed from murder or a missing child that they seemed offensive somehow, as though those who produced them weren't showing the proper respect for the grim situation we were investigating.

I took several sips of my tea before he finally spoke. His voice came slowly and heavily, as if he were speaking of something painful or embarrassing. "Money," he said, letting out a sign and rubbing his eyes. "Handouts. People lie about their health or their domestic situation or being made redundant and out of a job so the sympathetic minister will give them a couple of quid. Or a meal or a tank of petrol for the car."

It was the same as I had encountered during my first year on the beat. People giving you a hard luck story to finagle a few pounds into their pockets. Of course it was never much money, but multiply that by a 12-hour day, inducing donations from several constables and clergy, and you had a nice day's take. It was nearly as unkind as being lied to by a suspect. You have witnesses who saw the bloke do it, a surveillance tape that shows he did it, yet when you question him, he says 'Who, me? I was never there.' It was very difficult to deal with, being lied straight to your face. So yes, I could understand Graham's disappointment with humanity. Greed seemed to rear its head constantly and attacked anyone and everyone. It conned the gullible and generous; it drained coffers and pockets, reducing funds and supplies for the deserving; it penalized the truly needy through the hardened hearts of the duped. Greed was indeed a sin. And it knew no societal division.

"It doesn't take much experience," Graham said, abandoning his contemplation of the village green and concentrating on me, "to know that if someone tells you he needs money to buy petrol for his car, you go with him to the station to pump and pay for the petrol yourself."

"You think you've outsmarted him, then."

"Perhaps he's outsmarted you. Perhaps he had the money and he's just getting a full tank thanks to you. Now he's ahead ten pound or so and can spend his petrol money for something else." He picked up his mug, stared at the coffee, then took a long gulp. The mug thudded back onto the tabletop, like a judge's gavel pounding for order. Graham snorted, his jaw muscles tensing.

I said, "You have no way of knowing, sir. Most of us are probably deceived countless times. Isn't it better to err on the side of generosity rather than let some deserving person go hungry?"

Without raising his eyes from the coffee mug, he said, "Like freeing a guilty suspect rather than hanging an innocent person? Then I'm one of the Kingdom's least employed executioners. I've probably given handouts to hundreds of con artists. What does that make me?"

"A sympathetic person."

"I suppose." He drained the last of his coffee and looked at me. His eyes seemed tired, almost haunted. He flashed a grin, but his eyes didn't. I knew he was forcing himself to be positive. "You think I'm earning stars or points by falling for these agony stories? Does St. Peter look kindly on the fool? What is that saying about God looking after fools and drunkards...?"

"I don't think you're a fool, sir, and I think you're being smiled upon."

"Just so *someone's* smiling, that's fine."

I wanted to ask if he had had problems this morning when he had driven to that undisclosed place, but decided that if he had wanted me to know, he would've told me. I smiled tentatively, couldn't think of a reply, and sought refuge in my salad.

The pub began filling up with people unwinding after work or wanting to catch a quick meal before heading out for the evening. The table near us held a family of four, the children about ten and twelve years old and chanting that they wanted sticky toffee pudding. A dating couple occupied the table on the other side of us, the woman leaning toward the male and giggling at something he had whispered in her ear. Someone at the bar cheered and pumped his fist, immersed in the televised rugby match. The fragrance of sautéed onions and broiled steak drifted over to us as the waiter passed our table. I picked up a cello-wrapped packet of breadsticks, ripped it open, and crumpled one of the sticks on top of my salad.

"You need some croutons?"

I blinked, momentarily thrown.

Graham pointed his fork at my salad. "Croutons. You want some?"

"I don't think they have any. This is fine. I'm used to it."

"That's as may be, but croutons are nicer."

I angled my head and smiled at him. "You sound like a connoisseur of croutons."

"I've had my experiences."

"Is that the only thing you're an expert on?"

"Food, you mean?"

"That's always good for a start."

"For a *start*? What else do you want to know about?"

I wanted to say 'your love life,' but knew that would be detrimental to my career and my relationship with him. Not that there was much. And not that I should be pursuing it. I had made a date with Adam, and I was trying to wean my heart from Graham. About as successful as rehabilitating Dillinger by placing him in a bank teller's cage, but I had promised Margo and Scott that I would try. And even though Graham had hinted last month about a date, he still hadn't made it official. So I passed up the love life opportunity, mentally panicked for some conversational subject, and said, "Your opinion of—" I scribbled the judge's name on a page in my notebook, not wanting to speak it in case someone would hear it.

Graham looked at me, clearly surprised. The judge solicited extreme reactions in law enforcement officers, lawyers and defendants—either ecstatic or outraged at the rulings, depending on how it went. And it usually went in favor of the defendant. Graham sighed, settled back and said, "He's too old, for one thing. That's obvious. He should've retired years ago. It's not that he's a particularly bad judge—he probably was extremely competent, maybe even top rung, in his day. But the problem is that his day is over and he hasn't realized it yet. He's still on the bench. He's retirement age and he should retire."

"I have noticed he falls asleep during court."

Graham cringed. "Don't remind me."

"Not the best image for a judge, no."

"One of his problems."

"And the other?"

"You really want to hear this, don't you?" His eyes surveyed me, suddenly alert, infused with light because he was talking about something that interested him.

When I nodded, he said, "He's out of touch. With current day criminals, with the system, with life. He doesn't really hear what's being said in court. He bases his rulings on *his* life experience, on what seems pertinent to his world of forty years ago, not on the case evidence or what happened to the victim or what we coppers testify to. He mentally takes this criminal and the case back to the era he feels comfortable in and replays it there, applying his own experience to it. His decisions are usually not good. He's let off too many criminals who would've been serving time if another judge had tried them."

HORNS OF A DILEMMA

He stopped suddenly, his face flushed in the heat of his address. He shrugged, signaled for more coffee, and said, "Sorry, TC, but you wanted my expert opinion."

"You've nothing to apologize for, sir. I thought you felt that way, but I wasn't sure since we've never discussed it. I'm glad you told me."

"Why?"

It was the first time I felt he was opening up to me, revealing bits of his personal life so I could establish a connection between us. Not as boss and subordinate, but as one person respecting another. But with that one question I felt challenged. I felt my face flush. I stared down at my salad, needing time to compose myself. The tines of my fork flipped through the bits of broken breadstick. I said, "It just makes it easier to work with someone if you know opinions, know what a person likes or dislikes."

"Like marriage, you mean?" He smiled and squeezed my hand quickly. "I'm just kidding, TC. But I do agree."

"Being partnered with someone is easier if you know how the person thinks and reacts."

"And knowing opinions is sometimes the first step. Perhaps we need more of these sessions. You can tell me what you think of the late-lamented fraternization between solicitors and police, and I'll let you in on my opinion of olives."

I laughed. I already knew that. "Does this loathing go back to childhood?"

"You mean, did I slip on olive juice, or eat too many and become sick?"

"My sister and I ate a whole pan of sticky toffee pudding one night. We sneaked down to the kitchen and sat there, the pan between us, each of us with spoons, attacking it. Part of it was because it was so incredibly good—my mother probably made the best I'd ever eaten. Part of it was because we were both involved, sitting in the dark kitchen, midnight..."

"Partners in crime at such a young age. I'm shocked, TC. But I applaud your decision to forsake your illicit path and turn to the Good."

"It took me years, literally, before I could eat sticky toffee pudding. 'Course..." I hesitated, glanced at my thighs, then back at Graham, and said slowly, "I don't know that that's a particularly great accomplishment that I conquered my revulsion."

Graham laughed and again squeezed my hand. "I don't think it ranks as one of the Seven Deadly Sins, TC. But I know what you mean. My sister and I had similar experiences with jumbals. Mother had baked an entire batch—oh, I don't know how many dozen—for the church fete. My sister and I thought we'd each have one each. Well, one biscuit led to another, and by the time we'd finished our crime spree, we'd eaten three dozen. Mother was not amused."

"Such a major crime must have brought a punishment. Anything besides the obvious?"

He smiled, dropped my hand, and leaned back in his chair, tipping it back slightly as he said, "Besides the tummy aches and the spanking? I can't remember anything else. Only that I, too, avoided jumbals for years. Pity. They're very good."

I nodded. The crisp, almond biscuit was one of my favorites. "I wonder if we could take a poll to see how many police officers have shady pasts."

"Perhaps it's not such a bad thing, TC. Gives us a better understanding of the crook."

It was my turn to laugh, and I found his eyes smiling at me this time. The easy conversation and the shared stories were linking Graham and me in a more personal, closer way than the job could do. I felt my heart jump with hope.

Graham's mobile rang, cutting into my mood and our meal. He glanced at the caller ID, told me it was Margo, then answered it. After several seconds of questions, he rang off, pocketed the phone, and said, "Margo called to let me know that WPC MacMillan has had a run in."

"With whom? Someone we're looking for?"

"Not a person. With a rock."

"Someone *assaulted* her?" I said, incredulous that someone would attack a police officer. "With what? Is she all right?"

"Not who, TC. *It*. A rock. Margo assumes MacMillan was following the path through the forest. At any rate, that's where she found her—on the wooded section of the path near the church. She's still unconscious. Has a nasty head wound. Margo's rung up for the ambulance."

I felt fear building within me again. "Ambulance? It must be bad, then. Will she be all right? I mean, if her head's hurt—"

Graham nodded. "I know. There could be contusion of the brain if she hit her head hard enough. Of course she doesn't know. We'll have to wait until MacMillan's admitted to hospital to find out. Margo's staying with her until the ambulance attendants arrive, but she thought we should know about it."

I couldn't speak. My fright threatened to overwhelm me. So I simply nodded and let Graham talk.

"I'll trot on over there and see if I can lend a hand. Or an arm, if she's recovered sufficiently to hobble back to the church. Even so, she needs to be checked out by a doctor." He gazed out of the window. The landscape had darkened to the somber grayness that comes after sunset. Stars would have been blinking through the darkness, but heavy rain clouds were smeared across the sky, black smudges against the slate-gray backdrop. Several drops of rain hesitantly hit the window, as though not having the heart to spoil our view. Graham sighed, muttered something about little Johnny wanting to play, and stood up.

The rain had strengthened in that handful of minutes, pelting the window in a regular tattoo of sharp taps. Rain collected on top of the thin veins of leading that held the panes in place, then coursed down the glass in miniature streams to pool on the sill. Larger pools were establishing themselves on the pavement and the High Street, and throwing back the yellowish tint of the streetlamps floating somewhere above them in the murky gloom. A car splashed up the street, its red taillights mirrored and multiplied in the puddles.

Graham pulled on his jacket and peered outside. "Time and tide, TC. Time and tide." He straightened up and faced me. "I've got to see to this. You want to linger here in the warmth and finish your tea?"

"I'm finished," I said, getting up and donning my jacket. I glanced at our unfinished meals. "You want me to go with you?"

We left our money on the table, walked to the door and hesitated in the open doorway. The air was chilly and damp, and smelled of wet moss and stone. Graham zipped his jacket and peered at the sky. "Thanks for the offer, but no. If I need help, I'll ring you up. MacMillan may be able to walk. I'll find out. Hell of a night to be caught in the rain."

He stepped outside and I called, "You want a mackintosh? I've got one in the boot of my car. I can fetch it."

"No. Thanks anyway."

"If it doesn't rain any harder than this, you shouldn't get soaked."

"I hope I'm not out there long enough for that!" He grinned and dashed up the hill, disappearing into the darkness and rain.

I lingered beside the door, loathe to leave the shelter of the covered doorway, undecided what I should do. I would have liked to have gone with him, but he hadn't seemed to want me. I glanced at my watch. Half past five. There was time enough to type up my notes and get a few other things finished before I called it a night.

Clasping the collar of my jacket to my neck, I stepped onto the pavement. It was wet and glistened beneath the outdoor lights. Water lay in the gutter beside the street and would be a welcomed bath in the morning for the sparrows. As the rain showered my head, I chastised myself for not grabbing a newspaper inside. At least I could have used it for a hat. Lacking that, I held my shoulder bag over my head and trudged toward the incident room.

I'd avoided most of the puddles by the time I arrived at the corner of the High Street and Green Acre Road, where the community center sat. I stopped, looked both directions and was about to cross the street when a police car paused opposite me. When the window came down, a voice called from inside the car, "I know you like animals, but impersonating a duck is going a bit far."

I ran over to the car as the passenger side door opened. Scott Coral's face beamed at me in the glow of the overhead light. "If you've got time to pester law abiding women," I said, "you obviously haven't enough to do. Shall I let the Super know you need more of a work load?"

"That'll be the last thing you ever do. You busy?"

"Not officially."

"Good. Get in." He pushed the door open a bit wider and patted the upholstery of the passenger cushion. "You can get a refresher course on taking statements, then. I'm splendid in action."

I got into the car and shut the door. As I angled my body towards Scott, I said, "Who are you talking to? Where are you going?"

"To the manse," he said, taking his foot off the brake pedal.

"Graham's up there now." I cupped my hands around my eyes as I glanced out of the window, expecting to see something that would explain Scott's call. "Well, not at the manse. At the path close to the church. Has something happened? Did he—"

"Cool your jets. He's fine. At least, I know nothing to the contrary." His voice had taken on an edge, as though he were exasperated with the call or with me. "I thought you were forging new pathways in the romance department."

So that was the reason for his irritation. He thought I was anxious about Graham. "I am," I said, my voice not as strong as I would have liked.

"You don't sound it. In fact, you sounded more like the desperate wife, just then, instead of the lady who's dallying elsewhere. You and Erik are still—"

"Yes!" I snapped. "Still cohabitating, if you need to know."

"Then you ought to be fine. But you aren't, I take it." He glanced at me. "Don't wear your heart on your sleeve, Brenna."

I turned from the window and glared at Scott. "I *am* dating someone, if you have to know."

"And it's *not* Graham. Fine."

"And why should my courting status preclude my concern for my co-worker? He's my boss, which should count for some of my anxiety, and he's a smashing person, besides. I'd react the same way if I were worried about Margo or Mark. Or you," I added somewhat begrudgingly. "I'd been going to ask if Graham had called in something on Enrico, but you cut me off. *And* jumped to a conclusion. A false one, I might add."

"What's that adage?"

"What one? Don't count your chickens—"

"Me thinks the lady doth protest too much."

"Funny, Scott."

"Natural wit, Bren. I can't help it if I'm funny."

"Speaking of funny..." I leaned forward a bit, trying to see his face. "What was going on this morning with you and Roper? You acted like you had a problem with him. I've never seen you so edgy. You'd taken on the tactical stance. I thought you were going to leap at him, the way you were positioned. You know him?"

"Don't even know his name, but he certainly set off alarms the minute he walked in. He's obviously into physical combat—you know that without being told."

I nodded, remembering how my hair had stood on end, my throat had tightened and I had gripped my chair. There had been a warning, that unexplainable sixth sense that all cops develop, alerting them to felons or potential danger. Places evoked that—too dark, deserted, or silent,

HORNS OF A DILEMMA

something out of context or not making sense; people imparted that—a look, a remark, a presence that could nearly be tangible. But as soon as Roper had entered the incident room, Scott had discerned Roper's true nature and had immediately reacted, taking the tactical stance, watching his moves, ready for a fight. And Roper, conversely, had taken the same position. Was it an implied challenge to Scott, or was it Roper's natural posture, suggesting he was always ready for battle?

"The weird thing is," Scott said, "it was disconcerting. The guy's a mass of muscles, a walking danger. Yet he's eloquent."

"Most muscle-head bad guys are different," I agreed.

"They can barely create understandable sentences. Yet he carried on this conversation filled with innuendoes. He had total control of the situation—physically and psychologically—and he knew it."

"If he wasn't staring at Graham, he was sizing you up, grinning all the while."

"I hated his guts the moment he walked in. Who is he?"

I told Scott about Roper's inelegant past and that Graham had arrested him.

Scott whistled softly. "That explains a lot. I'm sorry for Graham. Having a berk like Roper in his past must give him a few nightmares. He's an imminent threat, no matter if he's involved in a current case of Graham's or not. He'll always be lurking in the background. His type always is."

"You think Graham's in immediate harm?"

"No. Roper's too smart to pick a deliberate fight. But if he's ever in the main frame and Graham closes in on him..." He shrugged and steered the car around a fallen tree branch. "Don't go sitting outside Graham's room, Bren. And don't appoint yourself his bodyguard. Roper's not going to do anything. He's no cause."

"If he hates Graham for former convictions—"

"We can't protect the entire populace of the world, Bren. Graham knows Roper's in the village; he'll take precautions. Besides, as I said, Roper won't do anything stupid. I doubt if revenge is his style."

I muttered that I hoped so, then asked, "So, what's going on at the manse, then? Something new on John's disappearance?"

"Not that I know of. I'm responding to a report of a burglary." I must have looked incredulous, for he added, "Yeh, who'd steal from a parson? Well, in this case, a parsonage? Doesn't seem right. Won't win you any points in heaven."

I refrained from saying that Graham and I had just had a similar conversation and instead said, "Lloyd and Darlene made no mention of the burglary this morning when Lloyd reported John missing. Did it just happen?" I could well believe it had. March and October seemed to be favorite times of the year for residential break-ins, what with the time change and early dusk making homes dark.

Scott turned the car into the church lane before replying. "I don't know anything more than that they just reported it. Could have just discovered it; could have just returned home and surprised the burglar in the act. I don't know. We'll find out soon enough."

Like a black cat snuggling into a hollow to avoid a wetting, the vicarage crouched under a canopy of dripping trees. Dark but for two small lights, it was difficult to place exactly, a dark shape camouflaged by other dark shapes, lying somewhere ahead of us in the somber surroundings. The evergreens waved their long-needled arms over the rain-soaked tiled roof, as if rendering an incantation against further ill fortune. One of the lighted windows sank into blackness, to be replaced by a dimmer light elsewhere within the bowels of the house. It seemed to be settling down for the night and for bad news.

The rain strengthened and plunked into the widening puddles wallowing in the lower areas of the road. In the sweep of the car's headlights I could see the wizened stalks of dry grass bowing beneath the alluvial beating, the puddles alive with bubbles that seemed to boil and burst as other raindrops crashed into them. Scott flicked the wiper switch, and the wipers' rubber blades skated across the glass, corralling the water and pushing it aside. As the car's headlights panned the front garden, a huge tower bell came into relief, unexpected and menacing in the brightness. The bell rested to the right of the front gate, near an exuberant yew tree. Possibly why I hadn't seen it last night, I thought, marveling at how even now it melted into the darkness of the spruce as the car lights moved beyond it. I thought it must be an old bell from the tower, then wondered why it sat here. Had some affluent parishioner willed it to the manse? If so, why not add it to the ring in the tower?

A tree branch crashed to earth, missing Scott's car by inches. He parked the car outside the front door, muttered that it was going to be impossible to find tracks outside, then grabbed his torch. I dashed after him into the wetness.

"God, what a night," Darlene said as we entered the house. It was sparsely lit, as if too much light would reveal her suffering.

We wiped our shoes on the scatter rug by the door and Scott pulled out his notebook. I followed a few steps behind them as Darlene talked, her voice high and rapid.

"Normally I'd be at work," she said, leading us to another room.

"And where's that?"

"In Chesterfield. I work as a secretary. I would've been there today, but with John missing...well, I couldn't go to work, could I? I mean..." She stared at Scott, looking as though she was wrung of tears. Her eyes were red and puffy, and her hair was in disarray. "Well, with John missing, I can't concentrate on anything but him." She lowered her head, took a deep breath, then looked again at Scott. "Anyway, that's why I'm home today. I was out for a while—talking to neighbors and such."

"And you think the burglary happened then, while you were out?"

"Logical, isn't it? I only just discovered it. I'll show you." She

HORNS OF A DILEMMA

motioned to us and we followed her into a room lined with bookcases and holding a large wooden desk. She stopped at the doorway and pointed toward the far wall. A window was open, the curtain blowing in the breeze, its lower portion wet from rain. "In here. I'd gone in to get a phone number from Lloyd's desk and found the window open."

"I suppose," Scott said, walking into the room and pushing aside the curtain with his pen, "you know for certain you were burgled. I mean, there's no possibility the window was left open last night."

"We always lock up on going to bed. I know we were burgled. Look at it. The window's been forced open."

Chapter 14

"Don't come in," Scott said, his voice sharp with Authority.

I nodded and talked to Darlene while Scott shone his torch on the window frame. He must have found splintered wood or a broken latch, for he let the curtain fall closed and got out his mobile. When it became apparent that the room was off limits and a contingent from Buxton was going to take over, Darlene asked if I'd like some tea while I waited. I followed her into the kitchen.

It was warm, large, and in need of renovation. A white enamel cooker, spotted with chips where people had dropped pots or banged filled tea kettles on it, sprawled along one wall, companion to the sink and an ancient dishwasher. Opposite those appliances were a small refrigerator and wooden table. Four ladder-back chairs clustered around the table, the same apple green color as the table. White and green painted wall cupboards and two large windows consumed the walls. The floor was white, black and green speckled lino, so abused that some of the tiles were warped or had corners missing. The entire room smelled of lemon washing-up liquid and fresh coffee.

"I'll brew up a pot," Darlene said, indicating that I should sit at the table. "That way there'll be some for the constable, too." She filled the electric kettle, flipped on the switch, and moments later I heard the sound of simmering water. Darlene filled the teapot with hot water from the water tap and set it on the counter. She then opened a cupboard door and brought out three mugs. Their green and pink floral design blended well with the colors of the kitchen. Had they been bought to coordinate with the décor, or were they hand-me-downs from the previous vicar? Did any family ever own anything, other than their clothes and a few personal items, in a vicarage?

Darlene turned on the light fixture above the working top, swirled the water around in the teapot, walked over to the sink and poured out the water. She then spooned tea into the warmed teapot. "Do you take sugar?"

"Two, please. And white."

"What about the constable—do you know how he takes it? I don't have any biscuits, but I've got a nice pound cake. Baked this afternoon. I—" She stopped, self-conscious. "I had to keep busy. To take my mind off John. I'm—I can't think of where he could be. If I didn't have something to do, I don't know how I'd keep my sanity."

"Baking is no sin, Darlene."

"No, it's not. But there are some in this village who'd condemn me for it, saying I should be out looking for him. Where am I supposed to look, besides school?"

"And why not let the police do it? We've more manpower than just you and Lloyd, and we can make more inquiries."

She nodded, her eyes wide with concern. "Anyway, that's why I baked today. I had to keep busy. I never was much of a housekeeper."

I doubted it—the kitchen was spotless.

"Anyway, you've not come to hear about my reason for baking. Would the pound cake do for you and the constable? It's lemon—the cake, I mean."

I asked her not to go to any trouble—we weren't here to eat—told her of Scott's and my tea preferences, then asked, "If you were home all day, waiting for news of John, did you hear anything that—thinking about it now, after the discovery—you believe was the break in? Did you hear something that you just put down to usual unexplained neighboring sounds?"

Darlene turned off the kettle, poured the boiling water into the teapot, and set the timer. She turned to face me, leaning against the edge of the working top, and said, "I've been trying to recall something. Anything that would help pinpoint this. Trouble is, I was either in the kitchen or in the front garden doing a bit of work. It's too soon to ready the beds for spring planting, I know, but I had to do something in the garden. You might think it daft, with the ice and snow lingering in the shadier spots, but I had to rake up the dead leaves and dry grass. I needed that as much for the garden as for my nerves. So, you see, I wasn't in that part of the house much. I'm sorry." She glanced at her hands, which were clasped and held against her midriff, as though fearing a scolding.

I said, "Can you give us an approximate time, then?"

"Well, I know the window was locked last night after the stone turning because Lloyd always checks the windows and doors before going to sleep." She lifted her head, shifting her attention to the room where Scott was still working. Seconds passed as she stared, oblivious to me and her surroundings, her eyes and mind fixed on something beyond the kitchen's wall. Perhaps she was trying to divine her husband's actions, recall a scrap of conversation with her son. She was silent so long, immersed in her world of voices and vision, that I prompted her with another question.

"Could your husband have forgotten last night? It may be his routine to always lock up, but could last night's custom have disrupted his schedule? Was he talking about the turning, for instance, and forgot to lock up?"

"I suppose it's possible," she said slowly, as though my voice had dragged her out of some mental quagmire. She blinked, perhaps not sure of where she was, then said a bit more emphatically, "But highly unlikely. The turning was over fairly early—I think we were back here and having a last cuppa at 9:00. The Ash Wednesday service was over around 7:45, then we had the rock cakes and such in the church hall after that."

"And the gathering broke up around 8:15 or sometime before."

"Yes. So by the time we cleaned up a bit, turned out the lights, and Lloyd locked up the church, well, we were home by nine. We talked a bit about the turning and were in bed around 10:30. John had left the church long before all this and was most likely asleep at ten. He usually is on weeknights. He's not one of those teenagers who keeps late hours. He always goes to sleep at a decent hour."

"So, presuming your husband saw that everything was locked up for the night, you've no idea when this break-in occurred, then."

She shook her head, her eyes and mind now fully on me. "When I came inside from my gardening work this afternoon, I turned on the radio. It helped distract my thoughts from John. So if someone was here...well, I might not have heard anything, you see. I—I'm sorry, miss. I can't help."

Inwardly I was exasperated, but I hope I didn't show it. John could have gone missing any time since 8:00 last night, but without an approximate time to work with, it would make our job a bit harder. I asked, "Is anything missing? I know the entry point will be confirmed by our investigation, but if the burglar did enter by the study window, did you notice anything stolen from the desk? Or any other rooms in the house?"

"I can't imagine what the thief could have been after. We're not rich—everyone knows that! A vicar isn't exactly in the same league as the bishop. Even my secretarial wage doesn't shoot us up into that strata. Everyone knows we're poor as church mice. So no, I can't think of a thing that would attract a thief. Even if it's a stranger, it's obvious this is the vicarage—the house is practically attached to the church. Besides, there are no other houses close by. This has to be the vicar's home."

"That's as may be, Darlene, but perhaps you were chosen just for that reason. You *are* fairly isolated. Not in the woods, perhaps, but you haven't the proximity of neighbors as the village proper has. You are up on the hill."

"Affords a nice secluded spot, you mean? No one to peek out her window and see what's going on across the street. Yes. It works against us at times."

"So," I repeated, "did you check to see if anything is gone?"

"Not beyond the obvious, no. I mean, I was so startled when I discovered the forced window. Things like that have never happened to me before. I feel so..." Her eyes shifted to the right as she sought the correct words. "...So desecrated. Isn't that ridiculous? I mean, he didn't physically harm me—I don't even know what he looks like. But I feel so abused. It's laughable."

"Not at all. A stranger forces entry into your home, walks around, rummages through your personal items. Or course you feel intruded upon.

HORNS OF A DILEMMA

He's rifled through things you may not have even shown to your best friend. The refuge of your safe harbor has been destroyed."

Darlene murmured that that was it exactly.

I had not just spouted off police training phrases or echoed what other victims had voiced. It was a personal emotion born of my own experiences. The first time the offender had violated my car. I'd found it several dozen yards from where I'd parked it in the garage at my flat—outside and angled against another car. At first your mind tries to understand the oddity. Had I parked it like that in a hurry the previous evening? Had the parking brake failed, allowing the car to roll to that position? But when the implications of such ludicrous reasoning filtered through the confusion, it registered that someone had been trying to steal the car. And the feeling of violation was strong. I had the same emotions when my flat had been burgled. Only this time the outrage was overwhelming; he had flung my underwear onto the bed and floor in his search for jewelry and money. In my shame I had dumped them into the washer rather than let the police detectives see the exact crime scene. Yes, I may have destroyed useful clues, but I had preserved what dignity was left to me. I had not wanted the officers to poke through my knickers and bras. One man's hands had been more than enough. So yes, I could understand Darlene's indignation and anger at the trespass. It was the disrespect of your Person that hurt so much.

"There was nothing in the study," Darlene was saying as I pulled my concentration from my past wounds and refocused on her problem. "Nothing that anyone would consider valuable, I mean. Just Lloyd's books and papers, his correspondence and computer. That's all there. I looked for that straight off. Well, computers are sometimes taken, aren't they? But it's there."

"Yes," I said, remembering its bulk on the desk. "Did you look through the desk drawers? Is money kept there?"

"No." She cut some slices of pound cake and put that, two plates and forks on the table. Wiping off her hands, she said, "At least, nothing much. Perhaps a few pounds. But nothing of consequence."

"And your wallets and purses and such?"

"In our own bedrooms. That was my second thought, of course, so I looked. My wallet's in my purse and the money and credit cards are there. Lloyd has his wallet with him. I suppose John..." She took a deep breath and quickly changed the subject. "It makes no sense to me. My jewelry's here."

"Any valuable pieces?"

"Hardly. But I have my mum's wedding ring and her sapphire earrings. They're still in the dresser drawer. What in heaven's name did the burglar want?"

The timer went off and Darlene poured out the tea. As she brought mine over to me, she asked if she could take Scott's tea to him. "I know he's busy. And he said for us not to go into the study, but—"

"I'll take it to him, shall I? He'll appreciate it." I got up and grabbed his tea just as he walked into the kitchen.

"So." He grabbed the mug from me, stared at it and forced a smile. I knew what he was thinking: *tea*. Not his beverage of choice, especially when working. He would have liked coffee, but he was polite, so he accepted it and thanked Darlene for her thoughtfulness. He took a sip before asking, "Have you remembered anything you haven't told me, Mrs. Granger? Can you pinpoint the time that this happened? It would help with the investigation."

She relayed the pertinent bits of our conversation and again apologized for not being more observant.

"It's not exactly something everyone does, Mrs. Granger. It's not human nature to clock everything we do during the day. No need to feel bad."

She murmured her thanks and offered us some cake. I declined, but Scott accepted, although I knew he would've preferred Welsh teacakes. I rarely saw him eat anything else for his elevenses, given the choice. He ate several bites of cake, commented on how good it was, and said, "Although the logical time for the burglary is while you and half the village were at the stone turning—it was dark, no one was home—we can't rely on that."

The quietness of an isolated house, devoid of the child and his activities, lapped up Scott's words, and wrapped around us. In the silence, the electric kettle purred as it cooled, a tree branch rubbed against a gutter, a pipe in the kitchen gurgled as it slowly cleared itself of water. I looked at Scott, wondering if he was feeling Darlene's pain and imagining his own children missing. A handful of rain pelted the kitchen window, startlingly loud in the quiet of our separate contemplations. I was the only one who looked; Scott and Darlene were concentrating on John and the burglary.

"I—" Darlene stared into her tea, as though afraid to voice her idea. She said slowly, "I hope, if he was inside the house, we didn't scare him away. I don't think I will ever feel safe here again if that's the case. God! To think that someone was in my house, a few feet away, while I was…"

"I think it highly unlikely," I hastened, hoping to alleviate her fears. "It would have to be a bold burglar to risk entering your house with so many people several hundred yards away."

"But Lloyd's study faces the wood," Darlene said, talking through the imagined scenario. "He wouldn't have been seen. Maybe that's why he chose the study window."

The room grew silent again as we considered the timing of the crime and the layout of the house. The electric kettle clicked off and a radiator gurgled before Scott said, "Did you and Lloyd come back earlier than usual?"

Darlene looked confused.

Scott said, "Earlier than you normally do after the stone turning. Like, do you usually—oh, I don't know—go to someone's house for coffee, or wash all the dishes in the church hall, or go to the launderette, only this year you didn't. You skipped the coffee with friends and came home an hour earlier than normal. If so, and a villager knew your yearly routine—"

Darlene's face drained of color, her mouth dropped open, and she stared at Scott as though he had just told her the Church of England was merging with the Church of Rome. She stammered, "Why th— You can't...that would mean one of my neighbors, a villager who's a friend..." Her teeth clamped down on her knuckles as though she could stifle her thoughts as well as she stifled her words.

Scott said, "It's just a thought, Mrs. Granger. I apologize if I've upset you. That wasn't my intension. I merely wanted to know if your schedule had altered any this year from previous years."

"So you could concentrate on those who might know about our routine." Darlene nodded, seeming to rouse herself from some inner reserve. "Certainly. It makes sense, doesn't it?" She took a minute to consider something before saying, "No, I don't think so. Once a few of us lingered in the church hall to talk over tea, after the main group had left, but we haven't done that for ages. And it's not a regular gathering. So, no, Constable, I don't think that theory is valid. We've never gone to anyone's home after the stone turning, and we don't usually go anywhere else. It was just dumb luck that we scared away the intruder—if we did."

"And you've no idea what he may have wanted. You're not collecting for a specific fund or storing church relics here." Scott paused, looking hopeful, waiting to take another sip of tea.

Darlene again declared that they were poor, that everyone knew it, and the annual church jumble sale was in the autumn. "We've made no grand purchases lately. No telly or CD player or rare books."

"What about your son? Could he have bought a leather jacket, say, and one of his classmates was envious of it—"

"He hasn't that kind of money, Constable. Besides, I'd have seen the jacket if he has one. I can't for the life of me understand this whole thing. We've nothing worth stealing—*nothing*! But if John has something..." She hesitated, perhaps afraid of saying what was gripping her heart.

I said, "We'll ask him when he gets back, all right?"

Darlene forced a smile through quivering lips and said that would be fine.

I thanked her for the tea and Scott said he'd wait for the detective contingent, if that would be all right with her. As we stepped outside, Scott handed me his key and nodded toward his car. "You'll catch your death if you walk back to the incident room. It's still bucket-down rain. You'll be soaked and catch pneumonia and I'll end up visiting you in hospital, plying you with flowers and get-well cards and cases of chocolates. You wouldn't want me draining my bank account like that, would you?"

"To say nothing of wasting your time off," I added, zipping up my jacket.

"Time off is a precious commodity, Brenna."

"And you'd use some to visit me? Cheer my dreary hours? I *am* touched."

"You should be. Especially since I spend most of my time at the poker tables."

"True friendship, Scott. There's nothing else like it. As I said, I'm touched. And to trust me with your car—I must rate right up there with a royal flush."

"Take the car, Brenna, and save me the visits and the buying marathon."

A rumble of thunder rolled across the heavens and I glanced upward. The rain splattered onto the flagstone walkway, ricocheting off the hard surface and onto the surrounding soil. Darlene's carefully raked flowerbeds had already turned into a mound of mud. My fingers closed around the key and I thanked him.

"You want to ring me up when you're finished and I'll come get you?"

"I'll get a ride back with one of the CID team. He can drop me at the incident room—where is it?"

I told him, then added, "Scott, isn't it weird that we've two cases of forced entry? The vicarage and the church hall?"

"You're suggesting the events are linked in some way?"

"Well, they seem to have happened very close in time and proximity. What do you think?"

"I think we need some evidence before you make anything more of it."

"But it *is* odd. Even if you discount the church hall break-in to something else, what about *this* one?"

"You think the burglar is a villager?"

"I know the timing may be crucial to this whole thing, but like Darlene said, they've nothing a burglar would want. You saw their house—they *are* poor as church mice."

"That kitchen *is* fifty years out of date," Scott conceded.

"They've one tiny microwave, but even that looks tired and like it's about to bite the dust. It's got to be an outsider, perhaps a crime of opportunity."

"Like the guy's a hiker on the local stretch of the Pennine Way, but took a detour to burgle houses while he's tramping through picturesque Derbyshire? Are you serious, Bren?"

"That, or could be one of John's mates. He crawls into the house, bent on doing something teenager-ish with him—that's why nothing's stolen."

"Fine. Something teenager-ish. Like what—smoking pot? Why not come to the front door, say 'Hi, can little Johnny come out and play?' or go into John's bedroom and close the door? Why run the risk of being seen breaking and entering, or—perhaps worse—stumbling into the study occupied by Lloyd? Besides, if they wanted to smoke pot they wouldn't do it in his bedroom. The odor would give them away. This whole thing doesn't make sense."

HORNS OF A DILEMMA

"Neither does the village angle, Scott. It's too obvious. The bloke should know we'd consider locals first. They know the layout of the land, the habits of the household."

"We could look at it another way, Brenna."

"How?"

"John's gone, isn't he? It's not a burglary—it's a snatch."

Chapter 15

"Talk about wild ideas!" I said. I'm sure I stared at Scott as though he'd lost his mind.

He snorted, pulling in his lips into a near pout. "All right, Smarty, have you a better explanation? When did John go missing?"

I opened my mouth for a quick retort, then hesitated, trying to remember Lloyd's words this morning. I said rather meekly, "John wasn't seen after the Ash Wednesday service ended last night—around 7:45."

Scott grinned like he'd just nabbed a sack-carrying burglar exiting a house. "Your Honor, I rest my case. No one saw him at home. *He* could have sneaked out of the house—he had a date with a girlfriend, or he wanted to do something later that night with a mate of his. Whatever it was, it was *John* who *left* the house—not a burglar breaking *into* the house. *Compris?*"

The strange picture rolled through my mind in slow motion, the actors nearly comic in their actions—John wearing black clothes and sneaking into his father's study, raising the window, perhaps digging at the woodwork to make it look like a burglary or else inadvertently damaging the frame or latch in his haste to get out; Lloyd and Darlene sitting in the front room, chatting quietly over their tea or an evening program on the telly; John's chum or girl friend hovering beside the house, trying not to make a sound, waiting in the darkness…

I said, "But why would he go to all that trouble? If he left the church hall at 7:45, why wouldn't he go to meet his girl—or run off to wherever he was going—right then? Why go home and leave later when he'd have his parents' eyes to avoid? Seems like he'd be taking a greater risk sneaking out later. Why are you so keen on your sneaking-out-of-the-house theory?"

"Because," Scott said, his tall form even taller as he stood close to me in the dark, talking softly so his voice would not carry in to Darlene over the din of the rain. "He knows that sometimes mum and dad look in on him. He knows that sometimes mum brings him a cuppa to ease the strain of homework, or he knows Uncle Heinrich rings up to help him with his algebra. How the hell do I know? I'm not acquainted with him. John knows his household routine and thought it expedient to stay in his room until his parents went to bed. It's just a theory, Brenna. I haven't said it's fact."

A fork of lightning stabbed the darkness and I nearly jumped. In the brief brightness I could see the white puff of my breath as I exhaled in the cold air. I shivered.

"Well, it still sounds absurd. How many kids sneak out of their houses at night?" Scott opened his mouth and I quickly said, "All right. More than I would guess. I guess I was too content with my home life—"

"Or too attached to creature comforts—"

"—to sleep on the ground or drink rain from a leaf. But I'm still banking on it being a burglary. It's more logical. Your set-up smacks of a Hollywood plot."

"I should make you bet me. It'll teach you not to doubt my superior reasoning skills."

"This isn't a poker game, Scott."

"Maybe not, but I'm still winning." Even if I couldn't see his face, his voice told me he was grinning.

"Do you wear sunglasses when you play?"

"Get into the car." He pushed me into the rain and returned to the house without looking back at me.

When I returned to the incident room, I glanced around for Graham, but he wasn't there. The few constables who were there hadn't seen him, didn't know where he was, and didn't seem to care. Graham's absence was odd, I thought, as all he had been going to do was to see about WPC MacMillan. Unless her injury was more serious than Margo had thought, and he had accompanied MacMillan to hospital. He certainly could have gone any number of other places, too. I sighed, slightly disappointed, for I had wanted to tell him about the Grangers' burglary. I was about to grab my mobile and punch in Graham's number when I saw Mark.

When I had hurried over to him, related the burglary incident, and asked him if he thought Harry was a likely suspect, he looked at me quizzically, perhaps not certain if I were serious. "Your motive being..."

"He wanted to hear the church bells this morning—remember?"

"So he breaks into the *vicarage* to get to the *church* bells? Wouldn't even *he* know the bells would be in the church?"

"I don't know what he knows," I said, slightly annoyed with the burglary, John's disappearance, the hour, the weather, and Graham's absence. Besides, I was tired. "Anyway, the house isn't that far-fetched. It has an old tower bell in the front garden. I saw it tonight. Not particularly large, but it's as big as that small bell we saw last month in Lord Swinbrook's bell tower."

"Couple hundred pounds, probably," Mark said, nodding. "One meter high, so he'd no doubt have seen it."

I glossed over Mark's scientific tally and surged ahead with my theory. "Maybe the bell at the parsonage was replaced with a new one, which is now hanging in the church tower. Maybe the old parsonage bell was cracked and they had to get rid of it."

"The bell foundry couldn't have fixed it?"

I sighed heavily. "God, Mark, cut me some slack! I don't know! Maybe it's unfixable, maybe it cost too much."

"Could be another of those loony legal things, I guess. You know how some wills are. 'My voice shall ring until I die,' or something."

"The thing is," I said firmly, trying to establish control, "the bell's sitting there, plain as a pikestaff, and that could be the association Harry has with bells and the parsonage."

"He sees that bell, so he believes other bells are there," Mark said slowly, thinking over the possibility."

"Maybe he—or someone—has also broken into the church. We don't know that, either."

"Seems a bit roundabout, though. Breaking into the house to get to the bell tower. Even if Harry was frustrated—and people with a personality disorder do become violent if they are frustrated—would Harry have broken into a house just to hear a bell?" Before I could answer, he hurried on. "Anyway, Harry seems more IQ-challenged than psychotic. You'll have to check with Harry's sister to see if he was home, anyway."

"*Me*? Why not 'us' or 'you'?"

"Because *you're* the one who's brought it up. I'm content to let the investigation proceed leisurely. Anyway, it's not our case. We're not in the burglary division. Let it rest, Bren." He took a sip of coffee, staring at me as though challenging me to squawk.

I did. "What kind of detective are you who lets a golden opportunity slip through his fingers?"

"A detective who's had enough brushes with discipline to know when discretion is the better part of valor. Look, Brenna, I know you want to help—help solve Enrico's murder, help find John, help discover who broke into the parsonage. But you can't do every bloody thing yourself. You're one woman—competent and skilled as you are—and you can't possibly do it all. That's why you're part of the CID *team*, not Brenna Taylor, Private Investigator." He smiled—not mocking or impudent or superior—but warmly, as friend to friend.

"Surprise, Mark. I agree. But it drives me crazy—"

"It will, if you let it. You've got to go by the book on this one, Bren. Don't get personally involved. I know the missing boy freaks you out, but we'll find him."

"So you don't think he sneaked out of his house, then?"

"I don't know. Kids do that. One of my brothers did when he was sixteen." He shook his head, as though reliving the event. "But it could very well be a simple burglary that got no farther than the intruder prying open the window or entering the home. If it was a person outside the village, he wouldn't know about the Grangers' plans for the evening. He wouldn't necessarily know about the stone turning or when the Grangers would be

HORNS OF A DILEMMA

home. He just found a dark, empty house and responded to Opportunity knocking. The fact that nothing's gone missing can be explained by the Grangers' arrival home, spoiling our felon's lark. Satisfied?"

I sucked in the corners of my mouth and nodded.

"Besides," Mark continued, "we've two strangers right here we can focus on, if you're keen."

"Tourists at a B-and-B, you mean?"

"Closer to home, Bren. Conrad and David."

"Conrad's visiting his aunt. And David Willett is visiting his sister."

"Exactly. Who better than those two? They're local in the sense that they wouldn't arouse suspicion if they were seen wandering about, but they're enough of strangers to not know the finer points of the evening's schedule."

"But a villager would also know about the stone turning."

"Granted. But if he doesn't participate, as Conrad and David didn't, then he wouldn't know when the Grangers would come home. He'd just know the house was empty, the Grangers are presiding over the rock cakes and tea, and so he takes a chance. He opens the window, hears them returning..."

"Conrad's a friend of John's," I reminded Mark. "Why would he break into John's house? John left the church hall at a quarter to eight. Conrad could have arranged to meet John at the pub, say, or somewhere on the green. He wouldn't have to break into John's house."

"That's why I've placed my money on my friend David Willett. He looked suspicious to me in December's little drama, and he looks suspicious now. Two murders in two villages where he pops up, and now a burglary. I don't trust that bloke."

"If I may echo you, we've no proof yet that he's involved in either the murder or the burglary. You better be careful where you voice your opinion."

"I won't say anything," Mark said, sniffing, "but I'm sure as hell gonna keep an eye on David." He glanced at his watch. "You want to have dinner? We've got a date scheduled for this evening, you know."

I blinked, my brain racing to remember what day it was, trying to remember what I had agreed to about our date. Mark was right—we'd made arrangements for dinner tonight. And I'd had a salad with Graham earlier in the pub. Damn. Sometimes I just couldn't do anything right. "I don't feel much like eating, but it's all right."

"Too early?"

"No. I'm worried about Graham. We've not heard from him. It's been two hours. He should've called in."

"You're too much a cop, Bren. He's probably doing something. Perhaps he's at hospital with MacMillan."

"Well, I feel like a cop. I always feel like a cop. I think I've always felt like a cop, even as a child."

"So, what pulled you into the job? Burning desire for heroics?" He said it without humor, his eyes looking steadily into mine, really wanting to understand me.

"The reason I wanted to become a copper..." I hesitated for a moment, wondering if I was going to regret this, if I was opening myself up to ridicule. But one look at Mark's intense gaze told me there would be no repercussion. I gave him a quick smile and said, "Why I wanted to be a copper was probably the same as most other officers. I wanted to help people. Making the world a better place was a close second, but that could be accomplished by helping people."

"Many people can help others, Brenna," Mark said, his eyes serious as he studied my face. The lighting indoors wasn't particularly bright, but even if I couldn't see it I knew the skin at the corners of his eyes was ingrained with coal dust. A physical reminder of his years in the mines, infiltrating his skin as coal dust also infiltrated a miner's lungs. Luckily for Mark, he hadn't stayed long enough to develop that dreaded disease. His eyes held me, lured me into telling him about my life. He said, "Society's filled with helpers—medical practitioners, teachers, vicars..." He paused, probably seeing if I'd say something about Graham. When I didn't, he added, "It had to be something more with you. Helping people is noble. We need more people who put that first as a career choice. But why become a copper to do that?"

"I could ask you the same thing."

He smiled, showing his perfect white teeth. "You're the one who's being interrogated at the moment. You can grill me later, if you wish."

That was almost how I felt, too. Interrogated. Still, I put on a brave smile and said, "Of course it's the drama, the adrenalin rush when the call comes in. I felt that as a response officer, and I still feel that. Only response drivers see more of it. Still, I won't lie and pretend that the feeling isn't part of it. I like my heart kicking into high gear, the prickles that surge through my blood. I feel more alive at that moment than I ever do."

"Nothing beats a high-speed car pursuit, no."

"Unless it's arresting some creep you've been after for months."

"That's a different kind of thrill."

"Still, I get a great pleasure out of it. Physically as well as morally."

"I know," Mark said. "If it was just the rush, I would've been a fire fighter."

I laughed.

Mark went on. "But there's a bit of the protective quality about coppers, too, isn't there? A lot of us want to protect society, a way of life, good people...people we care about...or love." He stared at me, his eyes wide and expressing his statement.

I fought to keep the heat from my cheeks, realizing that would tell Mark more than I wanted him to know. I didn't know how to respond. Things were turning around between us—that had been evident since December. But I had no interest in dating Mark or falling into his arms. There was no denying he would be a handy polestar as I struggled to wean my heart from Graham. But I had vowed never to go out with co-workers, which was another reason I had decided to steer away from Graham and concentrate on Adam. How many times had I heard about conflict of interest when married coppers worked in the same department? I wasn't about to get trapped like that, and I wasn't about to change divisions or careers. So I focused on my upcoming date with Adam and tried to answer Mark's implication.

"I think," I said, fiddling with my left earring, "that I would fight to the death to protect my parents. Despite the problems we've had."

Mark exhaled slowly, conceding defeat at drawing out a declaration of love from me. He said, "Being odd-man-out does make for strained family relations. You don't have to tell me."

And he didn't have to elucidate, either. He, the only son not in his family's business, must have had to deal with his share of problems. He must have felt like the outsider when they talked about rose shipments and damper trouble and regulation. Just as I had disappeared into the background when my parents and siblings talked of concert schedules and house takes.

"Still," I said, "there is something deep within us, never mind problems with kin, that calls us to respond and help. We do it for strangers—why wouldn't we do it for our parents?"

"But strangers haven't wounded us as our family has. Strangers don't have the years of verbal abuse or cold shoulders connected to them. They don't conjure up images of hurtful arguments and such. You help strangers because that's your job. It's easier. There's no emotion with it."

"But you're letting *your* emotion get in the way with this case." The minute I said it, I regretted it. Mark frowned and his neck muscles tightened. "With David Willet," I said in answer to his question.

"That's not emotion, that's logic. He was in Bramwell when everything was going on, and he's here in Hollingthorpe when everything's going on."

"Guilt by association? Smashing way to build a case, Mark."

"I'm not building a case yet, Bren. I'm simply observing."

"Don't you think that a bit obvious, though? Murder in Bramwell, murder here? Wouldn't he assume we're smart enough to link the two?"

"David didn't know we'd be called here when he killed Enrico, did he? Anyway, why are you so defensive? You keen on him?"

"Of course not! What an idiotic thing to say! Why must you make everything personal?"

"I haven't made it personal. I'm simply stating a fact that's obvious to any observer—or to you, if you'd step back a distance and look at this objectively. You evidently like the bloke."

"Oh, fine. Now I'm supposed to turn apathetic and callous."

"God, Bren. Why do you always misconstrue everything I say? I did not say that! I said that you are too close to the subject to see it clearly. You took it the wrong way—as usual."

I lowered my head and squared the corners of the stack of papers on the table, avoiding Mark's eyes and his judgment. "I only want you to give David a fair chance, Mark. Which you aren't. You've already mentally tried and convicted him."

Mark snorted. "If I have, it's because he's an obvious suspect. I said it a few minutes ago and I'll repeat it—he's been at the scene of two murders in two different villages. I don't care if we haven't found evidence yet to connect him to Enrico's murder. We will. A bloke like David Willett is slick—he stole material for his book. I'm convinced of that even if he denies it from now till the end of time. He's cagey. I don't know his connection with Enrico yet, but I'll find one. And when I do, I'll be grinning from ear to ear as I slap the cuffs on him."

"And drive him some place where you can carry out your own verdict. Don't look at me like that, Mark. Coppers are supposed to let the law take its course. We're supposed to *enforce* the law, not pronounce sentence as judge and jury. Oh, I know that hasn't stopped coppers from getting a little rough and abusive with prisoners. Watch any nightly newscast on the telly. Read the bulletins dished out at the station. You accuse me of letting my emotions get in the way—well, other coppers have done it. Only, they've done it with their fists and boots and night sticks against prisoners' bodies. I may be guilty of emotional involvement, but to date it's only been an outpouring of sympathy. There's a good reason why coppers aren't also judges, Mark. We'd be standing people we envisioned guilty against a tree and beating the hell out of them. Do you really want that? As an officer sworn to uphold the peace and protect the innocent, do you really want it to come to that?"

I looked at him then, needing to see his reaction and if he were angry with me.

Mark had turned his head and was gazing at the far wall, perhaps out of the window, up at the church. Twilight was claiming the land, embracing the church and the crest of the hill in its dusky embrace.

His eyes still on the far wall, Mark said slowly, "I thought you knew me better than that, Bren." He closed his eyes briefly, as though silently counting to ten, then opened them and looked at me. They were filled with anger and hurt.

I said, "I thought I did, but when you start sounding like a vigilante..." I stopped, listening to the voice in my head that whispered I was crossing the line.

Mark's eyebrows lowered and his voice hardened. He shoved a nearby chair into the next table and kicked the table leg. I stepped forward, closing the space between us, wanting to hug him, to take away his hurt. I was too close to him at the moment to be comfortable, but I remained where I was—less than an arm's length from him, smelling his aftershave lotion, feeling his breath as he sharply exhaled. To a casual observer, we might look as though we were sharing an intimate discussion. But Mark's frown and my flushed face betrayed the nature of our chat. He said, "If you label me a vigilante, you better familiarize yourself with the meaning of the word again. I have never physically abused anyone. *Anyone!* I have never doled out punishment—not so much as locking handcuffs too tightly. I have never illegally arrested anyone or committed any infraction of the police code. There has never been a report written up against me, nor have I ever been reprimanded." He paused, glaring at me, and I was reminded again of my recent verbal rebuff from Graham. I felt my cheeks grow hot and I opened my mouth to reply, but Mark rushed on. "Vigilantes break the law. I have never—*ever!*—broken the law. I don't speed, I don't steal, I don't lie or bare false witness or disobey any other of the Ten Commandments or civil laws. Vigilantes deal out punishment personally to those whom they deem guilty, and while I have my own views of who is guilty, I have never acted upon them illegally or immorally. Do I think David Willett has something to do with this? Hell yes, I do! But other than talking about it and keeping my eye on him while I work on the case, I won't do a damned thing to him. And if you don't believe that, then perhaps we're not suited to work together. I thought you knew me better. And frankly, your lack of trust in me hurts like hell."

A silence that was almost tangible fell between us. I slowly lifted my gaze from my clenched hands to look at Mark, afraid of what I would see in his face, afraid to hear his next words. I picked up my shoulder bag and said softly, "Perhaps we should have our dinner some other time. I don't think either of us is hungry right now."

He kicked another chair, sending it careening into the adjoining table as he said, "I've never refused a lady anything. If you wish to call it a night..." He handed me my jacket and sat on the edge of the table, his arms folded against his chest. He made no move, seemingly content to stay in the incident room.

I took my jacket, my eyes nearly level with his, and fought to find my voice. His eyes overflowed with pain. "Mark, I'm sorry."

"Needn't be. You've your opinion of me—which doesn't make it necessarily right—only, I know the truth. I know who I am and what I feel and what I'm capable or not capable of. I'm shocked you don't know any of this. I thought you did. Maybe we're not as close as I assumed. Or kidded myself into thinking we might be. Night."

He got up, ignoring my call to him, and walked over to a constable, asking if he'd like to get a beer at the pub. I watched the two men grab their jackets and head out the door. They were halfway to the pub before I could force my legs to move.

Chapter 16

My anguish didn't last long. Nor did I have a chance to follow Mark. The ringing of my mobile phone checked my impulse and when I answered, Margo's voice checked my misery.

"Is Graham with you?" she asked, the concern evident in her voice.

I shook my head, then realized she couldn't see me. I stammered, "No. Uhh, why? You haven't heard from him?"

"I wouldn't be ringing you up, Bren, if I had."

I exhaled heavily. "I'm not in the mood to worry about precise syntax or to be chastised by you, Margo. What's going on?"

"I don't know. That's why I rang you up. It's nearly 8:00."

I blinked and stared at my watch. It indicated 7:50. And Graham had left me just after 5:30 to attend WPC MacMillan and look at the scene. A little over two hours to look at a patch of ground? I walked over to the window and glanced outside. The rain had lessened somewhat in intensity, but it still fell steadily. Where would Graham be? Even if he had finished at the scene, he would have rung up someone in the incident room. I leaned my head against the windowpane, trying to see outside.

"Margo, where are you?"

"On my way back to the incident room. I went to the hospital with MacMillan, but now that she's taken care of, I need to come back to type up my report and do a few things. I haven't seen Graham here. I rang up the incident room to inquire. *No* one saw him there, either. That's when I got concerned. He should be either place—or at least let someone know what he's doing."

"Did you see him at all? I mean, he left the pub at tea time to go see you..."

I paused, my mind whirling. Of course she knew that. He had told her when she'd rung him up. I said, "Was he there? He was going to see to MacMillan."

"I never saw him, Bren! That's why this is so crazy! He told me on the phone he was coming, and I thought for sure he'd put in an appearance. I mean, when one of your own coppers gets clobbered, you kind of expect the boss to show up. But the ambulance attendants came and went, and Graham still hadn't arrived." She made a clucking sound, as though thinking over something. "I wonder if he went through the woods. You know, maybe took the back route, joining the path on the other side of the church."

"Why would he do that? We were in the pub. He should've simply walked up that path and found you." Had he said which way he was going? Had he mentioned that he was going to check on the terrain before seeing to MacMillan? I couldn't think; I couldn't recall his exact words. I'd been so certain that he'd be back within a few minutes, or even ring me up from hospital should he decide to accompany her there.

"I don't know why he'd do that, Bren." Margo's voice bored into my confusion, laser-sharp, concentrating on the current problem. "I didn't talk to him after I rang him at the pub."

"Look. Get here as fast as you can, Margo. Come to the incident room. I think we need to do something." I stood up and set my shoulder bag on the table.

"Yeh, but what, exactly? Form a search team? Where do we look?"

A rumble of thunder rolled over my response. I repeated it. "Ring up Mark, will you? Maybe he knows where Graham is." I doubted it. He was either still imbibing at the bar, or had picked up a woman by now.

"Mark's not, uhh, with you?"

"He is not. And don't you say another word, one way or the other, about that. Have you inquired at headquarters? Did you check with the constable on guard at MacMillan's hospital room? Do you know where they took her? Maybe Graham was doing something else while you were with MacMillan, and he slipped in the room when you left. I know it's probably a waste of time, but if Graham drove back to Buxton for something..." I squashed the mobile between my left shoulder and my ear as I struggled into my jacket, then grabbed the phone again. "You know, sometimes he just kind of gets involved with the case, and goes off on a tangent."

"For two hours? You're joking!"

I conceded that I didn't believe it either, and said again that I'd be in the incident room. I didn't care who knew it—I was more frightened with each heartbeat that something had happened to Graham. He wouldn't have remained silent for so long; I would've heard from him.

I rang up Graham's mobile phone, pressed my phone against my ear, crossed my fingers, and listened for an answer. The rain drummed against the window and I instinctively moved away, bending forward to hear more clearly should Graham answer. After a dozen more rings, I rang off, fear needling my heart. If Graham was unhurt, surely he would answer his phone. Even if he was home, his feet propped up in front of a fire—which I knew he wouldn't do—he would answer his phone. My fingers closed around my mobile. Something had happened to him. He never ignored our calls. It was procedure he had drilled into me when I had first been partnered with him—keep in contact. I jammed my mobile into my jacket pocket and turned to PC Fordyce. After telling him the situation and that we would need to form a search team, I dashed outside. I needed to do something physical, even if it was only running in circles and screaming.

127

My car was parked close to the door, and as I slid behind the steering wheel I tried to think where Graham could be. I glanced out the windscreen at the black sky that was ripped apart periodically by the white jags of lightning. I didn't relish the thought of beating the undergrowth, but it was a place to start. Maybe Graham had slipped on wet rocks or moss, as MacMillan had, and had twisted his ankle and broken his mobile. If so, he'd be soaked to the bone, mad as hell, and happy as a kid on the last day of school to be rescued. I started the car's engine and drove to the pub.

Sure, I had told Margo to ring Mark, but I wasn't good at waiting. So even though the mobile phone call was faster, I had to see Mark, to ask him if he had talked to Graham.

I double parked in front of the pub's door, thinking this pardoned any breaking of the law, and ran inside. Pausing in the doorway, I glanced around the room. I couldn't see Mark at the bar or at a table. Fine. Let Margo track him down. I wasn't going to his room and pound on the door to see if he was in. I might surprise him in a cuddle, and if so, the only person embarrassed by that discovery would be I. He'd either be amused or gloating at my discomfort. And I wasn't going to show him I cared about his evening trysts.

I ran back to my car and drove the long block to the incident room in nearly certain record time.

The incident room was alive with light and I could see a dozen officers inside. Some were about to form a search team. One man was talking on a phone and pointing to something outside. I set the parking brake and got out, leaving my bag on the car seat.

Margo dashed out when I ran up to her. We stood beneath the canopy over the door, the rain drumming on the metal roof, the puddles consuming the asphalt. My hair was wet and lay plastered to my head, and my shoes and socks were damp. But I ignored my discomfort, too anxious about Graham.

"Did you get a hold of Mark?" I shouted over the noisy downpour, not particularly wanting to work with him so soon after our argument, but knowing we needed help. And, argument aside, Mark was a good cop.

"Yeh. He answered immediately, so at least I didn't wake him up. He said he'd go over to Enrico's place, thinking maybe Graham got a lead on the case and went there to look for something. He said he'd check that out first, then come back here to join the search team. If we need him elsewhere we're to let him know, but right now he'll concentrate on the wood right outside the pub."

The dark images of childhood fairy tales threatened to burst from the dark recesses of my mind. Everything wicked and terrifying had happened in the wood—Hansel and Gretel imprisoned in the witch's house, Red Riding Hood threatened by the Wolf. The forest may have been an allegory for the dangerous world beyond the village, and begun as a way for parents to teach their children the evils of life, but at this moment the forest was a very real symbol of Graham's danger. I tried to ignore the dark consequences of *The*

HORNS OF A DILEMMA

Robber Bridegroom tale and cleared my throat. "Can we go back to the scene of MacMillan's accident, Margo? If Graham went there..." I paused, suddenly afraid for the second time this evening. A fork of lightning lit up the western sky behind the church tower, and I sensed it was God making an ominous statement. I trembled, anxious to know where Graham was.

"You have an extra poncho or something I can wear?"

Margo's practical question lifted me from the mental picture I had of Graham's broken leg. I nodded and we ran to the boot of my car. She put it on while I said, "I think we should at least look at MacMillan's accident scene. I don't think Graham would be up there two hours later, but it's a start. We may find something."

"Find what?" Margo fastened up the rain jacket and shoved her hands into her pockets. "What do you want to find?"

"I *want* to find Graham. But unless you have any other suggestions of where to look—"

"That's fine. You're the sergeant. You're in charge."

I didn't feel in charge. I felt apprehensive and hopeless and cowardly. It would be easy to hand it over to Mark and Scott Coral and the other male officers, and then I could play at being Command Center in the incident room, safe and dry and not having to make decisions. But my nerves were too taut to sit around and wait. Even if we didn't find Graham, I'd at least be actively searching, which helped stifle the voices in my head. By doing something physical I would at least know the status of the search.

"Right," I said, staring into the rain. Hopefully he was not out there, injured or sick, lying in the mud. Hopefully he was in his office in Silverlands, or somewhere else warm and dry, merely suffering from immersion in the case. I choked back my growing panic, nodded and said, "Let's start there. You'll have to lead." I grabbed two torches from inside the car's boot, slammed it closed, and followed Margo into the darkness.

The path winding up the church hill, through the graveyard and skirting the wood was wet and slippery. Under the beams of our torches, tops of gray limestone rocks loomed like backs of whales breaking the surface of muddied, black water. Grass, mature and tall before the end of its growing season, bent nearly double from the weight of dozens of raindrops collecting along their deeply veined ridges. Several drops ran together, creating a miniature waterfall as the water cascaded off the grass's tips and plopped onto the ground. The long grass grabbed at our shoes and ankles, threatening to trip us, and snapped in two as we tugged free. Water ran down our faces, collected at the base of our necks, chilled our hands. It turned the soil into miniature mud pits, reflected our torchlight back at us. As we passed the Devil's Stone I shone my light into the area. The white geometric stretches of the police tape jumped out of the night, startlingly brilliant in the blackness, while the blue, alternating patches melted into the night, leaving the white sections disjointed, like dashes of Morse code floating in the blackness. Graham was not there. I hadn't expected to see him, but I had to look.

We split up at the outskirts of the graveyard, Margo taking the western half near the parsonage, I taking the eastern section nearest the church. Again, it seemed a futile hunt, but I had no idea if Graham may have walked up here after he had checked out MacMillan's accident scene. Our torchlight swept from side to side as we walked through the rows of headstones, looking for evidence that Graham had been there, checking that the area was vacant. Rows of gray tombstones, pock-marked through centuries of storms and smothered with lichen, seemed to wobble in the darkness as our lights continuously panned over them, back and forth, left and right, falling back into near oblivion as we eventually passed and left them to sleep once more. Finding nothing of Graham, we came together again and turned northeast toward the wood.

As we stopped at the top of the path where it divided on its run down to the pub, Margo yelled above the din of the rain. "We're just about there. MacMillan tripped a few hundred yards into the wood. You want to see it, or wait here while I check it out?"

"Why should I wait here? It's not strewn with blood, is it?"

"No, but I didn't know if you wanted to wait here, in case Graham comes along the path from the pub or somewhere. If you go with me, you might miss him."

It made sense. We didn't know where Graham was. He could very easily be at the pub and come strolling up the path. It would be my luck to miss him. But as much as I could see the wisdom of splitting up, I wanted to search the location myself. Not that Margo could miss seeing a man's figure, but I had to satisfy myself that we had gone over the entire area, poke about in spots where she might not. I motioned her onward and fell in behind her, my torchlight alternately spotting each side of the path.

When we came to the accident spot, I was disappointed. There was nothing to indicate Graham had been there. Still, I suggested we look around, just to make sure, and we again split up. I had not been poking about the bushes for more than two minutes before I found the body on the ground.

I yelled for Margo as I ran over to the limp form. The first thing that struck me was that he was wet—soaked. As if he had lain here during the entire storm. The second thing I noticed was his position. He lay in a comma shape on his left side, his right palm dug into the mud as though he had tried to break his fall, his left arm slightly bent and about shoulder-high. His face was angled from me, but I could see the broken skin and matted hair on the back of his scalp. His blood had run through his hair, over his cheek, and down his neck to collect on the ground and his shirt collar. I screamed Graham's name, stepped around the body, and shone the torchlight onto the face. It was John Granger.

I don't know how long I stood there, staring at the boy's face, alternately crying in my relief that it wasn't Graham's form before me and trying to choke back my tears. I knew it wasn't professional to let my feelings snap. Our police schooling had taught that; Graham had stressed that; I was learning that. But my emotional release overwhelmed anything I had heard, and it was another minute before I could breathe deeply and turn into a copper once again. Margo ran up from the other side of the path, her hair wet and specked with bits of leaves, her face wet and hopeful. As she stared at John's face I bent down to lay my fingers against his neck. There was no pulse. His body was cold. Margo was grabbing her mobile as I felt his wrist. The caring human in me wanted to turn him to see the extent of his injuries, but at least I had returned to cop mode and knew not to disturb him. There could be other injuries to the left side of his head, but it would be up to Jens to find them. As Margo called in for police and medical help, I stood up and played my torchlight over the ground. It was soaked from the rain, a leaf-littered forest floor that is a Scientific Officer's nightmare to work. I could see nothing damning such as a coat button or lost wallet that would identify John's attacker. And it had to be murder or a quarrel that had led to John's death—even if he had stumbled, he couldn't have hit the back of his head on a tree root.

I glanced at my watch, wanting to make a note of the time we'd found him. Quarter past eight. And John had been missing for twelve hours that we knew of, perhaps twenty-four. I stepped onto the path and looked down its dark length, feeling like a character in a forest-filled fairy tale.

Margo finished her call and came over to me. "Jeffries and his team are on their way." The simple statement told me she had put the CID inquiry into motion.

I nodded and rang up Mark. He had the manners not to say anything about our disastrous dinner, listened as I hurriedly related the situation, then said, "We'll try to find Graham, Bren. He could be at the vicarage, talking to the Grangers, maybe still trying to learn more of John's schedule. He won't know of John's death, of course. He would've rung up headquarters to get the team out here if he had." He stopped and I could picture him leaving Enrico's house, perhaps getting into his car and looking at his watch. Several seconds later, he added, "Unless you want me up there with you."

Was he extending an olive branch, a hint that he was anxious to patch things up between us? I opened my mouth to tell him I was sorry about the argument, to say I wanted him up here, to ask for his comforting presence, but instead I swallowed back my anxiety, glanced into the wood, and said, "No. Thanks for your offer, Mark, but I'm fine here. I think you need to find Graham. He's not answered his mobile, I guess—"

"I tried just before you called, actually. Still no answer. It just keeps ringing."

"I can't understand it."

"Well, maybe he lost it. It's happened to others."

"Could have done, I guess." I paused, my mind racing, trying to sort out the mysteries of Graham's disappearance and John's death. Finally I said, "Look, Mark. Why don't you go to the vicarage first? See if he's with the detectives detailed to the Grangers. Inform the detectives about John, of course, but if Graham's not there..." I wondered who he could be talking to, what lead he might be following. "If he's not there—"

"I'll look everywhere I can think of, Bren. So will the search team. We'll comb the area. Don't worry about me. Or him. You take care of the scene. I'll let you know after I've been with the Grangers."

I thanked him and rang off. The reassurance I'd felt with Mark's voice in my ear quickly vanished as the silence and the dark forest engulfed me. I stared into the rain, nearly overcome with fright as the cold air wrapped around me.

Margo's quiet, strong voice seeped into my agitation. "One of us needs to direct Jeffries' team here. You want to go, or you want me to?"

Turning my head and thoughts from the wood, I blinked. She repeated the question and added, "I told him approximately where we are, but we may be a bit hard to find in all this rain."

"I never was much good at semaphore," I said.

"Even though I told them to take the path behind the pub, with all this rain...well, I thought it might be hard to see the correct path. The trail branches again farther along the main track, did you know? If you don't know the area..."

I nodded, envisioning the CID team wandering around in the rain and the dark for hours. "I'll stay here, if you don't mind. I want to look around. Not that I'll find anything."

Margo nodded. Darkness and rain made a search difficult enough. Add the fallen leaves and tree branches and dead vegetation that cluttered the forest floor, and searching was nearly impossible. Still, as with physically hunting for Graham, it was an activity that occupied my mind. Margo flipped the rain hood back over her head, said she shouldn't be gone long, and left for the pub. I watched the light from her torch grow smaller and dimmer as she walked away from me, until her black figure and the light disappeared over the brow of the hill.

I stood alone in the palpable blackness for several minutes, trying to make sense of John's disappearance and death. Nothing I could think of seemed plausible except that he'd had an argument with someone. Why else would he be attacked and left for dead? If that attacker was the person whom he had sneaked out of his house to meet, that was more than criminal. A rendezvous gone so horribly wrong was reprehensible.

The nearby oaks quivered in a gust of wind, unloading their wetness. Raindrops fell heavily, thudding onto the muddy path and leafy ground. The wind moaned in the pines, stirring the great boughs so their long needled-branches looked like ghostly arms waving from out of the gloom. Rain slid down oak leaves and rocks, collected in puddles, and ran downhill in tiny streams when the puddles could not contain all the water. Standing amongst the great trees, I listened. For what, I still don't know—the murderer, Mark, the bogeyman of my childhood. I could hear stealthy steps beneath the thud of raindrops, feel the ogre's raged breathing on my face, imagine ghouls hiding behind trees, waiting to grab me. But as I played the beam of my torch over the sodden soil, nothing revealed itself but falling water and sodden leaves. The monsters remained at bay—at least while I shone my light. I shivered, the cold penetrating my clothing. Or perhaps it was fear. I shone the torch on John again, wanting the certainty that the ghoul hadn't made off with him. Another flash of lightning stabbed the sky. In that brief illumination John seemed to jerk, to jump. Which was impossible. But as the night closed around me again, I wavered between my growing uneasiness and cowardice. Neither was becoming to a copper.

I was desperate to know where Graham was, more so now than before finding John. I squelched the urge to investigate, to look for that torn-off button or lost wallet that would lead us to John's killer. Tramping through the crime scene was a bad idea in the first place, but in these less-than-ideal circumstances, it was sheer destruction. Without daylight I might have trod on something valuable and destroy our only clue. So I stood, useless and anxious, trying not to think about John or Graham, rehashing the facts of John's disappearance, listening for the tell-tale rustle of leaves that spoke of a watching murderer.

Yet, for all my good intention, Graham's face kept creeping into my mind. Something had happened to him—I was certain. He wouldn't have lost his mobile; he wouldn't have ignored our calls. And as a rumble of thunder rolled across the sky, I felt that sudden surge of protection that Mark and I had talked about. It was more than what police officers feel for victims; it was the great need that engulfs you when someone you love is missing or hurt, and your only thought and desire is to hold him in your arms, seeing his face before you, having him safe by your side. This is what I felt about Graham, never mind my friendship with Mark and Adam, or my living arrangement with Erik. I needed to see Graham safe beside me.

I also needed to let Simcock, our divisional detective-superintendent know what was happening. An investigation team needed a leader and, as Graham's immediate superior, Simcock would be that person. So I punched his phone number into my mobile, waited for the call to be answered, and tried not to think past this exact moment. The call was answered almost immediately by a stern yet surprisingly warm voice. I took a deep breath and blurted out, "Hello, sir? This is DS Brenna Taylor. Yes, sir. Well, we've a bit of a problem..." I told him about the situation with Graham, answered his questions, said we'd be in the incident room, and rang off. The wood seemed slightly less menacing after that.

It was just after nine o'clock when the torchlights bobbed up the path from the pub.

Margo's voice floated up to me, sounding both concerned and supportive. When the team had begun setting up lights and cordoning off the area, I told Margo that I still had heard nothing from Graham or Mark. She said we were bound to find him eventually and not to worry.

Which was easy to say, but she wasn't emotionally attached to him as I was. I mumbled something like 'Of course we will,' forced a smile, and watched some of the lads set down the crime scene tent. They would process the scene at first light tomorrow, it being impossible to see adequately in the dark and rain, and thereby increasing the chance of making mistakes. But for now, a constable or two would stand guard over John and the scene, protecting it as good as could be expected, given the weather and the hour. I watched the lads run through their maneuvers. Had we really played out the same roles only twenty-four hours ago? Was it so soon on the heels of Enrico's murder that we were doing the same thing again?

I stood for some moments after the lads had finished with the lights and the crime scene tape, the rain still falling. Margo was talking with Keith Jeffries, the detective-sergeant in charge of John's case, and I suddenly felt a great desire to accomplish something, anything. I rang up Mark, hoping for some good news.

"Nothing yet," Mark said, his voice cheering me even if his words didn't. "I asked the detectives if Graham had dropped by, or if he had rung them up. I didn't mention why I wanted to know. They hadn't heard from him. I let them know about John, and they've just broken the news to the Grangers." He paused, as if wanting to say something, and I could hear subdued talking in the background. The Grangers had two detectives assigned to them—a male and a female—experienced in dealing with murder victim families. Though at the offset, no one had known, of course, that John would become a murder victim. But these officers were highly trained in dealing with any such event. Not only would they impart the news of John's death with delicacy and grace, but they also would advise the Grangers on the identification of the body and inform them of the postmortem examination results. It was a position I never wanted.

"Are you finished there, then?" I asked Mark.

"Yeh. What's going on at your scene? You need help?"

I relayed what had happened, that the medical team and the SOs would come in the morning, that search teams had been started and were exploring the wood and the village.

Mark said it sounded like I'd done all I could do.

"I rang up Simcock. He's on his way. Someone needs to take over if—" I couldn't finish the sentence, so instead I said, "Don't scold me, Mark, but I'm worried. Graham would've let one of us know where he was by now. This isn't like him."

Instead of the laugh or lecture I expected, Mark agreed with me, adding that a superior would never be out of touch with his team for this length of time. "Especially Graham. He's unusually thoughtful about keeping in touch."

"So where is he? What's happened to him? God, Mark, I can't stand this!"

My fright had become so apparent that Mark said, "Don't worry, Bren. We'll find him. It's probably some stupid mistake."

"Like losing his mobile," I said, echoing Mark's previous explanation. "Even if he had, he would have stopped at a pay phone and contacted us. Or driven back here."

"Or sent a message with someone," Mark finished, avoiding

mentioning the obvious officer's name. Graham would have sent Scott Coral or some other officer to let us know where he was. This four-hour silence whispered of trouble. Mark snapped, "Meet me at the incident room. I don't care if it takes all night or this is the end of the world—we're going out right now to find him."

Chapter 17

The incident room was full of activity when I burst through the doors. Everyone not recruited to do preliminary work at John's crime scene or employed in one of the search teams was working on one of our two murder cases. There seemed to be no letup in the pace even if it was nearly half past nine. PC Byrd was at a newly assembled whiteboard, jotting down the time we'd discovered John's body, and Fordyce was tacking up photos pertaining to Enrico's case on that chalkboard. Even with Graham missing, the two cases were still moving ahead. I grabbed a couple of powerful torches, glanced at a packet of crisps—which I might have eaten under different circumstances but my stomach was too tense for food right now—and rang up Graham's home phone. I acknowledged defeat after his ansafone message clicked on.

Two minutes later beams from a car's headlights shone through the window and fanned across the far wall of the incident room. The light cut off abruptly, plunging the room into the dimness of the overhead florescent lights. A car motor shut off, and the sounds of rain dripping off tree branches and hitting copper gutters filtered through the windows. A car door slammed, the retort dulled by the gurgle of water through the downspouts. Footsteps crunched against the gravel of the car park, growing louder as the runner neared the building. The door squealed open, let in a blast of cold, damp air, and banged shut. Wet footsteps squawked on the linoleum floor and moments later Mark barged into the main room, wet and wild-eyed and incredibly Authoritative. He rushed up to me and reached for one of the torches.

"Heard anything?" he asked, glancing at the clock.

I shook my head, saying I'd just tried his home number again.

"Well, we best get started. I don't like this."

He didn't mean the weather; he meant Graham's disappearance.

I agreed, and we rushed out of the incident room and back up the path to the wood.

The spot where WPC MacMillan had fallen was becoming familiar to me by now. I'd seen it first when I'd walked this area after Enrico's murder. Then, tonight, I'd canvassed the ground when Margo and I looked for Graham. Now, an hour later, I was back and determined that we'd find Graham here—or at least somewhere in Derbyshire. Never mind that more

HORNS OF A DILEMMA

organized search teams were combing the village. I needed to look for him on my own, as my instinct directed. An organized, slow-plodding team did not suit my emotional requirement at the moment.

Mark and I stayed together, scuffing through the grass and leaves on either side of the path, our torches shining into the wood as far as they could before distance and undergrowth stopped their illumination, and making slow, methodical sweeps through the bases of the trees and small bushes. Mark was only a few feet from me, near enough to talk to, close enough to lend physical and emotional support, but in the darkness of the forest, with the question of Graham's whereabouts still unsolved, I felt vulnerable and alone. The crunch of Mark's footsteps and bounce of his torchlight offered little comfort to my growing fears.

We had worked our way, snail-paced, up the path for half an hour, passing the tent where John's body lay, when Mark called out to me. My heart jumped into my throat. Had he found Graham? I rushed over to him, half hoping half dreading to see Graham's body, but Mark merely stepped onto the path and suggested we call for help. "He wouldn't have gone up this far, Bren," he said, shining his light farther up the path, his voice strained against the arboreal sounds. The beam of his torch revealed nothing more than a pockmarked muddy path, wet leaves and a sheet of drumming rain. Beyond the reach of the light the din seemed louder, ominous, as though curtaining another crime scene from our eyes. I watched a dry leaf snap in two from the pounding of the rain; one half floated in a water-filled depression, the other half pounded into the nearly liquid mud rimming the indentation. A moment later the raft-like leaf floated over the edge of the miniature pond and plowed into a rock. Another victim of a stone. I lifted my gaze from the spotlighted ground. The blackness of the wood closed around us and I moved closer to Mark. "I don't know what he would've been doing here anyway, Bren," he said, his voice strangely comforting. "If he'd found John's body, he would have rung us up. Even if he'd lost his mobile, he would've gone down to the pub or to the incident room to report it. Why would he walk into the wood?"

I stared into the rain that seemed to isolate us from the rest of the world. The usual night sounds of crickets and owls, and the rustling leaves that betrayed the presence of voles and mice, were oddly missing. Instead, I was assaulted with the constant drip of rain on stone and soil, assailed by the aromas of wet leaves and earth instead of Mark's aftershave lotion. The cold air crept into my clothing, bore into my bones and seeped into my heart, mingling with the fear that threatened to consume me, despite my best effort to ignore it. I looked at Mark's face, now taut from his increasing concern.

"I don't know," I finally replied, tired of trying to fathom Graham's actions. "It doesn't make sense when you put it like that. What do you think we should do?"

"Get some help. We can ask for the dogs to be here in the morning."

"And until then?"

Mark drew in his mouth, his neck muscles tensing. He didn't reply.

I said, "I want to keep on looking. Just another five minutes," I added as Mark was about to speak. "Please, Mark. Just five minutes. I'll be okay by myself if you don't want to go any farther."

A bolt of lightning lit up the sky and I involuntarily leaned against Mark.

He smiled and hugged me. "When you use such persuasive arguments..." He shone his torch into the wood on his side of the path again and said, "All right. Five minutes. As you were, Sergeant." He walked back to the edge of the trees and we resumed our search.

It didn't take us my negotiated five minutes. We had two minutes to spare when I found Graham. I remember screaming to Mark, the beam of my torch focused on Graham's body, my lungs gasping for air, the forest toppling down on me. Mark ran up to me just in time to catch me, for my knees had suddenly decided to fold up. I started sliding down a tree trunk when I felt Mark's hands grab me and hold me upright. He stood with me for a moment, staring at Graham's body, before he said, "God, what the hell's going on around here?"

I whispered something incredibly clever like "I don't know," and Mark left me leaning against the tree while he squatted beside Graham. He looked up at me, his eyes merely black voids beneath his brow. He laid his fingers against Graham's neck, then held them up for me to see. Before the rain washed them clean, they were bathed in blood. He barked, "He's alive, Bren! God, he's alive! His pulse is damned weak, but he's breathing." He closed his eyes, shaking his head, then looked at me again as he yelled, "God, oh God! BLOODY HELL!" His shout sounded muffled in the woods, barely audible against the counterpoint of plopping raindrops and dense trunks. But I could see the anger and fear mixed in his dark eyes. He leaned his head back, bellowing at the treetops, pounding his fist against a tree trunk and letting the rain beat his face. A minute went by. Another minute, as he remained rooted to the spot, screeching to the heavens. Slowly, sometime later, when his anger had been spent, he exhaled deeply, wiped the rain from his face, and slicked back his soaked hair. He bent over Graham again and shone his torch onto Graham's head. I fought back a wave of nausea as I stared at his wound. His scalp was bloody and deeply cut, similar to John's.

I murmured, "What happened, Mark? What's going on?"

The night closed in around me, the forest whispered threats as I stared at Graham. Mark took off his jacket and laid it over Graham's back. Standing up, he said, "I don't know when this happened, but I'm glad we arrived before—"

He broke off, leaving the inference unsaid. I nodded, unable to shift my eyes from the side of Graham's face, and suddenly began sobbing. Great body-shaking cries that released the pain of childhood snubs and parental put-downs. And lost loves. And the death of hope.

Mark hurried over to me, grabbed me by the arms, and pulled me to my feet. Shaking me violently, he barked, "For God's sake, Bren, snap out of it! You're a cop. Start acting like one instead of a lover!"

I gulped for air and choked back another sob, drowning in raging emotions. Mark's hand grabbed my chin and forced me to look at him instead of at Graham. His eyes were alive with fire, speaking of his anger, as they had been the night of David Willett's house fire. I wanted to avert my gaze, to ignore his rage, but was powerless to do so.

Mark eyed me for a moment, perhaps accessing my mental and emotional condition, then barked, "I'm calling for an ambulance. Can you get yourself back to the pub and guide them here? Are you fit enough to do that?" He paused, as though reconsidering his request of me. A roll of thunder broke into the silence. When I didn't flinch, he said somewhat calmer, "I need you, Brenna. Graham needs you. You could stay with him and I could bring up the lads, but I think it best if you do something active. Are you all right with that?"

I didn't give him time to analyze my situation. I blurted out that I could do it, and shook off his hand. "We'll need to preserve the scene, of course." Perhaps my police training was finally kick in; perhaps I subconsciously felt better now that Graham would be heading for hospital. I rang up Fordyce in the incident room, told him of the situation and that we needed another tent, possibly from an adjoining Division if he couldn't procure one from ours, and to get another team of Scientific Officers up here, then rang off. Mark, in the meantime, had called for an ambulance. When he had finished, I told him I had already talked to Simcock. "He should be here soon."

Mark nodded, perhaps thinking ahead to the next few hours. "What did he say?" He didn't really want to know—it was just something to say to ease our tension while we waited.

"He—he was glad I phoned. Well..."

Without looking again at Graham, I turned, picked up my torch from where I'd dropped it, and shone it onto the path. The rain was more intense there, in the open, with no canopy of trees to deflect its fall, than here beneath the huge, cradling arms of pine, yew and holly. I hesitated for a moment, grabbed the collar of my rain poncho with my free hand, and looked at Mark. He was smiling encouragingly, like a father watching his child trying to swim. Before my throat tightened, I said, "He'll be fine, won't he, Mark?" Then, without waiting for his answer, I ran down the path, aware only of the darkness, the rain, and my need to bring help.

I knew exactly when the ambulance crew arrived. I'd been staring at my watch, pacing up and down in front of the pub, eyeing each set of vehicle headlights that approached the village from the Buxton road. There were more cars than I would have thought for a late Thursday evening, and I stared at each passing one, hoping to see the familiar flashing blue light. Of course the minutes felt like hours, but in actuality the lads made great time—33 minutes. I was at the vehicle's side as it braked to a stop.

In that half hour I would have had plenty of time to mull over my relationship with Graham if I could have willed my brain to think. I could have analyzed the problems of a married couple serving in the same Division; the chance for an enduring marriage when the couples had been boss and subordinate; the likelihood of fights due to both partners being in high stress careers; the possibility that I'd latched onto Graham because he was handsome, intelligent and available—and that my former colleague and future date, Adam Fitzgerald, had the same qualities and seemed anxious to make a go of any relationship between us. But I couldn't think of that. I couldn't think of anything but Graham. I couldn't do anything but pace, clock watch, glance at the heavens and pray.

I don't know for certain if there is a God. I have greater suspicions now that there is one, but I wasn't certain then. And I didn't know if God heard prayers offered while walking and staring into the night. But I presented them with all my strength, even momentarily stopping my pacing and closing my eyes to squeeze every last bit of ardor into my request for Graham's continued life. When I opened my eyes again, the rain was still falling, the night was still black. If there had been a comet, or a flash of lighting different from the others, or a heavenly winged messenger, I hadn't seen it. I tilted my face skyward, staring for some sign that God had heard me and that everything would be all right. But I saw nothing extraordinary. So I ran back to the protecting overhang of the pub and watched the cars splashing up the High Street.

In the remaining time before the ambulance came, I rang up Adam on my mobile. I remember pulling the phone from my shoulder bag, flipping it open, ready to punch in Erik's phone number. But actions, as they say, speak louder than words, and for some reason I hesitated, my fingers above the keypad. Then, just as oddly, as though an unseen presence was guiding my hand, I tapped in Adam's number and seconds later was talking to him, pouring out my heart, listening to his voice. Though Erik had placated me with similar soothing phrases last night, Adam's words penetrated my anxiety; they weren't mere panacea, as Erik's sometimes seemed to be. His voice, while particularly deep, held a depth of concern and assured me that he would work off-duty on this, should I want him to. I declined, but just the offer lessened my apprehension.

I stood under the eave of the pub, staring into the rain still pelting road, plant and ground, my mobile still in my hand. For some odd reason, I hadn't automatically closed it when I'd finished talking with Adam. Was my mind nudging me to make another call? But to whom? Our entire Murder Team knew or would very soon know about Graham, so that wasn't it. And I'd told Adam, the man I was beginning to lean on and open my heart to. A bolt of lightning slashed the sky to the west. Sure, Scott Coral. He would want to know about Graham. Besides, being one of Graham's favorite coppers, Scott should hear it from me and not from office gossip. With my fingers shaking, I punched in his number and prayed he would answer. He did. Immediately.

A few succinct, emotional sentences had to suffice with Scott, for I was afraid if I poured out my heart—which I was aching to do, needing his laid-back, analytical response—I'd lose what slender control I had on my near-hysteria. So I rang off after giving him a handful of details, thanked him for listening, and let a 'Thank you, dear God' slip from my lips as the ambulance braked beside me.

The entire episode was probably over quicker than I thought, for I watched the preliminary first aid and transfer of Graham to the stretcher in what seemed like slow motion. Mark had been sitting beside Graham when the ambulance attendants and I arrived, looking very wet and cold, his jacket still covering Graham. He had angled his torch onto the pathway, giving us a beacon to find them. Now, looking back, I applaud the wisdom of Mark's decision to send me for the ambulance crew—I doubt if I could have sat in the dark like that, waiting for an eternity, suffocated by the blackness and the wood dwelling devils, willing Graham to survive. Activity had been my talisman warding off my emotional collapse, and Mark had sensed that at the beginning. But back then, when I was close to hysteria, I couldn't see that.

"The SOs are on their way," Mark said as Graham was laid onto the stretcher. The action had the ominous familiarity of John's transport nearly two hours ago. I closed my eyes again, praying with all my heart that Graham would not meet the same end.

When I finally looked at Mark, he was hanging his damp jacket around his shoulders and brushing off the seat of his slacks. I nodded and followed him to the muddy path, now littered with footprints, wet leaves and twigs. We stood there for a few minutes, talking until the SOs arrived. They ran a strip of police tape around the area, Mark directing them so they didn't trample the vicinity where Graham had fallen. Byrd lit the lanterns, placing two just outside the cordoned off area and two on the path opposite the site. He checked with Mark about any other instructions, then walked over to me, squeezed my arm, told me Graham would be right as rain, and wished me some sleep before he joined Fordyce.

"With any luck, Simcock might be here," I said as we walked back to the incident room. "I hated ringing him up, but..." I checked my watch. Just after 11:30.

"Hell, it's an emergency," Mark said, sounding like Graham. I knew Mark was tired, cold, wet and as emotionally drained as I was. But he put duty ahead of his comfort. "I don't care if it's three a.m. and we destroyed his dream of playing at 007. Besides, he would have expected to get a call when he heard what happened. He would've been mad as hell in the morning if we hadn't told him at the earliest moment."

"He needs to take charge of the case. Physically, I mean." Although I was still emotionally drained from discovering John and Graham, the ritual of police work shoved me into a type of comfort zone. The familiarity of routine and work would redirect my mind and numb my emotions.

Mark nodded, as aware as I was that Simcock, as detective superintendent, was in charge of each case even if he didn't actually appear at the crime or incident room. Mark shone his torchlight onto the SO tent still enveloping the Devil's Stone, sidestepped around a puddle, and swore. "Damned, idiotic custom. If they'd not had it, we'd not be here."

I refrained from pointing out that the customs was centuries old and that this was the first murder associated with it. Mark wouldn't appreciate being corrected at this hour of the night. "Ta," I said as I slipped on a slick clump of leaves and clutched Mark's arm.

"What a hell of a long night."

"At least he didn't lecture me about the obvious when I rang him."

"I should bloody well hope not. Don't we know enough by now to preserve the scene?"

I let him fume, releasing his anger and frustration and fear over Graham's condition and the two deaths we now had to deal with.

We finished the walk in silence, busy with individual thoughts, trying to quell the devils that plagued our minds. When we were seated at a table in the incident room and had taken a few sips of hot tea, I asked Mark if he'd had time to think of anything while I'd been waiting for the ambulance.

"Think of what?" he said, holding the warm mug chest-high.

"Motive. Why Graham would be attacked, for one. I presume you looked at his wounds more closely after I'd gone."

"I didn't move him, Bren." His voice hardened, the anger creeping into his tone. "Don't even suggest I crossed the line."

"I wasn't suggesting you had moved him, Mark. I just thought you might have got a good look at his head wound while you sat there. I know you wouldn't disturb the scene. Even if you wanted to start with the investigation."

Mark took another sip of tea before answering. "The cowardly bastard struck Graham from behind, Bren. I know it! The wound to the back of his skull was the only thing I saw. There was nothing on the forehead or right side of his head. There could be another wound on the left side, but since he was lying on his left side..." He set down his mug but still enclosed it with his hands. "I hope to God it's not serious, that the surgery—" He broke off and bowed his head.

The room seemed to dim, then brighten, the lighting fixtures fluctuating in an apparent confusion as to how luminescent they should be. Computers and printers and the other equipment brought in for our investigation seemed farther away, as though it would take an eternity of walking to reach them. The lights, now hundreds of feet above us, took on halos. I was conscious of the cold metal of the chair biting into the backs of my thighs and I leaned back, exhausted.

In a small voice, I asked, "What was he doing up there, Mark? Have you figured that out?"

"I didn't rifle his pockets! I didn't check his notebook."

HORNS OF A DILEMMA

I sighed. This wasn't going well. And Mark accused me of getting emotionally involved. I said, "Right. He and John are found in the wood. Both have head injuries. Granted, Graham was farther into the wood. Does this suggest anything to you?"

Mark picked up the mug, held it without taking a sip, and said, "He might have found John, perhaps saw or heard something that he wanted to follow up on right then—"

"Which was why he didn't phone us—"

"—and trailed that person through the wood."

"Getting attacked for his efforts. Perhaps the assailant sneaked around behind him, or Graham was looking for something else and the assailant just spotted an opportunity to take care of him."

"Graham might have found something connected with Enrico's death. He might not have even found John. He could have been checking out something in that patch of the wood, was assaulted without being aware anyone was behind him." Mark grimaced and swore quietly.

"We'll go over the area tomorrow morning. Fortunately, the rain's forecasted to end tonight."

"Won't be too soon for me." He finished the last of his tea, put down the mug, and leaned forward, his forearms on the tabletop. He looked incredibly tired; there was no spark in his eyes. His hair still glistened from the rain. "God, what a night—John, Graham, freezing temps, rain..." He gazed out of the window, muttering he should've been a fire fighter, that at least he'd always be warm.

Two constables were seated at computers, either entering data or doing research. Neither spoke. The soft click of the computer keys gradually dimmed beneath the drumming of the rain and my own thoughts. Then these, too, faded into the silence born from disregarding familiar sounds.

The quiet claimed us again, terrifying and comforting at once. I coughed and Mark stared at me, expecting some explanation, perhaps of events. I muttered it had been a tickle, and he went back to staring out of the window. The clock over the entranceway boomed through its slow countdown of Time, keeping us aware of our wait. Mark cleared his throat. I asked what he wanted and he replied he'd had a cough. We lapsed back into quietness. I straightened a pile of papers on the desk, read the top sheet several times, then watched the clock's second hand travel full-circle several times before I broke the stillness.

"Alibis might be the key," I said, startled at hearing my voice after so much silence.

Mark gave up his contemplation of the outside world to look at me.

"We need to find out who has a rock-solid alibi so we can concentrate on someone else."

"You're talking about opportunity."

"Many people had opportunity, Mark, but if they have an unbreakable alibi, like they were lecturing before a hundred people, then they're not a suspect."

"Like I said—opportunity. If they're lecturing before a hundred people, they have no opportunity."

I gave up. Fine, let him go with that. I was too tired to fight.

I glanced at the small puddles of water we'd tracked into the room, the blobs of mud and bits of wet leaves. By the time the rest of the CID team had wandered to and from both current scenes, the place would resemble a well-used rugby field. I got up, grabbed a mop from the utility closet, and cleaned up the mess, thankful for something to do while the clock inched toward Simcock's arrival. Mark shook out his jacket, refilled our mugs, brought them over to the table, and rinsed out the mop. One of the constables printed a page on the computer printer.

"What I don't get," Mark said, returning to the table and taking a seat, "is why Graham didn't phone in to us if he found something. That's the first thing we do. It's automatic."

"Maybe he wasn't certain he had found something. Maybe he was following up on a hunch. We don't know if he even saw John's body. He could have been coming through the wood from the west, beyond the church and vicarage. He could have been attacked before he came upon John. There's nothing written in stone that he had to join the path from the pub."

"So where's a convenient spot to get on the path, if he came at it from the west?" Mark grabbed an ordinance survey map of the area, opened it, and we leaned over it, searching for the walking trail.

I jabbed the spot and looked at Mark. "Here! While there's no official footpath from the building itself, it's very close to the group of millstones."

"And the car park."

We exchanged glances, wondering if we'd found a possible explanation.

"Green Acre Road winds slightly north at that point," I said, thinking aloud and tracing the road with my finger. "The car park sits in the little curvy spot before the road winds westward again. That's where the millstones are."

"And the forest trail is not so far away that someone can't park in that area, walk over the hill, and get onto it easily."

"You'd kind of have to know the trail's there, though. I mean, with the hill and the wood, I'd think the trail was hidden from the road."

"I'll check it out in the morning," Mark said, folding up the map. "Which will be here too bloody early. I know we could wait until Graham tells us..." He stopped, his face suddenly flooding with color. He broke his gaze from me and concentrated on creasing the map closed.

I said that it might be another day before Graham could talk to us, and we'd be losing time in the investigation. "We ought to go ahead and do it. He'll be impressed that we figured it out." Though not as confident as I sounded, I smiled, and felt better when Mark smiled back.

"But it doesn't have to be a local, does it?" Mark said, moments later after we'd watched a car's headlights pan across the room's windows. We had waited, nearly holding our breath, hoping it was Simcock. But the car moved on, and we were once again listening to the rain and our internal voices expressing our worries. "I mean," he went on, sighing, "anyone can get an ordinance map and see what we just saw. It doesn't really get us anywhere. Damn."

"Locals are the most obvious, I agree. They know about the path and the millstones and such. But Graham's attacker may have been in the wood before Graham even started up the trail. Or he could have come up from the pub, very respectable looking, just another rambler tramping through the village. No one would pay him any mind."

"He'd be more invisible if he were a local."

"I'll be happy if he hadn't been invisible to Graham when he hit him."

Chapter 18

We were finishing our tea and talking about any subject other than Graham—mundane topics that ordinarily we would never waste time or thought on, but desperately needing to take a break from the horror—when car headlights swept over the window of the incident room. Mark and I stood up, staring out the window, asking each other if it was Simcock's car. I shielded my eyes from the headlights' glare, trying to see beyond the brilliant light to the car itself. The headlights switched off just as I said I couldn't be sure, and moments later the door to the incident room banged open, letting in a stream of wind, rain, cold, and Detective-Superintendent Simcock.

I'd had contact with Simcock before, of course, but now that he was subbing for Graham, in a sense, he seemed larger than life and more authoritative. It was the personal contact and the absence of Graham that did it. The intrusion into Graham's patch. Which was a ludicrous way to look at it, since Simcock was Graham's superior officer, and therefore mine, and we were all working in the same division. Plus the tacit implication of Graham's serious condition—if Graham hadn't been attacked Simcock wouldn't have been here. And I couldn't help feeling that surge of protectiveness when Mark brought Simcock a mug of tea and we had briefed him on the entire evening.

"Bloody awful evening," Simcock said, settling back in his chair and glancing around the room. I knew he meant Macmillan's accident and the two attacks, not the weather.

I agreed, not knowing what else to say and feeling the strain again of the attacks now that we were about to get to work. He took several deep breaths, as though preparing to throw himself physically into the investigation and I wondered about the next few days. I'd never worked CID with anyone other than Graham. I felt as though I were in the head master's office in school and I didn't like it.

I watched as Simcock jotted down some notes. He was a large man, in his late fifties. I knew he was married and had one grown son, who was living in Bolton. I also knew he was a distinguished graduate of some university. But that was about all. Just a veneer, an impersonal handful of facts. Now the man who had always been a shadowy figure lurking somewhere behind Graham was metamorphosing into flesh and bone and personal vignettes. I glanced at him as he took a sip of tea, curious as to his personality. If he'd been shorter, he would have looked portly, like a caricature of an old English squire, but his great height helped diminish the excess weight. Advancing age and a desk-demanding job contributed to the slight swell of his belly. It had confined itself to the area over his belt buckle, giving him a leaner look when seen head-on than was suggested from a side view. Yet, he moved gracefully, as though he'd taken ballet lessons in his youth, and everything about him suggested speed and aggression. His sharp-edged nose, like the prow of a clipper ship, seemed to be built for sniffing out clues in a case, and his long, graying hair was worn swept back from his sloping forehead. All in all, he gave the impression of rushing into the fray, whether he was moving or sitting still. However, he had time to convey compassion, whatever he was doing. Glancing from Mark to me, he again expressed his concern for Graham, MacMillan and the Grangers.

When he had heard all the details of the cases, he angled his chair toward me. He leaned his left forearm on the table, bent forward slightly, and said, "Taylor, I'd like you and Salt to continue with the investigation of Enrico Thomas' death. Anyone else whom you're working with at the present? I know Salt is part of your team, but before I call in other lads from another division to help with all this, I'd like you to continue working with the team you're comfortable with. It makes for easier working conditions. You're no doubt anxious enough about Graham and MacMillan without me partnering you with a strange detective." His voice held the broad vowels of northern Lancashire, the area of his childhood. He was easy to target in a police station full of local Derbyshire speech. Yet, in a profession that tended to be cliquish and possessive of its own, Simcock had been taken in as one of Derbyshire's own and respected as a great copper.

I replied that I appreciated his offer, and that Margo Lynch and I also worked well together.

Simcock leaned back in his chair, looked at us and said, "Speaking of partners and easier working conditions, I suppose I should heed my own sermon and tell you a bit about myself. You'll then know why I think and act the way I do—which might help in the long run, don't you think? A little understanding usually goes a long way at such times."

I said it would be nice to get to know him, as I'd never worked with him.

He began with the obvious things, the non-personal aspects that contributed to him being who he was. He told us of his wife and son, who had followed a parallel career to end up as a sergeant in the Lancashire Constabulary. He told us he'd met his wife when they had both been constables and that she had left the job to rear their child. He told us that he had always wanted to be in the police or a related career and that he had graduated from the University of York, having read International Relations. Years after graduation he finally settled into police work. He skimmed over specifics of his career, making it seem as though he had struggled to attain the rank of superintendent. But I knew he'd been a flyer, a person who breezed through the ranks. Perhaps that was a byproduct of his brilliant, analytical mind. Perhaps he merely wanted to get on with his life, to attain the position he'd set as his goal back in his childhood. Perhaps his was a hyper personality, and he was dissatisfied with standing still, needing the challenge of new goals to keep him happy and mentally active.

He related it all in a languid voice, but the sentences were short, as though he was in a hurry to be on with the night's work. "I once worked for MI6," he added, almost as an afterthought. "Did you know, or am I adding to my legend?" Even though he had said it straight-faced, I could detect a suggestion of self-mockery. Did he know he was viewed as either a demi-god or a devil? "It was interesting work. I made a lot of friends, but I think I really came to life when I joined the Force." Running his hand over the top of his head, he said, "Right. Enough of this, however fascinating you may find it. We've two murders and attacks—all within twenty-four hours. What've we got out here—a gang or a maniac?"

"I don't know which would be easier to track down," Mark said.

Simcock took another gulp of the hot liquid and asked for our opinions of the case so far.

Mark voiced his and concluded with his thanks for the offer of more detectives to work the case. "MacMillan may or may not be back in a day or so. Same with DCI Graham. I suppose we'll be hearing fairly soon what their conditions are, sir."

"Yes," Simcock agreed. "I've put a call into the hospital, requesting an appraisal of their conditions the moment they know anything. Not only will we know who's available for work, but also we'll all feel a hell of a lot better once we're told how they are physically. I'm certain I echo all the officers' sentiments when I say I'm worried."

Mark and I murmured our agreement, then waited for Simcock to continue. We already felt the strain of the attacks and of working with a new boss.

Simcock turned to me, his face a map of frowns and concerns. "Is there someone we should contact? I know Graham's not married, but is there anyone who needs to know—parent, relative, close friend, fiancée...?"

I tried to ignore the rush of jealousy and the heat flooding my face. "Well, sir, I believe his parents have passed. He has a sister, but I don't know where she lives. And as for the other..." I let it slide, hoping Simcock would believe I was working on a name.

"I'll look up the info on his personnel record. Maybe he put her name and address down as an emergency contact. If not, I'll send a constable to Graham's house. There's got to be something—address book, letters, phone number."

I murmured my agreement, wondering if we would be able to contact the sister. Graham hadn't given me the impression that they were that close, but maybe there was something in his file.

HORNS OF A DILEMMA

Simcock slowly rubbed his jaw and took another sip before saying, "I don't have to tell you that it's highly unusual to have two officers assaulted and unconscious. I don't want to believe there'll be any more, either. But what I do know is that we need the help. Not just because two coppers are unable to work and in hospital but also because we need more manpower to catch this bastard." He set down his mug and gripped the edge of the table. His voice hardened. "I know I've got a reputation on the Division as an uncaring sod, demanding results, but by God, I want this more than I've ever wanted *anything!* I want this bastard caught. I'm not going to sleep, and I'm not going to allow you lot much sleep, until he bloody well is."

"None of us feel much like sleeping anyway, sir," I mumbled.

"I'm not threatening," Simcock reassured us, "and I'm not an inhumane git who's going to drive you 'round the clock. That's no way to get results." He paused, as though remembering a case famous in the Division. A murder investigation in Hope had been botched up due to officers pushed beyond their limit, working 18-hour days. Simcock's voice lowered and filled with sympathy. "I'm merely giving you advance notice of what I'll expect. Any problems with this?" He waited, shifting his gaze from me to Mark, his chest rapidly rising and falling, clearly eager to press on with the job.

Mark replied that he was as anxious as Simcock to see the guilty party behind bars. Which wasn't exactly how he phrased it, but I'm not used to writing such language. I nodded. Although I didn't voice my decision, I'd made up my mind before Simcock had arrived that I wasn't going to sleep until Graham's attacker was taken in charge.

Simcock flashed a smile, leaned back again, and said somewhat more calmly that he'd ring up for extra officers after we were finished for the night. "I hope to God that I can get limited mutual aid from Greater Manchester or North Yorkshire. I know it's damned expensive and almost never done, but I'll talk to the Chief Constable about it. We need the help."

Mark said he'd welcome the extra hands. "The more officers we've got on the cases, the quicker we'll find this flaming berk."

"Normally, of course, I'd request officers from other divisions within our Constabulary, but we're thin on the ground at the moment, what with an arson case in Matlock, a number of car thefts in Derby, and a kidnapping in Chesterfield. So perhaps the chief constable will consent to the mutual aid request after all."

Mark and I nodded, and I mentally prayed that we would get the help. We were wallowing in major cases.

"Anything else?" He picked up his mug and waited, wanting us to feel free to voice our concerns or make a request.

I said, "With this second murder, now, and with DCI Graham and WPC MacMillan in hospital..." I hesitated, unsure of how to phrase it. Simcock took a sip of tea, waiting for me to continue. He looked at me, neither glaring in impatience nor bored at my anxiety. "Well, sir," I said, taking a deep breath, "we'll need more officers to deal with the media again.

And the resulting crowd."

"Certainly. I'll take care of that. Is that it? Right." His mug thudded onto the table top, signaling the end of the subject.

When he had finished, Mark rubbed his forehead, perhaps already feeling the pressure to solve each case.

"We do what we can do, whether we get the mutual aid or not," Simcock said. "Of course I want results. There's not an officer in the constabulary who doesn't want to see the murders solved and the attacker of WPC MacMillan and DCI Graham up before the judge. But I'm past expecting miracles. Especially now, with what we've got right here." He nudged the mug around in a small circle, his fingertips tapping lightly against the surface. In the silence I was aware that the rain had stopped, and there was only the occasional drip running off trees and plopping onto the tarmac outside the window.

Simcock grabbed the mug, held it as though it were a recently captured felon. "It's easy to demand results when you're sitting in an office and taking the heat from the higher-ups." He glanced at me and Mark, perhaps to see our reactions. When I raised my eyebrows and smiled, he continued. "It's a consequence of the times, you know. The average citizen wants to feel safe in his home. He wants protection from burglars and robbers and the other scum that plague our society. And when murder happens, especially if it's an old-age pensioner or child, the cry for the apprehension of the killer goes up, and we who only direct the cases from our desks succumb to that demand."

"And we're caught between the wail for the felon's head and the pressure from the Divisional Commander," Mark said.

"Or even higher up," he added, nodding. "It's a hell of a mess. You run the risk of arresting an innocent person if you push the case through too quickly, and you risk being reprimanded by the ACC if you don't produce the culprit, don't show him something for the wage you're getting." Simcock sagged back in his chair, his eyes suddenly tired, his breathing slow and laborious. He seemed as though he were already exhausted from the added cases of this evening. "So," he said, tapping his pen against his open notebook. "You two, along with the original team, are working on the Enrico Thomas case. Who's in charge of the John Granger case?"

"Keith Jeffries," Mark said, sitting forward in his chair. "Mr. Graham called him in early on, when it was a missing person case. Now that it's turned into a murder investigation...well, Jeffries quickly adjusted and has got his team up to speed by now, I expect. He'll be talking with Jens Nielsen and Faye Usher when they get here in the morning."

"The Home Office pathologist and biologist, yes...." Simcock's voice trailed off as he stared at his notebook. One of the constables in the room got up from his computer, stretched, and walked into the kitchen. His footsteps sounded unnaturally loud. "And this was when?"

"Just after eight o'clock."

"So Jeffries has had...." He consulted his watch. "Four and a half hours, approximately, to get into the case. Fine. He should be making some headway. Where is he now?" He swiveled in his chair, looking around the room.

"I believe he's still at the scene. He got there immediately on our call. He wanted to look at the body and the area."

"Can't do much there until Jens Nielsen and Faye Usher have done their bit. I hope he's not mucking about, trampling on the ground. He should know a damn sight better than to do that."

"Yes, sir. No, sir, he's not. He viewed the body and the scene from outside the police tape and mentioned that he would stand guard for a while with the constables. Giving them breaks until other officers can relieve him."

Simcock muttered that we damn well ought to have the extra manpower that another constabulary could provide, then nodded. "I expect Jeffries will be in later in the morning. I'll catch him up then."

I stood up, collected my jacket and shoulder bag, and told Simcock I'd be in at the usual time, unless he wanted me earlier.

"Shouldn't think so," he said, glancing at the clock. "God, it's nearly one o'clock! No. Usual time—ten. We won't have anything on that requires an early start. That also applies to you, Salt," he said, grabbing Mark's empty mug. "Okay? Fine, then. Good night."

Mark and I left Simcock reading his notes.

I drove us back to the pub, incredibly relieved that Simcock had turned out to be human, and emotionally lightened that the sky was clearing. Maybe we could find something later this morning at one of the crime scenes.

When Mark paused outside the car, looking confused that I wasn't parking, I told him I wanted to see Graham. "They ought to know something by now. He's been there for several hours."

"You want me to go with you? I'm good at holding hands." Only this time he didn't mean that in a romantic way. He meant it as a friend who wanted to help alleviate my fear.

I shook my head.

"There's the phone, Bren. It's a handy invention. It saves an inordinate amount of drive time."

"I need to go, Mark. Don't get mad. It's just not the same over the phone. I need to see him. I'm worried about him. Maybe if I see—"

Although I could see his neck muscle tightening, Mark refrained from saying anything about my feelings for Graham.

"I'm just going to pop in, Mark. See what's happening. I'll be back before you know it."

"Just don't start by ticking off Simcock. He's awfully decent, isn't he?"

"More than I would've thought yesterday. Night."

I waved and drove off before Mark could voice another opinion.

The car park at the hospital was nearly empty save for a few cars huddled beneath the street lamps. *Other midnight visitors to emergency or accident victims*, I thought, getting out of the car and hurrying into the complex. The Devonshire Royal Hospital, as it was properly called, is surrounded by trees and a box of roads, north of Buxton's famous Crescent, which houses—among other interests—the town's library and access to the mineral springs. The hospital sat across from the cricket ground to its west, and opera house and swimming pool to its south. I always suspected it was rather unique—other than its claim to having at one-time the world's largest unsupported dome encasing its walls—for sporting an octagonal-shaped exterior and a circular interior. But tonight I ran past the gray bowl-shaped roof, ignoring its circular, windowed cupola perched atop it like some topper on a wedding cake. I had to see Graham.

The halls echoed from my rushed footsteps and housed that curious aroma particular to hospitals. Disinfectant mixed with lingering odors of food, and perhaps a whiff of soiled linens. And the underlying smell of sickness that defies description. It was more than unwashed bodies or dirty bedclothes; it seemed to scent the air with disease and death.

A constable was ensconced in a chair inside Graham's room, leafing through a coarse fishing magazine. I knew him from our office but I reminded him of my name, showed him my warrant card, and asked how Graham was. The constable grimaced, glanced toward the bed, and said there was no change yet. "As long as you're here," he added, standing up and tossing the magazine onto the chair seat, "if you'll be a minute or two, do you mind if I—"

"No. Take a break. I'll tell you if he says anything."

The constable nodded, thanked me, and quickly left.

There was no one else in the room other than Graham and me. Evidently the medical staff had finished for the moment, for Graham lay in bed, his eyes closed, hooked up to IV fluids, a mask covering his nose and mouth. I gaped at him, my heart racing. If I had been thinking, I would have expected to find him like this. But I was shocked to see this man, who was always healthy and fit, lying helpless and plugged into machines.

A sliver of orange-ish light from the outside street lamp slipped between the closed curtain and the wall, spilling onto an edge of the dresser beneath the window. The dresser top was littered with typical hospital items: a drinking cup, an insulated pitcher of water, a box of facial tissue, and a plastic tray that held notepaper, pencil and a laminated card of local phone numbers. The metal stand holding the infusion bottle stood close to the bed. A lightweight woven blanket was folded neatly across his lower legs, a pillow in a white, starched pillowslip beneath his head. It was unrumpled, giving the lie to the impression that he was getting a normal night's sleep. His head made the only indentation in the otherwise flat surface. The sheets and blanket covering him were still smooth and pulled taut, mutely speaking of his inactive state. The bed, which was located beneath the wall-mounted electrocardiogram monitor, seemed to be surrounded by beeping lights and ominous tubes. It looked incredibly sterile and incredibly frightening.

I slowly walked up to him, softly speaking his name. His eyelids never fluttered; his head never moved. When I stopped at his bed, I could see the bruises on the left side of his head, the torn flesh of his scalp. The matted blood had been cleaned off, but the purple discoloration of his skin worried me. What damage had been done to his brain?

I glanced at the respirator, watched the pump, heard the rush of air passing through the machine and into the tube leading to the facemask. If Graham needed oxygen to live, if it should fail... I studied his face, afraid to watch the drip of liquid seeping through the tube and into his hand. Overwhelmed with dread, I grabbed it. His fingers lay unresponsive in mine, like a limp fish that had been dead for days. I cupped my other hand on top of his, needing to feel that he was still with me. I bent closer to him, squeezing his fingers, talking softly. I did not want the constable to hear should he suddenly enter the room; I did not want to startle Graham should he wake up.

"You'll be all right, sir. Don't worry about that." I paused, wondering what to say that would cheer him if he was able to hear me. Maybe it wasn't the words as much as it was that someone was with him, someone cared. I gushed on, "Don't, uhh, don't worry about anything. I mean...don't think about a thing except getting well. Mark and I will catch whoever did this to you—I promise! You might think it daft, but I've vowed not to rest until he's caught. And Mark...well, he would never admit it to you, sir, but he's worried. About you and MacMillan. We—" I stopped, knowing both my banter and the fact that I was talking to an unconscious man sounded inane. Still, hadn't it been proven that people in comas heard conversation? Would it be detrimental to Graham's recovery if he heard that we cared for him? I glanced at the door. No one was coming. I leaned closer and whispered, "I'm praying, sir. I started this evening, after we found you. I—I don't know how to do it—not really the proper way, that is. But I'm trying. I know you'll be okay again. I've asked God to help you, to punish me instead, if that's why this happened." I brought his hand to my chest and placed it against my heart. In the quiet of the room I again promised him I'd find his attacker if it was the last thing I ever did.

He didn't move. God didn't roar. The respirator quietly sighed; the IV bag still dripped its slow, continuous liquid through Graham's incision, the lights of the mobile monitoring unit blinked beneath the bedside lamp, looking at once Official and Life-Saving and Ominous. The silence closed in on me as I waited for a response, either from God or Graham—a sigh or movement from Graham, a thunderbolt or flaming sword from God. The respirator continued pumping, the lights blinked unhurriedly. I felt smothered by the antiseptic, impersonal environment, angry at God's heartlessness. Squeezing Graham's hand, I laid it on his chest. I was wiping my teary eyes when the constable returned to the room.

Mark was seated by the doorway when I entered the pub. He looked exhausted and worried, his eyes dull and staring at me from the dark depths beneath his brows, made blacker by the traces of coal dust ground into the corners of his eyes. His colorless face and flesh seemed to sag from his cheekbones. Grabbing my hand, he steered me away from the door and asked how Graham was.

When I had told him, Mark shook his head. "It sounds bad, doesn't it? But I suppose the oxygen thing is just a precaution. Like they're protecting his airway. Just in case." His eyes searched mine for some reassurance. I couldn't give it.

Instead I said, "He's bound to be all right, Mark. I mean, they're monitoring him, which is good. And there weren't any doctors hovering around him, which is another indication that he's—well, I mean, if there was any doubt about his condition…if the doctors thought he was in danger…" I stopped, aware that I was babbling, yet unable to control my anxiety. "I guess they aren't afraid—Simcock, I mean—that Graham's attacker will try anything. I mean, even though the constable is there—"

"The constable is just a bit of procedure, Bren. Doesn't mean anything."

"Other than they don't want the bastard to come back and finish the job."

If Mark was surprised by my language, he didn't show it. "Anyway, he's most likely there to hear anything Graham might say on recovering consciousness. Simcock doesn't want vital information to be lost. It's just procedure." He had tried to sound reassuring, almost nonchalant, yet he pressed his lips together, as though he was sorry he'd said it.

But it was true. Constables always guarded hospital rooms in similar instances. It didn't mean anything medical, didn't signify Graham's imminent death. It protected him against someone posing as a hospital employee and sneaking into his room. It also afforded the constable the chance to speak to Graham about the attack.

I took a deep breath, stretched, and said I wanted to go to my room. Mark walked me upstairs and leaned against the open doorway of my room as I hung my jacket and purse on the back of a chair. He said, "I'm sorry about this evening, Bren."

"You couldn't help what happened to Graham, Mark." I came over to him. He hadn't stepped over the threshold.

Shaking his head, he said, "No. Not what I mean. At the incident room tonight. On our way to dinner. I'm sorry about the fight. I acted like a berk. *Again.* I'm sorry. Will you forgive me?"

My response should've been quicker, for as I was trying to put words to my emotions, Mark frowned. I mumbled, "It's partly my fault, too, Mark. I guess we're both overly tired. I'm sorry it happened, too. I'd also like your forgiveness."

Mark brought my hand to his lips and lightly kissed it before releasing it. "Can we start over? Nothing posh. Nothing too high-stress. How about breakfast this morning? You willing to risk your appetite seeing me first thing over a plate of eggs?"

Ordinarily I would have laughed, but our present situation had plunged all of our team into dejection. It was sobering enough to have injured officers, but our grief deepened at not knowing their prognosis. I stepped back into my room, my hand on the edge of the door. "Nothing to risk. I'll see you at nine. Thanks, Mark."

He nodded and walked down the hall to his own room. I lingered at the door, listening to the sound of his measured tread against the rug, wondering what the next few days would be like without Graham, dating Adam, and working with Mark.

Chapter 19

From the desk of Scott Coral...
My shift had been going well, nothing unusual, nothing overwhelming. My shift—Scott Coral, Constable in B Division of the Derbyshire Constabulary. Nothing unusual; just another hectic day of responding to a rash of calls: domestic violence complaints, two pub brawls, a cat up a tree, a car crash on the A5012, a residential burglary call, suspicious activity at a bank, and a supposedly stolen car. Nothing overwhelming until I received Brenna's phone call.

I had to stop my car on the side of the road while going home after my shift. I'd made it three minutes into the drive when I felt my head about to explode. The pounding rain hitting the car's windscreen was in perfect rhythm with the pounding near my temples. As I sat there, I could think of nothing but a superior officer, a very good man, lying in a coma. Graham had even been a man of the cloth at one time before oddly turning to police work. My anger was overwhelming.

A massage therapist once told me one way to cope with stress was to tighten up every muscle, starting with your eyes/nose/mouth, and working your way down to every single toe. To strain and tighten everything for a few seconds, and then relax, would actually relieve tension and reduce stress. At this point, anything was worth a try. As I got to my neck, I wondered how I looked to the passers-by on the road. Some bloke on the verge, sitting in his car, making faces as if he had just swallowed a bucket of sour lemons, tensing up, doing it again. A smile briefly forced itself on my face, but the anger and bitterness quickly returned. Besides, the pouring rain probably skewed any on-lookers' view, and in my current mood, I didn't much care either way.

Nine years as the Section's defensive tactics instructor, I'd never seen a thing like it—two officers down from hand-to-hand conflict within the last two days. Could my training of them have been so inadequate? What I would have done to trade places with either of them. What I would do to find the coward now. Two officers brutally attacked, and no one to answer for it. I didn't know which caused me to seethe more: the fact that it had happened, or that we had absolutely no idea who had done it. Or why.

But more than that—something did not seem right. Graham was not only one of the most respected senior officers in the Division, but I also personally considered him the finest I'd ever seen. He didn't have a large physical stature, nor appear overly muscular, but he did have what every cop strived to attain: Command Presence. Graham had an aura when he entered a room that clearly said, 'Do not mess with me; I am clearly in charge of this scene.'

So what type of criminal would even consider attacking a man such as Graham? How would that same criminal have been able to surprise him? It had to be an ambush. But that thought was ludicrous. No one in his right mind would assault an officer, especially a known Inspector in the community, in such a brutal manner without the intent to kill him or be killed in the attempt. How many people like that were even around? Those who were, we called the One Percenters—the one percent or less of the population who would use any type of violence, to any extent, to attain their goals at any given time. Those who made up that peer group were only partially human—meaning they had very little, if any, conscience common to the rest of us.

The wanted posters around the building at work showed the faces of several violent criminals, but almost all had 'made names for themselves' exclusively in major cities such as Manchester or London. Why would one of them be in this area now? The more I thought, the more nothing made sense. My mind raced back to the man named Roper. It had been a long, long time since someone had raised the hair on the back of my neck. Roper did that, and deep down I knew why.

I had been on two extended, behind-the-scenes tours of the Kingdom's maximum-security prisons. David Robinson, a childhood friend, had worked at HM prison Dartmoor as a guard for the better part of ten years and had taken me in to show me around. I had spent time with the guards and watched how the animals in the cells lived. These were experiences I knew I would keep the rest of my life. Growing up, I had heard family and friends say, when hearing of a prison sentence for a brutal criminal, "Ahh, now they get the telly and good meals every day! We should all have such a life!" That was the public perception. The reality was that life in the nick was the closest thing to hell on earth. Everyone—from the warden, to the molesters, to the cooks, to the robbers, to the guards—lived in FEAR. Twenty-four hours a day of non-stop living on the edge with no end and no hope in sight.

Roper had done time in a place such as that. Of that, I had no doubt. I knew every inch of his movement in the brief minutes I had seen him. He would be a challenge, and he had the capability to kill me. A One Percenter. As I closed my eyes, I shuddered at the memories of prison life. I shuddered at dealing with Roper. I just didn't know for whom I was shuddering.

The stress exercises were really not working, but then I thought of something most glorious: The Black Eagle Pub—near enough to warrant being called 'on the way home,' if I stretched the meaning of the phrase a bit. A shot of Tanqueray gin with a lime twist would be much more effective aid than sitting in a car making faces, would it not? Would Alexa and the kids understand? They would have to. I knew—from experience—I could snap at any little thing at home if the stress of work followed me from the street into my family life. I would call her in a bit, but for now, I had to get this resolved in my own way.

It was odd that I was viewed as one of the most laid back people in the Division. Very few people had ever seen me rattled, no matter what the circumstance or how volatile the situation. I had been spit on, swung at, cursed at, vomited on, and any number of other things in my career, with nary a rise in my blood pressure. But in this case I could feel myself losing control. That piece of shit was out walking, enjoying life as if nothing had happened, while one of the best human beings on the planet was in a hospital room hooked to a monitor.

Graham's CID team was excellent, and I was confident that they, along with many other constabulary resources, would find the attacker. Brenna Taylor was one of my most trusted friends, and I knew she wouldn't sleep until Graham was back on his feet or his attacker was found. But for now, that wasn't my immediate concern, for the Black Eagle was in sight and I needed to get in there in the worst way.

As I entered the pub, it happened. I immediately saw Keeler and took two steps toward him at the bar. Just to my left, two men were doing some drunken karate style dance, when one of them gave the other a shove with both hands to the chest. The man, a bit smaller than I, stumbled, hurtled toward me, and suddenly slammed with all his weight into my left shoulder. So I helped him. I had already positioned my feet for balance, so I grabbed his collar and briefly pushed him forward. I figured if he wanted to dabble in the martial arts, I might as well give him a lesson. I was in the mood. As soon as I had pulled him back upright, I violently yanked him down again as swiftly as I could. His shoulders and backside thudded loudly against the polished hardwood floor, and his eyes momentarily rolled back. Good. By the smell of him, he was also in no condition to drive. Better to let him rest on the floor.

Apparently none too keen on assisting his friend on the ground, the other bloke came running at me, swearing all the way. Aikido is truly an amazing art. To use a person's own momentum against himself is so simple, and yet so elegant and effective. As he came within an arm's length of me, I turned sideways, grabbing his right arm in the process. The slow, fluid turning of my body (with his arm in tow) and his continued forward momentum sent him sailing over his fallen friend and into the wall. As sloshed as he was, it really wasn't very difficult. But it did make me feel better.

"Coral! You stupid son-of-a…you're lucky I don't let them borrow my cricket bat and use your head as a ball!"

I knew the booming voice very well. Stanley Keeler. Owner-bartender of the Black Eagle Pub, and more importantly, a friend I could trust.

"Get up to the bar, Coral. The first round's on the house—a 'thanks'

HORNS OF A DILEMMA

for savin' me havin' to do what you just did. And you two..." He walked over to the two drunks, who were sitting up and rubbing their arms. It'd be another minute before their heads cleared and they could stand. Keeler leaned forward, gesturing toward the door. "Get the bloody hell up and off my floor before I mop it with the both of you. You're lucky I saved you from Coral, here."

They nodded and mutely got to their feet. Except for their groaning.

As they staggered toward the door, Keeler yelled, "I'll save your tabs for tomorrow. Now get out of here and sober up somewhere else."

As I took a stool at the end of the long bar, I knew the questions would come as soon as the large man came sauntering over to me. Two young couples were clapping and waving to me, obviously appreciative of my effort and apparently having grown tired of the two yobos' antics long before I had appeared. Keeler started the questioning before I could take a breath.

"What the bloody hell has gotten into you, Scotty? You haven't acted like that since you were a probationer."

I stared at him, not sure of my response. I didn't want to start talking about Graham. It wasn't Keeler's business and I was afraid that once I began I wouldn't be able to cork my frustration. And Keeler might witness another physical demonstration, but this time on his furniture.

Staring at me as though he was judging my level of sobriety, he said, "Why, I just saw the unflappable Scott Coral tossin' drunks about like in the old days. Come on, then? What's the story?"

I stared at the massive shelves behind the bar, crammed with every liquor known to mankind. At the moment, the bottles spoke to me louder than Keeler's voice in my ear. I snapped, "Keeler, if you don't want to wind up like those two, you'd be wise to get the big green bottle over there. Just look for the green bottle. Or maybe try to find the letter 'T', as I know you can't read."

Keeler's laughter, as deafening as his speaking voice, exploded into the air. As it went on, it became contagious. I hadn't even had a drink and I was already in a better mood. I'd just tossed two drunks around and was now sitting next to an old friend who could put me in my place just by looking at me. His laughter coaxed the rest of my anger from me and I couldn't stop laughing with him. But I did—abruptly, as if a pail of cold water had been thrown on me—with his next question.

"I heard 'bout the Inspector who's in hospital. Does this have anythin' to do with you bein' here, crackin' heads on a weeknight, when you should be home?"

I continued staring at the four bottles of Tanqueray about five feet in front of me, behind the bar. I just shook my head.

In a quieter, softer tone, Keeler said, "You find that bastard, Scotty, and you know what to do. Oh, I know you're 'by the book', but an attack on a copper is an attack on us all. If you don't take care of him, bring him in here for a pint. I'll put the mug so far up his—"

I had to interrupt. "Hey, are you a bartender or what? I'm a bit thirsty here!" Stanley Keeler had seen me through my days before becoming a constable and my days before marriage, chasing everything in his pub. In the last few years he had seen me advance in law enforcement and had watched my family grow. He knew I rarely drank anymore, and knew me being here during the week wasn't right.

Keeler answered, "Does Alexa know you're here talkin' to old Stanley, or does she think you're workin' late tonight? I don't know what that beautiful Yank ever saw in you, but I sure as hell would rather be with her than with me. Unless you're thinkin' of changin' sides, Coral. I heard you were gettin' soft. But you start winkin' at me, Miss Sally, and I'll have your head mounted on the wall by sunrise! Got it, young lady?"

I slid off the stool and onto the floor, doubled up, my eyes tearing up from laughter.

But as liberating as the banter was, I realized I still hadn't called Alexa at home. I'd been married now for twelve years, after first meeting her in the States. More beautiful than ever, she had adapted very well to a new country, a Brit constable for a husband, and me spending a lot of my off-duty time at poker tables around the country. But lying on a pub floor, on a weeknight after work—stone cold sober, no less—was probably not what she wanted to hear about.

"All I did was come in for a quick one, and look what happens," I said as I clambered back onto the stool. I scanned the room. It was relatively empty. Many of the diners were having the pub's famous fish and chips, and others were playing darts. "It's good to see you though, old friend."

"Okay then, boy, here's your drink," he said, setting the glass in front of me. "Better late than never, eh?"

By way of an answer, I downed the gin.

"Incidentally, Scotty, let your mates in the office know I'm givin' you uniformed lot half-off all drinks on Thursdays."

I nodded, still concentrating on my drink.

"I have to serve real customers now, but I expect a large tip before your ugly arse leaves my stool."

"I'm leaving now, old man," I replied, savoring the last ounce of the fine mix of Tanqueray gin, tonic, and lime. "I may bring the kids and Alexa in this weekend, if she's still with me, so watch yourself. My boys are almost double digit in age—quite old enough to rough you up if you rile them. Or me."

Keeler stopped, looked back, and smiled. "Who said they were your kids, boy? I met Alexa about the same time you did, don't you know." And with that, the 53-year-old bartender let out a booming "HAH!" and sauntered into the kitchen.

As I left, I realized that good friends, along with family, are what kept us all in good graces and good cheer. I would go home, hug Alexa and play with the kids. And for me, all would be right in the world for this night. Graham was strong and would recover, God willing. But as my headache vanished, I remembered that Graham's attacker was still out there. May he sleep well while he still could.

Chapter 20

After Mark left, I was too distraught to sleep. I wouldn't even try. If I hadn't just talked to Adam, I would have called him again, but I didn't want to wake him. And Erik, for some reason, wasn't an option. I leaned against my closed door, going over the events since MacMillan was found. John's death may or may not be linked to anything—it could have been a teenaged meeting that had ended as an argument and accidental death. Still, it seemed suspicious, for his body had been found in the wood. And the wood had also been the backdrop to MacMillan's and Graham's assaults. That they were both attacks, I was now certain. Their wounds matched John's. And Enrico's, I suddenly realized. I grabbed the doorknob to keep from sinking to the floor. All four victims—murder and assault—had identical head wounds. How common was that? I groped for the bed, unsure of my legs, and flopped on top of the duvet. Four victims, four head wounds, four crimes in the same area—the wood and church. Had this something to do with the Devil's stone custom, or was it personal, directed originally toward one person but enlarged as others came too close to discovering the perpetrator?

I grabbed my notebook and a pen and sat cross-legged on the bed, ignoring the rain pelting the windowpane, the lightning jumping from cloud to cloud. I listed the villagers' names in a vertical column on the left side of the page, then jotted down possible motives for either the murders or attacks opposite each name. Some I left blank due to lack of information. Some I had only a word or two. After a head-busting hour of work, I abandoned the list, determined to fill it in completely before Graham was out of hospital.

For the remainder of the night I tried to find out more about Enrico. I surprised the two constables when I walked into the incident room around three o'clock that morning. Clearly they weren't expecting anyone; Simcock was attending John's postmortem and other detectives such as Mark and I should have been in bed. I got myself a cup of tea, bid them good morning, and settled down at a computer. As the monitor screen woke up I wondered how the constables guarding the scenes were getting on. It was a bitter morning, seemingly colder due to the moisture hanging in the air. A raw wind carried the chill of rain-soaked earth. I had wrapped my scarf more tightly around my neck and hunched my shoulders against the frosty assault. The warmth of the incident room seemed practically tropical by contrast.

HORNS OF A DILEMMA

Every avenue I pursued in my search for Enrico's past ended in frustration. He not only had never attended school, legally owned a car, paid taxes or voted in an election, but he also had never been born. I stared at the computer screen as each inquiry crashed to an end. It was worse than simply unable to attain information; it was the alarm that went off in my head—there was no such person as Enrico Thomas! Was Mark correct with his assumption that Enrico was a terrorist, alive only for these three months so he could fulfill some mission? Could a criminal, as I had originally classified Enrico, cover his identity? What if he was a computer whiz, able to hack into governmental sites and delete his information? I trembled, aware again of the consequences such a criminal could cause. But for what purpose? What crime would require the erasure of his past?

I squelched the desire to visit Graham, needing to be near him, even if he wasn't able to talk, to quell my rising panic. So I rang up the hospital and inquired as to his condition. No change, the unemotional voice told me. I thanked her and rang off.

It was now nearly half past five. I would be meeting Mark for breakfast in three and a half hours. So I had another cup of tea and for two hours pursued David Willett via computer. Mark would be happy to learn that I was looking at his favorite suspect. No previous convictions, not as much as a complaint from a neighbor about a noisy party. He'd had several parking tickets throughout the years, but had paid them promptly. His property was well kept, he didn't mistreat animals—so there were no grievances lodged with the appropriate local councils. There was a ten-year-old question of his involvement in an arson case, but it had been dropped. Other than that, David Willett appeared to be squeaky clean. So at half past seven I logged off the computer, went back to my room, showered and dressed, and pondered the problem of Enrico's mobile phone.

If he had been a terrorist, surely he would have used it to communicate with members of his gang. How else would they know dates, times and other information such as target schedules and personnel? Yet there were no records of him ever having used the phone. I sank back in my chair, envisioning Enrico's house. There had been a BT phonebook in the front room. Was that a clue? If so, what type? If Enrico hadn't made calls on his mobile, why even have a phone book? For use at a phone box? But he'd run the risk of being seen by people, perhaps of being overheard. The calls would certainly be in the phone company's log, providing a clue to the police. It didn't make sense. Why have a mobile if you didn't use it?

The same thing applied to his car—no record of purchase or hire. It could have been a friend's, loaned to Enrico, perhaps, until the car he ordered arrived. But Enrico's death had been splashed across every newspaper in the Kingdom, been broadcast on television and radio newscasts. Surely the friend would have heard of it and come to claim his car. Unless the friend was out of town. Which might explain the loan of the car in the first place. 'You can use my car till you get yours. I'll be in

Holland on business for a fortnight.' But there was a flaw to that reasoning, too. Enrico had been in the village for two months; he had had the car for that entire time. Would he have a friend who would take such a lengthy trip? Maybe the friend had a second car that he was using.

I abandoned the puzzles and staggered downstairs to meet Mark.

He was looking brighter than I felt when I found him in the pub's dining area Friday morning. He stood up when I came over to the table, pulled out my chair for me, and presented me with a bright red oak leaf. "No flowers are blooming yet," he said as he sat down.

"So you stole this."

"I would've stolen a flower if I could've found one."

"Then let's be thankful some irate villager didn't catch you pilfering her garden."

"The forest will never miss a leaf. Anyway, they can't be valuable—you swept some outside last evening in the incident room."

"What's one woman's trash..."

"I know."

We stared at each other, aware we were babbling, trying to make the morning seem normal, forcing ourselves to be brave and cheery. But we knew it was a façade, so we dropped the chatter and picked up the menus. He waited while I scanned the page, though I was so upset about Graham that I didn't really care to eat. Perhaps sensing this, Mark suggested toast, fruit and coffee. "Guaranteed to give you a shot of energy and calm your stomach," was how he phrased it. I thanked him and gave the waitress my order. Seemingly satisfied with my food choice, me, and his morning so far, he told me he'd been to the millstone site already. "I've got to do something, Bren. I can't just sit about, hoping Graham will get better and be able to give us a lead on his assailant. I wanted to check for myself, to see if that was a plausible route."

I asked if he'd been able to see the forest path from there.

"Not so as you'd notice." He stared at me, looking suddenly very boyish in his maroon-color Aran knit. His hair was still damp, either from his shower or from his walk through the wood. "Green Acre Road looks closer on the ordinance map than it actually is in the village. The hill is a bit too high to afford a view. Then, there's the group of millstones dumped near the hill's crest."

"Should cut off a good portion of the line of sight close to those."

"They do. I drove down the road a bit, looked at the wood from my car and then got out and walked up the hill a bit. Still couldn't determine there was a walking trail there."

"Shouldn't think the casual tourist driving along would be searching for the trail, then."

"It's something a rambler or a villager would know about. But, to make sure, I left the car there and ran a bit down the road in both directions. Couldn't see a thing—and you'd distinguish less at night, when you can't see into the trees. The wood is incredibly dense along that bit. The trail can't

HORNS OF A DILEMMA

be seen."

"So Graham's attacker doesn't necessarily have to know about the proximity of the trail to the millstones, then."

"He could have wandered up from the pub, as we said last night, or just about from anywhere—other side of the church after he's been poking about in the church yard, for instance—good touristy activity—and come up behind Graham. It doesn't really mean a thing, this experiment this morning."

But it kept your mind occupied, I wanted to say. I saluted him with my cup of tea. "You get high marks from me, though, getting out so early and seeing to that. At least we know that Gra—" I stopped, suddenly afraid to say his name, as though it would jinx his recovery. I took a sip of tea, wanting to numb my mind. But my common sense whispered that he was all right. Simcock would have rung us up if he'd received bad news.

Mark's plate of eggs, ham, grilled tomatoes and fried bread, and my fruit and toast were set before us and we ate nearly half of it before Mark said, "I'm glad I could do something that made up for last night, Bren."

I put down my spoon, afraid of what he was going to say next.

"I mean, I always seem to be getting off on the wrong foot with you. First in the academy, then in our first few cases together. Then last night before dinner. I'd like to try again, if you'll let me."

I glanced out of the window, at the church tower and the rosy hue tinting its upper-most stones. Another day, perhaps another beginning in our relationship. But I suddenly heard Adam's voice in my ear, felt a warmth flood my body, grabbed his words and locked them in my heart. When I looked back at Mark, I knew it was hopeless and told him so. "I'm sorry, Mark. It's not just the timing—Graham and MacMillan in hospital, the two murders. It's us. No matter what our best intensions are, we always quarrel. We can't get through one meal without one of us misreading the other and exploding."

"Don't you think we could—?"

"No. We're just not suited for anything more than being coworkers," I said rather too quickly. I was tired from working the case on my nerves, fearful for Graham and MacMillan. Mark either didn't notice or put it down to my agitation. "I'm sorry. I like you—as a colleague. But I don't want to continue the dating game. I'm tired of trying and not having things turn out well."

His fingers gripped his teacup, holding it as a drowning man clings to a life preserver. I glanced toward the bar where the waitress laughed suddenly at a waiter's quip. They seemed as though they got along. Why couldn't Mark and I? He said, "But later on, Bren. We could try again. A real date. Without the pressure of work spoiling the evening. We don't always work cases through dinner."

I shook my head. "I'm sorry, Mark. It's not just our cases right now or the fact that I can't focus on anything else, though I feel like I'm going to crumble or be dragged to Bedlam if something else happens. I like you, Mark. I honestly do. But not as a person should a potential date. There's something incompatible about us. No matter how we try to get along, we fight. I'm tired of it. And if we continue trying, with the same results, I'm afraid I'll end up hating you." *Besides*, I thought, averting my eyes from Mark's face, *I want to focus on Adam.*

His eyes widened briefly, quickly, as though he hadn't been expecting that answer. He said of course he understood, that he'd be a first-class berk if he didn't, and stared at his teacup.

We finished our breakfast talking about our chances of locating anything significant at the crime scenes in the wood and about Simcock's soft work approach, but drove to the incident room in complete, strained silence.

Chapter 21

Simcock greeted us in the fashion of an uncle welcoming his favorite niece and nephew. He asked if we were rested, then informed us that he had had calls early this morning from the doctors. "Both DCI Graham and WPC MacMillan are in comas." He paused as I gasped and Mark swore. I don't remember much except that I grabbed Mark's hand, needing something to hold on to.

Simcock's voice droned from some nebulous direction. Words such as 'lacerations...head contusion...bleeding...stitches' seeped into my consciousness. All I could hear was the sound of the oxygen flowing from the respirator in Graham's hospital room, the squeak of wheels from trolleys as they rolled down the white lino hallways. Moments later, from some far-off existence, the haze dissipated and Simcock stood before me. He was saying that MacMillan would probably be up tomorrow, but Graham had suffered the greater trauma to his head and therefore the doctors didn't expect him to regain consciousness for several days. I must have looked anxious, for Simcock said, "It looks grave, but he's being monitored constantly. He'll pull through—don't worry." No doubt he added that last bit to assure us, to help take our minds from Graham's recovery to our immediate job of work. I nodded, not much more relieved with those words than I had been seeing Graham last night at hospital. Now that Simcock had briefed us about our cohorts' conditions, he told us he'd held an early morning briefing.

"But, sir," I stuttered, partially shocked because Mark or I usually conducted the briefings and partially because neither I nor Mark had been asked to attend. "Why weren't we—?"

"Because," Simcock interrupted, "I meant what I said last night, that I didn't want to see either of your faces before ten o'clock this morning. And, despite the fact that it's..." He consulted his watch, which had just gone quarter to ten. "...fifteen minutes earlier than you should be here, and you're already disobeying my order." His face showed no sign of amusement, but his voice suggested otherwise. His eyes held mine for a moment before he added, "Besides being up half the night, you were dealing with the stress of the boy's murder and with the attacks on our two officers. I don't want either of you going ill on me. We're thin on the ground already, and besides, you're both damned good coppers. You'll be hard to replace. Now. I've the Home Office pathologist and biologist at John Granger's scene. They got here at first light, along with the Scientific Officers, photographer and so on. Jeffries is already on the scene, so we're well under way. You will be pleased to know, no doubt, that we found what we believe is the murder weapon used on Enrico, if not on John. A constable found it in a tree."

"A *tree?*"

"Unusual, isn't it? Behind the vicarage, bordering the wood. Who would think to look for something like that above ground?"

I said something like it was a good thing the crowbar hadn't fallen on the constable's head.

"I agree. We'd be dealing with another officer in hospital. Clever spot, that. Even if it eventually fell, it won't really matter if it's wiped clean. We're testing it for prints and DNA traces. We won't find any, but it's somewhere to start."

I murmured that it was, then said that we had eleven of the twelve crowbars accounted for. "Do you think the murderer hid that after attacking Enrico Wednesday night, then thought he needed to do another murder, so he stole another one from the church hall? I can't see it, sir, because if he had the crowbar and could retrieve it, why not use it again on John? Isn't the murderer taking a bigger chance breaking into the church hall than he would be getting the crowbar from the tree?"

"Unless someone was at home at the time, or the murderer was afraid of attracting attention. The tree's only a few dozen yards from the back of the house."

"It'd take a lot of nerve to go back for the crowbar. He'd be afraid a family member would see him."

"It makes more sense to break into a deserted church to get another one. Besides, Taylor, we don't know if another crowbar was used. Perhaps *two* were misplaced, as Lloyd keeps insisting happens frequently in the village. And we don't know when the crowbar was placed in the tree. It could have been immediately after Enrico's murder or it could have been much later."

"After John was killed," I murmured, afraid to speak the words aloud.

"Unfortunately, yes. It's a damned chilling thought. There's someone in this village who's put a police chief-inspector in a coma and killed two grown men, all essentially with his bare hands."

"We've four people with gashes and skull fractures—all due to one dangerous person."

"One person dealing out violence on a level this village has never seen. This isn't a crime of passion, where someone gets fed up with a neighbor's loud music. It's pure, undiluted violence laced with hatred or evil. And as such, it scares the hell out of me."

I nodded, unable to speak, envisioning the two dead bodies and Graham in his hospital bed. A crowbar may have been the agent, but violence had guided the attacks. And that, as Simcock has said, was terrifying.

HORNS OF A DILEMMA

Simcock said, "We have to concentrate on one person—someone plotting two murders, keeping the crowbar after he kills Enrico with it, using it on John, perhaps bashing MacMillan and Graham with it, then hiding it in the tree..." He rubbed the back of his head, as though he had a headache. It wasn't a pleasant situation to envision, but we had to. "But we don't know. It doesn't really make any difference right now. We have a crowbar that is undoubtedly a murder weapon—why else hide it, and in a *tree*, for God's sake! We go with that and test it."

"Are you still trying to locate Graham's sister?" I said, abruptly changing the subject.

"Her neighbor tells us she and her family are in Switzerland, tramping about in the Alps. We don't know where, though we've begun an inquiry through the airlines and passport control. We'll find her eventually. I just hope it's not too late."

A phone rang somewhere in the room, abruptly cutting into Simcock's comments. He glanced at his watch, said something about needing to get on with the day, and told us several detectives from the Greater Manchester constabulary were going to be arriving to work the scenes in the wood. "The Chief Constable agreed we needed the limited mutual aid, so that will be a help. I've asked WPC Lynch to take over in that quarter, show the lads to the various scenes. Didn't want to steer them wrong."

I agreed that John Granger's scene no doubt looked very much the same as Graham's, but there could be differences.

"Didn't want to muck up things from the start. I've asked her to show them what to do, then report back to me when they're on to something. And as for you two, I'd like you to work on Enrico's death. You know the details and have already questioned some of the villagers. I don't want to assign that to someone else who'd be not only wasting his time but also doing double work by going over the same ground. You alright with that? Right." He nodded, evidently relieved that the machine of police investigation was rolling.

Simcock got to his feet and turned to me. I felt positively dwarfed next to him. He buttoned up his coat and said, "I'm going back to the office. There are a few things I need to do there before the day's much older. I'll have a briefing somewhat later to inform everyone about John Granger's postmortem examination results. I know you're anxious about Graham, Taylor, but right now I need you to work on Enrico's case, since you've told me you're already into that."

"I'd like to question some of his neighbors, see if anyone knows anything."

"Certainly. You can get me on my mobile if you need me. I know you've got the number. I'll be back when I can. Thanks." He was out of the door before I could reply. All I could think of just then was Graham's sister rushing to Graham's bedside as he breathed his last.

The Dutton family—Noel, Rita and daughter Toni—lived on the other side of Enrico's house. Graham and I had questioned his other neighbor, Tad Mills, yesterday. That's when we had discovered David Willett lurking in Tad's kitchen. Feeling we had nothing immediate to gain from talking again to Tad, Mark and I drove over to the Duttons and were rather surprised to find Mrs. Dutton's mother. She seated us in the front parlor, offered us coffee, and settled herself opposite us in a chrome-and-leather chair that would have looked at home in a bachelor's flat.

Plump and with graying hair, Frances Cresswell epitomized the picture of the stay-at-home mother. But in her case, she was the mother-in-law. She moved a dusting rag out of the way, propped her feet up on the upholstered ottoman and asked what she could do for us. *So much more mannered*, I thought, *than asking me what I wanted*.

I told her we were investigating Enrico Thomas' murder and asked if she had heard anything Wednesday that might suggest he had quarreled with someone. "Or seen something," I added. "Were you at the stone turning Wednesday?"

"I was not," she said emphatically, crossing her arms across her ample bosom.

"Don't you like the custom?"

"It's fine for those who like such things."

"And you don't."

"Don't particularly like it or dislike it. It was going on way long before I came to live here, and it'll see me out. I'm just not one for having more connections with the devil than I can help. Which means," she said before I could ask, "the everyday cruelty I come in contact with and see on the telly. And no, I don't hold with Halloween, either. Too much emphasis on devils and evil ghosts and such. Downright scary. Oughtn't to be allowed. It wouldn't be, if I had any say-so. I'd get us back to God-centered lives. Films and books and such have made all this Satan stuff too exciting. It's bad for us."

Mark asked, "Did you attend the Ash Wednesday service at the church?"

"I did attend a service, yes, but it was in Bakewell."

"Is that a different denomination than St. Michael's? Is that why you didn't attend service here in Hollingthorpe?"

"I happened to be in Bakewell. That's the only reason, sir. I had been visiting a friend, stayed for tea, and we went to the service. I knew I couldn't make it back here in time for service, so we went there, to her church. Anything wrong with that?"

"So you didn't hear any quarrel that day, anything involving Enrico, then?"

"I'm not a nosey neighbor, sir. I don't listen at the walls or make a note of his company."

"He had visitors, had he? I understood he was a private person."

"He was a private person, yes. And of course he had some people over.

Not many and not often. But there were a few people who came over. He just liked his privacy, and I didn't intrude on that. I respected that."

Mark glanced at me, as though to say it would have helped our case if Frances had been a neighbor who peeked between closed curtains. I said, "Are you home most of the time, Mrs. Cresswell? I mean, do you usually see or hear Enrico during the day? I thought perhaps, if you were, you would know—"

"Look, miss. I appreciate your problem with sorting through his murder, but I'll tell you straight out that I'm gone weekday afternoons and some evenings. I work in the village, at the tearoom. As a waitress and cashier. So of course I'm at home here in the mornings. I don't leave till half past eleven."

"Would that be The Rose Petal?" I asked, amazed I remembered the name of the tearoom.

"It would. You been in? No, I don't think so," she said, chewing on the tip of her fingernail. "I would've seen you and remembered."

"You get so few visitors that you can recall every patron?"

"I've a good memory for faces," she said, straightening herself in her chair. "Besides, Enrico's death only happened Wednesday evening. Little more than twenty-four hours ago. You wouldn't have been there Wednesday evening, and I know you weren't there yesterday. I was watching people extra careful when they came in to see if someone suspicious happened in. I like to help the police when I can."

I thanked her and was reminded of the phrase 'helping the police'—a tongue-in-cheek statement that actually meant the speaker had been interrogated by officers.

"My husband was in the job, you know," she continued. "In the Metropolitan police. When he died four years ago, I came up here to live with my daughter and her family. I didn't want to..." Her voice slowed and softened, as though she was remembering a difficult decision to move from London. She clasped her hands, put them in her lap, and said more energetically, "But it was best all around. You know—me getting on in years, my daughter Rita having to work and not being able to look after the house as well as she'd like. And I can see Toni, my granddaughter, off to school of a morning. Noel doesn't mind, either. Noel—that's Rita's husband. He was the one who suggested I come up here, actually. It's worked out real well for all of us."

"And Noel...he works, I take it." I looked up from my note taking to glance around the room. There were no 'Chef of the Year' plaques, no posters of concert gigs. Nothing to suggest Noel Dutton's occupation. Just a room of modern furniture and black-and-white photos of people. All very monochromatic, soulless and clean.

"He works, yes. As does my daughter, Rita. They own the hair salon in the village. They're both hair stylists. They trained in London." She threw out the last remark with an unmistakable tone of pride. "Weekends I'm cashier in the salon. Oh, I don't get paid, mind you. It's my bit to help out with the household expenses. They wanted to pay me, but I wouldn't hear of it. I keep my waitressing tips from the tearoom, but my wage goes into the household account. It's hard enough making ends meet without the burden of another adult in your house."

Mark said that was very commendable, that he didn't know many people who would relinquish their earnings to the general bank account.

Frances looked at him, perhaps assessing if he were sincere. "I keep a bit for myself, sir, as I said, for mad money. If I want to take a trip or get myself something. But I don't miss the wages. I've a good roof over my head, a warm bed, three meals a day, and a family who loves me. If I've a mind to potter about in the garden, Rita's delighted to let me exercise my green thumb. So I don't miss my garden back home, which helps save my sanity and brightens up our home. Can't ask for much else from life. Besides, I like to keep busy. I need it. Keeps my mind from wandering back to my husband." She bit her bottom lip and gazed down at her hands. I wondered if he had died in the line of duty and was suddenly consumed with the image of Graham in his hospital bed.

I stood up quickly, startling Mrs. Cresswell. Her foot jerked, knocking the dust rag to the floor. She blinked, started to say something, then struggled to her feet and hurried to open the door for us.

The sky had changed to a dim blue, but it was enough. I stood in a patch of weak sunshine and thanked her for her time before we left to find the adult part of her loving family.

HORNS OF A DILEMMA

Chapter 22

The front window of Duttons' hair salon displayed a dozen plush, cuddly white rabbits and as many fuzzy yellow toy chicks sitting on or beside an assortment of hair and skin products. Several yellow and pink wicker baskets sat like sentries along the back of the window, their enthusiastic green and purple cellulose grass nearly spilling out of their woven confines, shimmering in the morning sun. Salon gift coupons, cans of hair spray, tubes of liquid foundation, cases of eye shadow, and bottles of shampoo—'not tested on animals'— nestled among these grassy mounds. Subtle marketing, even if it was a bit early for Easter.

Harry Willett had just left the shop when Mark and I got out of our car. Mark said something about not wanting a repeat of yesterday's bell episode, and I silently agreed with him, but hurried across the street, wanting to get on with our investigation.

Harry was humming to himself, waving to others on the street and repeatedly pressing his hand against his jeans pocket and peering inside. When I had introduced myself and Mark to the woman standing in the open shop doorway, I commented on Harry's behavior.

"He's a funny one, he is," said Rita Dutton. She was slightly plump, which would probably turn to significant overweight in her later years, and medium height. Her short hair, styled in a trendy cut, was a startlingly red hue that could come only from a bottle. She seemed to be a mass of red and silver, for her apron and slacks were red and she wore a mass of silver dangle bracelets. I wondered how she could work with so many rings on her fingers. Rita watched Harry pat his pocket closed and said, "I've lost count of the things he's stolen from us."

"Money, you mean?" Mark said.

"No, honey. Lord love you." Rita eyed Mark's tall figure before adding, "Things. From our shop. He's taken a comb this time."

We turned to watch Harry as he exploded in laughter and shoved his hand into his pocket.

Rita said, "They're for our customers. We keep them at the register so people can take one when they pay their bill. It's not much, but it shows people we appreciate their business."

"Does Harry always help himself? Does he confine himself to combs?"

Rita snorted. "Don't I wish. Lord, no. Sometimes we've small tubes of hand lotion, sometimes small samples of eyeliner or shampoo. Sometimes it's something a bit more pricey, like pocket diaries or pens. Harry doesn't mind what it is, as long as he grabs what he can. I suppose he thinks he's getting away with something."

"Well, isn't he?"

"Yes, I guess he is, since you put it like that, hon. Noel and I don't get too upset. Noel's my husband. We work together. Anyway, we don't usually get too upset with Harry's pilfering, but once he stole a pair of scissors. Expensive, they were. My favorite pair."

"It would be. Hard luck."

"And another time he took a customer's walking cane. Proper cane, it was. One of those old Victorian things with a carved ivory head. Ooh, heavy it was, too! I believe it had an iron tip. Anyway, we're used to Harry's popping in and grabbing things. Like I said, Noel and I don't usually mind, but when he takes expensive items—"

"Did you or the customer get your things back?" Mark asked. "I suppose you complained to his sister, Page."

Rita dug into her pocket and withdrew a packet of cigarettes. After she'd lit one and taken a puff, she said, "Wouldn't do no good, honey. We'd be ringing her up constantly, complaining that he'd taken another comb or tube of hair gel. We don't like it, but we'd rather chalk it up to business expenses and keep on good terms with Page than to cry over a few missing items."

Harry started mumbling and placed his hands over his ears. He evidently turned off his hearing aids again, for he began chanting "You can't hear me, you can't hear me...." He laughed, pulled the comb from his pocket, and held it over his head. He zigzagged down the street, waving the comb at everyone he passed until he stopped abruptly at the launderette. Something fascinated him, evidently, for he remained there, staring into the window.

I asked Rita if she or Noel had seen anything suggestive at the stone turning.

She took another drag on her cigarette, rolled the smoke around on her tongue and exhaled slowly, as though she hadn't a shop-full of customers or her smoking was the most important thing right now. Finally, she said, "By that you mean the murderer, I suppose. Well, no. We didn't."

"You can speak for your husband?"

"Yes. We talked about the evening when we got home. We would've discussed something so obviously odd as a bloke skulking about the tombstones."

"Enrico wasn't killed in the graveyard," Mark said, tiring of the conversation.

"That's as may be," Rita said, "but we didn't see anything odd. Just the same crowd as any other year. The same stone turning, the same tea afterward. Nothing varied from last year. Nothing even suggesting murder."

"You and your husband were present for the entire activity?"

"Yes. For the turning, the service and tea. Noel participated in the turning—he likes a bit of rough fun. And we went to the service after."

HORNS OF A DILEMMA

"Your mother go with you?"

"She wasn't home. She'd gone to a friend's house and didn't get home until later. But our daughter, Toni, was present. She watched the turning and went with us to the service and the tea. I doubt if she saw anything that would help you. She would have said something to me if she had. But ask her, if you've a mind to."

"When will she be home?"

Rita told me and added, "But she comes straight here after school."

"Why is that? Are you afraid for her to be home by herself?"

Rita took another puff on her cigarette before replying. "No, Lord love you. She's a cashier here. Works after school, weekends and summer holidays. I wouldn't allow her to have the job, of course, if her grades failed. But she's a superb student. Never had any problems in any subject." She seemed to beam, a proud parent expounding on her child. I wondered briefly if Toni knew how proud her mother was of her, wondered what it felt like to garner her mother's adoration. My brother and sister knew; they had grown up with it, beginning their musical careers early and winning my parents' approval and culling their favoritism. But I had chosen police work, something that took no talent, according to them, and as such reaped no praise. Mine was just an ordinary job, done by hundreds of people, whereas an outstanding concert pianist and operatic singer were countable on one hand. They were name making, unique. I was one of a team and had gone through schooling to become who I was. Their careers were spun from talent.

I shooed my parents' faces to the back of my mind and asked Rita about her salon.

She told us that they were just beginning their tenth year, having bought the salon from a stylist who wanted to retire. Many of their customers had come to them that way, but they had built up the business through superior products, superb haircuts, friendly service and by adding the skin care line. "It was a natural outgrowth," Rita said, flicking the cigarette ashes onto the pavement. "People want to look good. The hair cut or color is one part of it."

"And the other part?"

"Skin care and make up. We match the cosmetics to each client—skin, hair and eye color. So many women buy their lipstick and foundation at Woolies or Marks and Sparks. At best they'll come away with something passable in the hue that compliments them; at worse they'll get some shade that they love or that used to look fine on them twenty years ago before their skin sallowed or reddened. Our cosmetics are color coded to our hair tints."

I said it sounded mistake proof.

Rita smiled, perhaps glad I appeared impressed. "We've a licensed cosmologist in the shop. She works closely with the customers who want our total package."

It sounded like an advert I might have seen on the telly.

Mark asked if Enrico had been a customer.

Rita threw her cigarette onto the ground and stepped on it. "No. Perhaps if he'd lived longer..." She shoved her hands into the pockets of her slacks. "He was here for such a short time. Two months, wasn't it? We never saw him in the shop. Perhaps he patronized a barber or some hair salon in Buxton. All I know is that he wasn't a client. I'm sorry to hear he's dead. Seemed like a nice fellow."

"So you didn't invite him over for tea or anything, he being a neighbor of yours."

"No. Never got around to it. Well," she said, glancing up at Mark, "you don't think someone's going to get killed, do you? Or so soon after moving in. I mean, two months! He'd hardly unpacked and now he's dead. I would've got around to asking him over but..." She shrugged, as if to say it wasn't her fault.

"And then to hear about John," Rita continued. "Lord love us, was that a shock! I mean, who would've thought we'd have another death. And the next day! It's a real blow. I'm sorry for the Grangers. Nobody likes to think of losing a child, and John was such a bright lad. My Toni will take it hard when she hears."

"Particular mate of his, was she?" Mark asked.

The emphatic ringing of a phone inside the shop was followed by a shout. Rita called back, saying she was busy with the coppers. The voice yelled that he was busy applying color. Rita apologized to us and said she'd have to get the phone. Mark said he was going to watch Harry for a few more minutes, and I followed Rita into the shop, waiting while she took the call.

The shop was nothing exceptional, harboring the expected salon equipment. But a portion of the shop was obviously designated as the cosmetics corner, for not only did a beautician hold court behind a table crammed with make-up mirror, pots and tubes of cosmetics and skin cleanser, but there were also discrete signs proclaiming product ingredients and prices. The area was tastefully done up in understated lilac and green, a comforting change from Rita's dramatic red.

When she'd taken the call, she again apologized for the interruption and introduced us to the man standing at a salon chair. He was dark and short, with biceps the size of tree stumps and a bum not much bigger than my fist. The woman in the chair had a head full of aluminum foil strips, rather like an exuberant television aerial, and laughed at the man's remarks. He brushed a strand of hair with the purplish hair product and nodded to us.

"That's Noel," Rita said, leaning against the counter. "My old man. He does most of the hair coloring and I tend to do most of the cuts. We didn't plan it, but we've gradually discovered our strong points. That was Mrs. Smith, Noel," Rita called to her husband.

Noel looked up. "Oh, yes? She's my next appointment."

"No, she isn't. She can't make it. Something about having forgotten about her dentist."

Noel frowned, obviously disgruntled, but leaned forward, smiling at the woman with the foiled head. "All the more time for you, Mrs. Deaver."

The woman tittered and flushed, perhaps pleased with Noel's attention.

"About Toni," I said, returning Rita to the subject.

"Oh, right, hon. Well, I wouldn't say they were particularly close, but they went to school together. And of course, growing up in the village...well, it'll be a shock, there's no doubt. As it will be to everyone at his school."

"Has Toni made plans for when she leaves school?"

"She's going to university. She wants to teach. That's why she works after school and such. To save her money for university. She was working part time in the health club Page Hanley—that's Harry's sister, do you know?—works at."

At the name of David Willet's sister, I mentally said a prayer that Mark wasn't here.

Rita gushed on. "Page recommended her for the job, but it was too far from home, the drive was too long, and Toni didn't like the atmosphere of perfect-body and egos to match. I know David slightly from his visits to see Page. Seems a nice man. He's offered to help Toni any way he can, advising her on what university courses to take, maybe helping her get a job. Nice chap."

I remarked that it was fortunate that Page had a brother whom she was close to.

Rita agreed, mentioned that she was an only child and always envied people with siblings. "Noel, now," she said, smiling at her husband, "comes from a larger family. Four brothers. Haven't you, dear?"

"What's that?" Noel put down the highlighter brush and pealed off his latex gloves. At that moment, when his hands were exposed, I saw it —the capital letters A C A B tattooed across the four knuckles of his right hand. 'All Cops Are Bastards,' I mentally filled in the meaning. A classic prison tattoo. A bit milder than some, but strong in their statement and union with other inmates. A silent declaration of time behind bars and sentiments.

I would have ignored the tattoo but, perhaps agitated by Graham's attack, I couldn't let it slide. Besides, nothing is trivial in a murder investigation. I asked Noel where he got the tattoo.

As though seeing it for the first time, Noel glanced at his knuckles, held up his fist so the letters angled toward me, and said, "Oh, this? In prison, where else? I'd have thought you, being an old copper yourself, would know."

"I know," I said, exhaling heavily.

"Yeh, well, I've done my time. Two years. I'm not ashamed of my past. I did wrong and I paid for it, but it's behind me now. I've been out for five and been straight ever since. Haven't I, luv?" He cocked his eyebrow and looked at Rita, who smiled and pursed her lips.

"What were you in for?"

"Don't see what it has to do with your current case, luv. You've been asking around about Enrico. And now John. What's my little crime, committed seven years ago, have to do with these two deaths?"

"I can find out. Easiest thing in the world. But I'd appreciate your cooperation."

"Well, find out, then." Noel turned toward me and folded his arms across his chest, making sure the tattooed knuckles were still visible. "I'm innocent—of everything. I've done my time, and I haven't done anything illegal since. Got it?" He snorted, glaring at me, and turned back to his customer.

"I always thought," his customer said, patting Noel's hand, "that Always Carry A Bible seems such a fine sentiment for a man to have tattooed on his knuckles. So many tattoos are vulgar or have such vicious meanings. But you've taken your love of religion one step further and shown it to everyone who happens to look."

"I've always got my personal philosophy in the open," Noel said, loud enough for me to hear. "It's plain as a pikestaff for me to see and keep it in mind."

I turned to leave. Mark and I had a lot more work to accomplish this morning.

Noel glanced at me, smirked and said to the woman, "I try as hard as I can to live a good life, Mrs. Deaver. I've never made a secret of my past or my prison sentence, have I?"

"No indeed, Noel. And that's another reason why I like you. You're so forthright with everything."

"It's getting to where no one is innocent anymore."

"Too right," Mrs. Deaver said as she got up and moved to a hair drier. "I say if you've made a mistake and paid for it, that should be it. You're a free man, aren't you?"

"Not to hear the coppers speak. Are you fine like this?" He positioned the drier's hood over her head.

"Fine, dear, ta. Truer words, Noel, truer words. If I was to tell you what they did to my Tom…"

Her saga was lost beneath the roar of the hair drier. I thanked Rita, who was buffing her fingernails, and left the shop.

Harry Willett had wandered across the street and had begun singing again. Only this time it was his own version of "The Wraggle Taggle Gypsies," but it was rendered with feeling and in a remarkably fine voice. Mark was standing beneath a tree, watching Harry, but held the car door open for me.

"Daft as a mad hatter," he said, getting into my car. "He likes to pull his jacket up so it covers his head, and walk around like The Mummy."

"Can he see where he's going?"

"Not too well. He bumped into a shop window, then pulled his jacket back down, and started singing. Daft."

"At least he's harmless."

"So far." He voiced his frustrations—with Harry or the case or my

HORNS OF A DILEMMA

rejection of him—through the car, tearing away from the curb, and several minutes later we were drinking coffee in the incident room.

"You want to look up Noel's prison record?" I asked Mark after I'd told him of my chat with Noel. I'd looked around for Simcock but he wasn't back from Buxton yet. "Or should I do it?"

"I'll do it. Nothing would make me happier at the moment than to get something on that berk. 'Always Carry a Bible.' He's the last person who probably would do." He turned on the computer's monitor and started typing. "Where are you off to, then?" he asked, eyeing me.

"Oh, nowhere in particular. Thought I'd wander about, ask questions as I think of them."

"And wander over to hospital to see Graham. Fine. I'm not the one to tell you no, but I think you ought to concentrate on the case. The sooner we wrap this up, the better you'll feel about everything."

"I'll feel better," I said, taking a deep breath and glaring at Mark, "when Graham's out of danger. Don't lecture me, Mark. I'm in no mood for it. I've my mobile if you need me."

The High Street was swollen with pedestrians, cars and delivery vehicles that had double parked in front of shops to unload their shipments. A panel truck outside the teashop looked to have brought cartons of tea, sugar and digestives, for the shop door was propped open and the driver was loading his barrow with cardboard boxes. Tad Mills was opening the door of his house to a deliveryman who had several boxes stacked beside him. Art supplies, I guessed, seeing some sort of palette logo on one carton.

I turned down Well Hill Street and had driven for several minutes before I saw Page Hanley. Her car was on the verge and she was leaning against the side of her car, the rear door open. I parked behind her and walked up to her. She smiled and greeted me warmly.

"Flat tire?" I asked.

"Yes. I feel so stranded and so foolish. My mobile's at home and no one wants to stop."

I rang up the A.A. and then suggested we sit in my car until help arrived.

"Awfully nice of you," Page said, looking less anxious than she had on my arrival. "I can't believe I forgot the phone. I always carry it. But isn't that typical? It's never around when you need it."

"Like a copper," I said, smiling.

"But you were. And I'm very grateful."

"You going to be late for something—appointment or job? Should I ring up someone for you? Your brother?"

"I am on my way to work, yes, but you needn't ring. I left early so I could make a stop on the way. I'll still get there on time. And Harry's probably not home. Even if he were...well, he doesn't exactly care where I am. Just so long as I'm home for meal time. Thanks."

"Is David home? Do you need to talk to him?"

"I don't know where he is. He wasn't home when I left. But he could be visiting Tad. They're great mates. It doesn't matter. He knows I'll be at the club."

"And you work at..."

"A health club. Fancy name for a gym."

"Do you like it?"

"Yes. It keeps me fit and I enjoy helping others attain fitness. Our society's become too sedentary. We've got to do more physical activities."

"Computer games and the telly and films haven't exactly primed us for winning 100 meter races, no." I was conscious of my extra weight and felt myself reddening. I glanced at Page, who shifted her gaze from my thighs to her car. Silence settled between us.

"It must be super to help so many people," I said after a string of cars had passed. My car, a Fiat Punto, swayed in the tail wind of a passing lorry. "They must be very thankful to you, for giving them guidance and support."

Page abandoned her contemplation of something outside the car window and turned back to me. She was frowning, as though considering her reply. "I suppose they must do," she finally said, her words slow. "Some do, of course. They thank me at the end of each session, give me small gifts at holidays, but others..." Her upper teeth clamped down onto her lower lip.

I asked if she was having trouble at work.

"Not really. Nothing like harassment. But there are a few customers I try to avoid."

"Why?" I sat up, wondering if I needed to make a police report. "Someone been threatening you? Anyone hurt you?"

"No. I'm sorry if I gave that impression. I avoid them because they're rude and demanding."

"Who are they? Would I know them?"

"Richard Linnell—he owns the launderette in town—do you know him?"

I nodded, saying I understood he washed the clothing of the participants in the stone turning.

"And Richard's mate, King Roper. He's not a resident, thank God, but he's here often enough. *Too* often! He comes for the stone turning and sees Richard sporadically throughout the year. Personally, miss, I think King shows up at the turning simply to exhibit his muscles. He's a bit vain about his physique."

"Likes a bit of adoration, does he?"

"Likes it and feeds off it. Which is why I'm afraid of him."

"Afraid?" I stared open-mouthed, about to ask if Page had been attacked, when she said, "I saw him beat up someone in the car park."

I shook my head, trying to make sense of what I was hearing. "Did you ring 999? Was the person all right?"

Page lowered her head and clenched her fingers together. She sat quietly for several moments, then raised her head and said, "I'm ashamed to say I didn't, miss. I—I didn't like the victim, so I never reported it." She briefly closed her eyes, as though shutting out the image of the beating, then looked at me. Pain and embarrassment flooded her eyes. "I've seen people get beat up before. It was fairly common when I grew up—kids who didn't like other kids would lie in ambush and attack one lone kid. Always a gang beating up a single person. Did it give them a sense of superiority, six against one? Or was it some implied threat?" She chewed on her lower lip, perhaps reliving an event.

"But this attack, with King..." I prompted.

"Right. I've never seen such intensity, such raw hatred. It was vicious. Incredibly violent. I—that's why I'm afraid of him, miss. It wasn't a simple black eye he gave the bloke. There was no mistaking his anger. It was like he had all this hatred bottled up within him and it broke loose, uncontrollable. I was terrified!"

"Do you know the reason behind the attack?"

Page nodded. "It sounds inanely stupid now, months afterwards, but the bloke had been taunting King in the gym."

"Taunting? About what—his inability to do something?"

"No, miss. About his build, his muscles. The bloke accused King of taking steroids. King cursed him and shouted that he didn't need anything like that. He prided himself, as I told you, on his physique and his workouts. He had an ego from here to China, always boasting about what he could bench lift and such. I'd never want to cross him. Just one look at him, at his eyes and muscles, told you he'd be hell if he was ever crossed."

"So King was angry about the perceived insult."

"Never seen anyone so full of anger. I thought the bloke was going to be permanently injured or something, but he recovered. I feel bad now that I never rang up for help, or reported it, but..." She looked at me, wanting a pardon or some understanding.

I thought of Graham and MacMillan, victims of attacks, and wondered if their attacker would ever feel remorse or turn himself in.

Page said. "At least King's not a full member. And he's not at the club that often."

"Just when he visits Richard?"

"Yes, thank God. He gets into the club as a guest of Richard's. I can hardly wait until he leaves."

"Do you see him often?"

"Several times a year. But even that's too much!"

"Has this been going on for a while? I don't mean the assault on the club member—King's presence there."

"Couple of years, I know. Probably more. I try not to think of him. He's a hard person." She shuddered.

"What's he like—his personality, I mean."

"Egotistic, like I said. Thinks he's the only male in the room when he thinks I'm watching him. Likes to show off, talk loud." She paused briefly, then added, "I would have thought he'd have tattoos. You know, something else to call attention to his body."

I murmured that would have seemed likely.

Page said, "You can't help looking at a tattoo. You may not be interested, but you look to see what it is. A rose or anchor or something on his arm or chest. But he doesn't. At least, not where people would normally see it. And if it's hidden like it is, why have it? I mean, isn't that the purpose of a tattoo—to make a statement? Not much of a statement if others can't see it." She looked again out the window, clearly anxious for her flat tire to be changed.

I said, "So King has a tattoo? If it's not obvious, how'd you—"

"I see a lot of tattoos," she said, giving up her search for the A.A. van and looking again at me. "A lot of our clients work out in sleeveless Ts and briefs, so I see their biceps and thighs. But King's...well, not only was it more obscurely placed on his body, but I also had never seen anything like it."

I asked for a description of his tattoo.

Page replied instantly, needing no time to recall it. "It's on his upper thigh, close to his hip. He doesn't wear such immodest shorts—he wears longer ones that hit him mid-thigh. But they rode up a bit during one of his workouts."

"So..." I know I shouldn't have prodded her, but I was intrigued.

"It wasn't a picture or a word. They're the usual thing, you see. This was like modern art."

"What?"

She nodded, her words coming faster now that I obviously was interested. "The tattoo was like a design—well, the bit I saw, which was only a few inches. But it was black and red and cream colored, some geometric design or swirls that fit together into squares, like a mosaic. I was trying not to stare. But it was beautiful. I was fascinated by the design and astonished that such a brutal person would have something so delicate and lovely tattooed on him. And, like I said, covered up and in such an unlikely place as his upper thigh. I didn't know what to make of it."

I said that I'd never seen a tattoo like that either.

The A.A. van arrived and Page thanked me again for ringing them up. I left her with a promise I'd talk to her again, and drove to the hospital.

It wasn't the best time to come. I knew that when the constable met me at the door to Graham's room. Two doctors and a nurse were inside. I must have looked panic-stricken, for the constable assured me he had heard nothing to cause alarm. "They're checking him over," he said. "Seeing how he's doing and such." He gave me a reassuring smile, said he'd been told to keep everyone out just now, and suggested rather strongly that I wait to hear from Simcock. "He'll be notified of the Vic's condition, so don't worry." I nodded, glanced again at the closed door, and walked back to my car, not knowing if so many medical personnel were reassuring or alarming.

Mark had left the incident room by the time I returned. None of the constables knew where he was, which not only was sloppy police procedure but also irritated me. But he had left the information on Noel for me. The page was lying across the computer keyboard, my name written boldly and diagonally across the lower section of the page. I took off my jacket, hung my shoulder bag on the back of the chair, and picked up the paper. Noel had received a custodial sentence of two years for grievous bodily harm committed during a domestic violence attack.

Chapter 23

I know I sat there for a minute, staring at the paper, unable to move. Mark had typed in additional information, no doubt gleaned from the evidence given in court by a police detective. Noel had received several phone calls from concerned friends and neighbors during his incarceration, some of which were from King Roper. Mark had checked out the phone number. Noel's wife had never visited him, which wasn't surprising, since she had been the victim of his attack. I slowly sat down, laying the paper on the tabletop. They evidently had put all that behind them, for she had blown him a kiss in the salon.

Clearly Noel had procured his A C A B tattoo during this prison sentence, for he had no other record. Noel's tattoo was expected, then. But King's wasn't, for there was no police record of him having any tattoo—which was standard procedure every time a prisoner is detained. Numbers and descriptions of all tattoos were filed along with fingerprints, photos, and a DNA sample. So he must have got it after his release from prison. Fine, but where would he get something like that? It seemed a bit more complicated than the usual anchor and heart or skull. I was painfully aware of Graham's absence at that moment. Graham, who was more than my superior officer; he was the person I automatically turned to with my questions. But this time I couldn't turn to him. I had to rely on myself.

I hit the space bar on the computer keyboard, bringing the screen to life. I typed 'tattoo' into the search window and was instantly rewarded with hundreds of sites I could read if I had the time. Opening a few of the first listings produced nothing like what Page had described was mentioned. Finally, in increasing exasperation, I logged onto a New Zealand site. Photos, drawings and explanations of *ta moko* leapt onto the screen. This certainly looked like the thing Page had seen. The colors were correct; the design was a complicated pattern of swirls. I leaned forward and read about the Maori *moko*.

A half hour later I leaned back, completely fascinated and convinced King sported a Maori tattoo. But did King have Maori ancestry? According to the website site, the *moko*—the intricate tattoo design first cut into the skin with a chisel and the slash then dyed—was used as individual identification, ancestral declarations, tribal rank and history, and statements of warrior ferocity or female beauty. Any Maori could not, in good conscious, wear the *moko*. It was traditionally only for the wealthy and for those whose tribal status decreed they were worthy of such identification—chiefs and warriors. As such, the *moko* incorporated the person's lineage, tribal history, and the wearer's personal identification. The *moko*, then, was truly unique to each person and involved months of designing and tribal approval. It was a rite of culture and a spiritual experience. This is in direct opposition to gangs who wear the *moko* for identification and thus, in the eyes of many Maori, are not only degrading their heritage but also using it out of context and cheapening something that should be used only as a rite, not a designer element by the non-Maori. Those who wore the *moko* proclaimed their pride of Maori ancestry by making this irreversible commitment.

I paused in my reading. If King was of Maori lineage, why was his *moko* not of the facial type? Every picture I'd seen on the website was of facial *mokos*, either full face, one half, or—for women—just the lips and chin. I scanned farther down the documents. On a following page I found a mention of other *mokos*, those applied to the buttock, arm, thigh or full leg. Placement, according to the article, conveyed various other meanings. As with anything consisting of numerous, independent elements, *moko* symbols had no universal meaning from tribe to tribe. Still, if designed according to tradition, the *moko* supplied personal information about the wearer.

As good as identity theft if someone copies your moko, I thought as I printed the pages. So, was King a New Zealander who happened not to have an obvious tribal tattoo, or was he sporting it merely as body art? I looked once more at the vivid spirals, chevrons and rays, the intricate placement of negative and positive space. Cost aside, I wondered how anyone could endure the pain of so many cuts, for the lines comprising the tattoo designs were extraordinarily fine and close together. No wonder warriors were some of the only people who wore the *moko*.

Even though it was past lunchtime, I still had no appetite. Graham and MacMillan were consuming my energy and pushing me to get the case closed. I was about to make a phone call when Mark and Simcock walked over to me. They both looked like they'd been dragged through a hedge backwards. Both men sat down and Simcock produced the postmortem report from his pocket.

"I have the PM report. I won't bore you with the lot, but the salient points..." He scanned the page, then looked at us. "John Granger did not die immediately upon being attacked, as is probable with Enrico's death. Jens surmises this was due to classic defense wounds to John's fingers and fingernails. Blood was brown and congealed, signifying death had occurred as much as twenty-hour hours previous to your finding the body. Both livor and rigor were present, and the body had significantly cooled. There was no massive skull fracture, as would indicate a frontal attack and therefore instantaneous death."

"And the boy's front teeth?"

"Knocked out. His nose and left cheek were broken, and he had massive bruising to his left forearm."

"He saw his attacker and tried to defend himself."

"One blow from the murder weapon hit him over the left hip, causing a large bruise over that area and a ruptured spleen within. There was bleeding from his scalp and from those facial lacerations, of course, but the mechanism of death was bleeding within the abdomen."

"Did Jens find anything under John's fingernails?"

"No. Not foreign skin or bits of the assailant's clothing, if that's what you mean."

"So we've no clues from them."

"Just that he tried to ward off the attack, as shown by the broken fingernails."

"And the lacerations to his face, this broken teeth, nose and cheek," I added.

"And the murder weapon?" Mark asked, his voice strained.

"Some heavy, round-edged object. Not too large in diameter. About the size of—"

"A crowbar," Mark added. "You said the weapon was heavy, sir. It makes sense. Something like a branch would have broken. Has to be a crowbar. We've another murder and two attacks with the same types of injuries."

I refrained from looking at either man, too frightened from the idea that we had an individual who was responsible for both murders and assaults.

Mark voiced my next thought. "Could we have a copy cat murder, sir? Or a coincidence? Crowbars, if the weapon is a crowbar, were plentiful the night of the devil's stone turning. Mightn't someone have picked up one, either expecting to use it later on John or perhaps borrowing it for personal reasons and intending to return it to the church later?"

I asked, "How many people walk through the wood with a crowbar, Mark?"

He shrugged. "All right, so it's a bit far fetched. But all I'm saying is that both attacks and John's murder are close to the church and therefore close to Enrico's murder site. A crowbar was used in his murder, and these later three attacks all sport the same injuries."

"Suggesting crowbars were used in all assaults," Simcock said, nodding. "Yes. But it seems unlikely that we'd have more than one person responsible for these assaults. The events happened too quickly: John's death followed within twenty-four hours of Enrico's, and WPC MacMillan's and DCI Graham's attacks were within hours of each other, and within twelve hours, perhaps, of John's. We'd not even discovered them, let alone had time to make them known—either to the villagers or to the press."

Mark nodded. "So it's more than likely we're dealing with one bloke."

Simcock put down the PM report. "As certain as we can be right now, yes. The cause of death is a big giveaway that it's one person."

"And manner of attacks," I said. "I don't know if I'm comforted or alarmed that we're looking for only one berk."

Mark murmured that it made little difference to him and grabbed his cup of coffee.

Simcock asked how I was getting on. I wasn't certain if he referred to the case or to Graham's continued hospitalization, but I replied that I was making headway with my questioning.

"The family liaison officers and I have decided what to tell the Grangers with regard to their son's postmortem examination." He looked at Mark and I, making sure we understood. I nodded. Simcock handed us a small, white card, upon which was written the information that could be termed 'public knowledge.' He waited while Mark and I read it, then said, "I don't want any slip-ups on this. As far as you're concerned, this is what we know about the case. You're to say nothing more, nothing less. Of course I've held some things back, but that shouldn't concern you at the moment."

I nodded. Of course he would do that. So had Graham. It strengthened our case when a person confessed and gave us details that were not known to the public.

"Anything else?"

Mark shook his head and I murmured that I had things I had to do.

"Fine. I'm going back to John's crime scene. I shouldn't be gone long. You're doing fine. Continue with what you were doing." He was gone before I could reply.

Mark set down his cup, shoved the card into his slacks pocket, and said he had to see someone. He grabbed his car key and left.

I picked up my mobile and rang up headquarters to request any information on King Roper. Even if there was nothing criminal about him, I might learn if he was Maori and, by default, morally eligible to wear a *moko*. I left the tattoo information on the table, grabbed my jacket and bag, and left the incident room, needing to clear my head and get my blood moving.

Afternoon sun washed the village in insipid warmth, but it brought a bit of cheer, keeping alive the hope of spring. I turned left out of the community center, crossed Green Acre Road, and hiked the short distance up the church hill. The crowd of the curious and idolatrous still milled around the devil's stone—or as near as the police tape and constables would allow. The onlookers had dwindled slightly in number from the first day, perhaps disappointed that they couldn't touch the boulder or unwilling to brave the weather. The several dozen people who had come to gawk, either at the murder scene or to display their beliefs pro or con about the stone's devilry, were well-behaved for the most part, content to gaze, snap photos and chat up villagers. One person had been removed in handcuffs when he had tried crawling under the crime scene tape to attach a notice to the boulder. The message had proclaimed that Unbelievers had been shown the Truth, that Enrico had been struck down because he had scoffed at the devil's stone.

The statement was signed 'Divination Congregation.' I wondered if one person could purport to be a congregation, but then considered others may have been there—he may have been the only one brave enough to act on their urges. The current group had no placards, merely picnic baskets, thermos bottles, lawn chairs and cameras. And maybe a camera phone or two, I mentally added, seeing a woman hold a mobile out at arm's length, angled at the boulder. I watched a constable direct a man to pick up the crisps packet he'd discarded, and walked on.

The vicarage roof, a patchwork of vivid grays and blacks beneath the melting frost, sparkled in the sunlight. The tower bell, I noticed as I crested the hill and approached the front garden, still held onto a patch of ice on the north-facing rim of its mouth. I paused, looking for an inscription, but could not read the embossed lettering. Perhaps in sunlight, out of the gloom of shadow...

One of the liaison officers answered the door and, on hearing I wanted to talk to Lloyd, directed me to the kitchen. He was pouring hot water from the electric kettle into a large pottery teapot. When I called his name, he turned around, momentarily surprised, yet cordial at seeing me. He ran a damp sponge across the plastic tablecloth, apologizing for the informality but saying it was the warmest room in the house.

I told him I preferred to sit in the kitchen and that it looked fine.

"I don't like to have the electric fire on in the front room if I can avoid it. It's so expensive. John always liked it when it was on. He'd pretend that he was camping in the American Wild West or that he was a caveman huddled in front of a fire. He had so much fun. I wonder why he gave it up. Perhaps I'll light it for him tonight..." His eyes were red-rimmed and moist, looking at me from beneath puffy eyelids. His voice, too, held the remnants of his grief—rough and strained as though from crying or talking. We sat at the table, cups of tea in front of us, listening to the faint notes of the wind chime in the back garden, the popping of woodwork as the house warmed, the scraping of a tree branch against a back room window.

Wanting to break the strained silence, grabbing for something to say, I mentioned that it seemed to be windy.

Perhaps my comment hadn't registered. Or Lloyd hadn't heard me. He thanked me for my condolence on John's death and said Darlene was lying down. "She's not doing well," he said, glancing behind him. "She's taking this very hard. The officers are very nice, very comforting." He glanced at the open doorway to the front room, perhaps seeing an officer sitting on the couch. "They've been such a blessing to us. So easy to talk to. That's important, you know."

I told him I understood, then asked if he felt up to answering a few questions.

"If it's about John..." He began, hurt welling within his eyes.

I assured him it wasn't, and he nodded, sinking back in his chair.

"And how is Geoffrey? And the WPC. I forgot her name, I'm sorry."

I related Graham's and MacMillan's conditions and agreed when

HORNS OF A DILEMMA

Lloyd said he was worried about them. "Geoff is such a good friend of mine, Brenna. I—I don't think I could continue if something happened to him. Especially after John." He looked at me, leaving unsaid what we were thinking, then asked what I wanted to know.

I told him I'd visited the hair salon, heard about Noel's conviction and wondered if it had been an on-going occurrence.

He seemed as though he was concentrating on something else, for I had to repeat my question. Blinking as if just waking from a deep sleep, he sighed deeply and said in a faint voice, "The domestic violence? I'm afraid so. Despicable! He'd slapped Rita about several times, I know, though I never saw bruises or black eyes or such on her. And yes, I do know it happened because Rita confided in my wife."

"How long had this been going on before Rita contacted the police?"

The question remained unanswered for Lloyd was staring at something outside the kitchen. I waited for a flock of rooks to settle in the top branches of an oak before asking him again. He looked startled, as though he didn't know I was here, and answered the question.

"I can't recall. It was some time, though. Years, probably. Isn't that the norm with many women—stay with the abuser even though it endangers her life? I just remember his prison time. Well, you would, wouldn't you, with something like that? He was gone from his family for two years. I don't know about his first wife, if he beat her. But I suppose if that's part of your behavior you'd batter whomever your partner is." He sat quietly, again focused on something outside. "I've never laid a hand on my wife. Or my son. John is such a good lad…"

I said, "Did you say Noel's *first* wife? I didn't know he'd been previously married."

"Oh, yes. I can't recall her name—I don't know now, all these years later, if I ever did know it. My wife and I had just moved to the village soon after he and Rita were married. They've been married ten years, I believe. Just this past December."

"So Toni…"

"Isn't Rita's…child. No." He had said the word 'child' haltingly, as if it hurt his tongue when he moved it. He lowered his head, glancing at his hands so it seemed like he was in prayer. Perhaps he was. Or perhaps he was just thinking of John. Again I repeated my question before Lloyd replied that Toni was about to go to university.

"So why isn't Toni living with her mother?"

"She…she was for a bit, but her mother, uhh…" He paused, took a deep breath, and said, "She died in a house fire when Toni was five. Toni has a sketchy memory of it. Probably best, when you lose someone." He swallowed noisily and dabbed his eyes with his handkerchief. I apologized for the questioning, but he said he was fine. "You have to know these things if you're investigating a crime, don't you?" He took another sip of tea before answering my next question. "No, I don't know what caused the fire. He wasn't accused of arson, if that's what you're implying. It was put down to 'suspicious.' I believe that's the correct phrase. Noel and his first wife lived here. It was natural that he would remain here after he remarried. He'd grown up here, had roots here. He loved the village and had friends here. Rita's a local girl, too."

"Does she get along well with Toni?"

"As far as I know, she does. I've never heard of any fights or abuse. Well, not meaning Noel would slap Toni around like he slapped Rita around, but you hear so much of child abuse these days. It's all over the newspapers and evening news on the telly. But no, I've never heard anything. Thank goodness for that! Toni seems a good student, has never been in trouble. She and John... Why isn't he going out with her more often? She's such a nice child. I'll ask John tonight why he stopped seeing her."

A scuffing of shoes in the hall drew Lloyd's and my attention. Darlene stopped in the kitchen doorway, glancing from me to Lloyd. In a voice strained from tears and sleep, she asked what we were talking about.

I apologized for intruding into her grief and offered to come back another time. She said I may as well stay and get whatever it was over with so I'd leave them alone, and crossed the room rather like a child just learning to walk. She grabbed the handle of the refrigerator, then leaned forward to grasp the back of a chair before Lloyd could scramble to her side and seat her at the table. He poured her some coffee, set it in front of her, and explained that I was asking questions about Noel and Rita.

"Charming," Darlene said, ignoring the coffee. "You suspect them of something? Or can't you say? Is it all too hush-hush? Have you got your man...or woman?"

"It's too early to accuse anyone, Mrs. Granger," I said.

"Well, when you do, dear, I'm sure we'll all hear about it. This damned village excels at grapevine news—pardon my French." She stared at Lloyd as if seeking pardon for her language.

"Brenna's just gathering information," Lloyd said, moving Darlene's mug out of the way of her gesturing arms.

"Charming," she asked, looking at me. "How about *giving* us some information."

"What would you like to know?"

"When I can have my son."

I glanced at Lloyd, took a deep breath and said I couldn't give them consent to proceed with funeral arrangements. "I'm sorry, Mrs. Granger. I have nothing to do with it. It's up to the coroner. The liaison officers will let you know."

"So he's still by himself, on a cold slab." Darlene sagged onto the tabletop, her arms knocking the mug to the floor, sobbing.

I walked into the front room where the two officers were and asked them to help with Darlene.

Lloyd hurried over to Rita and lifted her upper body off the table. He squatted and embraced her. I wiped up the spilled liquid, picked up the pieces of the broken mug and deposited them in the waste bin. Lloyd was soothing her with words and light kisses, asking how she could say that, reminding her that humans cannot possibly fathom God's reason for anything that happens.

The officers had approached her and were talking calmly to her.

Darlene leaned back slightly, separating herself from her husband. Her face was twisted into a caricature of something inhuman, her eyes red and glaring. She shouted that if God is so cruel as to take her only son, she hates God. "If he's abandoned me, I abandon him!"

Lloyd said she couldn't mean it, that she was just hurt and was trying to hurt God.

Darlene yelled again that she would never love God, that she hated him for taking away her life, and pushed her palm against Lloyd's chest.

The female officer stepped forward, quietly asking Lloyd if he wanted help getting her to bed or if there was some medication she could get for Darlene.

He shook his head, repeating biblical verses in a low voice, trying to soothe his wife.

I slipped from the room as the officer guided Darlene to her bedroom.

The report on King Roper had come in via fax while I had been at the vicarage. And while it wasn't the longest or most chilling account I'd seen, it did tell me that King had previous arrests involving violent behavior, and had served prison time. I stared at the page, not seeing it, my mind trying to take in the meaning of everything I'd learned. King's previous record didn't concern me as much as the fact that he was here, in Hollingthorpe. I sank into the metal chair. Why would a hardened criminal appear in a sleepy village? Certainly, he was a free man and had a right to travel wherever he wished, see whomever he wished. But it seemed out of character with what I knew of him.

I picked up the paper again, rereading it. I was probably slandering the man. He was probably trying to go straight and I was already suspicious of his behavior even though I'd no proof he was involved in anything illicit. After all, if anyone should be under suspicion of murder in the village, it should be a villager—they know each other!

I tossed the paper onto the table and stared at the printout of the Maori *mokos*. Were King and Noel acquainted? If so, had they met in prison? Just because both men had tattoos, I was linking them in some as yet unnamed crime. I shook my head, amazed at the ridiculous turn I was putting on the case. King had done time in Winston Green; Noel had served in a lesser facility. There was no connection there. *Anyway why would there be*, I chided myself. But King had phoned Noel several times when Noel was serving time. The records showed that. Did that mean anything now, for this case? I exhaled deeply. I was looking for connections that probably didn't exist, wanting a nest of criminals hiding in the village so we could wrap up all four cases with one arrest.

"What's the news?"

I probably jumped a foot in the air on hearing the voice practically in my ear. Looking up, I found Mark standing beside my chair. He took off his jacket, tossed it onto an empty chair, and asked what I was reading that was so interesting.

"You're assuming, Mark. A good copper never assumes."

"I did *not* assume. I deduced it. It has to be interesting to grab your attention like that. You didn't even hear me come up to you, and I'm wearing hard-soled shoes."

I handed him the Maori tattoo article and explained the major points as he skimmed the pages.

"See? I was right. It *is* interesting. Well, well. Our friend Roper is definitely becoming a person of interest."

"Just like the article," I said. "And what have you been doing—interesting or not?"

He tossed the pages onto the table and said he was considering suing Richard.

"Why? What are you talking about?"

"My clothes," Mark said, hooking his foot around a chair leg and leaning forward to glance at the computer screen. It still had the Maori website up. I logged off. "Or not," he added. "Depending on how you phrase it."

"And how do you phrase it, Mark?"

"I dropped off my jeans and jacket at Richard's laundry this morning—I'd got them muddy last night when we were poking about in the rain and mud looking for Graham."

I nodded, recalling the less than pristine crime scenes and Mark sitting in the rain while I waited for the ambulance to arrive.

Mark said, "So I went to the launderette. The shop was open but I couldn't raise anybody."

"What do you mean 'raise anybody'? If it was open—"

"Just what I said. I called, even wandered into the back room. I couldn't find anyone. Maybe the attendant had sneaked out back for a smoke. I don't know. Anyway, I thought how hard can it be, washing a pair of jeans and a jacket? So I go over to the soap dispenser, only it was empty! Nothing. No soap anywhere. So I go to the back room again, calling. Nobody's there. I saw some large cardboard cartons of soap powder—one was open but evidently whoever it was hadn't unpacked the soap powder yet. So I grabbed one, dumped my money on top of the cardboard carton, and went back to the washing machine. I poured some of the soap powder onto my clothes and ran them through the wash cycle."

"Good so far. What's to sue Richard about?"

"Because," Mark said, his neck muscles tightening as he leaned forward, "the damned clothes were still dirty when the wash was finished. And they didn't even *smell* good!"

"You must have done something wrong, Mark."

"What's to do wrong? I poured on some washing powder, turned on the machine, watched it fill with water and start washing. What could I have done wrong?"

"Well, something, obviously, if your clothes aren't clean. Are you sure you chose washing powder? Perhaps it was water softener or—"

"I can read, Brenna! Of course I'm damned sure it was washing powder. How stupid do you think I am?" He kicked the leg of the table. "I do my own wash at my own flat—despite what you may think. I can do my own wash here. Bunch of wide boys. I ought to run them in for false advertising. Launderette. How's he stay in business if this is how his customers' clothes look?"

I replied I didn't know and that had to have been some mistake. "Perhaps the boxes are mislabeled. You know, like a mix-up at the factory. Wrong boxes used, so it's really something else in the boxes."

Mark settled back in his chair, looking thoughtful. "Could have done, I guess. It didn't particularly taste like washing powder. Or smell like it."

"You *tasted* it?"

"Only afterwards, when the clothes were finished. I was curious that the mud hadn't come out, so I tasted the powder. Just a few flakes. I don't know why. I was just curious."

"Well, good thing it wasn't cyanide. You'd be flopping on the launderette floor."

Mark snorted and glared at me.

"But it *is* curious," I said. "Remember Graham telling us that the launderette always does the laundry for the stone turning participants? That wouldn't happen if the clothes didn't come out clean. Nor, as you said, could Richard stay in business all these years if he had problems with the wash."

Mark sat up, tapping the tabletop. "It's damned odd, Bren. Odder than I first thought. What if..." He nodded his head as his words tumbled out. "What if Richard's in some smuggling racket. And it's not washing powder in that box I got, but something else?"

"Like drugs? Did it taste like a drug?"

"No, it didn't. I would've spotted that instantly. It was bitter and salty. I've not tasted anything like it before. I don't know what it was."

"And no smell, you said."

"I've some left, if you want to see it. I used only a partial box because I washed only my jeans and jacket. I thought I'd save the rest for another load. The box is in my room at the pub. You want to check it out?"

"Wild horses, as they say." I hurried after him, wondering what we were getting into.

I practically bumped into Margo as Mark and I entered the pub. Margo stood just inside the door, her attention on Harry, who was talking to a woman at the bar. Mark said he'd be right down with the box, and took the steps two at a time. Margo came up to me, nodding toward Harry.

"Local Romeo," she said. "I've been here for a few minutes. You won't believe what I've heard."

"Try me," I said, feeling overwhelmed with everything that was happening.

"Just listen. It'll give you a laugh."

"I could use one," I said, then listened to Harry.

He was smiling, telling the woman she was beautiful and would she like to pose for a book he's doing on the region? She quickly said yes, wonder in her eyes.

Harry reached into his jacket pocket, frowned, patted his slacks pocket, then said he seems to have left his business cards at home. But if she would come back tomorrow at the same time, he'd have a contract for her to sign and he'd tell her more about the project. She assured him she'd be back and gushed that she'd always wanted a break to get into modeling or acting. Harry said he could always spot talent and that she should stick with him. He leaned his elbow against the bar, looking the epitome of a sleazy casting director. She finished her drink, squeezed his hand, and left with a flutter of her eyelashes.

"God, it's enough to make me ill," Margo said when Harry had turned back to his drink. "Where's he come up with such a line?"

"Must be something he saw on the telly."

"Even a television program can't be that inane."

"I might have lost my breakfast if I'd heard any more. Do you believe that woman fell for that line? It's older than I am."

"Speaking of food—"

"Which we weren't."

"—have you had any? Today, I mean, Bren. I didn't see you at breakfast, and you didn't ask me to meet you for lunch. So I can only conclude—"

"That I'm busy, Margo. I'm working on this murder and I'm worried sick about Graham and MacMillan—"

"—and you're not taking care of yourself. You can't work on your nerves, Bren."

"I've heard that before. And quite recently, too."

"Then heed it. Isn't there something about repetition, like drops of water?"

"Maybe that's Harry's life line. Maybe he thinks if he says something often enough, someone will bite."

"Maybe women have bitten, Bren. We don't know much about Harry. Maybe he's got a good thing going here. Maybe he uses the same line over and over."

I said, "Then I feel sorry for them."

"Because they're that gullible, you mean?"

"Yes. And because there's no book for that woman to be in. It's sad to have your dreams crushed."

"Well," Margo said, "we've all got to grow up sometime. For some it takes a bit longer and a bit more of a jolt."

"Speaking of jolts," I said, glancing at the stairs to see if Mark was there. I told her about Darlene's breakdown, adding that I was sorry she had the double blow of feeling betrayed by God.

"Have you ever felt that?" Margo asked.

"To a degree, but I've never had the loss of a child or family member."

"So what made you mad at God?"

"Usual disappointments. Life."

"Like not getting the man you love to fall in love with you?" She looked at me, unsmiling, willing to listen and offer solace.

I said this was not the time to expose my wounds, and was relieved when Mark galloped down the stairs.

Margo pointed to the box. "You need clothes if you're going to do your washing, Mark. Or is this some male ritual to impress the ladies—bathing in the stream?"

"You're so funny, Margo, I can hardly stop laughing." Mark jiggled the laundry powder box. "All set?"

I turned to Margo and told her we'd be back soon.

"Where you off to, then? What if Simcock asks where you are?"

"I'll ring him up on the way," I said, heading for the pub door. "We'll be back for tea."

Margo pointed to the box of powder. "I just hope you're not brewing *that*!"

Mark drove us to Silverlands, theorizing the entire trip about what the contents of the box might be. I rang up Simcock, told him the washing powder story and that we were dropping the box contents at headquarters. He said he'd authorize it to be taken to the regional Home Office forensic science laboratory, and added that he'd be interested to see if it was linked to our cases.

I thanked him and rang off, settling back in the car as Mark rattled on, letting off steam on subjects as varied as his unwashed clothes to the Harry's beer mat collection.

"How do you know?" I asked. "When did you have time to find that out?"

"When I had lunch today. Harry was in there, pestering the publican."

"Harry seems to be always pestering someone. Poor Harry."

"Don't pity him too much, Brenna. He's getting what he wants."

"How would you know? You an authority all of a sudden?"

"I know a psychopath when I encounter one. And an unstable mind. Harry was at the bar, talking to a customer about putting money into Harry's book. The publican told the customer that Harry has no book, that he shouldn't give Harry any money, and then told Harry to leave. Harry got mad, yelled that he was going about the village taking photos for his book and that just for that, he wouldn't include the publican in his book. The publican told Harry to mind his own business. To resolve the situation and restore some semblance of order, the publican gives Harry a beer mat and tells him to go home."

"The long arm of the law didn't step in to accelerate the coming of peace and quiet?"

"I was going to help, but the publican had obviously dealt with Harry before. Harry grabbed the beer mat, cradled it to his chest, laughed, and ran out the door."

I sighed. "Could you live in that village, putting up with that constantly?"

"Might be better than living in a neighborhood ruled by toughs."

"I'm scared, Mark."

He glanced at me, concern etched on his face. "Scared? About what? About what we'll find out about the washing powder? I know we've got officers from other divisions working the other cases, but we'll have the help we need if this turns out to be something we need to investigate. We won't be working so hard—"

"No, Mark. I'm scared about Graham and MacMillan. We haven't heard anything since this morning. You don't think—"

"No, I don't. If something had happened to either one of them, if the doctors had discovered something on the x-ray or if one of them had worsened, we'd know. Simcock would tell us. He would have told you just now, when you talked to him. No matter when he heard anything, he'd ring us up immediately because he knows we care. We're more than just people working together, Bren. We like and respect each other. We've been through tough times together, helped each other out of life-threatening situations. He would let *us* know as soon as *he* knew." He smiled, conveying confidence in his words and encouraging me to believe, too.

The remainder of the trip to headquarters was quiet except for Mark's singing. And by the time we'd returned to the incident room and to talk to Simcock, I shared Mark's belief.

Chapter 24

I hadn't planned to eat dinner, but Margo nagged me into taking the break. "You're losing your skin tone," was actually how she phrased part of her argument. Lord knows I struggle enough with my looks—I didn't want a sallow complexion scaring away my coworkers. "You need some food. You look like hell, Bren. I mean that kindly, as a friend to a friend, but you really do look bloody awful."

I wondered how she would have phrased it if she weren't my friend. When I said I was going to ring up Adam and cancel our date, she came back with, "Just as well. It's not really the thing to do, taking a night off at this stage of the inquiries. But you've got to eat. Even Graham and Simcock eat. Come on."

So I begrudgingly consented, changed clothes, brushed my hair, and allowed Margo to lead me downstairs. When she pushed me toward the door to the dining area, I understood her devious maneuvering. Adam was waiting for me.

I will admit that seeing Adam again after several years was good for me. Doctor Margo had diagnosed that correctly. Adam greeted me with a smile and a bouquet of astilbe—"which means," Adam said, "I'll be waiting." The bouquet was more than I had to give him. I thanked him, rather more seriously than I had intended, perhaps because I was astonished he knew the traditional symbol of the flower. At least it wasn't a red rose. I must have stared at the flowers too long, for he said, "Wrong choice? Should I have given you a variegated tulip?"

"That was years ago, Adam."

"What's a few years when I have your eyes to remember?"

I told him he was either too much of a romantic or desperate. "A good bunch of Bells of Ireland might be more in order, though," I said, after we were seated and had ordered. He laughed and I discovered that I was suddenly quite hungry and glad of a meal.

"Why do you particularly need good luck?" he asked.

I told him the main points of the murder cases and the attacks. Adam shook his head slowly and leaned forward in his chair. His after-shave lotion was again discernable. "Sounds like you need help. Has Simcock made any move? Other divisions?"

"He's requested help from Greater Manchester, I believe."

"Mutual aid?"

I nodded, saying it was actually limited mutual aid. It fooled me into thinking things weren't as bad as they were.

Adam nodded. "With all that going on, he needs it. God, what a muck sweat he must be in to solve this. And Graham being in hospital doesn't help. One of the best detectives in the Constabulary, in my opinion." He paused as the waiter brought our salads, then said, "You must be worried sick, Bren. I know what you think of him."

Perhaps he knew my professional opinion of Graham—that he was ethical, idealistic, compassionate, committed—but he didn't know my personal feelings. That had erupted after I'd attained sergeant rank and been partnered with Graham. Adam had moved to Ripley six months prior to my ardor. I looked at him from over the rim of my teacup, briefly wondering how our lives might have evolved if Graham and I hadn't been paired together. Though I hadn't the same feelings for Adam, I liked him immensely and was willing to give our relationship a chance. He obviously wanted it to go somewhere—the astilbe bouquet implied that. And his serious, dark suit also hinted at the regard he gave our date—at least it wasn't torn blue jeans and a football jersey. I smiled, losing myself in his blue eyes, letting the richness of his voice lull me into a happiness I had no right in feeling while in the midst of a double murder investigation. Still, Adam pulled this sensation from where it had been imprisoned in my soul, and I let myself float. I was ready to make a serious commitment with someone, something more long term than what I was currently experiencing with Erik, my live-in companion.

"So you're thick with Margo," I said.

"Sure! She suggested it. Great little arranger, that woman."

"Yeh, great."

"She explained how the case was developing, that you wouldn't be able to take the time off for a proper date—"

"She's in the wrong line of work."

"—and said even Simcock couldn't refuse you a quick dinner in the pub. So, here I am."

I shook my head, amazed at the plotting. "Well, for once, I'm glad of her scheming. I can't believe how much I've missed you."

He smiled and blew me a kiss.

I set down the teacup.

Richard and King were among the villagers having drinks or dinner. They were seated at a table near the bar, more interested in trying to see the dart game than in their drinks. At a roar from a group near the board, Richard stood up, knocking over his beer, which spilled onto King's lap. King jumped back, bringing a laugh from the game group and a curse from King.

I closed my eyes, not wanting to be reminded of the case, letting myself unwind and enjoy my time with Adam.

"Either you're finally relaxing," Adam said, breaking into our silence, "or I've got spinach between my teeth and you're repulsed. Which is it?"

I looked at him, apologized and replied that I was just enjoying the atmosphere.

"It *is* rather different from your crime scenes," he agreed. "And, if it doesn't sound too corny, I'm glad you rang me up—to suggest we get together again, *and* while you were waiting for the ambulance. I like being part of your life again. I only hope this time you won't drop me."

"Did I do that? I'm sorry!"

He smiled. "It's not as cruel as it sounds, Brenna. I was transferred to Ripley and you'd just made sergeant. Our jobs got in the way."

"Are we any more stable now?" I asked it seriously, but meant for it to sound light-hearted. I was enjoying being with Adam again and I didn't want to lose him. But the weight of the investigation was threatening to spoil our time together.

Adam scratched his head. "Don't know. Shouldn't think it would do. We're both in better positions, I think, to manage our time. *I'd* like to continue this evening—on a more regular basis. If you are, that is. I can't fathom a woman's heart nor do I have the ability to read your body language right now. You're staring at me."

"Am I? I'm sorry. I didn't mean to."

"Like I said—it's either spinach between my teeth or I'm utterly fascinating to be with."

"Did you have spinach for lunch?"

He shook his head.

"Well, then, you've got your answer."

He grabbed my hand, gave it a quick kiss, and released it. "Good. I hate multiple choice. Simple yes-no or true-false statements are easier to understand. Thanks, Bren."

"For what? Wanting to go out again?"

"Certainly that, yes. But for confiding in me last night. You sounded terrified when you rang me up. Don't be afraid to do that, Bren. I'm always available for you—in person or by phone. I'm glad I could at least talk to you if I couldn't be there while you endured that. God, what a night! MacMillan, the Granger lad, and Graham..."

I nodded and suddenly trembled.

Adam looked at me skeptically. "Are you all right, or would you rather leave? I mean, if you're too worried about Graham and MacMillan..." He peered at me as though trying to discern my well being.

I attacked my salad with the vigor I didn't feel and said yes, I was deeply worried, but that I'd like to have dinner with him. "I'm sorry. This isn't the best night for this, is it?"

"*I'm* having a splendid time. I'm just sorry you're not."

Putting down my fork, I said, "It's not you, Adam. You can't think that—not after I rang you up and asked if we could see each other again. It's just that..." I fingered the edge of the tablemat, trying to phrase it so he wouldn't take offense. "Yes, you're right. It *is* Graham. *And* MacMillan. The attacks were vicious, violent. You haven't seen the crime scenes. The one with Enrico Thomas was the worst. It was like some overdone setting in a cheap horror film. And the others—John and MacMillan and Graham. The wounds were savagely dealt out. It was like a personal statement against them."

"It has to be bad for your team that they're both in comas."

"But it's the implication of the attacks, you see. If someone was getting frightened that we were getting close to identifying the murderer, he might lash out. I can accept that. But to beat them both so brutally..."

"Like using a lorry to deliver a paper clip. Yes, it is rather extreme."

"Why beat up someone like that? It's more than fright, Adam. It's like making a statement."

"Of course, I don't know all the particulars of the case," he said, leaning back in his chair, "but it kind of smacks of hatred. But against Graham and MacMillan personally, or the police in general?"

We finished our meal catching each other up on our lives since we'd separated—Adam joining the firearms unit, learning to play poker, considering writing a crime novel, avoiding marriage; me joining the CID team, learning to sketch, considering a holiday in New Zealand, desiring marriage. I most likely chattered inanely, desperate to avoid conversation about the case and wanting to leave Adam's last question unanswered. But after we'd kissed good night and promised we'd get together again soon, another question screamed at me after our stroll around the village. Graham and MacMillan were assaulted in the same vicinity. Perhaps the wood held more than the terrors of fairy tales—did the wood hold the key to the case? I'd go out tonight to look.

I hadn't time to consider the significance of my idea, for Harry Willett eased into the shadows clinging to the pub as I walked back to the establishment's car park. I stood beside someone's car for a moment, watching him keep to the darkened patches of landscape as he scurried to the neighboring building. He plastered himself against the teashop's wall, blending into the black night. I walked around the car, hugging Adam's flower as though it were some talisman, aware that I was being watched. The night was silent and still, harboring many living things beneath its murky mantle. That knowledge never bothered me—it was the reality of night-dwelling creatures such as the owl, bat, moth and fox. But knowing that Harry stood there, breathing and watching silently, melting into the shadows, alarmed me. That he should have been at home was one thing; that he was clearly bent on some mischief was another. I took a few steps toward the shadow-wrapped wall, calling his name. A sound, like a squelched intake of breath, shot out from the blackness. I called again. The grate of hard leather on concrete reflected against the side of the pub. When I stated my name, there was a snuffle, the clatter of falling metal, and a rattle of gravel. A moment later the slap of running shoes and the clank of a rolling dustbin echoed off the stone walls. The dustbin crashed against the corner of the pub; the footsteps diminished into the distance. Quiet descended, abrupt and absolute, thickening the shadows with the lingering unease that intimated Harry wasn't the only bit of devilry haunting the region.

In my room at the pub I made myself a cup of tea with the small electric kettle now so common in small establishments. As the water boiled I gazed out of the window. The High Street held the occasional car driving past or small group of people walking to their cars or over to the green. From this height, my room over the barroom afforded me a hawk's-eye view of the village main street. The street lamp at the corner of the High Street and Well Hill Street, at the far corner of the green, shone faintly, like a moon nestled among tree branches. The park bench nearest the pub was nothing more than a dark blob against a darker background. Rectangles of yellowish, dim light from the greengrocer and launderette stretched, irregularly-shaped, across the pavement, as though trying to escape the confines of the windows. Other than these feeble lights, and a few indicating other darkened businesses along the street, the village seemed to have shut its eyes to the night and lay beneath the cradling blanket of darkness. I lifted my gaze from the street, searching for the moon. It had struggled free of the clouds that had held it at bay and now painted the landscape in silvery light. I wondered how the churchyard looked, the lines of slanting tombstones white and luminous against the ebony curtain of night, like rows of teeth in a blackened, gaping mouth.

The whistling kettle drew me from the window. I made the tea and quickly downed the hot beverage. Another cup and some note-taking failed to ward off the fatigue overcoming me. I'd been up forty-eight hours, having vowed I'd work until Graham's attacker had been caught, but my body was betraying my efforts. My mind wouldn't work. I stared at my notes, then realized I was re-reading the same sentences, trying to understand the words. I slipped off my shoes, lay down in bed, and pulled the duvet over me, promising myself I'd grab a few hours of sleep before tackling my notes again. I should have set my alarm clock. The next thing I was aware of was the sunlight of mid-morning streaming into my room and my cramped muscles complaining because I'd slept in my clothes.

Simcock led the briefing Saturday morning. Graham was still in a coma, but MacMillan would be released from hospital late today or early tomorrow. While not fit to return to work, she would be at home and would soon be with us. Simcock paused for the murmurs of relief and thankfulness, then announced that although the House-to-House Team was conducting door-to-door inquiries, no new leads had surfaced about the identity of DCI Graham's or WPC MacMillan's attacker. He also announced that the lab analysis of the powdery substance in Detective Salt's laundry detergent box should be coming in tomorrow. Getting no questions, he dismissed us with a minor pep talk on lawlessness, victory and action.

When he had seated himself at a table, I walked over to him. He put down the phone, smiled and repeated the medical information about Graham. I murmured "Yes, sir," and asked if he wanted me to continue my same investigation. He nodded, then called me as I turned to leave. He looked up at me, frowning slightly, and said, "The person who did all this...."

"All what, sir? The assaults?"

"No. Well, yes. Both, I mean. The assaults and the original murder—of Enrico."

The three scenes loomed menacingly in my mind. I glanced at the table, at the handwritten note on MacMillan's condition and concentrated on that good news, trying to ignore my mental images of the bloodied bodies. I nodded, encouraging Simcock to continue. He looked confused. Or tired.

"Well," Simcock said slowly, as though he didn't know what to say. "There was a hell of a lot of blood, wasn't there?" Without waiting for my confirmation, he hurried on. "Every attack—even that lad's, John—had the same signature."

"Violent blows to the head."

"Yes. Most probably by the same weapon, since we've yet to find it. Anyway, what I'm getting at, with that much violence and the way it was carried out... Well, with all that blood about—" He paused and I said, "Our suspect wouldn't escape in pristine condition." The words had tumbled out as I recalled Mark's complaints about his muddy clothes. And he had merely helped with Graham, not engaged in a blood bath of an attack. I thought of the crime scene we had worked on last month, the blood flung about on the walls and ceiling. Surely our present attacker would have been splattered in blood.

As though reading my mind, Simcock said, "We're working on the assumption one person is responsible for everything here."

"Since the acts of violence, whether murder or assaults, are the same, yes, it makes sense."

"So we have one person, we presume, who's committed four bloody assaults. What would be your first thought if you were him?"

"Disassociate myself from my clothes," I said quietly, envisioning the attacks. "My clothes would be spotted with blood."

Simcock nodded. "And your next priority?"

"To hide them—either bury them or clean them without anyone knowing."

"Would you have four sets of clothes you could easily chuck?"

"Neither monetarily or physically, no. I'm not that wealthy that I can afford to lose four pair of jeans and four jackets—not even if I bought cheap ones for the occasion. It's still money spent or money I'd have to spend to replace my bloodied clothes. But that's me. Other people may have four sets of clothes. I suppose, they almost must have, for not many folks would keep bloody clothes lying about, waiting for the police to spot them should they arrive with a search warrant."

"And as for physically getting rid of them," Simcock added, "that's a huge risk. The average person has no idea how hard that is."

"You think you'll just dig a little hole in the back garden and bury them there. Well, maybe you can, but the earth will show signs of having been disturbed, for one thing. And four holes to bury four sets of clothes is stretching our belief a bit thin if you tell us you've just dug up dead rose bushes."

"There's always the wood. You could bury your clothes in the wood and we'd probably never find it. It's rather vast."

"But that would entail four trips. Each with a spade."

"Even if you go at midnight, would you be certain no one's seen you?"

"There's the pub. I can check it out, but I bet you anything you like, sir, that you can see a good distance into the wood from the pub's upper story. The trees aren't in leaf."

"Yes, it'd be hard to spot someone at midnight in the wood."

"But who's to say that's the hour when you'd be seen? I could be walking to or from, bloodied clothes in a sack, spade in my hand, and be seen. No, sir. If I were going to dispose of my four sets of bloody clothes, or even one, if I had the nerve to wear the same set for every attack, I'd dispose of them at home. No prying eyes. It'd be safer."

"There are other ways…"

"And we've dogs who are rather keen on ferreting out things like that. Burial has never stopped them from discovering a body. Same for water, if you were to weight them down and drop them into a pond. Water magnifies the smell for dogs. And burning clothes is also risky—you've got ashes to dispose of, then. And how do you know we won't find partially burnt fabric somewhere?"

"Is that all?"

I screwed up my mouth, thinking through the scenarios. I said I couldn't think of how else to dispose of clothes, unless it were to drive them to some town, like Manchester, and dump them into a street-side trash bin. Then again, it'd be a war of nerves that someone wouldn't spot me.

"What I'm getting at, Taylor, in my roundabout fashion, is that there's another method to get rid of bloody clothes." I must have looked blank, for he said, "Washing."

Chapter 25

"Sure, we've got luminal and phenolphtalein to indicate blood," Simcock said. "And tests can be made with the light beam. But does the average person know that? Even with all the crime programs on the telly, how many would think of that in the heat of trying to wash them? And the odds that we'd test his clothing are probably pretty low, this berk would think, for he's got the typical ego. They all do, this type." He picked up the handwritten note and read it again.

I cleared my throat and he looked up, waiting, for he knew I wanted to say something. "Sir, about the clothes—"

"The washing or the hiding?"

"Well, the washing, I think. Yes, sir," I replied when he nodded. "Would our suspect wash his clothes between the four attacks? That's a lot of blood to get rid of. Would he risk the four washings, which would comprise quadruple the amount of blood and therefore four times as likely that we'd spot residue in his washer?"

"Do you want him to put them in the clothes hamper or hang them back in his closet, ready for his next adventure?"

"No, sir. That's ludicrous. But what's he do with them between the assaults and murders?"

"Either wash them, or don new clothes each time he commits a crime. There's not much else."

"And he'd bury the clothes—or burn them or dump them in Manchester, say—when he's finished. How does he know when he's finished?"

Simcock frowned and asked what I was implying.

"Well, sir, if he killed Enrico, how did he know he was going to kill John? I can't see a link between Enrico and John—they didn't really know each other, and Enrico had just settled in the village a month ago. So there's no long tie between them. So how did our murderer, having killed Enrico, know he was going to kill John the following night? And how did he know he was going to assault two police officers?"

Simcock exhaled heavily and said something rather strong.

I added, "I don't know if the murderer had a personal vendetta against DCI Graham and WPC MacMillan, or if it was just coppers in general. But MacMillan was assigned that area to search, if you'll recall, sir. She went up

HORNS OF A DILEMMA

there near the church to photograph the rose left after Enrico's death. I was wondering if she'd found anything there—a clue or something odd. And if the murderer discovered later that he'd lost his latch key, let's say—"

"That could explain the assault. Yes, I see your reasoning. But we still can't conclude what the murderer did with his bloody clothes between crimes. And until we have a definite suspect, we can't go about the village spraying luminal or phenolphthalein into every washer."

"No, sir."

"Whatever has become of the clothes, we're dealing with premeditation, Taylor. *Planned* attacks. Nothing spur-of-the-moment here. No crime of passion, caught up in any argument."

"No. Uhhh, yes, sir." My reply came slowly, haltingly, as I struggled to make sense of his words and their implication.

He dismissed me with a verbal pat on the back, said I could reach him via his mobile, and left the room.

It was some time after Simcock had left that I pushed myself into work mode. My head seemed like it would explode from the tension of two murders, two assaults and Simcock's latest revelation. I took some aspirin, hoping that would at least alleviate the pounding at my temples, and looked for Mark or Margo. I wanted to work with them; I needed their company if just to keep me from slipping into insanity. Our case was bad enough, but after feeling a burgeoning tingle for Adam, and tossing through a nightmare about Graham's paralysis, I wasn't ready to be alone. But neither Mark nor Margo was in the incident room, so I took a deep breath and walked to the parsonage.

The day was chilly, with shafts of straw-colored sunlight slipping through the cracks in the gray sky. But a hint of warmer, vernal temperatures laced the breeze and I smelled the first blush of thawing earth. Under different circumstances I would have reveled in spring's whisper, but as I paused on the path and glanced at the wood where Graham and MacMillan had been attacked, my emotions boiled up and burst forth in sobs that racked my body. I sagged against the lych gate of the church, not caring if it was disrespectful or not, not caring if anyone saw me, and let my anger and frustration and fear explode. After I'd cried myself numb many minutes later, I wiped my face, pushed my hair back, and walked the rest of the way to the Grangers'.

Page was gathering fallen twigs and dead leaves from a grave in the churchyard, but stopped her tidying when I called to her. She stood up, shoved the forest debris into a large paper sack, and informed me that she'd seen Darlene going into Ian and Colleen's house. "To sort things out," she said, as if echoing Darlene's departing words.

I glanced at the vicarage. "What's to sort out? Did she get permission for the funeral?"

"Something about her future. She said something about Lloyd and God both failing her, then pushed past me. That's all I know."

I thanked her and made my way to the vicarage to see how Lloyd was handling this new blow.

No one answered the front door, though I heard some noise in the kitchen. I walked around to the back of the house and peered through the window. Lloyd sat at the table, a mug in front of him, the electric kettle whistling vigorously, the small television set on the working top blaring away. I pounded on the door but got no response. Ringing the house from my mobile didn't push him into action, either. I closed my phone and again pounded on the door. A minute later Lloyd finally stirred and shuffled over to the door. When he opened it, he remained in the doorway, his hand on the edge of the door, his eyes staring past my shoulder into the churchyard. When he made no acknowledgment of my presence, I said I'd come to tell him how Graham was. The words seemed to roll over him, unheeded, but I steered him back to the table, turned off the television and the kettle, and made him a cup of coffee. He remained unresponsive, staring at something behind me, outside. Or concentrating on something in his mind.

I said that I was sorry that he and Darlene were going through such a terrible time, and commiserated with him on his troubles. Even if Lloyd wasn't responding, he might be hearing my words, so I continued.

I said it was always harder to do anything when it involved someone so close, that perhaps Darlene expected more magical words from Lloyd, or greater healing since he's an instrument of God. That, finding nothing instantly healing or logical, she sank into a deeper depression than others might have done. I reminded him that we could not begin to understand God's schemes, that though they seemed cruel and heartless, even evil at times, we could not judge, and that *that* was where our faith came in. We had to believe in something beyond ourselves and our petty plans, in something more infinitely good than we could perceive, and believe that we would be united beyond this life.

Lloyd's eyes remained fixed on the eastern horizon, as though I weren't there.

I wondered what else I could say to help him, for he seemed caught in the middle—devastated by John's death, hit by Darlene's abandonment and Graham's physical condition. I opened my mouth, not sure of what I could add, then stopped. I was talking like Graham! Me, the agnostic, the woman struggling to make sense of indifferent parents and hateful school mates and broken love affairs, who tried to push through the life-sucking morass of shattered dreams and every day bills and violent crime.

I glanced at Lloyd, afraid he could see the Unbeliever in my eyes, afraid for my soul that I had blasphemed, that the words I had uttered would be judged by my previous thirty-five years of impiety, not judged by my slow, emphatic epiphany. But Lloyd only murmured Darlene's name over and over. I could see past him, into the front room of his home. A blanket was bunched up on the sofa, a pair of slippers on the floor near the piece of furniture, one of the throw pillows indented—all implying he had grabbed a few hours of sleep there, waiting, perhaps, for Darlene to change her mind and return home. Or avoiding their bed because it held happier memories.

HORNS OF A DILEMMA

The table and floor near the sofa held several mugs and books that were placed open-page down. A partially eaten orange lay on a folded newspaper, its juice seeping into the paper, darkening the page and plastering it to the one beneath. A piece of toast bookmarked a selection in a closed Bible. Lloyd felt his pain and struggled against his own maelstrom as deeply as I battled mine. We both had our own ways to conquer it.

I pushed the coffee toward him, patted his hand, and urged him to ring me up if he needed to talk. His vacant eyes merely stared past me, into the churchyard; the coffee sat ignored. I closed the door slowly and silently on the pathetic figure.

Darlene wasn't at Collette's home, as Page had told me. Nor was Collette or her husband, Ian. But, as it was Saturday late morning, I assumed Collette could be showing houses to prospective buyers. Ian might be coming home from his night job in Maccelsfield. Still, if Darlene was so distraught, she wouldn't have gone anywhere. She'd be unresponsive, zombie-like, as Lloyd was, in no mood to answer the door and chat. Perhaps she was lying on the couch, or having coffee in the kitchen.

I glanced at my watch and decided that even if she'd had a late night of talking to Collette, Darlene could be up, so I walked around to the back door. It wasn't logical that she wasn't home.

I knocked on the door, now slightly worried that Darlene had harmed herself in her grief. Overdosing on sleeping pills was not uncommon in such situations. When I'd knocked twice and received no answer, I paused, wondering what to do. In that brief silence someone or something bumped against a wooden chair leg, a china cup rattled in a saucer, and a soft cry was smothered. I stood on my toes and peeked through the curtained window. Had she fallen or slumped to the floor as the overdose took effect? I might have felt better if she had. Darlene Granger and Collette's nephew, Conrad, were on the floor, leaning against a table leg, their chests touching. Her eyes were closed, her head was tilted backwards, exposing her neck to Conrad's kisses. He was bare-chested and had his hand beneath her jersey.

I turned from the window and lurched for a shrub, unable to keep my stomach down or my thoughts from racing. I wiped my mouth on a facial tissue, disbelieving Darlene would jeopardize her marriage like that. Or have so little thought of her husband. As I got into my car a more disturbing idea trickled through my nausea: had Darlene used John's death as an excuse to leave home? Had she and Conrad been planning to disappear all along? Conrad had a new photo assignment; no one would think a thing of it when he left. And now Darlene, the wife who couldn't cope with her son's death, would conveniently need time away to heal. It was like stumbling onto a gold mine—suspicions wouldn't be raised when either departed and they would meet up later at some prearranged spot.

The teashop was not busy when I walked in. Perhaps late morning on weekends didn't bring the custom that workdays did. Still, several tables were occupied, and the two waitresses were carrying pots of tea and trays of scones and buns to the tables. I explained to the cashier I was joining a party, and walked over to Frances Cresswell, whom I knew worked there. She and a teen-aged girl whom I assumed to be her granddaughter, Toni Dutton, sat at a small table in the middle of the room. Not the best place for a police interview, I thought, but it would have to do. Receiving permission to join them, I grabbed a chair from a nearby table and sat down.

Frances introduced me to Toni, who was tearing apart a rock cake, playing with it more than eating it. She asked how the investigation was going, asked after Graham and MacMillan, then excused herself as a group of customers entered the shop. "I've had my break," she said, smoothing her skirt before going back to the cash register.

I told Toni why I wanted to talk to her, that I was sorry about John's death. Toni nodded, silent, and focused on the rock cake. Her right hand went up to her eyes and she blotted her tears with the back of her hand. Wiping her hand on her jeans, she looked at me and said, "John was a good friend. We grew up together, liked to do things together. He had so many dreams and now..." She tore off another chunk of bun and tossed it onto the plate. Seconds later she continued. "He wanted to go to university. Not like some of our crowd who wanted the fast track to success by impossible goals."

"Such as..."

"Such as making it big as a rock star, or winning the pools. John wasn't afraid of hard work. He knew what he wanted and how to get it."

"And what did he want?"

"He was going to read chemistry, maybe get a job in a police lab or at a major university doing research. He—" She wiped her cheek, this time ignoring her damp hand. "He wanted to do some good in the world. He always said there were too many people wanting the easy ride to the top, too many people who sponged and never gave back. He wanted to help people, to find medical cures or do police lab work so he could help catch suspects and bring peace to the victims' families. He was like that, you know. Caring. Worried about the world and environment and people's lives. He was so brilliant like that! And funny, too. I'm going to miss him awfully."

I let Toni eat some of the rock cake before saying I, too, wanted to catch the person who killed John. As Toni nodded, I suddenly wondered if the burglary at the parsonage was a result of John's ambition. Had John been experimenting in the medical field, perhaps already dabbling in drug research, only a mate of his got the idea that John's basic medicines would be better used as a means of getting high, or making money if sold. Perhaps they had argued and the argument had escalated into a killing. I asked Toni if she shared any of John's dreams.

"I thought I'd go into teaching. Maybe nursing," she said, lifting her eyes from the plate to stare at me. "But I'm not so sure now. If I can't save someone like John, what good would I be?"

"Sometimes," I said rather slowly, fighting the pain already rising in my heart, "all the best medicine in the world can't heal or save, Toni. Sometimes the person is beyond our medical limits and we have to relinquish him to God, or whomever you believe in. I hope you do, for we've a bleak existence if there's no hope for a reward after this life." I paused, the blood rising to my cheeks. I couldn't believe I was offering spiritual crutches. What would Graham say? I glanced at the torn rock cake. Would he ever recover so I could tell him? I said, "Medicine is still a noble profession, Toni. It saves thousands of lives. Isn't it super when it heals and family members don't have to mourn a loved one's death?"

Toni shrugged, in no mood to think about her future. She mumbled that perhaps she'll just get married and stay at home, then she won't have to deal with such tragedies as sickness and death.

I said that was the horn of the dilemma—immersing yourself in such tragedies, whether through medicine or police work, so you could do some good and produce a satisfactory, if not happy, ending.

"I suppose so," Toni said, then answered my question about a boyfriend. "Nothing official like an engagement, but I've been going out a lot with Tad."

"Tad Mills? The friend of Page Hanley's brother?"

"That's him. And sometimes Conrad when he's in town. But it's not often enough. I mean, even though I like Conrad, if he's never around. Well, what's the use? So I went out with Enrico. To fill the gap, like. But..." She trailed off, perhaps thinking that Enrico, like John, was now dead. "Well, it was only twice. We—we didn't have time for any more dates."

"Enrico Thomas?" I asked, trying to believe it. The age difference between them was more than twenty years.

Toni evidently saw my mind working, for she said, "He loved me. He told me so. It doesn't make any difference if he was older than me. He loved me. We kissed a lot. I liked it. He taught me how to kiss good. I know he wanted to go further, but I wouldn't let him. Some of my girl friends have already gone all the way, only to be dumped. And who needs that?" Tears again filled her eyes and I said I was sorry Toni had had to suffer two losses.

"We did go out twice, though. He liked to bird watch on the hill above the village. He said it gave him a great view of the wood and the stream and such. He had amazing field glasses. He'd sit so still, squat down in the grass or lie on his stomach with the tall grasses or a log in front of him so he'd blend in better with the land. Camouflage, he called it. So he wouldn't frighten off the birds. I got a bit bored, sitting there for hours, but I could be near him that way, so I didn't mind too much."

"What did he like to look for? Any particular bird?" I asked because I, too, loved to bird watch, and there was always something on your life list that you were desperate to check off as having seen.

"He just liked looking around the village and in the wood, I think, but I did hear him say he'd be over the moon if he could spot a white-tailed eagle."

I stiffened, staring at Toni. The white-tailed eagle habituated coasts, nested on cliffs. It was a bird not even found in England, being a very rare bird of the Inner Hebrides. I grabbed the edge of the table, afraid the room would tilt. Enrico obviously was no birder; so what was he really looking for?

Chapter 26

"I felt so bad when Enrico died," Toni was saying when I drifted back from my imagined scenarios. "I had to do something. He had no family, you know, and, well, I couldn't bear to think of him dead like that. Alone, at night, on the ground. It—" She sniffed and blinked back a tear. "It was indecent. Especially with all that blood. I wanted to show him I cared, to give him one last kiss, like."

"What did you do?" I said, my voice sounding far away.

She smiled faintly, as though embarrassed. "I—I laid a rose near him. Well, as close as I could get. Near the wood, on the side of the path. Near the church. A red rose. I wanted to show him I cared, that I loved him. That I'll always remember him and love him."

Red rose, I thought, recalling Adam's and my dinner conversation. Red roses meant love. An appropriate flower between lovers. I thought of the astilbes still crammed into a glass in my bedroom at the pub and wondered if Adam and I would ever exchange red roses.

"I wanted to do it," Toni said, bringing me back to the present.

"Because no one else was his friend?"

"Not a *real* friend. The vicar's wife talked to him, and he chatted to people at the bookshop where he worked, but he didn't go out with anyone but me. I wanted him to be remembered. So I gave him a rose."

I said that it was a thoughtful, loving tribute.

She sniffed. "I won't be giving red roses to King. I know that much already."

"King?" I said, amazed Toni could still astound me. "King Roper, Richard's friend?"

"Yes, that's him. I went out with him twice when he visited Richard. He's good looking in a rough, sensual way, and I thought he might be fun. A different kind of chap from whom I'm usually attracted to. But all he wanted to do was park and neck, and..." She looked down at her hands, as if they held some history. When she looked at me again, she said quietly, "I had trouble keeping him from taking me."

The sounds of the teashop washed over us as I considered her words. Toni had turned scarlet, embarrassed to be talking about so intimate a subject. I swallowed uncomfortably and asked if she'd been raped or beaten.

"No, miss," she said, her voice growing stronger. "Only scared at his strength. He was so determined to...well, you know. I don't know how I got him off me, how I got him to stop. I was scared for days after."

"Was this recent, Toni? Can I do anything?"

"This last time—last week—made me realize I had to break off our relationship. He'd just come to visit Richard again. I'm not going out with him anymore, miss. He was rough, rougher than he was before that. He—he felt up my skirt before I could get him off me. I don't want to go through that again. Even if Enrico was passionate, he never forced me. I felt safe with him."

"About your bird watching. You said you went out twice with Enrico. Did he use the field glasses any other time?"

She shook her head rather emphatically. "Not that I saw. Of course, like I said, we didn't have much time together. But he wouldn't have used them to spy on his neighbors. He wasn't that sort—not the kind of person to look through people's bedroom windows. Anyway, the glasses weren't out, sitting on a table or chair in his front room, when we left to bird watch. He always had to get them from his back bedroom."

And, I thought, remembering the layout of Enrico's house, there was nothing behind Enrico's house but the village green.

I repeated that I'd help her if she wanted me to, then told her again I was sorry about John. She thanked me quietly, her large eyes staring at me, and I left.

Simcock wanted a brief main frame meeting with the CID team, so I wandered back to the incident room, generally angry, confused and running on adrenalin. A good deal of anger seemed to link everything in this village, from the vicious assaults on Graham and Macmillan, to the violent bludgeoning deaths of Enrico and John, to the attempted physical violation of Toni. Even Darlene, John's mother, was angry at God. And, though it sounded ludicrous on the surface, I wondered if Harry, who had cussed out the publican, had any link to these cases. I said so at the meeting.

"Could be," Simcock said, directing Margo to sketch the grid onto the large, white boards we used to map out suspects, motives and opportunity.

In spite of my exhaustion, I inwardly bristled. It should be Graham directing this meeting, not Simcock. It should be Graham's voice I heard, asking for suspects and reasons why I considered them suspects. I averted my eyes from Simcock's face, drowning in frustration and helplessness, worried sick about Graham, wanting to find who did it, wanting to be at his side. I didn't give a damn at the moment who killed Enrico.

But I had to pretend I was concerned, so I put on an interested face. It was a large group. Besides our own team, Keith Jeffries was there with his team, anxious to hear anything new about John's case. Three men whom I didn't know also sat with our group. Probably from the Greater Manchester Police, I thought, knowing officers had been recruited to help work on our cases. They jotted down everything put up on the board, made copious notes of what was said, and looked incredibly serious. They would, Simcock assured our original teams, disseminate the information back to the others who had joined them here. We nodded to them and I wondered how much experience they had had in CID. Evidently enough to please Simcock; he would brook no incompetence. I glanced at Mark, wondering what he'd been doing all morning, then related Toni's experiences with King.

"Unless he committed rape," Simcock said, "we can't arrest him. There's no crime other than an over eagerness on his part."

I exhaled loudly, soliciting a hand pat from Mark.

Simcock asked if Toni could have killed Enrico or John in some jealous rage. "After all, she seems to have been dating a lot of blokes. Maybe one of them got tired of her, told her in no uncertain terms to clear off, and she killed him in anger. Do you think she's the type, Taylor? You've talked to her. What's she like?"

I admitted that I didn't know if she could have been so physically violent, but added that it very well could dwell within each of us and rise to the surface if we were angry enough. I related the deliveries I'd seen yesterday morning, the art supplies for Tad and the boxes of tea and biscuits for the teashop. "Ordinarily I wouldn't pay them any mind. After all, businesses and the self-employed need supplies. But we've got at least one box of laundry soap that doesn't seem to be laundry soap. Am I too suspicious?"

"Some clues you grab onto and assume something," Simcock said as Margo jotted down my observations. "You need a starting point in every case, and you learn to grab and hold onto that clue until it turns to dust or to gold. It's a lead. Anything else? Why suspect Tad Mills or the teashop owner?"

I said that the only reason right now that Tad could be a suspect is because his friend, David, had been a suspect in December's case.

"Guilty by association?" Simcock said.

"Or," Mark said, letting go of my hand, "guilty because he's the mastermind and David Willett is just his henchman."

"And what is this dubious cause or activity they are undertaking? Why murder Enrico or John?"

"They saw something?"

"Fine. They *saw* something," Simcock sniffed. "*What?* I can't arrest some bloke because he saw something. We see things every day, Salt. I thought you favored Enrico as a terrorist, anyway."

"It still makes sense. He being alone, hardly any furniture to speak of in his house so he can leave the area quickly, no history further than two months ago. There are no such people! Everyone has records—school, health, tax…" He took a deep breath, as though calming his heart rate. "There's something about him, something false. You just don't pop into existence two months ago!"

I related the episode of the bird watching and the field glasses.

Simcock asked if I had made anything of that, to which I replied that he must have been watching something or someone in the village, since he sat on the hill for so long. But at the moment I had no idea who he might have been observing.

"Could you get Toni to show you where they sat? We might get an idea what he was watching from there, project a sight-line from up there."

I said I'd ask her.

One of the men from the Greater Manchester Police said he had questioned the bookshop owner about Enrico, but had come up with nothing. "He was friendly with the customers, never late to work, and knowledgeable about several subjects, which helped him answer questions."

"What subjects? Did you find out?"

"Not crowbars or village history."

Or birds of Britain, I wanted to add, but kept quiet.

The man added that the owner had been saddened to hear of Enrico's death, for not only was Enrico a model employee but also likeable.

"Well," Simcock said, "That got us no nearer to knowing anything about him. And unless we can deduce what he was watching through his field glasses, we'll be out of luck with that line of inquiry."

"I suppose," Mark said, "he wouldn't have been watching deliveries. How would he know when the teashop was due for another shipment?"

"Precisely. And even if we were to examine the cartons delivered to the teashop and to this Tad Mills' home, we'd be a day late. They'd have had time to hide the illegal items, if there were any. Well, that gets us damn all. So..." Simcock slapped his palms on the tabletop, dismissed us with 'good work,' and Mark and I grabbed lunch before heading to the hair salon and our pursuit of Enrico's killer.

We separated as we approached the salon, Mark going in first and asking for a hair cut, I following several minutes later for a manicure. I was taken immediately, for the manicurist had an opening. Noel told Mark he'd be able to take him in five minutes, so Mark flipped through some magazines while he waited. Though Noel didn't say anything to me—perhaps not wanting to make a scene in front of clients—I felt his eyes following me as I sat at the manicurist's table.

I hadn't had my nails done in so long that I was slightly uneasy about presenting my work-roughened hands to the woman. But I was soon relaxing and chatting up the manicurist, who had attended the stone turning, plus the church service and the tea afterwards. "After all," she said, filing my nails, "it *is* the beginning of Lent, Ash Wednesday is. And the stone turning's not really a boisterous event like Guy Fawkes. We're just watching a handful of people straining to roll over a great stone. Not much to it. I don't consider it a sacrilege to watch."

"It has its origins in religion, I understand."

"I go have a look-see. It's not an evening's-worth of activity like Guy Fawkes is, but then," she said, pausing in her attack of my nails and looking at me, "most customs aren't, are they? You hunt for Easter eggs, it's over.

HORNS OF A DILEMMA

You get your valentine and flowers, it's over. You participate in clipping the church or you attend the Goose Fair, it's over."

"Yet, you can make it what it is, I suppose. You can extend most of those, like Valentine's Day. Dinner, go to a film, something for the two of you."

"I suppose we really don't have many all-day affairs, like Christmas or wakes festivals. Still, it's a bit of fun, the stone turning, and even though there's lots who don't go, I do."

She reiterated nearly verbatim the names of people I'd already heard. There was no one new to consider, at least from the manicurist's memory. She said, as an after thought, "Of course, King Roper was there. He's not a villager, but he was clearly with Richard. And Page Hanley's brother, David, was there. Colette's nephew, Conrad, watched, too, but I know him. Sorry, miss, I don't recall any strangers."

I thanked her and agreed that I'd not let my nails get so unsightly in the future. Mark was chatting with Noel as he clipped with enthusiasm. Mark's lovely curls were cascading to the floor. I shut my eyes, afraid to watch the transformation to flattop, paid, then left the shop.

I found Toni in the teashop and asked if she would show me the exact spots where Enrico had bird watched. After getting permission from the owner, Toni grabbed her jacket, followed me from the shop, and was soon seated in my car, directing me to park at the millstones site on Green Acre Road. It was the place Mark had checked out earlier to see if the path through the wood was visible from the road.

We hiked for nearly twenty minutes up the hill, behind the church, finally coming to a spot just outside the edge of the wood. The land rose steeply here, angling more obliquely beyond the church but not yet one with the near-vertical rock face. A sharp wind laced with cold and scents of pine and damp wood raced down the cliff face, bending the tall grass and stirring the tree branches. The land skirting the forest was littered with chunks of broken-off mountain, like the church expanse below us. Huge tree boughs or dead tree trunks fringed the edge of the wood here, some embossed with lichen and fungi. Tufts of tall grass nuzzled the trunks, enthusiastic in its protected habitation.

It was a perfect place for surveillance—tall grass, boulders and tree trunks to camouflage your presence. I didn't say as much to Toni, but I wondered if Enrico had deliberately sought out such a spot with the activity in mind or if he had come upon it by chance and thought it would be fun to see what his neighbors were up to. I squatted at the area that Toni pointed out. Only matted grass spoke of long hours of lying in wait; there were no cigarette butts or forgotten pieces of paper or lost buttons that signified Enrico's obsession—or disquieting hobby. I scooted down on my stomach and raised my head slightly so I was just peering over the trunk. A curtain of dry grass waved slightly to my left and on the other side of the hunk of wood. Ahead and below me the village sprawled, its streets and homes and village green spread out and visible like a model railroad layout. Inch-tall people and toy cars moved through the landscape, unreal yet somehow significant. From this sharp incline and great height, Enrico could surely have watched someone's activities. But whom or why was still unanswered. The answer lay down there and I was probably staring at it, but I couldn't understand what I saw. Nothing held any significance.

"Could we look in on Lloyd as long as we're here?" I asked. "It'll only take a minute, and I'll get you back to the teashop right after that."

Toni said that was fine and added that she'd heard that Darlene had left him.

We walked down the hill, coming upon the back of the vicarage. I went around to the kitchen, assuming it the most obvious place for Lloyd to be. I didn't even knock, but tried the door. It was open and we walked in. The two liaison officers were not there; Lloyd was not in the room.

We walked through the house, calling his name. He was in none of the rooms. I told Toni that I thought that was odd, since he had been so grief stricken the last time I'd seen him.

"He could be talking to Darlene," Toni offered, "or in the church. He could be praying."

I nodded, thinking that a likely possibility if Lloyd had finally stirred himself. We had walked through the house in our search and now stood in the doorway to John's room. The thing that struck me immediately was John's desk. It was very neat, though whether from Lloyd's manic cleaning spree or because John was tidy, I couldn't say. Notebook, schoolbooks, computer monitor, keyboard and mouse, calendar, pens and pencils were lined up neatly, like soldiers on parade. Toni said, "That's odd."

"What is? Is something wrong?"

"It's gone! It's not here, and it should be!"

"I'm sorry, Toni. I don't know—"

"John's camera. It's gone missing." She walked into the room, gesturing to the desk chair. It was an ordinary swivel chair that went with many computers.

"Does the camera hang from the back of the chair?"

She nodded, swinging the chair full circle, as though she were a magician proving to her audience that there were no wires or human assistants attached. "Just here. On the knob that adjusts the backrest. John always hangs it there. *Always.*"

"I suppose it couldn't be elsewhere in the house..."

"No. It hangs here when John isn't using it. You see," she said, relaxing a bit and leaning against the edge of the desk, "it was a rule. I know because we grew up together, we've been in each other's houses so much that we know about each other's families. That camera always hung there. Has been ever since we were young and he had binoculars or other, cheaper cameras. He had to keep all his things in his room, not scattered about like is the norm in so many households. You may not be familiar with parsonages, Miss, but they're owned by the church, not the vicar or minister. The cleric merely lives in it, one of a long line of occupants."

"So, since the house isn't actually the Grangers', it is subject to church members dropping by."

"Oh, they usually ring up first, John told me, giving them a chance to put on something else besides bathrobes." She paused, as though remembering a story about that incident. "It no doubt sounds odd to you, but that's life in a parsonage."

"Like living under a microscope, or on 24-hour call, I suspect."

"Yes, miss. And, since they were subject to moment's notice-visitors, he learned early on that the front rooms must always be tidy. It saved them and their visitors embarrassment, not to mention the last minute rush to make the place look presentable."

"So John was extremely tidy."

"Certainly! There was no reason why he shouldn't be responsible for his own things. That's why I can state so emphatically that he always hung his camera on the back of his chair, that his things were never in any other rooms in the house. If you want to walk through and look again," she said rather haltingly, as though debating the odds that I would gossip about John's underwear drawer, "you can do it. I mean, it's a murder investigation, isn't it? I heard about the burglary, about you and that nice young man who came with you that night. What was his name? The uniformed chap."

"Scott Coral," I said, half amused and wondering about Scott's reaction when I told him how Toni had referred to him. Probably nod his head and murmur that even young girls were perceptive and could see into men's souls.

"That's the chap! Yes! Anyway, Darlene mentioned to a friend that he had a look through the house that night, after you'd gone. Then the other officers arrived, the ones who worked on the case. None of them found the camera. They didn't find it stuffed into a drawer or beneath a bed. It must have been stolen!" She broke off, glancing at me to get my reaction.

"What type of camera is it? Is it expensive? Does it warrant the theft?" I wondered if it might explain the burglary.

"Not that I would have thought! That's the odd thing about this. It's just a cheap 35mm. Not a digital or camera phone. Rather old fashioned, I suppose, by today's technology standards."

"Still, it's a camera. It would bring something if he sold it."

"I hate to see it go missing. Not that it can't be replaced—as I said, it wasn't expensive. But it's John's and, as such, is a part of him. His parents would like it for no other reason than that. To...to hold on to." She glanced again at the chair and dabbed at her eyes with her jacket sleeve.

I knew how difficult this was for her, John's friend—trying to make sense of John's death and rising above the anger and depression that were surely clawing at all his friends.

Toni said, "John wasn't really a photographer. He didn't take many snaps. That's why he bought that particular camera. It was used and cheap.

John—he even said it would be crackers for him to invest in a digital model just to be in vogue when he only used the camera for holiday snaps and the like. He wasn't a great one for snapping his friends; he has no albums like that. So you see, miss, why I'm so confused by all this."

I agreed that it seemed odd, then asked about John's part-time job at the launderette. "I see a pay stub." I nodded toward the top of his dresser. A small stack of stubs lay neatly next to a small lamp.

"Not much to tell, actually. He worked after school, on holidays and through summer. Well, so did I. Only I work in the teashop and he works in the launderette. He needed the job; he was saving up to go to university. He was very reliable. Richard said that many times. He could always trust John to be at his job. He never had to worry about theft, either—monetary or supplies. I—it's a small thing, but it's comforting to know how others felt about him."

"Do you know if John's family patronize the launderette?"

"No. They've their own washing machine and tumble drier."

"You mentioned Richard being happy with John's work. Were there any problems at the launderette, any complaints that you know of?"

"I've not heard. But I would have done. John would have told me, for one. And villagers talk. Word gets about if any business—here in the village or in some other town—has inferior service or products. Well, you do, don't you? If you've had a bad experience with an item or were treated ill in a shop, you'd tell everyone. It's the same at the teashop. If someone thinks a scone is dry, or the tea's lukewarm, we hear about it. I suppose it's only right. I mean, you pay for it so you should get what you like. But no, there wasn't anything like that about Richard's place. It was very well run. Many people in the village use it."

I made a note of the camera model, thanked Toni for spotting its absence, said I'd put in a report, and we left. As we walked back to the car, I thought about Conrad, the photographer's assistant. Even though it was thin and probably laughable, he was the only link I had with the missing camera. But why steal the camera? Because the film showed something incriminating? What was incriminating in a village other than people having affairs? I thought of Enrico's field glasses and what he might have seen with them. He wasn't likely to have been a Peeping Tom. Not like me, peering through Colette's window to see her and Conrad necking. I kicked a pebble, angry with myself for spying, angry at the person who took John's young, promising life, angry that Graham had been attacked. At least MacMillan was getting out of hospital today—one spot of sunshine in this claustrophobic darkness. Yet, what could the camera film hold if it wasn't a couple engaged in an affair? From what little I knew of Darlene, I didn't consider her the type to have a sexual relationship outside her marriage. Had it started innocently—Conrad trying to console her on the death of John, Darlene sobbing on his shoulder, one thing leading to another.

I bent down and picked up a stone. Though obviously smaller, it was the same color and type as the Devil's stone. Did the stone turning custom have anything to do with Enrico's death, or was it just a convenient time to commit murder, an opportunity seized because victim and suspect had been there, alone? Had Enrico's death a link with John's? Or with Graham's and MacMillan's attacks? It was certainly suspicious, all four crimes occurring in the same vicinity. I considered the weight of the stone in my hand, tossing it several times, feeling the smooth surface. If the stone turning was the center of every crime, perhaps the devil was indeed behind it all. Or a devil in human form.

I dropped Toni back at the teashop, thanked her again for her help, and tried to convince myself that we would eventually discover the meaning of Enrico's surveillance. For that was what it had to be. Even if he harbored a sick thrill from spying on his neighbors, I doubted he would lie on that mountain for hours, or in broad daylight. Voyeurs would peer close up through bedroom windows at night, hoping to see something scintillating. Enrico's operation smelled of something different, and it frightened me.

I stopped at the bakery and bought a prepared sandwich, which I ate on my drive to the hospital. The traffic was heavy and it took me a quarter of an hour longer than usual to reach the hospital car park. But the longer drive had given me time to consider suspects and possible events warranting Enrico's use of the field glasses. I left the bit of uneaten sandwich and the village's problems in my car and hurried in to see Graham.

The same constable whom I had encountered at my last visit was still in Graham's room. I wondered if the lad ever got a break as I showed him my ID. He nodded, said he'd heard nothing new on Graham's condition, then left as I put down my shoulder bag.

Nothing had changed—not the tubes running into his arm, nor the lights on the bed monitor, nor the oxygen supply. The curtains were still drawn, still allowing a paper-thin stream of outside light into the room. The table still held a water pitcher, paper pad and pen. It seemed frozen in time, as though Graham and his treatment had been waiting my return before resuming life. And this sameness was terrifying, signifying Graham had not gained consciousness and had not been out of bed to use them. But there was something different about the room. As I came up to his bed, I noticed a dozen or more cards laying on top of the bed monitor, as though a nurse had brought them in and laid them there, unthinking, concerned with Graham's condition. I leafed through the cards, curious as to who had sent them. Simcock's was on top; I was becoming familiar with his bold handwriting. And there was one from Margo, her small, pointed penmanship easy to place. I was somewhat surprised to see it, for she hadn't told me she'd sent one. But, then, we'd hardly had time to chat during this case. The circumstances didn't invite conversation. I finished shuffling through the small stack, noting cards from others at headquarters. I returned them to the top of the monitor and spoke softly to Graham. His eyelids didn't open, his head didn't move, his body lay rigid. Nothing to show he'd heard me. Nothing to convey he was alive but the lights on the monitor and the rhythmic whoosh of air through his oxygen mask. I reached out my hand, hesitated momentarily, then touched his cheek. The flesh was warm and pliable, though unresponsive. I touched his hair, called his name again, then bent over his chest and sobbed.

I don't know how long I cried, pouring out my anxiety, relieved that he was still alive. As the minutes passed, so did my fervency. In the end, I stood up, wiped my eyes, and felt incredibly limp, as though all the passion had been swept from me along with my tears. Graham had not moved; the depression from my hands was the only disturbance in the otherwise taut blanket. I smoothed away the wrinkles, pushed the blanket farther beneath the top mattress, and, on an impulse, leaned over him. A noise in the hallway froze my movement. I glanced over my shoulder to the door and counted the seconds. The noise had faded; the constable had not spoken; the door remained closed. As I turned back to Graham, I heard footsteps approaching the room. Again I paused, my heart racing, my mind and heart offering prayers that this moment would not be spoiled. The footsteps faded and again it was quiet beyond the door. Taking a deep breath, I bent slightly closer to him and squeezed his hand. I whispered his name, then with my free hand slowly removed his oxygen mask. The whoosh of oxygen was louder with the mask lying on the pillow, but I hardly heard it as I leisurely and possessively kissed his mouth.

An eternity later, I stood up. There was no difference in Graham—he had not moved or uttered any sound. I brushed his lips with my fingertips, replaced the mask, told him good bye, and was reaching for the door when it opened.

Mark walked into the room. He looked concerned and rushed. He also looked odd—his curls were gone and the hair was cropped short along the sides of his head. I wanted to say something, but didn't. It was his hair; he had sacrificed it to chat with Noel. He stopped short, the door nearly hitting him as it began to close. He grabbed the edge, looked at me, and asked if I was all right. I nodded, shifted my eyes to Graham, and said that there was no change.

Mark let the door close and remained where he was, looking like he wished he were anywhere else. I made an attempt to step around him and grab for the doorknob when he said, "I didn't know where you were. I considered ringing you up on your mobile, but I didn't know if I'd be interrupting an interview. I should have known you'd be here."

"What's that supposed to mean? Why shouldn't I stop by? He's our boss. I care about him, the same way I care about MacMillan getting hurt. Or you, if it came to that."

"How many times have you been to see MacMillan?" His voice was low, accusing.

"What's it matter? Why bring that up?"

"Because," he said, folding his arms across his chest, "I think your visits to Graham are a bit more than a subordinate's concern for a boss. I think you're in love with him."

I opened my mouth to shout my denial, then closed it. In the short silence I heard the soft rush of the oxygen pump, reminding me that Mark was right. I mumbled that my personal life was not under Mark's command and that he was imagining things. "Graham's been in a coma for several days," I said, angry at Mark and angry that he had destroyed my visit. "I'm worried sick about him, as you should be. And if you weren't such a flaming berk, if you weren't jealous or hating Graham or whatever your problem is, you'd know that."

"Why should I be jealous? That implies I love you."

I felt my cheeks flood with heat. Tucking my shoulder bag beneath my arm, I snapped, "There's very little chance of that. Get out of my way." I nudged him to one side, knocking an envelope from his pocket, and yanked open the door. Mark's bellowed reply followed me into the corridor. The constable had the good manners not to appear to notice.

Though it was slightly cool for an alfresco break, I sat on a bench outside the building, trying to sort through my feelings. Yes, I wanted Graham sexually, but I didn't want a tawdry fling as Darlene and Conrad seemed to have. And yes, Erik and I lived together on weekends, but that was purely out of physical need. We wanted each other only to stem our loneliness. My need and attraction for Graham was different. I loved every aspect of him—physically and intellectually. And yes, while there could be someone else who fulfilled every aspect of my desires, I had yet to find him. But I was willing to look. That's why I had made the overture to Adam.

As though reading my mind, he appeared. I hadn't heard him approach, but he was suddenly there, standing beside the bench, looking at me. His voice, when he asked if I were all right, was low with disquiet. I smiled, said I was just concerned about Graham, and asked why he was here.

"Same reason," he said, putting his foot on the end of the bench seat and resting his forearm on his thigh. "Graham. I heard he was still in a coma. How many days has it been?"

"Two. A bit longer than forty-eight hours. He was attacked Thursday night."

Adam nodded, as though counting two days forward from Thursday. "He's bound to be fine, Brenna. I mean, it's a good hospital, good doctors. They won't skimp on anything."

"Two days is too long a time, Adam. MacMillan's already been released. Why hasn't Graham improved? I couldn't stand it if—"

"MacMillan's physical condition wasn't as bad. I don't know why because I don't know who attacked her or the reason behind the attacks."

"You think Graham's condition is more serious because the attacker hated him, struck him more violently?"

"I can't say. But I doubt it. In the wood, at night? How could Graham see who it was—because that's what you're hinting at, that Graham saw his assailant and was hit more violently in hopes to kill him?"

"Graham had a torch. That'd show him to his attacker."

Adam shrugged. "Perhaps. I'm not going to concoct a scenario or motive about something I don't know. Maybe MacMillan or someone else scared off her attacker before he could beat her as severely as he beat Graham. I don't know! But don't dwell on it, for God's sake! You'll drive yourself into Bedlam."

I mumbled that I was very nearly there.

"Well, I'll be first in line to visit you, then." He said it without smiling, but there was genuine concern behind his voice. He stretched and stood up. "Damn, it's chilly. How long have you been sitting here?"

I said not long, then hinted that I should be getting back to the incident room. "Are you coming or going?"

"Coming." He pulled an envelope from inside his jacket and wiggled it between his thumb and index finger. Another card, like Mark came to deliver. I watched the white rectangle flop up and down as Adam said, "This isn't brown nosing. I've nothing to gain by this. I like Graham. Always have, since day one. I learned a lot from him when I was starting my career. Probably still would if I ever got the chance to team with him." He shoved the card back inside his jacket. "I best be getting on, then. You up to having dinner with me?" He glanced at his slacks. "Obviously nothing fancy."

"The maitre d' might be tempted to kick you out," I agreed.

"Back luck for him, too. I'm a big tipper. And I know you can't take a formal break like a terribly romantic date would dictate. But we can grab a bite at a pub. What do you say?" He looked at me, assessing my vulnerability and need of companionship. "I won't be half a tick. Just wait here while I run this up. Or, no." He dug into his slacks pocket and pulled out his car key. "Wait in my car. It's warmer."

He was about to shove the key into my hand when my mobile rang. I apologized and answered it. It was Margo, telling me Simcock was asking after me. I said I was just leaving the hospital and I'd be there in thirty minutes.

As I flipped my phone closed, Adam said, "So much for romance. And dinner. Another time, obviously."

I nodded and turned on my heel, but not before I saw Mark leaving the hospital. He stopped short when he saw me and changed direction. I quickly headed for my car, regret and despair flooding my soul.

Chapter 27

Sunday morning dawned with a glut of sunshine and a sense of dread. The sun felt good on my face as I walked through the green on the way to the incident room. I wondered if Lloyd would be struggling through his sermon this morning, if he had steeled himself with some inner resolve and would conquer the weight of devastation that jeopardized him. Even the brave bunch of sparrows hopping among the cold daffodil leaves in search of breakfast did little to lessen my anxiety. As I came to the edge of the green, I noticed Darlene and Conrad sitting on a bench, holding hands. Whatever had gone on between them yesterday, then, had led to this—a public slap of Lloyd's face.

Passing the couple, I glanced between the two buildings on the opposite side of the street. Like an object viewed through a telescope, the lych gate of the church was visible, framed between the tearoom and pub. A short man with a clerical robe draped over his arm stood on the opposite side of the gate, looking down on us. I stopped, wondering who it was. Was Lloyd too ill to preside over the service? The figure turned, retreating toward the church. Moments later the slamming of the south door rolled down the hill.

I walked past the launderette and hair salon, gazing into the shop windows, recalling snippets of conversations. The shops were closed and dark, the pavement along this side of the street harboring only a scant number of people. Two of whom were David and Harry Willett, standing outside the bakery. David was talking, Harry was eating. I paused, interested in what had obviously got David so agitated, for he was speaking very loudly.

"You shouldn't lie, Harry," David was saying, his hand on his brother's shoulder. "Everyone in the village knows you. They know what you're like, about your condition. They know you're no damned film agent—or photographer's model rep or whatever the hell it is you fancy yourself at the moment. What're you trying to prove by lying?"

Harry mumbled something and crammed half of the bun into his mouth.

David yanked Harry's hand away but Harry brought it back to his mouth, yelling for David to leave him alone, that he wasn't hurting anyone.

"You're hurting our sister," David said, the veins on his neck bulging. "She has to live here and be subjected to neighbors' reactions. Why don't you consider living in a home where trained people can look after you? You'd have things to do, people to talk to."

"I *got* things to do. *And* folks to talk to. I don't need to go nowhere to do that."

"You're always sneaking about, getting into fights, getting mad. Especially with people who've done you no harm. I've had enough of this! Page has had enough! We're sick to death of your disturbances. They'll land you in trouble, if you're not careful."

Harry smiled, his eyes half closed. "I *am* careful."

"If that's what you call being careful..." David's teeth clamped down on his lower lip as he exhaled loudly. He grabbed Harry's hand and said, "Look, Harry. We've all got to make sacrifices in life. We've all got to do things at times we don't want to do. For me it was taking my damned teaching job. For Page, it was going through her divorce. This is your time. You've had a great life. Over thirty years of doing what you want—"

Harry shook free of David's grasp and struck a boxing position. "Not by half. I wanna box. I wanna be a boxer." He took a few swings at the air. "Damn, I'm good!"

"You're good, Harry. Nobody said you weren't. But we can't always be what we want to be. You can still be a boxer—that doesn't depend on where you live. We'll find you a place to live where there's a gym. You can practice all day long. Would you like that? Hours at the gym, maybe get you a trainer..." He peered at Harry to see if he was listening or considering David's suggestion.

Harry just continued swinging at the air, bouncing about in his boxing stance, and making little grunting sounds.

David said, "You've got to think of Page, Harry. For once in your life—*please*! Think of someone other than yourself. She's taken care of you for twenty years. She needs a rest. Won't you do this for her, move into a home so she can have a rest? She'll come to visit you. I will, too. We'll come often, every week. We'll bring you little gifts. How'd you like that? Things to brighten your room. But you'll be so busy with your boxing lessons and such—"

Harry froze as he was about to punch his imaginary adversary. He glared at David and shouted, "I'm not going to no home! I'm staying with Page."

"Page can come see you—"

"Page knows how to care for me; she knows what I like and what I don't like. And I *don't* like to go to no home!" He dropped his arms to his side.

"Now, Harry—"

"I'm *not* going nowhere! It sounds like prison, that home. I'd be shut up inside, where I can't see the sunshine or the birds, where I can't get out to walk around outside. It'd be like me being in the nick again, only this time I wouldn't be out in a year. I'd be in *forever*." He punched David's arm.

"Page would be able to see you, Harry. So would I. I'd come—"

"No you wouldn't. I know you. You'd keep me in there."

"Harry, be reasonable. It's a home, not jail."

"Not jail in name, or with bars, but a jail. Maybe it's better than being in the nick."

"You'd have your own room, Harry, and be able to train and have good food—"

Harry shook his head. "Maybe I wouldn't be looking through bars this time. But I'd still feel like I was in prison again. I'd still be watched and I'd still be limited in what I can do."

"We're all limited in what we can do, Harry. We're a society of laws. We can't just go out and do anything we feel like. If we do, and that act is against the law, we have to be punished. We spend time in jail. Even though I need money, I can't just go up to someone and grab his wallet. I'd be caught and punished and go to jail. Don't you see, Harry?"

"I see you're trying to send me back to jail. *That's* what I see! It may not have bars, this place you're so keen on, but it'd be like prison. I'd suffocate in there. I'd die. I'm not going back!" He took a swing at David, who backed up quickly to avoid Harry's fist, and ran off. David called after him to wait up, but Harry kept running. David swore, turned and saw me, and nodded. He waved to someone behind me and crossed the street.

I turned to see whom David had greeted. Ian was dressed in his security guard uniform and looked as though he hadn't slept in forty-eight hours. Perhaps he'd had a hard night at work or was worried about the murders. He ignored Darlene, walked straight up to Conrad and grabbed his nephew's arm. It seemed nearly the same scene I'd just witnessed with David and Harry, for Ian snapped, "Isn't it bloody awful early for you to be parading your affair in front of the village?"

Conrad frowned and stared up at his uncle. "Early? It's just gone—"

"I don't care what the hell time it is. I mean you two. Sitting together, your hands all over each other, in plain sight of anyone passing by. What the hell are you thinking, Conrad? Darlene's married. Or have you conveniently forgotten that fact? Not to mention she's—" He stopped abruptly, his face reddening, as though he'd been about to mention their age discrepancy. Instead, he said, "I want you to go home. Now! I'll not have you disgracing your aunt, or start idle tongues wagging. You'll not be having an affair while you're under my roof—you understand?"

Conrad stood up, his hands doubled up into fists. "I'm an adult. Or have you ignored that fact?"

"I know your age."

"Then you also know I *am* of age and can do what I bloody well like. Which means doing the sort of work I want, living where I want and living with whoever I want! Being of age means you can't do a ruddy thing about it, either!"

"I can stipulate and enforce the laws in my own household, Conrad.

And while you're staying with us, you'll abide by them."

"Well, that's easily changed. Maybe I'll just pack my gear and mosey off, then. That'll suit just about everybody, won't it? I'll be out of your hair, Aunt Colette won't be disgraced, you won't be a party to my affair, and Darlene and I can do what we want. Fair enough?"

"I don't want you to leave, Conrad. Your aunt will be upset to see you cut short your visit. I'm only saying that..." He took a deep breath and paused, as though mentally counting to ten, and said in a somewhat calmer voice, "I just don't want to see you doing anything rash, making a huge mistake you'll have trouble rectifying. Or that will haunt you for years. Just think about it before you do anything drastic. Step back and think. Of course I want you to be happy—your aunt does, too. We love you! But sometimes in the heat of the moment, without thinking, people act on impulses. They make rash decisions they usually regret later. That's all I'm saying."

"Yeh, well, all *I'm* saying is that Darlene's also an adult, and we've decided we should be together. She's left Lloyd and now we're both free to love as we wish."

Ian stared at his nephew, his mouth slightly open. He stammered, "You—you're not serious! Conrad! She's *married!* You can't run off with a married woman. Have you thought about this?" He looked at Darlene, frowning in his concern. "Do you know what you're doing?"

She nodded. "I'm going to live with the man I love. What's wrong with that? What's wrong with being happy?"

"Nothing's wrong with being happy, but you're married, for God's sake! You've a husband who desperately needs you now, Darlene. He's had a nervous breakdown. Someone else is preaching today. Lloyd's too ill. He's given up on everything—on his faith, on you ever loving him again, on the cops finding John's killer, on the recovery of his friend—that other copper, Graham, is it? He's an absolute wreck, a mere shell, nearly a mental case! He's gone to pieces. You're leaving him at the *worst* possible time, when you should be helping each other through your shared tragedy."

Darlene pointed her finger at Ian. "Don't you *dare* tell me about duty or how I should feel or act! You've not lost a child. You've not waded through years of duty and regiment and served on mind-numbing church committees until you want to scream. You've not sat in church Sunday after Sunday because as the wife of the vicar you must be there, bored out of your mind, wishing you were anywhere else, doing anything else. You've not given up your life to help a husband in his job, ignoring your own desires."

"You've got your own career. You've got your office; you have a boss who depends on you—"

"Depends on me!" She barked a laugh into the air. "God, what a goal for an employee. I've got my secretarial job to keep me from going insane, to keep my mind occupied. I get no more thrill from answering phones or typing letters than a horse does in pulling a plow. I do it because it gets me out of the house and away from the church and the old biddy committee. That's why! And I've put up with it long enough. It's time I live my own life, not follow some man around as though I were on a lead. Sit. Stay. Fetch. Nice wife." She stood up, standing close to Conrad. "I'm ready to go with Conrad."

She linked her arm with Conrad's. As they started to walk away, Ian grabbed Conrad's arm, pulling him to a stop. Conrad instantly turned and landed a punch on Ian's jaw, knocking him to the ground. Without glancing at his uncle, Conrad stepped over the man's legs, and murmured to Darlene that they best be going. The couple walked down the street while Ian sat there, nursing his jaw.

Lunch was typical, which is to say that it was hurried, inexpensive and barely tasted as I gulped it down. I'd left the teashop and was walking to the incident room when Page waved to me. I waited for her to cross the street before asking what she wanted.

"I can't find Harry," she said, worry in her eyes.

I asked if that was unusual, to which she replied it was and it wasn't. "Depends on Harry's state of mind and emotions. He'll sometimes hang around the house all day, working on his stamp collection or gardening. Some days he's all over the village, bothering the vicar at the church, popping into the hair salon and bakery, talking to anyone he meets."

I told Page of the incident with the tourist and asked if Harry could be somewhere with the woman.

She shrugged. "I suppose he could be. I don't know. But I would have thought the woman would have seen through Harry's tale. He's good at handing you a line, is Harry. But if you talk to him long enough you realize it can't be true. Why would a talent scout—one of his favorite stories—be in such a small village? Nothing he says makes sense if you take the time to think it through. You—" She paused, perhaps fearful of her own imagination. When she continued, her words were barely audible. "You don't suppose, do you, that he's done something with her?"

"What do you mean? What would Harry do?"

"Usually nothing. That's why he's at home with me and not in an institution. He's gentle, he is. Just a big kid. But he can get angry. He gets frustrated, you see, and when he's frustrated he gets angry. He—I don't know what he's capable of at those times. He lashes out, strikes and hits without thinking. Reacting to his anger. He's very good with his fists. I—I hope he doesn't hurt her."

I nodded, seeing Harry in the role of our murderer, attacking Graham and MacMillan. Page knew Harry better than I did; if she said his anger became violent and we were now dealing in deaths and attacks from four violent incidents... I told Page I'd look around and she should ring me up if

Harry returned.

"Certainly, miss," Page said, gazing at the church. "Last time I saw Harry was early this morning. Around half six or so. He was walking up the hill, making toward the church. He likes to go there, to sit in the graveyard, trace his finger over the chiseled names on the tombstones. He also likes the bells. I know it's way later than that, but Harry has no real concept of time. Oh, he knows morning, afternoon and night, but he's not too keen about clock time. He'll show up at seven, thinking he's home at five." She thanked me, apologized for giving me something else to worry me, and left.

Thinking I could quickly check out the last sighting, I walked up to the church. The graveyard was empty; no one lingered among the rows of tombstones. Same was true inside the church. Then, thinking Harry might be outside, perhaps behind the building, I walked outside again. The bench opposite the south porch was empty, holding nothing but a few dead leaves. I walked toward the rear of the building. A rapid drumming, as of someone tattooing against wood, caught my attention. I glanced toward the direction of the thumping. A great spotted woodpecker clung to a tree on the outskirts of the copse. Its black-and-white body blended in amazingly well with the tree, but the red patch on the back of the head spotlighted the bird's location. When it moved, I caught the flash of crimson coloring beneath the tail. It was common to both genders, but only the male carried the red smear on his head. I glanced at the lump of suet tied to a tree branch, a favorite food of this bird. Had one of Darlene's duties included feeding the birds? Or did she do it out of love? Or did someone else do it—Harry, perhaps? Was that one reason he gravitated toward the church? I left the bird to its foraging and stepped around a fallen oak bough. Clumps of daffodils, their buds tightly closed but showing a trace of the yellow that would soon burst forth, bobbed in the slight breeze that trickled down the hill behind the church. Masses of dead leaves skittered across the ground, coming to a halt against the stone wall or tree trunks or the church itself. I was wondering who cared for the church grounds when I turned the far corner. I drew up suddenly and flattened myself against a large oak. Ahead of me, half hidden by a huge rhododendron, King and Tad were talking.

"So, is it taken care of?" King's sharp, nasal voice floated over to me, his words more chilling than the cold wind.

Tad must not have responded, for King repeated his question more emphatically.

"I told you," Tad said reluctantly, "I don't like this."

"I don't give a monkey's what you like and what you don't like. Have you taken care of it?"

"Yeh. Don't lose any sleep over it."

"And you weren't seen?"

Tad's voice rose in anger, either from King's distrust or from Tad's obvious unwillingness. "That's my risk, isn't it?"

"Mine, too, if you talk."

"You've kind of seen that I don't, haven't you?"

"I like to keep things neat. Makes less stress in my life."

Tad snorted. "I'm all for that. Anything to help you sleep better."

"I've a clear conscious, mate. Don't know about you, but I sleep like a baby."

"Or the dead."

Dead leaves rustled, a few tree branches snapped, followed by a dull thud—as of a softer object hitting a harder surface. There was a soft gagging sound and another, louder, snap of tree branches. After a few moments of silence, King said, "Watch your mouth, mate, or you'll experience it first hand. Or wish you were."

An unintelligible reply followed, then more silence. I left the anonymity of the tree and walked up to them, smiling.

Both men were surprised to see me. Tad patted his hair back into place and rearranged his jacket while King returned my smile and saluted.

"I'm looking for Harry," I said, pretending I didn't see Tad's hasty grooming. "His sister hasn't seen him for hours and she's worried. Have you seen him anywhere?"

"Now, that's what I call helpful," King said, turning his head to include Tad in the conversation. "Gives you a warm feeling, doesn't it, to know our tax money's put to good use? Where else will you find the CID—and a detective sergeant, at that—stepping in to look for a bloke? Yes, real efficient use of our money, Tad. Don't mess about with a constable when you've got a gawd-almighty sergeant who can walk around. You solve the murders, then? You got time for tracking down half wits?"

I looked at Tad, not giving King the satisfaction of a reply. Tad said the last time he'd seen Harry was on the High Street. "He was peering into the hair salon window again. He does that a lot. I don't know if the place fascinates him or if he just likes the attention he gets from being obnoxious."

"I wonder who he got it from," I said, smiling at King and then refocusing on Tad.

"It's his favorite pastime," Tad continued, "discounting eating."

I nodded, remembering the scene earlier today with David and Harry outside the bakery.

"I don't know what direction he took. I was driving to my house, you see, and I didn't stop to chat. I'm afraid I haven't seen him since."

"And that was..."

"Close to seven, I should think."

"Awfully early to be up and about."

"Yes, well..." Tad colored, glanced at King, then said, "I'd been out early. I like to walk. It clears my head, gets me going for the day."

"Have you seen Harry?" I asked King, who was still grinning like a smart-mouthed felon who has contempt for the law.

King shrugged and said no, and that he has more important things to do than to keep track of a loony.

"Such as?"

"If you don't mind, miss. It's rather personal."

"Your conversation as I came up to you sounded rather personal, too. What was that about?"

"Like I said, it's personal. And, as such, is just that—*personal*. None of your damned business." His voice had taken on a sharpness that warned me not to press him. Perhaps sensing he had reacted too harshly and might have made me suspicious, he said more easily, "But I'll let you know, luv, if I come upon him. We can't have the old boy getting lost or hurt, now, can we? Is that it, then?"

Tad glanced nervously at King, who had turned toward him. He cleared his throat and said, "King and I were planning a surprise party for a mutual friend."

"You sounded awfully serious to be talking about such a pleasurable event. Are you having trouble with caterers or something?"

"It's—" Tad glanced at his feet, as though his response was written on the ground. "It's just that it's a big event. We don't want anything to go wrong, or have any of the details leaked to spoil the surprise." He wiped his palms on his jeans, then crammed his hands into his pockets.

King said, "Why don't you help the sergeant, Tad, and look around the graveyard? Harry likes to sit there," he added, grinning at me.

I said I'd already walked through the graveyard.

"Well, Harry could be there now. It's been some time since you were there, hasn't it?" He nodded to Tad, who glanced at me as though I would give him permission and then walked off. "Don't mean to do your job for you," King said, "but I just want to help. You've a big job. A murder—no, two, isn't it? That poor boy. *Two* murders and two assaults. Now Harry's gone missing. And the vicar, I hear, is a nut case. Sworn off God. What'll that do for his soul?"

"It's nice of you to worry."

"I've some time on my hands, miss. I may as well be beneficial to those who need it."

"Anything else occupy your time?"

He gave me a slow, easy smile, his eyes traveling the length of my body. "Many things."

"For instance."

He shrugged. "Are you that interested in me, then?"

I remained silent, returning his stare with a matched strength.

"Oh. Is it me personally, like you'd like to get to know me better..." He rolled his shoulders back and flexed his biceps. "Or me professionally, like 'Where were you the night of January 20?' If I had a vote, sweetheart, I'd choose the former."

"Just an example of something you're interested in, like a hobby, will do."

"I like to play tag."

"The children's game?"

"Yeh, like in 'tag, you're it.' It's your turn to try to catch me. Or hide-and-seek. I'm smashing at that. Lot of blokes never find me when I hide. And, long as we're on the subject, have you caught the person responsible for the attacks? You lot must be fair knackered, what with the cases and worrying about two of your own. Who's done it, then? He in the nick yet?"

"We've several leads."

King laughed, one short, loud explosion blasted into the air. He shook his head, smiling, and ran his fingers through his hair. "God, what a safe answer. So standard. They teach you that in police class? Too bad your attacker has no discernible identifying marks such as a mole or beard. Or tattoo. Personally, I feel that if you're going to engage in something criminal like that, you shouldn't adorn yourself with tattoos—they're too easily recognizable. You ever listen to police descriptions of fugitives? 'Five foot ten, dark hair, green eyes, wearing jeans and a red shirt, tattoo of a snake on his left wrist.' Sort of makes it easier to identify the criminal, don't it? You wouldn't catch me doing that."

"Catch you at what—a felony or getting a tattoo?"

Again his laugh exploded into the afternoon quiet. He leaned against the corner of the church and said, "Oh, both, luv. Or catch me during hide-and-seek. I'm a very law abiding bloke. But I'm talking about tattoos right now. No, not for me. It's a dead giveaway and it spoils the game."

"You consider enforcing the law and keeping people safe a game?"

"On the order of hide-and-seek, I'm afraid. At least, that's how criminals probably view it. I've got the loot; tag, you're it. Come and find me."

"I'll find you—or them. All I have to do is look under a rock."

"But that's for the coward, isn't it? If I were to hide, it'd be in the open. It's more sporting, more of a game."

"With the loot on you, or stuffed under the rock?"

"You won't know until you find me and search me. If—" He again flexed his biceps, though he made it look as if he was tired and merely stretching. "If you can get close enough to lay a finger on me."

"If I do, it'll be with gloves on. I detest touching garbage."

I left him speechless and leaning against the church wall.

Chapter 28

I envied King Roper that evening. Not his life style or his mates or anything so obvious. I envied him his nerve, his easy, confident bravado. For I had none of that when I visited Graham later in his hospital room. I stood by his bed, looking at him as I had the previous visits, listening to the whir of the oxygen pump and looking at the blinking lights of the wall-mounted monitor, and wished I had King's conviction. That Graham would fully recover. And recover not only to return to work but also to go out with me. I said as much to Margo afterwards when we were in my room in the pub.

"It's been two nights, Margo," I said, squeezing a handful of duvet. We sat cross-legged on my bed, our pints empty and sitting on the dresser top, our shoes kicked off. "MacMillan's released. Why isn't Graham?"

"We've been through this, Bren. Graham's attack was worse. He'll take longer to recover."

"He will, though, won't he?" I stared at Margo, searching for hope in her eyes. "I mean, it's a good hospital. He has good doctors. They'd tell us if—"

"Don't go brewing up troubles where none exist. Focus on work. Ugh. Focus on Erik. How is that going?"

I shrugged, saying we spent weekends together and that it was convenient to have someone around.

"What a way to phrase it. Convenient. So you aren't head over heels about him. What about Adam?"

"We've just started seeing each other. Besides, this isn't the best time for romance, with MacMillan and Graham..." I broke off, mentally seeing Graham lying unresponsive in his bed.

"You can phrase it anyway you—what?" Margo broke off as I punched her arm.

"*Phrase.* That's what's been bothering me!"

"Phrase? What phrase? Something Mark or Simcock said at a briefing?"

"No. That postcard in Enrico's house. We saw it that first night, remember? In his front room."

Margo frowned. "What about it? It was from someone on holiday. What's so odd about that?"

"Because it *was* so odd, the phrasing was so convoluted. Don't you remember?"

HORNS OF A DILEMMA

"Maybe so, but I wouldn't worry about it. Don't you jot down phrases, use shorthand, almost, so you can get more on a card? They're not graded by schoolteachers, Bren. So what if the writing resembles code or English as used for a foreign—*now* what?"

"That's it, Margo! Code!"

"What? Are you serious?"

"Look." I grabbed her hand, needing something to hold on to. "The sentences were ridiculous. Even if you put it down to squeezing as many words as you can onto a postcard, it didn't make sense. They jumped around and didn't even follow normal grammar. And don't say the sender didn't know correct grammar. No one writes that oddly."

"I might if I were in a hurry."

I closed my eyes, envisioning Enrico's front room. We'd found the postcard on his chair...an up-scale hotel was pictured on the front...the words of the message were... I opened my eyes and stared at Margo. "For one thing, the word 'sunshine' was written as two words. And the word 'excursion' began with the letter X."

Margo shrugged. "You can put that down either to a hastily scribbled message, cramming the message into the allotted space, or the sender's bad spelling. I don't see where that gets you, Bren."

"So to get more words onto the postcard the sender makes 'sunshine' into two words and cuts off the E of 'excursion'? Doesn't make sense. He's adding a space when he makes two words out of 'sunshine' and he's eliminating a space when he cuts off the E."

"So?"

"So, the sender had to do that because he couldn't come up with anything else to fit the code. He needed two Ss and an X. So he made 'sunshine' two words and chopped off the pesky E in 'excursion.'" I stared at her, waiting for her reaction. She nodded her head slowly and I said, "It's got to be a simple code, then, like the first letter of each word spelling out the message. It could have been something like every third word being the real code—"

"Which is difficult to build an authentic-sounding sentence around and which may explain the convoluted sentences of the postcard."

"But if you go with that theory, it doesn't explain the missing E from 'excursion.' That, in my mind, is the key to this—that makes me believe it's a code using the first letter of each word. That is why the sender needed the X."

"And talking about xylophones wouldn't work. Okay." She pressed her lips together, perhaps trying to figure out the significance of a coded message. When she spoke, her voice was slightly unsteady. "So we've got our terrorist getting orders from his boss. Probably about when to hit his target."

I nodded, too nervous to vocally respond.

Margo said, "God, Bren, what do we do? This scares the hell out of me!"

"What we do is try to look at that card to make sure I'm not going off on a tangent. If it *is* the first letter of each word, we can easily scan the card to read the message. Then we'll know what Enrico read and if the message does indeed seem to be terrorist-linked."

Margo screwed up her face, as though trying to visualize the postcard. She said, "Can we get a look at it again? Who has it?"

"I don't. It's wrapped and logged in with the other case exhibits."

"*What* others?"

I ignored her. "But maybe we can get it." I grabbed my mobile and punched in the phone number of the SO who had charge of the items from Enrico's house. When he answered, I told him I wanted to look at the post card—"I won't tamper with your seal, I just want to look at it and make some notes"—and hung up shortly afterwards.

"Well? Do we get to decode?"

"I'll rephrase his answer."

Margo exhaled sharply. "Never mind. I can guess. So there goes that idea."

"I'll ask Simcock tomorrow. He may like the idea. He's an old spy."

"*What?*"

"OK. Not really, but he worked for something like MI5 or the likes. He'll be keen on codes and ciphers. You'll see."

"I don't know, Bren. Maybe you should think about this. Talk to Mark."

"What's to talk about? Simcock's not going to demote me. All I'm going to do is ask him to see the postcard."

"Seems to me, if he thought it contained something, we would've heard by now. If he is an old spy, he would've seen through a code, if there is one. I think you'll be ruffling feathers, implying he's incompetent, if you ask him. Talk it over with Mark. Or Scott, if you think that's better."

"I don't need counsel, Margo. This isn't that big of a deal. We need to know if that postcard says anything that will give us a lead. Simcock will be impressed that we remember that." I grabbed my mobile and sagged against the bed's headboard. "Good night, Margo. I'm bone-tired and want to get some sleep."

"You're not too tired," she said, getting up and grabbing her shoes. "Give Erik my best."

"Tell him yourself. I've broken off with him."

She stopped, bent over from retrieving her shoes from the floor, and stared at me, her mouth open. Finally recovering, she straightened up and said, "What?"

I told her briefly about my decision to concentrate on Adam. "You may not believe in Freudian slips, Margo, but I made one the other night. I called him 'Adam' instead of 'Erik' a few nights ago. I think that means something."

"It's bound to. Anyway, you had a super time with him at dinner, you said. Go for it, Bren."

"I am. Now, out."

"Sweet dreams." She left the room, closing the door as I rang up Adam.

A short conversation, conveying the day's events and firming up another date, eased some of the tension bottled within me. But I took a sleeping pill anyway, afraid the day's events and the enigma of the post card would keep me awake. Even with my drugged sleep, I dreamed about Graham, covert messages, and the meaning of King's and Tad's secretive conversation.

I was up early Monday morning, anxious to get the day over with, determined to break the case. An air of depression or tragedy seemed to smother the village—people walked slowly along the High Street, barely speaking or nodding to each other. Shopkeepers kept inside their establishments, their placards or window displays advertising in their absence. There was even a dearth of cars parked on the street, as though people were afraid to come outside. The sun, too, must have felt the fear, for it cowered behind a solid wall of gray clouds. No breeze played down the street, no dogs sniffed along the curbs. It felt more like a Sunday morning, with people dawdling in bed or over breakfast, than it did a weekday morning. Life seemed suspended until the killer was apprehended.

Life also seemed suspended for Lloyd. Scott Coral had rung me up at breakfast to tell me Lloyd was in hospital.

"Hospital!" I cried, drawing every eye in the pub. I turned my head toward the window, hunched over my mobile, and said more quietly, "Where? When? What happened?"

Scott relayed it succinctly and as gently as he could. "He attempted suicide, Bren."

"You're kidding! A *vicar*?"

"He must be as depressed as a man can get—his wife walks out on him, his son is dead, his friend, Graham, is in a coma and may never recover...sorry, Bren, but you have to face the possibility."

I let the comment slide. "But, *Lloyd*, of all people! How he must be hurting! How come I didn't see this coming?"

"What would you have done if you had—slept at the foot of his bed, hidden all his knives—"

"Is that how he tried to kill himself, with a knife?" I shuddered. It would take a very determined person to cut his wrists.

Scott sighed heavily. "Overdosed on sleeping tablets."

"How was he found? Did you find him?"

"No. It was Fordyce. He was walking around the church last night, noticed a door slightly open, so he goes inside, remembering that someone had previously broken in to steal a crowbar. He found Lloyd at the foot of the altar, on the floor. There was one candle burning beside him, near his shoulder. Fordyce thinks he took it off the altar table and—"

"Why—" I took a deep breath, not wanting to talk about the subject, unwilling to think of Lloyd either as desecrator or suicide attempt. But I had to know, so I said, "Why did he do that? Why didn't he leave the candle on the altar?"

"I can't answer that. I don't know what the man was thinking. Or if he was. It's common for people attempting suicide to want to stop the pain—it's an emotional medication, if you will."

"I know, Scott, but there's a great difference in people completing suicide and those attempting suicide. So, Fordyce is certain it's suicide and not an assault? I mean, with MacMillan and Graham—"

"It's suicide, Bren. Lloyd said so in his note. Oh, I didn't mention that, did I? He'd written a note, which he still had in his hand. He said he had no reason to live—citing those three reasons I just told you—and said he wasn't afraid to die because God had evidently forsaken him in his pain. Maybe that's why he took the candle off the altar. An act signifying his abandonment of God. The small cross was lying on the altar, too. It could've fallen over when Lloyd grabbed the candle, but I'm thinking maybe Lloyd pushed it over on purpose. You know…shoving away his religion." Scott paused and I could picture him frowning, his mouth screwing up as he fought to keep the anger out of his voice. He couldn't; it spilled out in his next sentence. "God, what a bloody awful thing to do! What the hell was he thinking?"

"He wasn't," I said, my heart still pounding. "But if you're in pain like that, you can't think. You can just feel. Or you're numb. You can't see anything else but your anguish and the interminable empty road stretching years into the future."

"At least Fordyce found him in time. He called in the ambulance request. They got there very quickly."

"And when was all this? Why didn't I hear—" I stopped, suddenly recalling I'd taken a sleeping pill last night. The absurdity of the situation struck me as though I'd been hit with a shower of cold water. I'd taken the pill to help me sleep; Lloyd had taken the pills to help him die. I briefly closed my eyes, trying to breathe more slowly.

Scott said, "He's in the same hospital that Graham's in. Reports this morning were that he's expected to be fine, but the medical staff don't want to release him yet. They're afraid he'll try it again—this time with a quicker, irreversible method."

I nodded, thinking of guns or jumping off a cliff or some no-changing-your-mind manner.

"They'll get him counseling, Bren. It's a good hospital. They know their stuff. They won't release him until he's emotionally stable. It's just too much for him to handle right now."

"I wonder if seeing Graham would help or hinder Lloyd's recovery."

HORNS OF A DILEMMA

"You mean, if Lloyd sees Graham's helplessness, Lloyd would either want to live to help Graham or he'd want to die because he's powerless to help Graham and he'll be losing a friend if Graham remains in a coma. Yes. It's hard to say. But the doctors will come up with something. They're trained for that."

I cradled the phone to my ear, wanting the assurance of Scott's words that Lloyd and Graham would be fine, wanting to hold on to a voice that I'd always considered a helping hand. I didn't know if I could face the day after all. Finally, I said, "Uhhh...Scott?"

"Yes?"

"Do you think suicide is a sin?"

I heard the sharp intake of breath, as though the question had been unexpected. He said, "What brought this on? Why are you worried about Lloyd's suicide attempt? You're not contemplating anything are you, due to Graham's—"

"Of course not! I'm just wondering. I mean, Lloyd's a vicar. It goes against everything he—well, what he used to believe in. Do you think it's not a sin, that Lloyd doesn't consider it a sin? Because, if he does think it is, and he tried it—"

"Look, Bren. I don't know about this stuff. You'd have to delve into C of E theology. Graham's a Methodist, isn't he? I know a bit about that. My uncle's Methodist. It states in their affirmation from Romans that nothing will separate a person from the love of God. *Nothing*. Something like 'neither death nor powers nor things to come nor anything else in all creation' will separate us from God's love. There's no list of exceptions. It says *nothing*. Like the old joke 'what about 'nothing' don't you understand?' So I don't think it's a sin to Methodists and, as such, won't separate you from the love of God. But like I said, I don't know much about it."

"I guess someone in Lloyd's present state isn't thinking about that, anyway."

"He just hates God. He's angry about all that he's going through. Don't worry about it. You can't change it."

I stared out of the window at the church, wondering what the interior looked like, wondering about the hatred and despair that had caused Lloyd to attempt his own murder. I was silent for a long time. Eventually, Scott's voice murmured in my ear.

"Are you all right, Bren?" He asked it slowly, hesitantly, as though I were just waking up.

I mumbled that I was just thinking, then thanked him for telling me.

"I'm sorry to bring you news like this first thing in the morning, Bren, but I knew you'd want to know. Hope the rest of your day is better. See you later." He rang off, assuring me he'd phone if he heard anything different in Lloyd's condition.

I nodded and walked slowly to the incident room, feeling the ground shake beneath my quivering legs.

237

Two reports had come in overnight, and Simcock briefed us during our meeting. In short: there were no fingerprints, blood or other DNA samples on the crowbar that killed Enrico or the others we'd taken from the church hall. The powdery substance in Mark's laundry detergent box was pulverized rhinoceros horn.

"I won't lie to you all and put up a superior front," Simcock said, addressing our team. The officers from the Greater Manchester Police again had joined us. It was beginning to feel like they'd always been part of our team. Simcock cleared his voice and continued. "I'm as shocked by the report as you are. I can conclude from this that someone in this village is smuggling the rhino horn into the country."

The silence was thick as each of us tried to decipher what that meant. Margo asked if other illegal items such as tiger claws and hides or elephant ivory had been found.

Simcock shook his head. "So far, we've no reason to suspect other items, no. But that's not to say there can't be. Just because we've found only the powdered rhino horn doesn't mean there aren't other items."

Mark swore and said he hoped to God this wasn't the tip of the iceberg. "Are we going to execute a raid on the launderette, sir?" He leaned forward in his chair, his eyes already alive with the thought of the search and seizure. He tapped his pen against his thigh, anxious to get going.

"PC Byrd should be here any minute with the search warrant. When he gets here, we'll execute it. Meanwhile..." He walked to the front of the table, leaned against it. "Do any of you know about rhinoceros horn? Other than it being illegal to bring into the Kingdom?"

Margo shook her head, I murmured that I didn't know a thing, and Mark mumbled that its status was all we needed to know. The other officers murmured their ignorance, too. Simcock said that it was a bit more than just being illegal, like some street drugs. "It's an endangerment," he said, staring at each of us in turn. His voice was unusually heavy, as though the subject concerned him deeply. "The exportation of tiger skins, claws and teeth, rhinoceros horn and other illegal items are banned due to the fact that these animals are endangered. The African black rhino, which the pulverized horn comes from, has been hunted to the brink of extinction in many countries."

"I thought," Mark said, "Africa had game wardens. Countries like Namibia and Zimbabwe. Don't they nab poachers?"

"To a degree, yes. And there's been some success, especially in Namibia. To protect the animal, game wardens saw the horn off the living rhino—the same thing as you cutting your fingernails. They're all the same substance, by the way—your nails and hair and the rhino's horn. But poachers in Zimbabwe began killing rhinos merely to demonstrate to the authorities that they were able to slip into the game preserves and kill anyway."

Smart Alec felons were the same the world over, I thought, envisioning King's taunting grin.

HORNS OF A DILEMMA

"This is why," Simcock said, "we're seizing the pulverized horn in the launderette and arresting these smugglers. Not simply because it's against some man-made law, but because these beautiful, gentle animals are hunted and can't defend themselves. It's a moral issue, an issue between us and our Creator. We can't let these creatures become extinct."

"Can't anything be done?" Margo asked, her voice sounding small and faint after Simcock's emphatic blast. "Education, substitute products?"

"Part of the problem is that rhino horn is perceived by its purchasers as a cultural object or a necessary medicine. In the Asian community, the powdered horn is used to reduce fevers. In Yemen, for instance, the horn itself is turned into handles for ceremonial knives, though there is some progress here and Yemen has stopped importing the horn. And the introduction of aspirin as an alternative medicine has met with some favorable use. But even though the medical use of the horn has been illegal since 1993, the trade flourishes. I won't even begin to tell you about the dwindling numbers of animals worldwide, how close they are to extinction in some countries, for the numbers change daily. One kilogram of rhino horn sells anywhere from £40,000 to £100,000." He paused while Mark swore and Margo gasped. I merely clutched my hands together, envisioning the numbers of animals killed to produce one kilogram.

Simcock continued. "That's a bloody great deal of money. Murders have been done for way less that this."

"And with the amount of money that's obviously obtainable from these smuggling operations, murder comes easy."

"It's nothing to these blokes to blow someone away if he gets in the way. Big money like this rules everything these blokes do. And a murder or two isn't going to deter them from their game. They're out for money and there's nothing that's going to stop them."

Mark added that we had to rope in these bastards if for no other reason than for avenging Graham.

"In a way," Simcock added, "I feel for these poachers. Many of them do it as a means of supporting themselves and their families. Take away the demand for the rhino horn, and you take away their living. How do they and their families then survive? They're on the horns of a dilemma—they need the rhino horn to live, yet the more they kill, the quicker they and their families starve."

Mark made some comment like 'let 'em eat cake,' then became silent as Simcock went on.

"It's a damned hard thing to stop. The horn has been used in Asian medicine for 2,000 years. Most every part of the rhino is used for something—treating skin disease, fevers and bone disorders, as an aphrodisiac, to detect poison." He stopped, his jaw muscles tight. He took a long drink of coffee. When he looked as us again, his eyes seemed darker, sadder. He said, "However, there is some hope in this doom and gloom. Some African countries are training and hiring their citizens to protect the animals from poachers. It's a start and, if you're of an optimistic nature, you'll grab onto that and pray like hell that the project continues, succeeds and saves these magnificent animals. Right." He slapped his hands together, said he'd preached enough, and asked if we had any questions.

PC Byrd strolled into the incident room, nodded to Simcock, and pulled the warrant from his pocket.

Simcock said now we could get rolling and opened his mobile. As he punched in a phone number, Mark said, "Horns of a dilemma is right. Those blokes need the animals to survive, yet their killing is threatening their own survival. And the money needed to educate these people about alternative medicines or ceremonial objects..." He swore again.

"It's not easy, is it? I mean, like Simcock said. If you've got a culture that's been using something for 2,000 years, you're not going to persuade them to use aspirin or a plastic cup over night."

"Hell of a mess," Mark said. "So we've got Richard's launderette as the receiving station for the powdered horn. We don't know if he's involved—it could have been John who set it all up, but that stretches the realm of belief, if you ask me."

"It would be one thing if John worked there full time, but he's only there after school and on holiday."

"How can he oversee an operation like that if he's not on the premises daily? There's too much of a chance of things going wrong, like it did when I grabbed that box of laundry powder. No, this smacks of a fulltime employee—or the owner."

"So," I said, "even if it is Richard who's receiving the powdered horn, his business is probably just the distribution center. Someone else has to pick up and sell the powder to clients. And I don't believe his clients come into the launderette and buy specially marked detergent boxes."

"There's got to be another person who picks up this shipment. Such a high traffic of buyers coming into the launderette would be noticed in a village."

"If he were in a city like Manchester no one would bat an eye. Launderettes probably serve hundreds of people daily. No, I can't believe his place is the end of the line. There's got to be someone who picks up the powder from him and distributes it. You were just lucky when you grabbed a box you weren't supposed to have."

Mark sniffed. "Well, we've got to get the entire ring, or they'll just set up somewhere else. We aren't saving any rhinos merely by slapping the cuffs on Richard."

I agreed, then stood up, and grabbed my jacket. Now that we were about to execute the warrant and hopefully make an arrest, my heart was pounding. I looked at Mark. His eyes were bright in his eagerness to get going. Simcock said, "We have probable cause to take Richard Linnell into custody because the illegal substance was found on his premises. Now, I don't want any heroics. Let's stay safe and keep within the letter of the law. Right. Let's go." Mark dug his car key from his slacks pocket and we hurried outside.

HORNS OF A DILEMMA

The warrant execution was a textbook operation. Richard Linnell looked stunned when we entered the launderette. He had initially tried to hide but had bumped into the edge of a washing machine and had fallen to the floor, making him an easy capture. Crates of powdered rhino horn—still nailed shut and labeled with what must surely be a phony company's stickers—were stacked in the back room, the individual boxes that were on the floor clearly a different design than the laundry soap being used by a patron in the launderette proper. Mark had brought his box, matched it to the boxes in the back room, and ripped open a carton. He sniffed it, held it out for me to smell, and said it was the same thing as far as he could tell, for it had no fragrance. The SOs took photos of the boxes, crates and back room while Mark handcuffed Richard.

"I don't know what you're doing," Richard said, his eyes wide with fright. "What's going on? You can't barge in here, scare the hell out of my customers, take my products—"

"Funny thing," Mark said, tugging at the handcuffs to make sure they were locked. "We're doing it. Come on."

"But why? What did I do? I just run a launderette."

Simcock told him why we had executed the warrant, then had Mark caution Richard.

Richard blinked several times, then yelled that he had done nothing wrong, that he was innocent. "That stuff must be a mistake," he said, staring at the officers measuring the shipping carton. "I don't know anything about it. Ask the delivery bloke. He brought it. It must be a mistake!" His voice was tinged with fear and desperation.

Simcock sighed heavily, clearly having heard the same lines too often. "Just like crack, Mr. Linnell. No one ever claims its his when the officer finds it in the car, but you're guilty by association if it's where you sat. Take Mr. Linnell away, Salt."

Mark nodded, grabbed Richard's arm and led him outside to a marked car. Simcock and I followed leisurely and watched as Mark handed Richard over to a uniformed officer. King Roper sauntered up the street, stopped several yards from the launderette and joined the small crowd of residents who were watching Richard's arrest. As the police car drove off, King waved at me, bowed and smiled. I glared at him and got into Mark's car.

"What was that all about?" Mark asked, settling behind the steering wheel and closing the car door. "Some private code?"

"Not so private, but it was a code."

"Easily discernable, I take it."

"Too easy."

"Let me guess. On a par with Noel's little A C A B tattoo?"

"Similar, yes. But not so crude. Just a victory salute."

"Who won?"

"King's side, I'm thinking."

"Yeh, well," Mark said, starting the engine, "not for long if I have anything to do with it. Never saw a nastier piece of work than that one. I'd like one minute with him behind the barn."

"He'd kill you, Mark. You don't know how muscular he is."

"Who said anything about me using my fists?" He stared at me, unsmiling. "Knives are quick. No one need ever know. You want to lure him to a rendezvous?"

Mark was serious. I could read it in his eyes and the tone of his voice. I turned slightly in my seat so I couldn't see King. "Shut up, Mark. If you keep on, you'll tempt me to say yes."

"And what's wrong with that?" He laid his left arm along the top of my seat. "Look, Bren. You hate the guy, I hate the guy. I've good reason to suspect he's linked with this smuggling racket. He's mates with Richard, comes into the village throughout the year—probably to direct some shipment—and throws his muscles and weight around like a bully throws out threats. Only difference is King's threats are implied, so we have nothing really against him. A bloke like him just doesn't come to a sleepy village to visit his mate, no matter how smashing the health club is. They could go to Manchester or somewhere and work out. So what's the reason King comes here if it's not to manage the rhino horn shipments?"

"Take me back to the incident room, Mark. I want to get away from his stench."

We assembled back at the incident room, chatting over the warrant execution and the other possible members of the smuggling ring. Simcock had insisted that we take a few minutes to relax, stating that the murder cases and Graham's continuing coma were taking their toll, never mind the agitation we'd just suffered during the seizure of the powdered horn.

He sent Margo across the street to the bakery, giving her a fistful of money, and directed her to come back with a great variety and no change left over. Fifteen minutes later, Margo staggered back into the incident room under several boxes crammed full of scones, jumbals, orange bars, Figgie hobbin, potted salmon finger sandwiches, maids of honor, and shortbread. Balanced on top was a cardboard carrier of hot chocolate and coffee. When Mark and I had helped her unpack everything and we'd all settled ourselves with a drink and something to eat, Simcock thanked us for our hard work and long hours. "I've said it before, so you'll excuse me for repeating myself, but working the cases are hard enough without the stress of DCI Graham's and WPC MacMillan's attacks. You're all to be commended for your efforts and devotion."

PC Byrd mumbled something behind me and another officer echoed his agreement. Mark finished his sandwich and asked if we were any nearer a solution to any of the cases.

"Which is why we're here," Simcock said, putting down his cup of coffee. "And why I wanted us to eat something. We need brain food. Right." He grabbed the dry erase marker and walked over to the large mainframe board. He turned toward us and asked for a discussion of motives for the murders and attacks.

"I think," I said, setting my hot chocolate on the floor near my chair, "there's more to the horn smuggling than a few crates of powder, though that was an impressive shipment we recovered."

Simcock looked interested and asked for particulars.

I reminded them of Enrico's 'bird watching' episodes, described the area he had selected for this activity, and that he had left his field glasses in the back room of his house. "The only thing directly in line with that room," I explained, "is the back entrance of Richard's launderette. I checked it out."

"You think Enrico was keeping surveillance on deliveries or people at the launderette? And watching for something in the village from his vantage point on the hill when he was supposedly bird watching?"

"Yes, sir. It makes sense. The night of Enrico's death, when Mr. Graham, Mark and I were searching Enrico's house, I glanced out that back window."

"The village green backs up to it."

"Yes. I thought at first Enrico *was* a bird watcher, and that he was looking at the trees on the green. But the more I got to thinking about Toni's statement, that Enrico had been looking for that eagle..."

"It didn't make sense."

"It was a story, told to cover up his real activity. I looked out Enrico's back room window. If you angle your body a bit, you see the back of the launderette. It's the first business bordering the green on the south edge. So, if Enrico wasn't a bird watcher, and there were no bedroom windows to peer into, what was he using the glasses for?"

I waited while Mark said, "Keeping surveillance on the launderette."

"That's got to be it. Plus, the thing that scared all of us—that Enrico didn't exist before two months ago—suggests he was up to no good. Now, if he wasn't part of Richard's smuggling operation—as is suggested from him spying on the launderette—what other explanation is there?"

"He's a cop, gathering evidence to arrest him."

We looked at Simcock, waiting for his agreement. Instead, he said he would ask the Divisional Commander or Assistant Chief Constable if they knew anything about a covert operation, and said we'd best concentrate for the moment on the murders. "What's the common thread through all this? The murders are chillingly alike, aren't they? I think we can safely say we've got one killer. What's the obvious link between them?"

The word caught in my throat but I managed to say, "Violence. Dealt by hatred and great strength."

Chapter 29

"And who has the strength to swing a crowbar—for that's the murder weapon," Simcock asked after silence had settled on us. "And strength enough to beat with his fists?"

"If this was an ordinary case," Mark said, "I'd say Page Hanley." Mark's matter-of-fact voice stirred me from the mental image I had of Graham lying battered in the midnight-dark wood. "Because," Mark replied to Simcock's question, "she works as a personal trainer at the health club. She's good with weights, has great biceps, and knows the two murder victims. We also could consider Ian Harmon. He's a security guard. As such, he may know self defense tactics."

"He's out nights," PC Byrd reminded us, "and the murders and attacks occurred at night."

"You don't think he'd be at his job?" Simcock asked.

"He works eleven to seven in the morning."

Mark said, "And the murder of Enrico occurred, according to Graham between 7:45 and 8:30. Yes, more than enough time to kill Enrico and get to work."

"And," Byrd added, "the other attacks were in the early evening. Again, more than enough time to present yourself at work. And we don't know when John was killed. But it could fit the same type of time table."

I slowly raised my hand and after Simcock asked me to proceed, said, "Ian's nephew, Conrad, may fit into the suspect mold. He's big, strong, and used to lugging heavy photo equipment about, being a photographer's assistant. He struck Ian, too. Landed a punch on Ian's jaw that knocked him down. I don't think I'd like to see Conrad riled and with a crowbar in his hand."

Simcock agreed and wrote all three people's names on the board. He asked for more suggestions.

Margo said, "As much as I like him—and I know, sir, we're supposed to play this impersonal and emotionless—I suspect Harry."

"Page Hanley's brother, the mentally-challenged bloke?"

"Yes, sir. I know he seems rather a gentle soul, but he's also capable of great anger. We've all witnessed it. He becomes agitated quite easily if he doesn't get his own way."

"And you think he may have struck out in anger?"

"That's his way of releasing his frustration, through punching or hitting. He's hit his sister several times, and there may be others in the village he's assaulted. They probably haven't reported it because they like Page and they know it's just Harry's way of responding to frustration."

"But a little of that goes a long way," Mark said, snorting. "I mean, I may like my neighbor, and put up with a bit of abuse because he's got a mental problem, but if he slaps me once too often, I'll report him to the police. Violence usually escalates. It's dangerous. You never know when it will turn from mere slaps on the cheek to a full-blown attack. Ask any of your murdered wives or girl friends about their abusive relationships."

"I know that, Mark," Margo said. "I'm not pardoning his assaults. I merely said that Harry gets my vote for being a suspect. His behavior supports the possibility and he's done time."

Simcock's eyes widened. "Oh, yes? On what charge?"

"Grievous Bodily Harm against a tourist in the bar." She glanced at me and I knew what she was thinking: we'd both witnessed Harry's anger in the bar. Harry fit perfectly into the role of Suspect. Margo said, "Besides, Harry's a fairly decent boxer. And his sister may have taken him to the health club where she works, helped him with his workouts at the punch bag."

I nodded, envisioning Harry wearing boxing gloves and pummeling the bag. "We all know he had opportunity He walks around the village at all hours. I—" I stopped, the late night pub scene reappearing in my mind's eye. "I met Harry late one night. He nearly frightened me to death."

"What happened?"

I related the incident, then added rather sheepishly, "He didn't do anything. He just lurked in the shadows. But it sure scared the—"

"How'd you know it was him?" Mark's question, so simple, had stopped me mid-sentence.

I stared at him, my mouth open. "Pardon?"

"If he kept in the shadows and it was night, how'd you know it was Harry?"

"Well—" I paused, suddenly more nervous than I had been that night. "I called to him."

"And he answered?"

I shook my head. "I just thought—"

"Because it's a common thing for Harry to roam at all hours. Right. What makes you so sure it wasn't someone else?"

"For instance..."

"Hell if I know! David. He's visiting Harry and Page. Maybe he was out looking for Harry."

"Then why didn't he respond when I called?"

"Because," Mark said, shifting his position in his chair, "he was up to no good. He was lying in wait for someone to rob. He was on his way to burgle a house. I don't know! I'm merely saying that since you didn't see the bloke and he didn't answer you, that you have no assurance it was Harry that night. It could've been anyone—King, for instance."

I shuddered. If there was one person who made my skin crawl... I swallowed, sent up a prayer at my near miss from being assaulted, and let Simcock continue.

"As Mark said, if this were a more common case—by which I mean a crime of passion where it's a spur of the moment attack from emotions—I'd say these were plausible suspects. But it isn't. This is cold, calculated murder. Well planned and executed. Besides the two deaths, we have two attacks on police officers who had done nothing to warrant their assaults other than their job. So in the light of these conclusions, I can't see us concentrating on these suspects." He looked around the room, waiting for our reaction. The place was dead silent. He went on. "But, there *is* a commonality that binds our two murders and two assaults. Violence." He let the implication sink in. "Each person we've just named is capable of physical force and violence, as far as we can surmise. Each one has opportunity. Everyone—or no one—has motive. And our physical evidence is damn all, with the rain at John's and DCI Graham's scenes. Anything could have been washed away. Enrico's scene, while not under siege by the elements, is hardly better."

"Too many footprints, too much mud, outside where at least a dozen people were mingling about."

"As I said before, even if we find a hair belonging to Richard Linnell, for instance, we can't prove he wielded the crowbar. The hair could have blown there. It *is* outside and, as such, is subject to contamination from all sources and places. I don't think we can go with physical evidence. Anything else?"

"I suppose," Mark said, leaning forward, his forearms on his thighs, "none of us has detected an unwilling witness. Someone who we've questioned, stated emphatically that he didn't see or hear anything, but who we feel is lying to save his skin." He looked around our small group. There were no responses. "Wonderful. I was hoping that one of us would have sensed someone like that. What a bloody break for our killer—no one sees a thing because it's night, it's in the wood so it's secluded." He swore under his breath and leaned back.

Simcock said quietly, "Just because WPC MacMillan didn't see her attacker doesn't mean DCI Graham didn't."

I stared at him, holding my breath, wondering if he'd heard anything on Graham's condition, wishing with my whole being that Simcock was about to deliver good news.

"The chief inspector's still in a coma, unfortunately."

I slowly let out my breath, perhaps more disheartened with this statement than I had on hearing that Graham was in a coma.

"But when he recovers he may be able to give us an identification. I know it was dark when he was attacked, but Graham's a good cop. He excels at self-defense and knows how to handle himself. Maybe he recognized something about the attacker. Maybe he didn't. But we don't know. We'll have to wait for him to tell us. So that's on hold for the moment while we wait for Graham's improvement." He had forced cheerfulness into his voice for this last pep talk. I wondered if he meant it as much for himself as for us. But for all his bravado, his eyes were lifeless, as though the late hours, the number and severity of the cases, and the lack of evidence were sucking the life from him. It was a strange contrast to the confidence we had just heard. He gestured toward the board but kept his eyes on us. "Well, that might be it if we were dealing with the usual type of case. But we aren't. The commonality of violence suggests one person to me. Does it to you?"

The name squeaked out as I stared at him. I whispered, "King Roper."

"I agree, but I want to hear your reasoning, Taylor."

"Everything — the murders, the assaults, and the smuggling—suggest him. He has the intelligence, too, sir, for the smuggling operation. Richard's bank account shows nothing out of the ordinary in deposits—we ran a financial background check. Richard is smart enough not to bank his money so obviously—maybe King told him not to—but Richard's *not* smart enough to run this operation by himself. Richard has no physical way of killing two people and harming two others, even though he had the motive. It's highly doubtful. He's tiny, uncoordinated..." I paused, remembering the several instances I'd been with him. Each time he'd knocked over something or stumbled into someone. "Which points to him *not* being a killer—because those assaults called for great strength. And since he's not the smartest guy in the world, he doesn't seem capable of being the instigator of the scheme."

Margo nodded. "And King *is* big enough and smart enough."

"Richard is alone—no relatives, wife or kids—so he leads a very private life. There's no one about to see what he's involved with. It's the perfect set-up for King's little game." I continued, warming to the topic. "DCI Graham knew King. I saw the tension between the men the first time they met in the village. Mr. Graham told me later that he'd previously arrested King. Mr. Graham knew King's history and I'm certain they didn't like each other. King could have some grudge against the chief inspector."

Simcock scratched his chin. "It would be odd that he didn't, if King is violent and still harbors bitterness for his arrest. There are a large number of cons and ex-cons who dream of revenge. Some of it is merely talk, of course—contributing to the illusion of their tough façade. But some have followed it through, unfortunately. And even though I hate to consider it—because I hate to think of any copper being purposely attacked and because I like Graham immensely and consider him a friend—we have to."

"King works out in the health club. He attacked one man, whom I know of, in the car park. He certainly has the physique for it. And the anger. Even if King just talked a good story and had no intension of revenging himself on Mr. Graham, if Mr. Graham had discovered something about King, maybe linked him to the rhino smuggling ring...well, maybe King attacked Graham."

"A murder attempt that failed," Simcock said, nodding. "Yes. It makes sense. Same could be said for MacMillan, though she didn't know King prior to this case. Still, we've the possibility that MacMillan unearthed something that implicated King at that damned site where the rose was left, and King wanted to silence her, too."

"He wouldn't have stopped with hitting her to keep her quiet for a few days. He would have attacked her with intent to kill."

Simcock agreed. "He's got the strength and he's so damned sure of himself. Only he couldn't finish his assault on MacMillan because he was scared off. Maybe someone walking along that path. Maybe he heard Graham as he came to look at the scene. Whatever the reason, King couldn't kill MacMillan or Graham. Let's be thankful for that! But, yes, Taylor, I think King is prime suspect for the assaults. I'm inclined to believe he's also our man for the two murders, too. After all, they're the same scenario and the same type of weapon was used. Still, we have no hard evidence. So we consider all who fit."

"I think," I said, thinking it through, "we've a common theme with all this—John's murder and Enrico's murder. We find powdered rhino horn smuggled into the UK with Richard's laundry as a probable distribution center. Fine. John works at the laundry. What if, like our clean-clothes devotee Mark, here, John couldn't find laundry detergent for the washers? What if John went into the back room where the supplies are stored and opened a carton, but *this* carton contained the disguised powdered horn? What if Richard walked in, saw John's discovery, and informed King, since King seems to be the ringleader?"

"Or perhaps King walked in on John."

"Either way, King now knows that John has determined something is fishy. Maybe John says something to a mate, maybe he doesn't. Maybe he took a photo of the boxes and carton to show to the police in case the cartons of rhino horn powder disappeared before John could fetch us. It doesn't matter. What matters is that King or Richard or whoever knew about John's camera and decided better safe than sorry."

"So one of these fellows breaks into the vicarage and steals John's camera to destroy any photographic evidence—just in case."

"Right. Besides, he wants to be a chemist on leaving university. Maybe his attacker was afraid he'd taken some powder to analyze." I looked around the group to see if they were accepting my theory. Interested, eager faces mirrored my own fervor. I went on.

"So King or one of his toady crew lures John to the wood. I don't know how—maybe they got him close to the church and then three of them jumped him and dragged him into the wood to kill him. It's a nice screen for that, the wood is. Especially at night. It's dark and deserted and you can't see a thing. So John's killed to stop him from talking about the smuggling ring."

"And Enrico?" Mark asked. If this were happening months ago, right after we'd been paired together, his voice would have been colored with sarcasm, as though he were challenging me to think like a police officer. But now, far into our working relationship, he asked it seriously, as a colleague would question and encourage another colleague.

"Enrico is harder to pinpoint. We've agreed we can't do much with him because we don't know his life beyond this past January."

"But if Enrico was a copper or some other law enforcement officer—and we may as well take that as read on the grounds of our previous conversation—he may have made a mistake and exposed his undercover operation to King or Richard."

"We may never know. But it's a logical assumption, yes, given what we can deduce from Enrico's field glasses and his 'bird watching.'"

"So, King killed him to keep him quiet about the smuggling, too. It fits his history of assaults. Richard has no record."

I nodded, my eyes threatening to tear. "That's the thread I was talking about. Not only do we have the same MO, as Mr. Simcock was saying, but we have the same connection of the launderette."

"We have John, who worked at the launderette; we have Enrico, who was probably spying on the launderette; we have King, who is friends with Richard, owner of the launderette, and who is beyond normality when it comes to body building and anger control."

"King's done time for previous similar offenses. And while Noel, the owner of the hair salon, also has served time for the same crime—G.B.H. during a domestic violence attack—I don't see the connection either between Noel and King or between Noel and the launderette. I believe one end of the thread starts with King and the other ends at the launderette, collecting murders and smuggling gang members along the way."

The room had taken on an ominous silence during my assessment speech. No phones or faxes had rung, no police officers had entered or left the room, no outside noises such as car horns or church bells had filtered through the windows. We sat, barely breathing, thinking over the situation.

"Well..." Simcock sagged against the edge of the table and looked at us. He capped the marker and glanced back at the board. It was one of the emptiest I'd ever seen after a think session. A few names that no one took seriously, one name that everyone agreed was the murderer, and nothing in the Motive column. Simcock looked around our group, then out of the window. I'd never seen him so tired. Maybe it was the non-stop work and the sleep deprivation. More likely, it was the frustration of not being able to prove our suspicions. He finally stirred, saying if he had to vote on a likely explanation, that would be it. But reminded us again we couldn't prove anything—*yet*. "But we will. In the near future, we will. I'll be living for that day when we have King doing time." He stood up, tossing the marker onto the tabletop, his lips pressed into a thin, straight line. Receiving nods and noises of understanding, Simcock dismissed us. We settled at our computers to turn them off and collect our papers, or left the building in silence, depressed that the case had ended without an arrest, feeling like we had failed.

Simcock called to me, and when I came over to him, he handed me a set of keys. "DCI Graham's," he said without smiling. "Do you know his house?"

I nodded, staring at the keys, the emotions spawned from our session welling within me and threatening to break forth.

"Fine. Would you mind going there and picking up some clothes? He'll need them when he gets out of hospital. No," he said in response to my anxious look, "he's no better, Taylor. But he will be. God, he *must* be!" He closed his fist around the keys, as though his determination and prayer could be telegraphed to Graham via his personal property. Shoving the keys into my hand, Simcock whispered, "Get his clothes, Brenna. Take them to him in hospital. He'll need them soon. Maybe tomorrow. *Yes*. Tuesday. He'll thank you for them tomorrow. I've got to pack all this lot up, now. We've got to give these folks back their community hall and get back to headquarters." He turned from me, his head lowered, his voice barely audible.

I knew how he felt. It was never easy to give up on a case, no matter if it was only temporarily. The sense of defeat, of the bad guy winning even briefly augured into your soul, haunted your dreams, laughed at you from the recesses of your mind. Besides leaving King, or whoever was the killer, free to kill again, it played with our morale. And we failed to bring justice to the victims' survivors.

"Oh, sir."

Simcock raised his eyebrow, probably wondering what I wanted. I told him about Margo's and my conversation and that I wanted to read Enrico's post card again for a coded message.

"What, like substitution or numbers standing for letters?" He lacked the enthusiasm I had expected. Perhaps he hadn't been an agent; perhaps he had said he'd been *wishing* he'd been one.

"I don't think there were numbers," I said, trying to recall any specific phrases. "But it could be something very simple, the first letter of each word combining with each following letter to create words. Like 'Come' would be written on the post card as 'Can Orville meet me.' Or every third word comprises the real sentence. I'd like to look, sir. It might help us with the case."

"I'll get someone on it, Taylor." He was back to calling me Taylor. My brief fling at being Brenna to him was over, signifying he had slid back into lethargy or his police mode. "You just stick to the job of work I've given you. I'll worry about the code."

"Yes, sir." I knew I sounded frustrated and angry, but I didn't care. I couldn't understand why he wouldn't let me see the postcard.

HORNS OF A DILEMMA

I put on my jacket, put Graham's house keys into the pocket, and told Simcock I'd drive back to Buxton when I'd finished, unless he wanted me to help pack up the equipment. When he'd said no, that he had constables to do that, I stood there for a moment, wanting to echo his words that Graham would be fine tomorrow, that we would eventually link someone to the crimes, but knew it would sound like a hollow, spiritless pep talk. So I grabbed my shoulder bag and strode from the room.

The sky mimicked my cohorts' and my feelings, for it was a sheet of gray that spread as far as I could see. Along the western horizon a bank of darker clouds was building, their bellies nearly black against the steel-gray backdrop. A sharp wind whipped down church hill to my left, stirring the daffodil buds into confusion, driving dust and dead leaves before it. The debris careened against the community center's face and lay panting in a heap or drifted eastward around the corner. The air smelled of dust and far-off rain. I pushed the ends of my muffler into the open neck of my jacket and got into my car, glad to leave Simcock and his ill-humor.

I was driving down Green Acre Road, approaching Ian's home, when I saw Darlene and Conrad. Conrad was lifting suitcases into his car. Ian was standing in the open doorway, a mug in his hand, staring at the couple. I slowed down, unabashedly interested in the scene. Darlene threw the end of her scarf over her shoulder, for it had fallen free when she had leaned forward to put a smaller case into the car's boot, and now rubbed her gloved hands together. Whether it was from the chill or excitement in anticipation of her adventure, I didn't know. But she smiled and looked adoringly at Conrad. He slammed the boot closed, opened the car door for her, and got behind the steering wheel. As he turned on the engine, I drove past, consumed again by frustration and the sadness of changing relationships, broken hearts and a nose-thumbing murderer.

Chapter 30

Even though I'd never been to Graham's house, I knew which one it was. He'd talked about it often enough, sharing homeowners' problems and exasperations. Once he even asked my advice on a decorating dilemma.

It was a two-storey stone house on Lismore Road, a quiet, tree-shaded street near the Pavilion Gardens and the cricket field. One of Buxton's nicer neighborhoods. As I sat in my car in Graham's drive and looked at the wooden chevron design on a protruding upper storey bay window, I wondered if Graham would ever live again in his house. The front garden was rather unique in that it had no encircling fence as most houses did; it also had no lawn, being a landscape of flagstone patio with benches, large terra cotta planters and a pleasing variety of dwarf conifers. A white birdbath claimed the center of the circular patio, a nice contrast to the greenery and the tan stone. It wasn't his garden of choice, he had told me when we had talked about bulbs and perennials during one tea break. But it suited his current life style. "No lawn to maintain," he had said, grinning. "Which also means very little need to weed."

The window frames and front door were the same reddish-brown color as the wood decorating the front of the bay, repeated again in the patchwork of tiles covering the roof. The same color scheme blanketed the roof of the projecting entrance. A pleasant, quiet house it seemed, on a pleasant, quiet street.

I sat in my idling car, imagining him trimming the Lawson Cypress or holly, planting the King Alfred daffodil bulbs we had chosen, filling the birdbath. I don't know why I'd been surprised when I had seen it; perhaps because I assumed Graham would have no time to bird watch or would consider it just something else to maintain in his busy schedule. But I was pleased to see it, for it linked us in another way. It revealed his concern for all life and his need to help. I briefly wondered if he kept a life list, if he got excited when he spotted a previously-unseen species. Then realized he wouldn't. I turned off the car's engine, feeling a bit of our connection die, got out of the car, and walked up to the house.

The door, a heavy wooden slab scored with varying depths and widths of grooves, swung open easily when I turned the key in the lock. A pile of letters and magazines were scattered on the area rug just inside the doorway. One letter dangled from the lip of the mail slot in the door, suspended above its comrades on the floor. I gathered them up and placed them on the small entrance hall table, then went upstairs.

The hallway was dark without the benefit of sunlight that probably would have beamed through the small window set high in the wall. A thick, oriental-patterned carpet ran the length of the hall and duplicated the cranberry, gray and blue colors and general floral design of the wallpaper. Several black-and-white photographs in silver-toned frames dotted the walls. Photos of landscapes and seascapes, the lighting dramatic in each one. Unsigned, too. Graham had probably taken them on holiday. I left them to the silence guarding the house and searched out his bedroom.

It was a large room in the back of the house, away from street noise and snuggling up to a gigantic Norway spruce. I crossed the floor, amazed at the apparent size of the tree, and gazed out of the window. Dark green needles crowded the curved branches, making a dense curtain that served as a windbreak and a haven for small birds. Cigar-shaped, reddish brown cones nodded on the gently swaying boughs. It was the Christmas tree of my youth, of many peoples' youth, and it had always been an unspoken contest between me and my brother and sister as to which of us could find the most cones on our trees. I watched a robin hop from a branch to the ground before I got back to the task at hand.

The room held no obvious masculine or feminine sense as I had expected it would—masculine décor because it was Graham's room, but feminine touches were not out of the realms of possibility, for Graham had been engaged. I didn't know how close to the wedding date his fiancée had left him. They might have begun decorating his home to include her style. I lingered by the window, my hand clutching the sill, ashamed that I was violating Graham's privacy, electrified to be part of his private world.

The bed was large, probably a queen- or king-size, with maroon and gray sheets and duvet and a carved wooden headboard. The dresser and night table were of the same wood and design. The only nod to femininity or relaxation was the upholstered chair, covered in a maroon, pink and green floral design. Perhaps it had been his mother's or he had bought it for Rachel as a wedding gift. It looked lonely and unloved sitting by itself in the corner, not even the recipient of a tossed-off robe or abandoned book.

I rummaged about in the dresser drawers and his closet, chose socks, a shirt, pullover and pair of slacks. I hesitated with the briefs, embarrassment flooding my face. Even though I wanted to sleep with him, this was personal in a different way. I looked away, pulled out the top pair of briefs, and stuffed them into the center of the roll of clothes. Blushing, I hurried from the room.

The living room, when I peered within, was done in shades of gray and blue, with accents of green. A large wooden desk and sofa claimed the biggest portion of the space, but a piano-sized and -shaped instrument took up residence along the far wall. I walked over to it, the blood rushing through my body, my heart beating faster. It was Graham's harpsichord, a blue painted, smaller edition from the larger wooden ones that Mark's family produced. The lines of the instrument were simple and straight, with no curved legs or scrollwork apron. The robin's egg-blue paint was as delicate as I knew the tone of the instrument to be. I slowly lifted the lid, holding it open at eye level. The underside of the lid was painted with baroque-style flowers and curlicues. Fat bumblebees droned around masses of flowers; butterflies hovered on flower petals or perched on leaves; an unidentifiable bird sang from the base of a rose. And the real rose—the metal, gold-embossed medallion shining beneath the dozens of taut wire strings? It was a swirl of three initials surrounded by more curlicues. I leaned over the bentside, my arm outstretched as I held the lid open above my head. G M G. I stared at the letters, trying to recall Graham's middle name. He had never told me, but yes, I *had* seen it once. In his personnel folder when I had filed it. M. Matthew. That was it. Geoffrey Matthew Graham. I ran my index finger along a long, silvery wire, feeling the tension, trying to imagine the sound of him playing. I slipped my fingernail beneath the wire and plucked. The tone rose clear and crisp, surprisingly loud. I leaned forward, chose a fatter string. This was wound in a coppery wire and gave off a more mellow tone when I plucked it. A few more randomly selected strings and the entire wooden case filled with the quick singing, quick dying notes. There was not the muddiness of held-over notes as the piano gave. The notes of the harpsichord sang sharply, briefly and then died, clearing the air for other sounds.

I ran my fingers over the tops of the metal pins that held the strings, enjoying the tactile feeling as much as the sound of the strings. They were cold and angular and leaned away from the tail of the strings.

Lowering the lid slightly, I glanced once more at the rose. It seemed to float out of its nest in the soundboard and dance before my eyes. I felt a rush of heat to my face and I quickly lowered the lid. It slipped from my hand, dropping the last few inches and thudding closed. The reverberation of wood against wood nudged the strings into protest and their voices echoed cacophonously for a moment before dying within the wooden case.

The room had been awake while I pulled at the strings; now in the sharp contrast it sat cold and quiet. I turned, leaning against the bentside, and glanced around the room. An old Bible lay on an end table, a large ribbon bookmarking some selection. Family photos clustered together on the fireplace mantle and behind the Bible. It was a personal room, filled with things that mattered deeply to Graham, and I had no reason on earth to be here.

I trailed my hand across the top of the harpsichord as I left it. But I stopped abruptly as I came to the desk. A photo or drawing of a massive design lay on top of the desk. I picked it up. It was a mass of geometric shapes in red, black and cream colors. I turned over the paper, wondering if there was some explanation printed on the back. Nothing. As I was returning the paper to the desk, I saw a half sheet of paper covered in Graham's handwriting. I picked it up and read it.

The Maori perfected ta moko, the ancient art of tattooing.

HORNS OF A DILEMMA

Finely chiseled into the skin, the moko was employed as individual identification as unique as a person in another culture might sign his name. The moko served in this capacity as chiefs 'signed' treaties or land grants, and were legally binding. As the Scottish tartan identifies the wearer's clan and family, the moko identifies the wearer's tribal history, genealogy and so on. It serves as a living, vibrant declaration of the person's Being, and, as such, cannot be copied. Because it is used primarily as a form of identification, the moko is usually carved into the face, so that tribe, marriage eligibility, ferocity and so on can be readily seen. However, the moko may be displayed on other parts of the body, such as the thigh...

The paper sank to the desktop. Page's words came back loud and terrifying. King Roper had a *moko* on his upper thigh.

I stared at the strange geometric pattern again and wondered if this was a *moko*, and if so, was it a photo of King's tattoo? But if it was, how did Graham have a copy of it? From King's time in prison?

I picked up the bible and left the house, frightened and desperate that Graham recover.

A constable I didn't know stood guard outside Graham's hospital room, but let me inside when I displayed my warrant card. The room was very dim, for it had started raining on my drive over. Either the nursing staff or Graham had shifted his position, for he lay on his left side. But he still was connected to the tubes and oxygen mask. I lay the clothes on the bedside table, unrolled them and slowly smoothed out the wrinkles. I walked over to the bed and put the Bible next to him, on top of the blanket. Graham didn't move.

I don't know how long I stood there, listening to the oxygen pump, watching his face for a flicker of his eyelids or a sound from his lips. The cruelty of his situation threatened to smother me, more so than last time, for I had been in his house, had seen his bed, touched his harpsichord. Dear God, he had to live, to be all right! I wouldn't survive if he became a sack of potatoes, if we could never work together again.

A gurgle from the infusion bottle brought me back mentally to the room. I gently touched the bandage on the side of his head, trailed my fingertips across his sideburn and down his cheek. A stubble of beard grated against my fingers but the rough growth convinced me he was still alive. I grabbed his hand and leaned over him, speaking his name. Of course I'll never know if it was the physical or aural contact, a God-thing, or merely 'time' for it to happen. Graham's eyes slowly opened. They seemed to see nothing, to acknowledge nothing, as though they were the stare of a dead man. But moments later, while I was still holding my breath and whispering my prayer, they shifted to my face. Then, as though he pulled something

255

deep from within himself to mentally grab or connect with, he slowly smiled. He murmured "Brenna" and several other words that I couldn't distinguish before closing his eyes and falling back asleep. The room filled with the sound of my heartbeat. Squeezing his hand, I brought it to my lips. Such a small thing, but Dear God, how wonderful! He was back with us and would recover! I floated from the room.

That evening, near teatime, Mark, Margo and I were called to Simcock's office at Silverlands. We speculated on what Simcock wanted to talk about, but were unprepared for the topic and the four men seated in his office. I recognized three of them as members of the Murder Team Simcock had assembled to help with the case. Since I hadn't known them, I had assumed they had been recruited from the Greater Manchester Police, some place I had never worked. He soon set me straight.

"Let me introduce you to Terbrock, Nelson and Klarsch," Simcock said, adding that they were from MI6. It had nearly the same effect as a bomb going off in the office. Mark, Margo and I stared at Simcock, at the men, and asked why they were here. "Before I tell you any more about that, I want to tell you, Taylor, that you were correct about your assumption that the postcard found in Enrico's house was a coded message. I apologize for not telling you or letting you see it again, but I couldn't jeopardize the case. It was what you suspected—the first letter of every word combined, in order written, to create words of a short two-sentence message."

Margo smiled and squeezed my shoulder. Mark merely looked confused.

"Now..." Simcock gestured toward the three MI6 agents. "You want to know what's going on. I called them in to supposedly work on the murder cases," Simcock said, leaning back in his leather chair, "but that was just a cover. They work for someone else and were on an assignment here." He paused, seemed to consider something, but turned back to us. "All the work you've done on the Enrico Thomas case has been for Britain and Zimbabwe. I commend you. It was a bloody awful mess. I can't tell you everything, but I *can* say that Enrico was an intelligence operative for the government of Zimbabwe." He let the information sink in as he watched our shocked expression. "I know you want to know more, to know what Enrico was doing here, but you'll have to be content with this now. What I've told you *cannot* leave this room. Everything else on the case is on a strict need-to-know basis."

The fourth man—whom I didn't know and hadn't seen in the village—stood up, nodded to Simcock, and took a step toward us. He was short, dark haired and gave me the impression that a person would be deadly sorry if he crossed this man. His voice, however, was soft. Perhaps due to the topic, perhaps it was his normal voice. But I listened with every fiber of my being.

"Enrico's real name was Mudada. His Christian name will have to suffice, I'm afraid."

I tried pronouncing the strange name.

The operative sounded it out phonetically. "moo DAH dah."

"Mudada," I repeated, envisioning Enrico.

"Mudada," the agent said softly, nodding. "The name in the Zimbabwe language means 'The Provider,' and he certainly did, whether for friends, his family or his country. This assignment was a perfect example. Everything you know, or think you know, of Enrico—Mudada—was false. He had no history prior to January and for this operation, for the obvious reason that we didn't think he would need it; he'd just slip into the village, make his observations, and slip out two to three months later. There was no need to provide him with a cover story and history." He took a deep breath, as though it was difficult to speak. "He was a good friend of mine. I...thank you for trying to bring his killer to justice. It will give me some peace in the years ahead. In our way of doing things in this business, the killer has *no chance* of getting away with this." He shook our hands, reiterated his deep thanks, and took his seat.

I asked if they knew who had killed Enrico and John.

Terbrock, I think, said, "We suspect King Roper. It's his MO, at least. We were just notified before arriving here, in fact, that there's been a beating in Derby that seems suspiciously like Roper's handiwork. He excels in great violence, unfortunately."

"Derby? What's he doing—?"

"I know you want him caught for his attacks on Mr. Graham and WPC MacMillan. *All* of us do! Even though he's left town he won't get very far. We'll track him to see where he leads us—hopefully to bigger fish. We'll know where he is at all times. He won't ever get out of our net. Thanks for your work."

Simcock also thanked us and told us to go home and get some sleep.

More questions than answers filled my head as Mark, Margo and I slipped out of the building. An operative from Zimbabwe! *Africa!* It *couldn't* be a coincidence that Enrico was in the same village into which African rhino horn was being smuggled. I turned and glanced at the police station, the massive stone building that housed Information. Simcock knew the entire story, I was certain. Though he may have simply taken orders from MI6 and filtered them to us in CID, he was part of the operation. And maybe one day we'd know the whole story. But for now, as Terbrock had said, this would have to suffice.

I walked to my car. Dusk had claimed the sky while we had been talking to Simcock. Mark and Margo waved good night and got into their cars, roaring off in an obvious statement. I sat in my car, my hands draped over the steering wheel, and stared at the world beyond the car window. The cloudy threat of this morning had materialized into a steady, slow rain. The street and pavement along the police station were wet and shone in the yellow light of the street lamps. Puddles had formed in the lower ends of the lopsided concrete slabs, and rain dripped off tree branches in a metronomic beat. The trunks of the trees were turning darker, nearly black in the fading light, stained in great vertical stretches by the rain and creating a harlequin look against the drier, lighter tree bark. Like life, I thought, shivering and cramming my hands between my knees. Light and dark, good and evil, life and death. Rain and sun. The rain increased in intensity, drumming on my car bonnet and roof. Rain trickled down the face of the street sign and splashed against the windows. A few lights flicked on in the station, and silhouettes moved against the light as people peered outside or pulled down shades. Acceptance or disregard for reality, I thought. In all its beauty and ugliness. And right now, no matter how dreary the weather, the world was indeed beautiful. Graham was recovering and would be back with us. I leaned against the passenger seat and sobbed in gratitude and relief.

Jo A. Hiestand

Books, Girl Scouts and music filled Jo's childhood. She discovered the magic of words and the worlds they create—mysteries, English medieval history, the natural world, biographies. She explored the joys of the outdoors through Girl Scout camping trips and summers as a canoeing instructor and camp counselor. Brought up on classical, big band and baroque music, she was groomed as a concert pianist until forsaking the piano for the harpsichord. She plays a Martin 12-string guitar and has sung in a semi-professional folkgroup in the US and as a soloist in England.

Such a mixture of adventure, foreign delights and music laid the foundation for her writing. A true Anglophile, Jo wanted to create a mystery series that featured British traditions and customs as the backbone of the plot, while combining the traditional flavor of an English police procedural and the intimate atmosphere of a cozy. The result is the Taylor & Graham series, featuring Detective-Sergeant Brenna Taylor and Detective-Chief Inspector Geoffrey Graham, C.I.D., of the Derbyshire Constabulary. Brenna is a nature lover and amateur folk musician, while Graham loves early music and playing the harpsichord.

In addition to these hobbies, Jo enjoys photography, her backyard wildlife, reading and change ringing. She founded the Greater St. Louis Chapter of Sisters in Crime, serving as its first president, and is a board member of St. Louis Community Tower Bells, a non-profit organization obtaining change ringing bells for the St. Louis region.

She has combined her love of writing, board games and mysteries by co-inventing a mystery-solving game, P.I.R.A.T.E.S., which uses maps, graphics, song lyrics, and other clues to lead the players to the lost treasure.

In 1999 Jo returned to Webster University to major in English with an Emphasis in Writing as a Profession. She graduated in 2001 with a BA degree and departmental honors.

Years of British travel have provided the knowledge and detail that fill Jo's books. With one-month intervals separating each novel, the reader can experience a year of customs and holidays flavored with Murder Most English.

Her three cats—Chaucer, Dickens and Tennyson—share her St. Louis home.

Learn more about Jo and her books by visiting her website:
www.joahiestand.com

Paul discovered his love of writing very early in life. With the help of a high school teacher and, later, a university professor, writing became a favorite past time well beyond his school days. A random encounter with Jo Hiestand at a citizen's police academy grew into a lasting friendship—and writing partnership. A four year active duty stint as a military police officer for the US Army kindled the interest in his eventual full time profession: law enforcement. As a police officer, Paul adds a unique/realistic perspective to the Taylor/Graham police mystery series.

Through the years, Paul has served as a military police officer, military site security specialist, police patrol officer, field training officer, defensive tactics instructor, and currently serves as a police Detective. Paul's interests include playing a variety of sports, and can often be found at any given professional sporting event in the St Louis area. An avid poker player, Paul continues to travel to poker rooms around the country, as he has for several years. A summa cum laude graduate from Lindenwood University, Paul plans to continue with his education, with emphasis on writing. A continuing partnership with Jo Hiestand will be sure to follow. Paul Hornung lives with his family in the St Louis, Missouri area.

Printed in the United States
80931LV00006B/36